WINDS OF EDEN

First Published in Great Britain 2014 by Mirador Publishing

First edition: 2014

ISBN: 978–910530–10–8

Mirador Publishing
Mirador
Wearne Lane
Langport
Somerset
TA10 9HB

Winds of Eden

By

John Bradford Branney

11-25-14

Bill and Mary Lou;
  Happy holidays and
enjoy the finale!
  Best wishes,

Mirador Publishing
www.miradorpublishing.com

**Dedicated to Chayton, the first character
I created for a book.**

From the Author

Welcome to the third book and finale of the *Shadows on the Trail Trilogy*. The seed for the *Shadows on the Trail Trilogy* germinated on a warm summer morning on a beautiful ranch on the high plains of northern Colorado. Since I was a young child, my passion has been to search for the artifacts left behind by prehistoric humans. For three decades, I had periodically hunted for prehistoric artifacts on this Colorado ranch. The ranch sits in a large bowl shaped valley, surrounded by prairie grasses, sagebrush, and sandstone bluffs. During prehistoric times, a natural spring supplied water to a small creek that meandered down the length of the valley. The water in this creek attracted animals from near and far, which in turn attracted predators. One of these predators was prehistoric humans. Over the years, I have found several hundred human–made prehistoric artifacts in this valley. Many of the artifacts are stone projectile points, known also as arrow points, dart points, knife forms, and spear points. From an archaeological perspective, stone projectile points are a reliable indicator for determining the culture and relative age of an archaeological site. Throughout the prehistory of North America, humans changed both the physical features of the stone projectile points and the technology used in making them. As an analogy, modern man has changed the style and technology of automobiles every decade or so while prehistoric humans changed the styles and technology of stone projectile point types every few centuries or so.

From the different types of projectile points that I have collected on this northern Colorado ranch, I have been able to put together a history of human occupancy. From what I have found, nomadic hunters and gatherers first came into the valley near the end of the last Ice Age, sometime between 13,000 to 11,000 years ago. Over several millennia, other small bands of nomadic hunters and gatherers periodically gathered in the valley, right up through the historical Indian tribes of the 1800s.

One particular day on the ranch I happened to be walking in the sand of a dry creek bed when I noticed a large piece of chert (a favored type of rock for prehistoric humans) lying on a small mound of sand. I could tell from a distance that I had found a prehistoric artifact of great antiquity. Before picking the artifact up, I studied it from every angle. Finally, I pulled a camera from my backpack and took several photographs of the artifact the way I found it. After what seemed like an eternity, I finally picked the artifact up and brushed away centuries of accumulated dirt and sand. One side of the prehistoric artifact had a thick layer of calcium carbonate deposited on it, the same type of deposit you would find on the kitchen faucet in a house with hard water. I gazed at the prehistoric artifact and smiled, knowing that I was the first human to touch this artifact in well *over* 10,000 years.

Archaeologists have named the type of prehistoric artifact I found a discoidal biface, a technical name for a large and flat disc–shaped tool made by prehistoric humans for a specific purpose. The prehistoric maker of this discoidal biface had hammered on both sides of the rock, creating a sharp edge around its entire circumference. The ancient human then used this artifact as an all–purpose tool for scraping animal hides, chopping wood, and cutting through animal bone and tendons.

Besides being an all–purpose tool, a discoidal biface served another important function. Since these nomadic prehistoric hunters were not always near a rock quarry or source of rock, they used a large discoidal biface as a portable rock supply. When the prehistoric human needed a new stone tool or projectile point, he or she simply hammered off a smaller piece of rock from the discoidal biface and made the new tool, right there on the spot.

The discoidal biface I found that day in northern Colorado had something even more interesting about it. The prehistoric human had made it from Alibates chert, a rock type only found in quarries located on the Panhandle of Texas. This led me to surmise that over 10,000 years ago, a prehistoric hunter made this discoidal biface in Texas and then transported it over five hundred miles north to this northern Colorado ranch where he either lost or discarded it. In our modern day era of planes, trains, and highways, five hundred miles does not seem like a long distance, but in prehistoric America where humans had no other means of transportation except their feet, five hundred miles was a long distance, especially to carry a rock.

Finding Alibates chert on the high plains of Colorado is not common, but it is not rare either. However, this was the very first discoidal biface I had ever found made from Alibates chert. Why did this prehistoric human carry this large piece of Alibates chert from Texas when there were numerous sources of rock within a stone's throw (pardon the pun) of where I found this artifact? I believe that one reason was that prehistoric humans were enamored with the mysterious power of Alibates chert.

Alibates chert is a very distinctive, multicolored rock with colors ranging from maroon to red and gray to black. Mix in some white and tan with banded shades of pink, blue, purple, and brown and Alibates chert exhibits a rainbow of colors. Prehistoric humans were fascinated with its bright and exotic colors and believed that the rock held magical power over the animals they hunted. When I found this ancient discoidal biface made from Texas rock, my mind wanted to know who made this artifact, what was he or she like, and what ended up happening to him or her?

The third book in the *Shadows on the Trail Trilogy* follows my version of the adventure that led to this discoidal biface traveling from Texas to northern Colorado at the end of the last Ice Age. The main characters of the adventure belong to a real culture of prehistoric humans called the Folsom People, a mystical group or hunters and gatherers who roamed western North America over 10,000 years ago. Folsom people left behind beautifully crafted stone projectile points that had the distinguishing characteristic of a wide flute or channel running from tip to base on both sides of the projectile point. Today, finding a Folsom projectile point out on the prairie or plains is the equivalent of finding the Holy Grail. Folsom projectile points are the rarest and arguably, the finest made projectile points in North America's prehistoric past.

I hope you have enjoyed the first two books of the trilogy, *Shadows on the Trail* and *Ghosts of the Heart.* Welcome back to the Pleistocene and please enjoy *Winds of Eden*.

Chayton's Travels

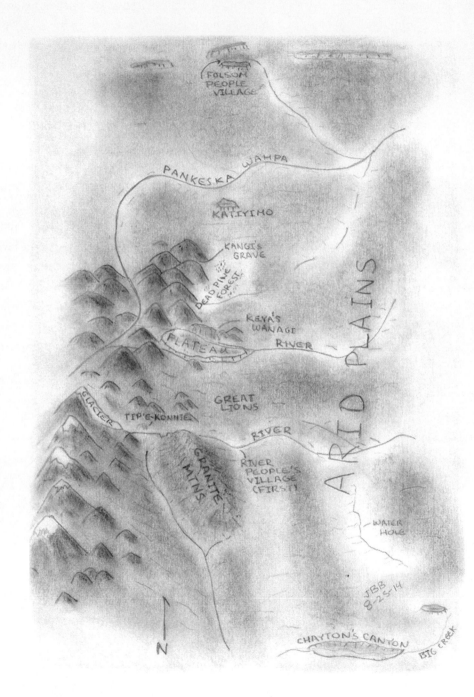

Cast of Characters
(In Order of Appearance)

Sica, whose name meant Bad in the tongue of the Mountain People and Folsom People. Shaman of the Mountain People.

To'sarre, whose name meant Black Dog in the tongue of the Mountain People. Originally, a warrior of the Mountain People until his family fled the tribe and the mountain village of *Tip'e–konnie*.

Honiahaka, whose name meant Little Wolf in the tongue of the River People. Chief of the River People. Son to **Avonaco** and brother to **Namid**.

Chayton, whose name meant Falcon in the tongue of the Folsom People. Hunter of the Folsom People. Husband to **Namid** and then **Tonkala.** Cousin to **Keya** and nephew to **Hexaka** and **Sheo**.

Hexaka, whose name meant Elk in the tongue of the Folsom People. Hunter and tribal elder of the Folsom People. Husband to **Sheo**, father to **Keya** and uncle to **Chayton**.

Wiyaka, whose name meant Feather in the tongue of the Folsom People. Hunter of the Folsom People and lifelong friend to **Chayton**.

Namid, whose name meant Star Dancer in the tongue of the River People. Huntress of the River People. Daughter to **Avonaco**, sister to **Honiahaka**, and first wife to **Chayton**.

Saril, whose name meant Dog in the tongue of the Mountain People. Shaman. Son to **Sica** and husband to **Huupi**.

Tah, whose name meant Moose in the tongue of the Folsom People. Hunter.

Tonkala, whose name meant Mouse in the tongue of the Folsom People. Granddaughter to **Tarca Sapa**, husband to **Kangi** and then to **Chayton**.

Hoka, whose name meant Badger in the tongue of the Folsom People. Son to **Kangi** and **Tonkala**. Stepson to **Chayton.** Husband to **Ptecila.** Father to **Cansha, Heesha,** and **Hogan.**

Lupan, whose name meant Gray Fox in the tongue of the Folsom People. Daughter to **Kangi** and **Tonkala**. Sister to **Hoka**. Stepdaughter to **Chayton.**

Cansha, whose name meant Red–Legged Hawk in the tongue of the Folsom People. Son to **Hoka** and **Ptecila**. Grandson to **Chayton** and **Tonkala.**

Heesha, whose name meant Owl in the tongue of the Folsom People. Daughter to **Hoka** and **Ptecila**. Granddaughter to **Chayton** and **Tonkala.**

Hogan, whose name meant fish in the tongue of the Folsom People. Son to **Hoka** and **Ptecila**. Grandson to **Chayton** and **Tonkala.**

Ptecila, whose name meant Small Bison in the tongue of the Folsom People. Wife to **Hoka** and mother to **Cansha, Heesha,** and **Hogan.**

Paco, whose name meant Eagle. Husband to **Moki** and father to **Gad.**

Moki, whose name meant Deer. Wife to **Paco** and mother to **Gad**.

Gad, whose name meant Juniper Tree. Daughter to **Moki** and **Paco.**

Satanta, whose name meant White Bear. Warrior.

Fala, whose name meant Crow. Warrior.

Kohana, whose name meant Swift. Warrior.

A Brief Return to *Ghosts of the Heart*

A hard winter came early to the Folsom People's camp along *Pankeska Wahpa.* – Shell River. The snows of winter were deep and the northern wind howled relentlessly, but with plenty of meat from the *tatanka* – bison kill, the Folsom People could stay in their tipis, protected from the brutally frigid weather. Chayton spent his days with Tonkala and her children, growing closer to all of them with each new sun. His romance with Tonkala continued at an unhurried pace. While Chayton could never replace the love Kangi had for his family, Chayton would always be there for them. Chayton had never been happier in his life. He was deeply in love with Tonkala and even though she had never admitted to loving him, he could tell she did. While Chayton and Tonkala shared their lives together, the Folsom People prospered at the camp along *Pankeska Wahpa.* They had finally found peace. On a particularly snowy day, Wiyaka came seeking Chayton and found him with the children and Tonkala.

"I was exploring *Katiyimo* – Enchanted Mesa and saw something to the south, heading north," Wiyaka told Chayton.

"Only you, Wiyaka, would be out exploring in this snow storm," Chayton replied.

"*Ai,*– Yes, we must go see what it is," Wiyaka said. "It may be humans."

"Humans in this storm?" Chayton questioned. "Have you told Hexaka?"

"*Ai,* most of the hunters are waiting, you were the last hunter I could find."

Chayton rose to his feet and replied, "I will go to my tipi and get dressed."

Tonkala looked at Chayton, her eyes filled with concern. Things had been going so well. Since the Folsom People had camped along *Pankeska Wahpa*, they had not seen any other humans and the tribe had finally lived in peace. Now, in the middle of a blizzard, there were humans approaching. Chayton walked over and embraced Tonkala, comforting her. "It is probably a herd of *tatanka.*"

The hunters waded through the knee–deep snow, heading south. The winds out of the north were brutal as the hunters slowly made their way to *Katiyimo.* – Enchanted Mesa. Chayton kept pulling his badger skin cap down further over his face, trying to shield his skin from the freezing cold. When the hunters arrived at *Katiyimo*, they climbed its icy slope so they could see further to the south. When they were high enough on the slope of the mesa, Wiyaka pointed towards the small figures, barely visible in the blowing snow, walking across the snow–covered prairie. Unaware of the hunters, the humans were walking right past them. Chayton counted the number of humans and stopped counting at thirty–six. Then the band of humans must have noticed the hunters standing against the mesa because they turned and walked towards them.

"Do they see us?" Hexaka asked, yelling into the wind.

"*Ai,* they see us!" Wiyaka screamed back.

"Spread out!" Hexaka yelled to the hunters.

The hunters spaced themselves out across the slope of the mesa, just in case the humans were hostile. The hunters nervously watched these humans walk across the prairie and then up the slope of the mesa. The humans were dressed in animal hides from head to toe, their eyes peering out through masks made from animal hides. Chayton's stomach turned over as the humans approached. He and several hunters notched spears in their spear throwers and hoisted the spears onto their shoulders. The human leading the band stepped in front of Hexaka and removed the mask.

"Namid!" Hexaka exclaimed.

Act I

Chapter 1

A lanky warrior stood at the top of a vertical cliff looking down at the ground below. A strong breeze out of the northwest threatened to carry him over the edge of the cliff. He was standing on top of a granite dome, peering down at an old man looking up at him from the valley below. On either side of the old man were two warriors, their spears ready to throw, in case the warrior above did anything to endanger the old man. The warrior above knew to be cautious. He was well within the range of a spear throw from the warriors on the ground.

"Come down, my friend!" the old man yelled at the warrior standing on the granite dome. "Think of your people…no food, no water! I will give them food and water! We can sing around the campfire, laugh about old times!"

"You come up here!" the warrior above yelled down at the old man. "Leave your warriors…come up here and visit me. Then, we can laugh about old times."

"Ha! Ha! Ha!" the old man howled with laughter. "I would then be your prisoner! I would have no food, no water! It is best that you come down here, my friend!"

"If my people come down there, you will kill them!" the lanky warrior accused the old man.

"No…no, I will not kill them!" the old man shouted back.

"You will make them slaves!" the warrior yelled.

"We all must work for our food!" the old man replied with a mischievous smile that the warrior could not see.

"You and your warriors should leave this valley!" the lanky warrior thundered. "Then, my people can come down from here and live in peace!"

This temporarily silenced the old man. He realized he was not getting anywhere with the lanky warrior. The old man retreated away from the base of the granite dome, outside the range of a well–placed spear throw. He gathered his underlings and told them what he wanted them to do. The warrior above watched the old man with suspicion. He knew the old man could never be trusted. The warrior on the granite dome nervously walked around the tiny perimeter of the flat–topped dome, peering down at the large contingency of warriors that had assembled around the base of the rock. He saw no way for his people to escape the granite dome without a battle and that would have to come soon. Either that or die of thirst and starvation.

After talking to his lackeys, the old man approached the base of the granite dome and yelled up at the lanky warrior, "Let your women and children come down! I will give them safe passage to my camp where they can eat my food and drink my water! There is no reason for them to suffer because you are so stubborn!"

The old man waved his left arm in the direction of his camp that occupied a hillside south of the valley. The lanky warrior peered in the direction of the large camp with its many huts and burning campfires. He gazed at the people walking around the camp, free to go about their morning chores. He could almost taste the bison meat roasting on the campfires. The lanky warrior thought about his predicament. His people may have a chance if he let them go to the camp. He took several steps back from the vertical cliff and looked down into a vertical fissure that split the top of the granite dome in half. Below, he saw his people kneeling and squatting with barely enough room to move. The stench of living in the close confines of the fissure reached the warrior's nostrils. He must do something. Even though it was winter, they needed water to survive and soon, they would be out of water.

The lanky warrior reluctantly walked back to the edge of the vertical cliff and peered down at the old man. "Sica, will you vow to me that no harm will come to our women and children?" he hollered. The lanky warrior heard Sica say something to the warriors surrounding him, but he could not make out the words. The warriors laughed at what Sica told them.

"Trust me, To'sarre!" Sica yelled up at the lanky warrior.

To'sarre backed away from the edge of the cliff and thought about what to do. A tall young man joined To'sarre on the top of the granite dome.

"What did he say?" the young hunter named Honiahaka asked.

"Sica will let the women and children join his camp," To'sarre replied.

"Can you trust him?" Honiahaka asked.

Preoccupied with thinking about the decision, To'sarre did not hear the young hunter.

"We should wait for Namid to return," Honiahaka insisted.

"How long shall we wait?" To'sarre challenged. "Our children are starving and soon there will be no water…"

To'sarre walked back over to the vertical fissure and looked down at the trapped people. Honiahaka followed him and repeated his question, "Will Sica honor his vow about the women and children?"

2

"*Hová'áhâne,* – No, Sica cannot be trusted," To'sarre replied and then after a pause, he added, "The Mountain People cannot be trusted, you know this as well as I."

"Then, we wait for Namid to return," Honiahaka suggested.

***

The two hunters were lying on a flat granite boulder on top of a rocky ridge that overlooked a wide–open valley. The two hunters were studying the terrain in the valley to the south. The bone–dry valley gently rose in elevation to the west where it eventually disappeared into the rugged mountains. To the east, the valley flattened out, becoming part of the vast grasslands that eventually became the Arid Plains. To the south of the valley, on a flat–topped hill, the two hunters noticed a large camp with huts and rising smoke from several campfires. The hunter lying on the left shifted his gaze back to the middle of the valley where a granite dome rose up from the grass–covered soil. He watched two humans standing at the top of the granite dome, looking down at another group of humans at the base of the dome. The hunter's eyes scanned the valley surrounding the granite dome and saw a large number of hostile warriors. The hunter studied the granite dome, looking for a way to climb to the top. On the near side of the granite dome, the hunter could see a thin, vertical crack rising from the valley floor and widening as it rose up the granite rock formation. Eventually, this thin vertical crack widened and became a fissure in the rock that split the top of the granite dome. The hunter counted at least ten warriors congregated around a campfire at the base of the thin vertical crack.

The hunter lying on the right crawled backwards and dropped off the granite boulder to the ground. He hid himself from the valley while stripping off his heavy hide coat. Although the winds were cold up on the ridge, it was much colder where this hunter had come from. The hunter then crawled back up on to the top of the granite boulder and lay back down. He continued to study the treeless valley in front of him.

"Too many warriors, Hexaka," the hunter on the right proclaimed.

"*Ai,* – Yes," Hexaka agreed. "We will have to surprise them, Chayton."

Chayton threw a handful of brittle grass high up in the air and watched the winds carry it across the valley to the southeast. Then, when both hunters had studied the lay of the land to their satisfaction, they pushed back from the lip of the boulder and jumped down to the ground. Chayton motioned for a third hunter to join them.

"What did you see west of here, Wiyaka?" Chayton asked the third hunter.

3

"There is only one way up that rock," Wiyaka declared.

"*Ai,* – Yes, a small crack with many warriors guarding it," Chayton said.

"We must find a way to make the warriors leave the valley," Hexaka declared.

"We can ask them to leave," Wiyaka quipped.

"I am sure To'sarre and Honiahaka have already tried that," Hexaka replied to Wiyaka's wisecrack.

"We can always show them the ugly face of Chayton," Wiyaka added. "That would frighten them. It frightens me. "

"Ha!" Chayton responded to Wiyaka with a smirk.

"I see that she is up on the ridge watching us," Hexaka stated.

All three hunters turned around and looked towards a higher ridge north of them. "She wants Chayton to attack the *ozuye,* – war party," Wiyaka added.

"I know," Chayton murmured.

"I will let you and Hexaka tell her why we cannot attack the *ozuye,*" Wiyaka said.

"*Canl waka!* – Coward!" Chayton blurted out to Wiyaka. "Are you afraid of my wife?"

"Even *igmuwatogla* – mountain lion is afraid of your wife," Wiyaka replied.

"She can attack the *ozuye,* – war party," Chayton replied, looking over at Hexaka to see if he had any suggestions on how to deal with Namid.

"*Hoppo,* – Let us go," Hexaka suggested. "I will tell her what we can do and what we cannot do."

"Ha! Ha! Ha!" Chayton laughed and then added, "Wiyaka and I will wait here while you tell her what we cannot do!"

Hexaka grinned and replied, "*Hee ya!* – No! She is your wife; you will have to come along!"

"Ha! Ha! Ha!" Wiyaka blurted out and then said, "I will be waiting here for both of you…that is, if you return!"

Chayton leaned over to punch Wiyaka in the arm, but stopped short. All of a sudden, he felt sick. His stomach rolled in anticipation of what he knew would be a difficult battle of words with his wife. He and Hexaka reluctantly walked upwind, headed straight towards the high ridge to the north.

The woman watched the two hunters climb up the rocky slope. Once the two hunters were on top of the flat–topped ridge, she stepped out from behind a pine tree. The two hunters stopped and greeted the woman called Namid. This woman was usually not in the mood for pleasantries.

4

"Did you see my people?" Namid questioned the hunters immediately. "Are we finally ready to attack the *ozuye*?"

"*Hová'áháne, Namid! –* No, Namid!" Chayton blurted out in the tongue of the River People.

"There are many warriors, Namid," Hexaka conveyed to the woman in a more reserved tone of voice. "We cannot attack them and survive. We will have to find a way to drive them out of the valley."

"I will not wait for you to find your courage while my people starve!" Namid replied.

"We do not have enough spears to battle the *ozuye! –* war party!" Chayton bellowed. "We will die and your people will still be on top of that rock!"

"Why did I come to the North Country to find you?" Namid asked herself loud enough for the two hunters to hear. "I should have known the Folsom People do not have the courage we need!"

Chayton started to respond to Namid's accusation, but Hexaka butted in. "We will help you, Namid," Hexaka interrupted, "but we must be crafty like *sungila. –* fox."

By now, Chayton was so upset with his wife that he began pacing back and forth in front of her. Namid paid no attention to him and turned her attention to Hexaka.

"There are many more warriors than hunters, if we are smart, we can surprise the *ozuye*," Hexaka stated.

Namid did not reply. Instead, she stared off towards the south. She had always had her doubts about Chayton's courage, but she had always respected Hexaka.

"Let us pray an answer and then come back to you," Hexaka suggested. "We will find a way to free your people before two suns are gone."

"Hexaka, we must hurry," Namid pleaded to the tribal elder.

Hexaka bowed his head in deference to the woman. Namid was satisfied that something was going to happen. Hexaka and Chayton turned and walked back down the ridge.

"Are you all right?" Hexaka asked Chayton as they walked north towards the first ridge.

"*Hee ya! –* No!" Chayton replied. "Sometimes I forget what Namid is like."

"That is something you should never forget," Hexaka declared and Chayton understood his uncle's meaning.

When the two hunters got back to the same flat granite boulder north of the valley, Chayton asked Wiyaka, "What has happened while we were gone?"

"There are now more warriors!" Wiyaka replied.

"Ha! Ha! Ha!" Chayton laughed and then replied, "That was what we needed, more warriors."

"I thought that woman would convince you to attack the warriors by yourself with only a stone knife," Wiyaka said.

"That woman has a name, Wiyaka," Chayton replied.

"*Ai,* – Yes," Wiyaka said, "I have many names for her."

"Besides, I am not that brave, Wiyaka," Chayton responded. "I would need more than a stone knife."

"I did not say you were brave, *le mita kola* – my friend," Wiyaka declared, "only *takuni slolye sni!* – stupid!"

Smiling, Hexaka listened to the two friends bantering back and forth. "The seasons never change for you two," he told them.

Chayton and Wiyaka laughed at Hexaka's comment and then they both became serious.

"Wiyaka, how do we free these people?" Chayton asked.

"*Slol wa yea shnee,* – I do not know," Wiyaka answered. "There are many warriors."

"I think I have a way," Chayton told Hexaka and Wiyaka. "It is something the Mountain People once did to us."

***

As the sun vanished behind the mountains in the west, the hunters and Namid were still debating Chayton's plan.

"I do not like your plan," Namid told Chayton. "You will kill my people."

Chayton was past the point of frustration with Namid's continuous arguing. Finally, he lost his patience and lashed out. "Namid, listen to us!" he scolded the woman. "Moving your tongue closes your ears!"

"Chayton, they are not your people!" Namid bit back. "You risk their lives!"

"Namid, we cannot save these people without risking their lives…and our lives!" Chayton blurted out.

"Namid, you asked for our help," Hexaka added, "It is time for you to listen to what is possible."

Namid said nothing. She did not need to speak. Her displeasure was obvious from the expression on her face. The debate continued deep into the night, until finally, the hunters wore Namid down and convinced her of a modified plan, one where she would participate. Then, knowing that there was no margin for error, Hexaka and Chayton brought together all of the hunters and explained to them what must happen. Once the hunters gave their input, the plan was set. For the rest of the night, the hunters prepared their weapons for the rescue.

***

At first light, the three hunters and Namid observed the valley from the flat granite boulder. Nothing had changed since the previous sun. Warriors surrounded the base of the granite dome and the main camp of Mountain People was still on the hillside south of the valley. The three hunters and Namid watched the activity in the valley until the sun had heated the earth enough to generate a light breeze. The hunters had seen enough and crawled down the back of the granite boulder. Chayton reached down and plucked some dry grass from the parched soil. He threw the grass high in the air and watched the breeze gently carry it to the southeast.

"The winds are not strong enough," Chayton suggested to the others. "We should wait."

"We cannot wait, Chayton," Namid replied, impatiently. "We must go now!"

"We go now!" Hexaka agreed with Namid.

Chayton started to argue, but decided against it. He reluctantly nodded his head. Chayton then turned to Namid and said to her, "Take your five hunters to the head of the valley, west of the granite dome."

Namid nodded her head and signaled her hunters. Chayton then turned to Wiyaka. "When we give the signal," Chayton instructed his friend, "take your ten hunters towards the grasslands, east of the granite dome."

While Wiyaka was gathering his hunters, Namid and her five hunters were already sprinting to the west, following the rocky ridge that paralleled the valley. Hexaka and Chayton crawled back out on top of the flat granite boulder to continue watching the war party in the valley. They wanted to ensure that Namid's hunters remained unnoticed. Hexaka kept his eyes on the sun and when he thought that Namid and her hunters had reached their destination, he lowered himself off the backside of the granite boulder and walked over to a small hidden campfire. Hexaka retrieved a special spear with the spear tip wrapped in rabbit fur, saturated in animal fat. Hexaka waved the tip of the spear over the flames of the campfire and the rabbit fur burst into smoky flames. Hexaka placed the butt end of the burning spear on the spur of his spear thrower and then standing on the ridge, he threw the spear as high as he could into the sky. The smoldering spear flew southward, out across the valley, leaving a smoky trail behind it. Finally, the spear fluttered to the ground and stuck in the grassy soil. It did not take long for the burning rabbit fur to ignite the dry winter grass. Aided by the breeze, the grass fire spread rapidly.

From their hiding place in the upper valley, Namid and her hunters caught a glimpse of the smoky contrail of the spear flying out across the valley. She and the five hunters walked over to their own campfire and lit two fire torches each. Then, Namid and two hunters jogged to the south, crossing the bottom of the upper valley while the other three hunters remained on the north side of the valley. As they trotted along, the hunters on the north lit the dormant grass on fire. Before long, the entire northern side of the valley was a series of small grass fires. Assisted by the awakening wind, the grass fires moved downwind towards the lower valley and the granite dome. When Namid and her two hunters reached the southern ridge paralleling the valley, they headed directly towards the Mountain People's camp to the east. As the hunters trotted along the ridge, they began setting the grasslands on fire.

Hexaka and Chayton watched as numerous gray puffs of smoke rose into the blue sky to the west. Chayton smiled and called out to Wiyaka, "It is time, *le mita kola!*"

Wiyaka and his ten hunters descended the northern ridge and headed towards the grasslands east of the granite dome. Hexaka and Chayton watched the gray smoke in the upper valley from their perch on the granite boulder. Soon, the grass fires would be burning out of control and then no one could stop them. Chayton looked up at the tops of the pine trees along the ridge. He saw that the winds were now strong enough to bend the crowns of the trees towards the southeast. The winds had finally arrived. Unable to contain himself, Chayton laughed aloud.

"What are you laughing at?" Hexaka questioned.

"*Wakan Tanka* has sent *thaté,* – wind," Chayton replied.

"*Ai, waste* – Yes, good," Hexaka said and then added, "We must be careful not to get caught in our own trap!"

The two hunters watched their plan unfold. Finally, Hexaka turned to his nephew Chayton and said, "It is time, Chayton!"

Chayton crawled off the boulder. He gathered the remaining hunters along the ridge and instructed them to burn the north side of the lower valley. The hunters grabbed their torches and headed down the slope of the ridge, burning the grass as they jogged along.

8

A warrior at the hillside camp of the Mountain People was the first to spot the smoke rising in the sky to the west. He screamed the alarm throughout the camp. Sica, his son Saril, and several warriors hurried to the northern edge of the camp to get a better look at what was happening.

"Smoke!" the warrior told Sica while pointing his finger at the gray smoke rising up to the morning sky.

"I can see that!" Sica roared, his eyes wandering to the granite dome in the valley to the north. Did the warriors at the granite dome see the smoke? Sica watched the warriors move about the valley without any sense of urgency. It was obvious to Sica that they were unaware of the smoke and the grass fires.

"Go!" Sica roared at a warrior, pointing in the direction of the granite dome. "Warn my warriors!"

"What should I tell them?" the warrior asked Sica.

Sica looked back to the west and saw that the entire upper valley had now vanished under a thick blanket of smoke. Without taking his eyes off the upper valley, he replied to the warrior, "Tell them to run!"

***

Chayton and the hunters continued to set the northern side of the valley ablaze with their torches. The dead grass burned rapidly, aided by a strong wind now coming out of the northwest. When the hunters were sure that the grass fires would sustain themselves, they headed east to join Wiyaka and the hunters on the grasslands. However, Wiyaka was no longer there. He and two hunters were sprinting to the southwest, directly at the Mountain People's hillside camp. When they arrived at the base of the hill directly below the camp, the three hunters lit the grasslands on fire in their attempt to cut the camp off from the warriors at the granite dome. When the warriors in the camp finally discovered Wiyaka and the two hunters setting the fires, it was too late; the three hunters were already running back to the northeast and out of range of the warriors' spears.

***

On top of the granite dome, To'sarre and Honiahaka watched the grass fires with concern. Thick smoke was now rising in the valley in every direction, except east. To'sarre and Honiahaka watched panicked warriors running around the base of the granite dome. To'sarre and Honiahaka knew that as a matter of life and death, the warriors would attempt to climb up the granite dome when the grass fires reached them.

"I told you my sister would return!" Honiahaka screeched into the wind.

9

"I am happy!" To'sarre replied. "I am not sure I like the way she returns!"

"We can now escape to the east while the warriors fear for their lives!" Honiahaka suggested.

"*Hová'áháne!* – No!" To'sarre bellowed. "We will remain here!"

"The fire will surround us, To'sarre!" Honiahaka argued. "We will be trapped on this rock!"

"*Héehe'e,* – Yes, we will be trapped on a rock that will not burn!" To'sarre countered and then added, "Trust me, my friend!"

With his heart pounding in his chest, Honiahaka glanced around at all of the grass fires. He wondered if the fires would cook them alive. Then, Honiahaka said words that no one from the River People tribe had ever said to anyone from the Mountain People tribe, "I trust you."

"Bring our people to the top of the rock," To'sarre replied, "except for the hunters who guard the only way up from the ground."

***

The hunters assembled on the grasslands east of the granite dome and watched their plan unfold. The entire valley was on fire, except for a tiny wedge of grasslands to the east of the granite dome. This small corridor of grass was the only escape route for the warriors at the granite dome and now the grass fires were threatening it.

"Spread out!" Chayton roared at the hunters. "Let no warrior pass!"

The hunters positioned themselves around the diminishing corridor of unburned grass. They did not have to wait long for the first warrior to come stumbling out of the thick smoke. Coughing and choking on the smoke, the warrior soon discovered he had stumbled into the hunters' trap.

Off to the west, Namid and her hunters had finished their work and now were making their way back to the north, around what was now a wildfire, so they could rejoin Chayton and the other hunters.

***

Saril and the remaining warriors in the hillside camp gathered around Sica, waiting for the shaman to tell them what to do. From his perch on the hill, Sica had watched the disaster develop and there were few options left if the Mountain People expected to survive the onslaught of the wildfire. "I will take the women, children, and slaves to the south!" he told his warriors. Then, he looked directly at his son Saril and said, "You will take several warriors east, around the fire. You will find those who started these fires and bring them to me, alive, if possible."

Saril was speechless, as were the other warriors. They wanted to head

10

south with the women, children, and Sica. None of them wanted to go anywhere near the wildfire, but they knew better than to argue with the old shaman. Seeing the hesitation from his son Saril, Sica blew up, screaming, "GO! BRING THEM TO ME!"

Sica's outburst frightened Saril and the other fifteen warriors enough for them to jump back when he screamed. They ran around the camp confused and looking for their weapons. Finally, they were sprinting to the east, attempting to get around the edge of the fast–moving wildfire.

***

Honiahaka ducked a spear thrust from a warrior who was climbing up the narrow crack. Honiahaka jabbed his spear downward, wounding the warrior in the chest and causing the warrior to fall from the dome. Another warrior climbed up after the first warrior only to have a hunter knock him off the rock. A third warrior scrambled up the crack, but this time the warrior let go of his handhold and grabbed the end of a hunter's spear, attempting to pull himself up the spear. The hunter merely let go of the spear and the warrior plunged to his death. The warriors that still surrounded the granite dome filled the sky with spears while others attempted to escape the oncoming wildfire by climbing the steep faces of the dome. Hunters, women, and children tossed anything they could find down on the climbing warriors in an attempt to knock them off the dome.

The smoke from the wildfire had grown so thick that To'sarre and the others could not see anything beyond the top of the granite dome. They stood on top of the dome, choking on the nauseous fumes and their eyes watering as the horrendous heat from the wildfire scorched the air. The wildfire had completely engulfed the valley. Fiery tongues of flames now reached the granite dome and licked its impervious sides. As the wildfire converged on the granite dome, the few surviving warriors sprinted east through the rapidly disappearing corridor of grassland. When the warriors finally wandered out of the smoke, hunters were there waiting for them. As each warrior appeared, hunters' spears were already flying through the air, speeding towards their targets. Before long, dead and wounded warriors littered the grassland in front of the hunters' trap.

***

"Hurry!" Saril urged the warriors as they sprinted to the east, attempting to outrace the wildfire. It seemed the faster they ran, the speedier the wildfire became. Saril and the warriors continued east until finally they were able to outflank the wildfire and turn to the north towards their enemies.

11

***

The deafening howl from the wildfire gave warning to the hunters of its rapid approach from the west.

"*Hoppo!* – Let us go!" Wiyaka yelled at Chayton and Hexaka.

"There are more warriors!" Chayton shouted back.

"Let this *kaga* – demon have them!" Wiyaka bellowed while pointing at the pile of warriors lying on the grassland. "We will join them if we do not leave!"

Hexaka and Chayton finally agreed and shouted at the other hunters to head east. The hunters took off running in single file, attempting to outrun the beast that they had conceived. As the hunters sprinted east, Chayton was the first to spot Saril and his warriors heading directly at them from the south. When the warriors spotted the hunters, they stopped in their tracks and unleashed a barrage of spears at the hunters who were still out of range. Chayton and the hunters raced towards Saril and the warriors. When Chayton was within spear range, he slowed down and took aim at the little man leading the warriors. He threw his spear and it missed badly, flying over the head of Saril. The little man readied his own spear, but before he could launch it, a spear from another hunter grazed him on his left side, just below the rib cage. Saril spun around, fell to the ground, and jumped back up to his feet. Saril had just regained his feet when Chayton crashed into him, knocking them both to the ground.

"You!" Chayton screamed when he recognized Saril.

Saril attempted to stand up, but Chayton plowed into him again, this time wrestling him to the ground. While Chayton and Saril fought for their lives, the remainder of the hunters and warriors did the same. Chayton kept trying to throw Saril to the ground, but the strength of the little man took Chayton completely by surprise. Saril remained standing with Chayton draped over the top of him. Then, Saril flipped Chayton over his back, throwing the larger man to the ground. Chayton regained his feet and reached out to harness Saril, but the little man kicked Chayton in the groin. Air escaped Chayton's lungs as pain shot up his abdomen and he doubled over. Saril then wound up and punched Chayton in the side of the head with his foot, knocking the large hunter to the ground. While Saril was giving Chayton a whipping, the rest of the warriors turned and ran, abandoning Saril, their leader.

"They are scared of us!" Wiyaka yelled at the other hunters.

"*Hee ya,* – No, they are not scared of us!" Hexaka yelled back.

"*Taku?* – What?" Wiyaka challenged.

"They are scared of that!" Hexaka roared while pointing at the wildfire advancing rapidly behind them. The wildfire had completely closed off the corridor and the blaze was rapidly approaching the hunters.

Still dizzy from Saril punching him in the head, Chayton wobbled to his feet. He reached out and attempted to grab the little man, but Saril sidestepped him. As Chayton stumbled past him, Saril stuck out a leg and tripped Chayton, causing the big hunter to plow into the ground, headfirst. Chayton rolled around on the ground, moaning. He slowly raised himself up to his hands and knees, just in time for Saril to kick him in the ribs. Chayton flipped over onto his back, choking on the dense fumes from the wildfire. He slowly got up, trying to stand on wobbly legs. Saril unsheathed his stone knife from its scabbard and waited for Chayton to get up. Chayton did not have the energy to stand up. He dropped back to his knees, too tired to get back up. Chayton then collapsed to the ground on his back.

Seeing what was happening, one of the other hunters tried to step in and help Chayton, but Wiyaka grabbed the hunter by the arm and stopped him. With a smile on his face, Wiyaka told the hunter, "*Hee ya,* – No, I want to see what happens!"

"The wildfire!" the hunter reminded Wiyaka of the approaching threat.

"This will not take long!" Wiyaka replied. "Chayton will beat this warrior...or he will die!"

The hunter glanced at Wiyaka, unsure if Wiyaka was serious or not. Seeing that Chayton had all but given up, Saril walked over to Chayton with his stone knife in his hand, planning to end the fight by taking the hunter's life. As Saril straddled the hunter's legs, Chayton scissor kicked and knocked Saril to the ground. Before Saril could respond to the counterattack, Chayton was sitting on top of him with his own stone knife jammed against Saril's jugular vein.

"I am not going to kill you!" Chayton told Saril. "You will be my gift to Namid!"

"Ha! Ha! Ha!" Wiyaka laughed when he heard that. He could not wait to see what happened when Chayton gave Saril to Namid. Wiyaka threw a length of hemp rope to Chayton and said, "This little man may prefer the wildfire over Namid!"

"You killed her father!" Chayton roared at Saril. "Now, she will have her revenge!"

Chayton stood up and while tying Saril's hands, he said to Wiyaka, "*Pilamaya!* – Thank you!"

13

"For the rope?" Wiyaka queried.

"*Hee ya,* – No, thank you for helping me!"

"I knew you did not need help," Wiyaka said with a smile. "Leave this little man here. He is wounded and will only slow us down!"

"*Hee ya!* – No!" Chayton roared while jerking the shaman to his feet.

"*Hoppo!* – Let us go!" Wiyaka bellowed, nodding his head towards the wildfire.

"You slow us down and I will let you burn!" Chayton warned Saril. Then, pulling on the hemp rope, Chayton led Saril away from the wildfire with the other hunters.

Chapter Two

To'sarre and Honiahaka stood on top of the granite dome, surrounded by their people. Everyone was coughing and choking, the effects of breathing the toxic fumes from the wildfire. The soil on the valley floor was scorched black, the grass incinerated to the ground. Random puffs of smoke still rose into the hazy sky while the charred remains of warriors smoldered on the valley floor. Through the smoke–filled sky, To'sarre could still see a massive wall of gray smoke, heading east. The wildfire was burning unhindered, destroying everything that got into its path.

"*Hahpanováhe* – Monster still lives," Honiahaka noted, referring to the wildfire.

"*Hahpanováhe* saved our lives," To'sarre replied.

"When does *hahpanováhe* die?" Honiahaka questioned.

"*Hahpanováhe* dies when it reaches the Arid Plains," To'sarre answered and then added an explanation, "There is nothing for *hahpanováhe* to eat on the Arid Plains."

"It is time for us to leave," Honiahaka suggested to To'sarre.

"I do not know," To'sarre replied. "We see the dead warriors, but we do not see the live warriors."

"Those who survived have fled," Honiahaka declared. "Our people need food and water!"

"I do not know," To'sarre repeated. "We must be sure the *ozuye* is gone."

Then, off to the north, Honiahaka spotted a black puff of smoke rising in the sky. The smoke was a different color than the gray smoke from the wildfire. "Look!" Honiahaka exclaimed, pointing at the black smoke.

To'sarre and Honiahaka watched the column of smoke rise and then stop. Then, after the first cloud of smoke had dissipated into the wind, another column of black smoke rose above the same ridge. Then, as suddenly as this smoke cloud had appeared, it disappeared. These puffs of black smoke happened two more times.

"Signal fire!" Honiahaka exclaimed.

"*Héehe'e,* – Yes, but who is signaling?" To'sarre asked, watching the billowing smoke rise into a gray sky.

15

"We shall wait," Honiahaka finally concurred with To'sarre's earlier suggestion.

"*Héehe'e,* – Yes," To'sarre replied, still watching the smoke. "We shall wait."

***

Namid and the five hunters stood on the ridge, throwing pinewood and wet cedar on the massive signal fire. After a huge cloud of black smoke filled the sky, the hunters covered the signal fire with wet bison robes, temporarily suffocating the flames. Then, when they pulled the wet bison robes off the signal fire, more black smoke ascended into the heavens. Namid watched the valley to the south, hoping to see any sign of life on top of the granite dome.

As the day grew old, higher winds returned to the valley and an icy grip whipped across the valley floor, freezing the charred landscape and extinguishing the last of the smoking embers. Namid remained on the ridge, continuing to search the hilltops and ridges for the war party. When Namid was satisfied that the wildfire had driven her enemies away, she and the five hunters descended the ridge and headed straight for the granite dome. To'sarre soon spotted the six humans trotting across the valley floor towards the granite dome. He focused his red eyes in an attempt to identify who was approaching. When To'sarre recognized the distinctive mane of hair on the human leading them, he smiled.

"Your sister returns!" To'sarre announced to Honiahaka, pointing his finger in the direction of the six humans. "It is now time for us to leave."

Honiahaka peered across the valley and saw the six humans trotting single file towards the granite dome. He smiled when he recognized his sister. To'sarre and Honiahaka gathered the people near the crack in the granite dome and one by one, they climbed down to the scorched earth below. When everyone was safely on the ground, the people began walking towards Namid and the other hunters. When the two groups met in the center of the valley, they celebrated with both laughter and tears. They had survived. Then, after the brief celebration, all of them headed towards the rocky ridge in the north where food and water was waiting for them.

While the people drank and ate their fill, Namid, To'sarre, and Honiahaka discussed what they planned to do next. Still obsessed with the Mountain People, Namid voiced her outspoken opinion several times, "We must track the Mountain People down and kill them!"

"We do not know how many survived or where they went," Honiahaka reasoned with his sister. "It is best for us to head to the north, away from this place."

"I sense the Mountain People are near," To'sarre proclaimed. "They will be back."

"That is good!" Namid declared. "We will be waiting for them!"

"When you escape the bite from a rattlesnake, you do not tempt fate by again sticking your hand in front of it," To'sarre reasoned with Namid patiently.

"This rattlesnake is wounded," Namid replied. "It is now time to kill it!"

"We have not seen the dead body of Sica," To'sarre reminded her. "A rattlesnake is dangerous as long as it still has its head. As long as Sica lives, the rattlesnake can strike."

"That is why we will head north, away from this place," Honiahaka butted in.

"If I find Sica, I will cut the head off the rattlesnake!" Namid proclaimed.

To'sarre did not respond to Namid's boastful threat. To'sarre knew that killing Sica would be almost impossible. Sica was both a shaman and a monster, born from a place the River People called *heávôhenēno.* – hell. To'sarre did not know Namid very well, but from what he could gather, she was both stubborn and arrogant. To'sarre knew Sica and the Mountain People. He was obligated to tell the River People what he thought they should do and then leave the final decision to them. With or without the River People, To'sarre was taking his people north as quickly as possible.

"You should let your people rest until first light," To'sarre suggested to Honiahaka. "Then, come with me to the north, away from this dangerous place."

"I want this to end here!" Namid bellowed. "We must find the Mountain People!"

"They are too dangerous," To'sarre responded to Namid. "Your people should go north and live in peace."

Honiahaka listened to both To'sarre and Namid and then said, "I agree with my sister, this must end here."

Namid smiled when she thought she was going to get her way.

"This is why we will go north with To'sarre," Honiahaka continued. "We must get far away from the Mountain People. If we fight, it only ends with more death."

Namid's smile faded into an angry scowl.

"That is the best decision," To'sarre added.

"Some of our people are still in the camp of the Folsom People," Honiahaka reminded Namid. "We must go gather them."

"Some of our people are there, as well," To'sarre added.

After another pause, Honiahaka proclaimed, "We will leave for the North Country at first light."

Honiahaka's decision troubled Namid, but she knew that her brother was the leader of the River People. She would reluctantly follow him and not argue with his decree. For now, she would forgo her revenge on the Mountain People.

"After you leave, I will remain here with a few warriors to wait for Hexaka and the hunters," To'sarre suggested. "Then, we will follow you."

"You may be waiting a long time for the hunters, they may be dead," Namid blurted out.

"I have faith that the Folsom People survived," To'sarre replied. "I have watched them in battle before."

"I forgot," Namid said. "You are their friends."

"I am your friend, as well," To'sarre added.

Namid did not reply to To'sarre's proclamation. She could never be friends with someone who began life in the tribe of her enemy, the Mountain People. Namid looked over at Honiahaka to make sure he had said what he needed to say. Then, she left the hunter and warrior to go prepare her people for their journey to the North Country.

***

Sica and the Mountain People had fled to the south, barely escaping the wildfire. They stopped running at a place where the wildfire could not follow, the Arid Plains. Sica was in a wretched state of mind. He had not only lost his prey, but the hunters had outsmarted him and left his war party in shambles. Sica was so obsessed with revenge that he had forgotten about his missing son Saril. One warrior somehow found the courage to speak to the ill–tempered and dangerous Sica.

"We have posted sentries," the warrior informed Sica.

"Good," Sica replied with little interest. Then he asked the warrior, "How many warriors are alive?"

The warrior hesitated to answer. Over many winters, he had watched what happened to other warriors who dared bring Sica bad news.

"Did you not hear me?" Sica demanded. "How many warriors are alive?"

"Uh," the warrior stammered.

"How many?"

Twenty–seven, shaman," the warrior mumbled.

"Twenty–seven?" Sica blurted out, his face contorted into a frightening expression. The warrior waited for the repercussion from delivering bad news, but Sica did nothing. Instead, he shooed the warrior away with a wave of his arm. Later that night, the four surviving warriors from the war party led by Saril snuck back into the Mountain People's camp, their tails tucked between their legs.

***

"*Inahni!* – Hurry!" Chayton warned his prisoner again, jerking hard on the rope that bound Saril's wrists. For even more persuasion, Wiyaka poked Saril in the buttocks with the sharp end of his spear. During the calmer winds of the night, the wildfire had slowed down as it continued on its path of destruction to the east. The slowing of the wildfire allowed the hunters to skirt around the edge of it. Now, they were backtracking to the west and heading straight for the valley and the granite dome.

To'sarre was standing on the same ridge and granite boulder that the hunters had planned the rescue. He was searching for signs of life in the charred remains of the valley. Out of the corner of his eye, To'sarre observed movement off to the southeast. He focused his eyes and determined that he was watching humans running straight up the blackened valley. To'sarre watched long enough to count the number of humans and then he warned his warriors. "Humans approaching!" he yelled, prompting five warriors to come running.

To'sarre pointed his finger in the direction of the line of humans. "Look!" To'sarre exclaimed. "Spread out and remain hidden until we know who it is."

The five warriors fanned out and disappeared behind rocks and trees along the ridge. To'sarre watched the humans run up the valley to the granite dome. Once at the granite dome, the humans walked all the way around it. They then gathered and suddenly took off running towards the ridge where To'sarre and the warriors were hiding. When the humans reached the bottom of the ridge, To'sarre recognized the leader as his old friend Hexaka. To'sarre managed a laugh and then shouted, "*Le mita kola, Hexaka!*"

Relieved that they did not have another battle on their hands, the warriors came out of hiding and joined To'sarre near the granite boulder. They watched the hunters clamber up the steep slope of the ridge. To'sarre noticed that the hunter at the back of the line was dragging a prisoner up the slope. To'sarre yelled out to the hunters to guide them to his location. Once the hunters were near the top of the ridge, Hexaka finally spotted To'sarre and the other warriors.

"*Was'te, le mita kola!* – Greetings, my friend!" Hexaka shouted, out of breath from running and then climbing up the rocky ridge.

"*Was'te!*" To'sarre shouted back.

Hexaka climbed on top of the ridge and embraced his old friend, To'sarre. They spoke for a moment and To'sarre craned his neck around Hexaka to see who the prisoner was. To'sarre smiled when he recognized the prisoner.

"Saril," To'sarre declared.

"*Ai!* – Yes!" Hexaka answered. "Chayton ran into him."

"We almost had to rescue Chayton from him. Ha! Ha! Ha!" Wiyaka quipped and then after laughing at his own joke, he added, "Chayton almost became the prisoner of Saril."

"*Enila!* – Be quiet!" Chayton blurted out. Chayton had lost his sense of humor from dragging Saril across the scorched earth for most of the night. Even though Chayton had warned Wiyaka to be quiet, he could still hear the snickers and giggles from the other warriors and hunters. This only managed to irritate Chayton even further.

"Saril was never much of a warrior," To'sarre declared. "I am surprised he put up a fight against such a worthy opponent as Chayton."

"Ha! Ha! Ha! Ha! Ha! Ha!" Wiyaka was now laughing so hard that tears formed at the corners of his eyes and drool ran out of his mouth. "If Saril is not much of a warrior, then Chayton is less than that. Saril had Chayton beat until we helped him! Ha! Ha! Ha! Ha! Ha!"

"Helped me?" Chayton questioned.

The laughing soon became contagious. Now, all of the hunters and warriors were laughing loudly with Wiyaka.

"*Enila, Wiyaka!*" Chayton exclaimed, but this only encouraged even more laughter from the warriors and hunters. Chayton looked around and noticed that he and Saril were the only two humans on the ridge not laughing.

"I will take the prisoner," To'sarre offered, still snickering.

"*Hee ya,* – No, I will keep him," Chayton replied.

"We will take him," To'sarre offered again, trying to grab the rope out of Chayton's hands. "We know how to deal with these people."

"*Hee ya,* – No, he is my gift to Namid," Chayton declined.

"*Ai,* save the prisoner from the wildfire only to give him to that woman," Wiyaka stated. "I actually feel sorry for Saril."

"The River People are gone...they left for the North Country, so this prisoner does you no good," To'sarre declared. "I will take care of him. You will never see him again."

"*Hee ya,* – No," Chayton repeated. "I will take him to the North Country and give him to Namid there."

"Dragging this prisoner all the way to the North Country to give to that woman?" Wiyaka questioned. "That woman has power over you, Chayton."

"*Enila, Wiyaka!* – Be quiet, Wiyaka!" Chayton blurted out, losing his last patience with his friend.

"I am trying to help you, Chayton," To'sarre jumped back into the conversation. "I will make sure no one ever sees Saril again."

Between Wiyaka's teasing and To'sarre's insistence on taking Saril, Chayton was now irritated at both of them. Somehow, he managed to hold his tongue. Instead, he just shrugged his shoulders.

Seeing that Wiyaka and To'sarre were beginning to irritate his nephew, Hexaka attempted to change the subject, "Do you remember Saril, To'sarre?"

"*Ai,* – Yes," To'sarre recalled. "I was there when his mother gave birth."

"The father of Saril is a *kaga,* – demon," Wiyaka announced, "The mother of Saril must have been *sintehlahla!* – rattlesnake! Ha! Ha! Ha!"

"His mother was my sister," To'sarre replied, turning and giving Wiyaka an icy stare.

"*Taku?* – What?" Hexaka asked, unsure he heard To'sarre correctly.

"The mother of Saril…was my sister," To'sarre repeated, still glaring with anger at Wiyaka.

"I am sorry," Wiyaka mumbled a rare apology.

"How can Saril…?" Chayton questioned To'sarre's proclamation. "Sica was the father of Saril!"

"*Ai,* – Yes," To'sarre interrupted having grown impatient with having to explain.

"You are the uncle of Saril?" Hexaka questioned, also finding it hard to believe. "You never told me."

"*Ai,* – Yes," To'sarre responded with impatience. "*Hee ya,* – No, I never told you."

"Your sister and Sica bore Saril?" Chayton asked, still dumbfounded by the revelation.

"Ha! Ha! To'sarre is the uncle of Saril, just like Hexaka is your uncle, Chayton!" Wiyaka blurted out. Wiyaka was the only one in the group who saw any humor in this irony.

To'sarre was now stuck with explaining Saril to his friends. "Sica was a powerful shaman…all Mountain People feared him, including our leader, Ei Hanit," To'sarre informed everyone. "As a tribute to the shaman, Ei Hanit allowed Sica to have any woman he wanted. When Sica was not sacrificing the women to his gods, the women were giving birth to his offspring."

"My father will kill all of you and hang your bones from the trees!" Saril swore.

"Quiet, Saril, or I will cut your tongue out!" To'sarre roared at his nephew in the language of the Mountain People. Then, speaking in the language of the Folsom People To'sarre continued to explain, "Sica brought shame to my sister with the birth of Saril…Sica allowed my sister to live long enough to raise Saril and then he killed her when Saril was old enough to start learning the magic from Sica."

"My father did not kill my mother!" Saril cried out.

"Be quiet, Saril!" To'sarre screamed, storming over to the little man. To'sarre raised his arm high in the air and swung downward, slapping Saril in the face with his open hand. With his hands still bound with the hemp rope, Saril spilled onto the ground. Saril attempted to get back up, but before he could find his feet, To'sarre kicked him viciously in the face. Saril flew backwards and rolled down the steep slope of the ridge until he ran out of rope. Chayton jerked on the rope, stopping Saril from sliding further down the ridge. Saril rolled over and laid there on the slope of the ridge, unconscious and bleeding from the mouth. The hunters looked at each other, surprised by To'sarre's violent temper.

"To'sarre, do not kill Saril before I can present him to Namid!" Chayton said with the slightest hint of a smile.

"Saril shamed my family! It is my right to kill him!" To'sarre stated, still breathing hard from knocking Saril into unconsciousness. Then, after catching his breath, To'sarre continued, "When the children from Sica were old enough, he always sacrificed the mothers."

"No one stopped him?" Chayton demanded. "You did not stop him?"

"*Hee ya,* – No, for that I am shamed," To'sarre replied. "Because of me, Sica did not sacrifice my sister…he knew better...but he killed my sister slowly."

"Namid told us that Avonaco died slowly," Hexaka observed.

"I have seen the magic of Sica that he has taught his children," To'sarre replied. "Some used it."

"Saril used it," Chayton reminded To'sarre.

"When we escaped *Tip'e–konnie*, my family stole Saril from his father," To'sarre explained. "He is all that is left of my sister…I vowed to do anything I could to keep him away from Sica."

"That did not work!" Wiyaka blurted out.

"Sica was always near…wherever we went, he found us," To'sarre explained. "Saril disappeared from our camp …then, Avonaco, the chief of the River People, died."

"I captured Saril, so he belongs to me," Chayton stated. "I am giving him to Namid and Honiahaka. They can decide what they want done with him."

"This is the way it must be," Hexaka agreed.

To'sarre looked straight at Hexaka. He was disappointed in Hexaka's decision, but knew that he had no choice but to accept it.

"We will rest here until first light and then we head to the North Country," Hexaka announced.

The expression on To'sarre's face finally softened. "You rest," he told Hexaka and the other hunters. "My warriors and I are rested. We will watch over the camp."

Chapter Three

Completely spent after their ordeal with the wildfire and the Mountain People, the hunters fell into deep sleep while To'sarre and his five warriors guarded the camp against unexpected trouble. Wiyaka was the first to rise at dawn from his restful slumber. Chilled to the bone from the frigid night air, he walked over to the nearly dead campfire and threw firewood on it. Then, he peered around the camp, searching for a warrior to ask him why they had let the campfire die. When he did not spot any warriors, he shrugged it off and thought to himself, *they are guarding the ridge.* Wiyaka crowded the rising flames, hoping that some of the heat would warm his freezing bones.

Tah was the second hunter to rise from sleep. He stood up and took a deep breath of icy air, quickly exhaling it. His warm breath left a trail in front of his face, crystallizing in midair. He walked over to the campfire where Wiyaka was warming himself and placed his hands over the top of the emerging flames, letting the heat warm his numb fingers.

"Where are the warriors?" Tah asked Wiyaka. "Why did they let the fire burn down?"

"*Slol wa yea shnee,* – I do not know," Wiyaka replied, bouncing up and down on his feet to warm up. "I had hoped for cooked meat, I am hungry."

Tah glanced over at the pine tree where the hunters had tied up Saril the night before. "Wiyaka, where is the prisoner?" he asked.

Wiyaka spun his head around and glared at the pine tree. Both Tah and Wiyaka arrived at the pine tree at the exact moment. Both of them bent down and searched the ground for Saril, as if he were hiding under a rock. Tah reached down and picked up the remnants of the hemp rope that once secured Saril to the pine tree.

"You go that way...I go this way!" Wiyaka exclaimed, pointing in opposite directions along the ridge. In the arriving light of early morning, each hunter jogged along the ridge, looking for any sign of the warriors or the prisoner. When they had run far enough to convince themselves the warriors and prisoners were gone, they turned around and joined each other back at the pine tree. They did not need to say a word to each other. They knew what had happened. It was time to wake up the other hunters and tell them what they had discovered.

"*Key kta yo!* – Wake up!" Wiyaka yelled at both Hexaka and Chayton. Hexaka bounced right to his feet while Chayton just rolled over and put his arm across his head. Wiyaka kicked Chayton in the leg and screamed, "*Kikta!* – Get up!"

After a large amount of coaxing from Wiyaka, Chayton finally gave up trying to sleep and staggered to his feet. Chayton's eyes were glassy and his face wore an early morning grimace. He stretched his back and then gave Wiyaka a disparaging look. "*Taku?* – What?" he demanded.

"The prisoner is gone!" Wiyaka announced to both Hexaka and Chayton.

"*Taku?* – What?" Hexaka demanded.

"*Hee ya!* – No!" Chayton exclaimed with disbelief.

"*Wayaka!* – Look!" Tah suggested, pointing his finger towards the pine tree.

"Where are To'sarre and the warriors?" Hexaka asked.

"They are gone," Wiyaka proclaimed.

"That cannot be," Hexaka replied with doubt in his voice.

"*Wayaka!* – Look!" Wiyaka replied, joining Tah in pointing at the pine tree. "The warriors are gone and so is Saril."

Chayton and Hexaka walked over to the pine tree to see for themselves. They spotted the fragments of hemp rope lying on the ground. Then, without saying a word, the four hunters separated and searched the camp, but none of them found any sign of the warriors or Saril. Chayton jumped on top of the granite boulder and scanned the valley, hoping that the warriors were there, but he already knew that would not be the case.

Wiyaka just shook his head in disbelief when he noticed Chayton looking out across the valley. "They are gone, Chayton!" he exclaimed. "Do you think they took Saril for a morning hunt?"

"The Mountain People discovered them!" Chayton insisted.

Wiyaka continued to shake his head. "*Hee ya,* – No," Wiyaka replied, "the Mountain People would not take them and leave us alone!"

"Chayton, Wiyaka is right," Hexaka agreed.

"We can find their trail," Chayton suggested.

"We can look for their trail," Hexaka responded, "but if To'sarre does not want us to find him, we will not find him."

"What do we do?" Wiyaka asked Hexaka.

"We search for the trail of the warriors. If we find their trail, then we decide what to do," Hexaka explained. "If we do not find their trail, we head north and protect our people. The Mountain People are still nearby."

"What about Saril?" Chayton asked. "He was my gift to Namid!"

"It appears To'sarre has fooled us...my friend has fooled me," Hexaka answered.

"Namid..." Chayton started to say something else about Namid, but never finished his thought. Wiyaka could not help himself and finished his own thought about Namid. "Namid will have to get her revenge on someone else besides Saril," Wiyaka said with a smirk. "She can punish you instead, Chayton. She is good at that. She has done that many times."

"Why you–" Chayton started to reply.

"*Enila!* – Be quiet!" Hexaka roared, interrupting the bickering between Wiyaka and Chayton. "Go wake the others."

The hunters walked through the camp, waking any hunters who could somehow sleep through the noisy ruckus. Tah walked over to one sleeping hunter and kicked him in the leg. When the hunter looked up, Tah screamed, "*Inahni! Hi!* – Hurry! Come!"

The other hunters ran over to see why Tah was screaming. Tah was not standing over a hunter; he was standing over one of the warriors. Hexaka was the first to find his tongue. "*Nituwe he?* – Who are you?" he asked the warrior.

"*Micaje Mo'pie,* – My name is Mo'pie," the warrior replied, looking around at the circle of hunters who surrounded him.

"You are a warrior with To'sarre?" Hexaka asked.

"*Ai.*"

"Where is To'sarre?" Hexaka demanded.

"He should be nearby," Mo'pie replied. "I fell asleep while I was guarding the camp...I should not have slept, but I was so tired."

Hexaka glanced at Chayton to see if he believed the young warrior's story.

"To'sarre is gone," Chayton informed the warrior.

"Gone?" Mo'pie questioned.

Hexaka and Chayton waited to see how the young warrior responded to this revelation about To'sarre. Mo'pie looked confused and did not say anything for a long time. Finally, he suggested, "The Mountain People captured To'sarre and the other warriors."

"Ha! Ha! Ha! Ha!" Wiyaka laughed, finding humor in the warrior's ridiculous assertion. "*Ai,* the Mountain People let us sleep like tired wolf dogs while they captured To'sarre? Ha! Ha!"

"*Slol wa yea shnee,* – I do not know," Mo'pie admitted.

"*Kikta!* – Get up!" Wiyaka barked at the warrior, kicking him much

26

harder than necessary. Mo'pie stumbled to his feet and peered around at the unhappy hunters closing in around him.

"*Taku wana?* – What now?" Wiyaka asked Hexaka.

"Nothing changes," Hexaka declared. "We look for the trail of To'sarre and the warriors, if we do not find it, we head north."

"Take me with you!" Mo'pie pleaded to Hexaka. "If the Mountain People find me they will kill me!"

"Leave this warrior right here, tied to the same pine tree that the shaman was tied to!" Wiyaka blurted out. "Or let me kill him right now!"

Hexaka glared at Wiyaka and then asked, "Wiyaka, have you not seen enough blood?"

"Do not leave me here!" Mo'pie pleaded to both Chayton and Hexaka. "To'sarre has left me and if the Mountain People find me, they will kill me."

Hexaka looked at Chayton and asked, "What should we do?"

Chayton looked over at Wiyaka. He could tell that Wiyaka was furious about the entire situation with To'sarre, the shaman, and now this warrior. "Wiyaka, this warrior is alone," Chayton explained to his friend. "We cannot leave him here for the Mountain People to find."

"*Hat'ugha?* – Why?" Wiyaka challenged.

Chayton glared at Wiyaka with a mixture of surprise and disbelief. Chayton knew that Wiyaka was now just being Wiyaka, meaning Wiyaka was being stubborn and obstinate. Chayton knew he would never convince Wiyaka that taking the warrior with them was the right thing to do. Chayton turned to his uncle to answer Hexaka's original question, "We should take this warrior with us. He can rejoin the rest of his people at our village."

"So be it," Hexaka replied.

"You are making a mistake," Wiyaka proclaimed, but no one was listening to him.

"We search until the sun is there," Hexaka told the hunters while pointing at a spot in the morning sky. "If we do not find the trail of To'sarre, we head north."

This was all the hunters needed to know. They dispersed and began searching for the trail of the warriors. Chayton waited for the last hunter to leave and then he asked his uncle, "Hexaka, what has To'sarre done?"

"*Slol wa yea shnee,* – I do not know," Hexaka mumbled.

The hunters searched, but just as Hexaka had anticipated, they found no trace of To'sarre and the prisoner. To'sarre was much too crafty for the hunters to find.

***

On the second sun of their journey to the north, the hunters reached the Dead Pine Forest and began crossing its windswept hills. Chayton passed the time by talking to the young warrior called Mo'pie. They talked about many things, but the topic usually ended about To'sarre's disappearance. Chayton wanted to know where To'sarre would go and why he had risked everything by stealing Saril. Mo'pie's answers were always the same.

"*Slol wa yea shnee, Chayton,* – I do not know, Chayton," Mo'pie replied. "I fell asleep and they left me."

Chayton finally gave up asking Mo'pie questions about To'sarre. He already knew the answers Mo'pie would give him. Either, the young warrior did not know what happened to To'sarre or he was lying. Mo'pie never admitted knowing anything about To'sarre's disappearance and was always trying to convince Chayton to let him stay with the Folsom People.

"If you let me stay, I will help the Folsom People," Mo'pie vowed to Chayton.

"I know you will help," Chayton declared. "You are welcome to stay with us as long as you want or until To'sarre returns for his people."

"He will not return," Mo'pie assured Chayton. "To'sarre understands your hate of Saril and he is blind when it comes to Saril."

Chayton did not reply. He could never understand why To'sarre would protect Saril and abandon his people. Chayton and the hunters made it across the Dead Pine Forest without incident and continued traveling north to their village. Mo'pie was true to his word and did everything he could to help the hunters. It did not take long for Mo'pie to become a favorite for most of the hunters. Everyone liked him. Even Wiyaka began to soften towards the young warrior. Mo'pie hunted, fetched firewood and always ate last, even when there was not much food left to eat. Around the campfire at night, Mo'pie joked around with the hunters, making them laugh with his odd sense of humor. Even the hardened Wiyaka smiled at the jokes and antics of the young warrior.

On the morning of the third day, the hunters spotted *Katiyimo.* – Enchanted Mesa. The hunters knew that soon they would be at their village along *Pankesha Wahpa.* – Shell River. Renewed energy surged through the hunters as each step brought them closer to their families. As Chayton and the other hunters walked past the east side of the Enchanted Mesa, he noticed that the snowdrifts that they had trudged through on their way south were almost gone. Only a few mud–covered snowbanks remained hidden in the

28

shadows of the mesa. East of the mesa, the prairie was already bone–dry. Chayton looked up at the blue sky above the vertical rim of the mesa, expecting to see the eagles flying overhead, but strangely enough, the sky was empty.

The hunters reached their village just as the late winter sun was dropping below the western horizon. When the people of the village spotted the hunters, a great cheer rose above the prairie. The people raced out of the village to greet the hunters. Namid led the way and walked right up to Chayton, grabbing him around the shoulders and embracing him with so much passion that they almost fell over. Namid kissed Chayton long and hard while holding him captive within her arms. Chayton fought the impulse to embrace Namid, but finally his willpower gave in and he wrapped his arms around her, holding her as tight as she held him. As the last of the hunters walked past them, Namid finally released Chayton from her clutches.

"They showed me our tipi," Namid announced to Chayton. "I put my belongings in there."

Chayton did not know how to respond. He did not want to share his tipi with Namid. After the winters that had passed, they were not ready for that. His life with Namid was in the past and Chayton had just begun a new life with Tonkala and her children.

"I have started a cook fire," Namid added. "I am cooking *tatanka*. – bison."

Chayton was at a loss for words. Namid cooking for him was a surprise. She had never cooked for him when they were married. She had always been just another hunter, not a cook. Chayton felt like telling Namid that he did not want her cooking for him, but for some reason, the words never left his mouth. As they walked along, arm in arm, Chayton spotted Tonkala at the edge of the village with her son Hoka and her daughter Lupan. Namid also noticed Tonkala and smiled at her while dragging Chayton off in another direction, away from Tonkala and her children. Eager to see Chayton, the small boy Hoka took off running after him, but Tonkala grabbed her son and pulled him away by his shirt collar. As Chayton walked away with Namid, he peered over his shoulder at the family he loved.

As soon as Namid and Chayton entered the tipi, she began preparing his meal. Chayton looked around and saw that Namid had spread out only one *tatanka* robe on the floor for sleeping. As Namid prepared the meal, she continued to smile at Chayton, making him even more uncomfortable. Namid was a stranger to Chayton and his feelings for her had changed over the past several winters. After the meal, Chayton lay down on the robe and Namid cuddled up behind him. Chayton thought about telling Namid about capturing Saril, the man who killed her father, but Chayton changed his mind.

"*Blue gxoe cha ah snee wa key yea,* – I am tired, so I rest," Chayton said to her, closing his eyes.

"Sleep, my husband," Namid replied. "I will always be here for you."

***

Hidden away among the fallen rim rock boulders on the northeastern side of a mesa was a small campfire with five warriors huddled around it. The warriors were trying to stave off the frigid temperatures from the late winter night. One of the warriors stood up, picked up an almost empty water pouch and headed towards a small natural spring near the base of the mesa. He walked past another warrior who was peering out into the darkness of the surrounding prairie.

"Cold!" the first warrior said to the sentry.

"It is cold, To'sarre," the sentry grumbled and then after a long pause, he asked, "What happens to us now, To'sarre?"

"I do not understand your question, Itsee," To'sarre replied.

"You have created enemies of the Folsom People," Itsee replied.

"Enemies?" To'sarre challenged. "They are not our enemies."

"We cannot go to their village and retrieve our families as long as this cursed Saril is with us," Itsee declared. "My family is with the Folsom People...your family, as well."

To'sarre did not directly admit it to Itsee, but he understood the concern. To'sarre missed his family, as well. To'sarre did not even know if his family was still alive, but he would not surrender his sister's offspring to Namid and the River People, even though he knew it was the right thing to do. To'sarre stared out into the darkness, torn with what he must do.

"We will wait," To'sarre finally responded.

"How long do we wait, To'sarre, hiding in these rocks like animals?" Itsee demanded.

"We wait," To'sarre repeated with a sharper edge to his voice.

Even in the dim light, To'sarre could tell that waiting was not something Itsee cared to do. The warrior wanted to see his family and as long as Saril was with the warriors, they would never see their families.

"You have destroyed a friendship because of this *kaga* – demon called Saril! You have made us outcastes with no place to go!" Itsee exclaimed,

30

unable to hide his contempt for Saril and a growing contempt for To'sarre. "We are now outcastes from three tribes."

To'sarre wanted to lash out verbally at Itsee, but he held his tongue. He knew Itsee had the right to speak his mind. "The blood of Saril is my own blood," To'sarre quietly replied in defense of his actions.

"The blood of Sica also flows through him," Itsee reminded To'sarre.

"That is why I must protect Saril from Sica," To'sarre replied.

"That is why we hide in the rocks?" Itsee questioned. "If Saril wants to join his father, you cannot stop him."

"This is my will, Itsee," To'sarre professed. "You and I have been through much together. You are like a brother to me. I want you to understand why I did this."

"I do not understand…the other warriors do not understand, To'sarre," Itsee bellowed. "I only hope that your decision has not brought an end to our families!"

To'sarre turned and walked back to the campfire, his thirst suddenly gone.

***

Chayton took the young warrior Mo'pie under his wing. He watched Mo'pie work tirelessly around the village of the Folsom People, hunting and carrying firewood for the families that To'sarre had abandoned. It did not take Chayton and the other Folsom people long to become very fond of Mo'pie. One particular day, Chayton was going hunting along the river and asked Mo'pie to join him. Mo'pie accepted the invitation and they took off downriver along the cottonwood trees and underbrush that lined the banks of the river.

"Chayton, do you not worry about the Mountain People attacking your village?" Mo'pie asked.

The question took Chayton by surprise. He and the others had not even thought about the Mountain People since the battle and the wildfire.

"*Slol wa yea shnee…hee ya,* – I do not know…no," Chayton replied after thinking about the answer. "Do you, Mo'pie?"

"I was raised with the Mountain People," Mo'pie answered. "I understand them."

"Are your parents with them?"

"My parents are dead," Mo'pie responded.

"My parents are dead, as well."

"They were slaves at *Tip'e–konnie,*" Mo'pie declared.

Chayton's mind flashed back to his memory of *Tip'e–konnie,* the mountain village of the Mountain People. *Tip'e–konnie* was where he first laid eyes on Namid and a great hunter called Waquini who died at the hands of the Mountain People. It was the first time he had ever seen the monster called Sica and the first place he met To'sarre.

"Have you been to *Tip'e–konnie*?" Mo'pie asked Chayton.

"*Taku?* – What?" Chayton asked, still lost in his thoughts.

"Have you been to *Tip'e–konnie*?"

"*Ai,* – Yes," Chayton responded, but did not say anything else. His memories of *Tip'e–konnie* were mostly bad. They were memories that Chayton had tried to forget.

"When my parents died, To'sarre and Puhi took care of me," Mo'pie recalled.

Chayton's thoughts drifted back to To'sarre. How could he abandon his family to save Saril, his sister's son? Chayton would always have respect for To'sarre, but he would never understand what the warrior had done.

"When To'sarre and Puhi left *Tip'e–konnie* they took me and the other children with them," Mo'pie explained.

"I have met you before," Chayton replied.

"*Tuktel?* – Where?"

"When To'sarre saved Hexaka from the snowstorm on the plateau," Chayton remembered.

"I do not remember," Mo'pie said.

Chayton remembered the cold winters he and Namid had spent along the plateau where two rivers came together. Not wanting to summon up more demons from his past, Chayton changed the subject. "Mo'pie, wait here and I will circle around," he instructed. "When the sun is midway, you walk downriver and we will trap the animals between us."

Mo'pie nodded his head and Chayton took off walking, circled out across the prairie to avoid spooking any animals resting along the river. When the sun reached midway, Mo'pie started his hike along the trees and underbrush along the riverbank. Mo'pie moved like a seasoned hunter, breathing slowly as he listened for the subtle sounds of animals fleeing a predator. As Mo'pie cautiously snuck through the underbrush, he listened to the ground through the toes of his moccasins, avoiding making any sound. He needed to get as close as possible to his prey and take its life quickly. He knew Chayton was waiting downriver, but he wanted to take this prey before Chayton ever had a chance to throw a spear.

Mo'pie walked along in the light morning breeze, swaying with the wind in the trees. He kept his eyes open for Chayton, knowing that the hunter was waiting for him to drive the prey towards him. Then, Mo'pie heard it, the soft padding of hooves on the leafy ground. He looked in the direction of the sound and saw the brown color of a deer camouflaged between the bark of the trees. Mo'pie slowly placed the nock of a spear on the spur of his spear thrower. He held his breath and quietly raised the spear to his shoulder. Then he quickly glanced over his shoulder, making sure no trees would interfere with his throw. Not wasting a moment, Mo'pie hurled the spear at the deer. The spear sped through the branches and leaves of the trees, finding its mark and piercing the hide of the deer. The deer only took two steps before falling to its knees. Mo'pie launched another spear. This second spear sliced through the deer's neck, knocking the animal over onto its side. By the time Mo'pie reached the deer, it was already dead.

Mo'pie shouted through the trees, attempting to draw Chayton's attention. Before long, the underbrush rustled and Chayton sprung out, smiling when he saw the dead deer. The hunters split the deer in quarters and then hiked back to the village. Mo'pie and Chayton's first stop was to the tipi of Puhi, To'sarre's wife, where they dropped off one portion of the deer. They then stopped at Tonkala's tipi where her children greeted Chayton.

"They miss you, Chayton," Tonkala told the hunter.

"I miss them," Chayton replied. "I would like to see them."

"Decide what you are doing with Namid," Tonkala suggested.

"I have no feelings for her."

"She is your wife, Chayton," Tonkala replied. "You must honor that."

"*Lotancila, Tonkala!* – I love you, Tonkala!"

Tonkala looked around and saw that Mo'pie was listening to their conversation.

"*Hi!* – Come!" Tonkala urged her children.

Both Lupan and Hoka reluctantly let go of Chayton's leg and walked over to their mother.

"*Lotancila!* – I love you!" Chayton repeated in a loud voice.

Tonkala was embarrassed that another woman's husband was creating a scene in front of her tipi. People from the village were now gathering as Chayton loudly proclaimed his love for Tonkala.

"*Dacos ya cheen hey, Chayton?* – What do you want, Chayton?" Tonkala demanded. "*Iyaya!* – Go!"

"*Hi, Chayton,* – Come, Chayton," Mo'pie insisted, grabbing Chayton by the elbow and dragging him away.

"*Pilamaya,* – Thank you…for the deer," Tonkala said to the departing hunters as Mo'pie pulled Chayton away from the family he loved.

After leaving Tonkala, Chayton went back to his tipi. The eyes of the village were now on him. People whispered behind his back, gossiping about the love triangle between Namid, Tonkala, and Chayton. To some observers, it appeared that Chayton and Namid were renewing their marriage. Namid was making Chayton his meals and keeping up his tipi. It appeared to Chayton that Namid had changed for the better, but he still did not know how he felt about her. On more than one occasion, Chayton started to tell Namid about Saril, but he never had the courage to finish. He was afraid of how Namid would react and what it would do to their potential relationship.

However, Chayton's heart still belonged to Tonkala and her children. He watched them from a distance, knowing that he could only see them occasionally and only when the possessive Namid was somewhere else. Wiyaka watched the drama from a distance, sometimes laughing while other times feeling bad for his friend. Wiyaka knew that the situation was ripping Chayton apart.

***

New suns came and went and the love triangle remained unresolved. On one particular morning, Namid was walking between two tipis on the outskirts of the village when she saw Tonkala walking towards her in the opposite direction. The two women had somehow managed to avoid each other for the most part, but in the confined space between the two tipis, avoidance would be impossible. Tonkala spotted Namid after it was too late. She stopped in her tracks and was about to turn around when Namid stepped in front of her.

"*Haw, Tonkala!* – Hello, Tonkala," Namid looked down at Tonkala while greeting her.

"*Haw,* – Hello," Tonkala replied, her eyes peering down at the ground.

Tonkala took a step to her left in an attempt to get past the much larger Namid, but before she could get past, Namid slid sideways and stopped in front of Tonkala. Tonkala then took a step to her right, but Namid quickly shuffled over and blocked Tonkala's way.

"I heard your husband died," Namid blurted out to Tonkala.

"*Ai,* – Yes," Tonkala murmured under her breath.

"Who was your husband?"

"He was called Kangi," Tonkala replied without looking up at Namid.

"How did *Kangi* die?" Namid questioned.

34

Tonkala did not want to answer this question. Everyone in the village knew how her husband died. Namid could find this out by asking almost anyone in the village. Why did this woman have to ask her? With each new sun, Tonkala had tried to forget that horrific day and now this woman was bringing it up.

"*Mato, –* Bear," Tonkala mumbled.

"*Mato?*" Namid said loudly.

"*Ai!*" Tonkala exclaimed.

Namid reached down with her left hand and grabbed Tonkala's right arm, jerking it up towards her face so she could take a better look at it. Tonkala tried to pull her arm away, but Namid was much too strong. Namid studied Tonkala's right forearm and noticed the three long scars that ran from wrist to elbow. With her index finger of her right hand, Namid followed the deep furrow from one of the scars.

"You must have loved your husband," Namid said, tracing the path of the self–mutilation scar on Tonkala's forearm.

"I did…I do," Tonkala proclaimed, trying to pull her arm away from the tightening grip of Namid.

"I know what it is like to lose one that you love," Namid replied.

Suddenly, fear overcame Tonkala. *Was this woman accusing her of stealing Chayton?* Tonkala renewed her efforts to escape the powerful grip of Namid, but she was unsuccessful. Namid only tightened her grip on Tonkala's wrist even more.

"Ah!" Tonkala yelped when the grip started to become painful.

"I know what it is like to lose one that you love," Namid repeated. "I lost my father Avonaco to the Mountain People."

Tonkala exhaled and relaxed her arm. *This woman is talking about her father, not Chayton!*

"I am sorry," Tonkala replied.

"My father was poisoned by a shaman called Saril and a snake of a wife called Huupi."

"*Ai, –* Yes, I remember," Tonkala mumbled, vaguely remembering the shaman and his wife.

Namid then repositioned Tonkala's arm so that she could look at Tonkala's hand. Namid took her index finger and fondled the blunt stub of where Tonkala had once had a little finger.

"This must have caused you pain," Namid suggested, rubbing the scarred nub at the end of what was left of Tonkala's finger.

35

"*Hee ya,* – No," Tonkala answered. "The pain came from losing my husband."

"I also know the pain of losing a husband, Tonkala," Namid said, now running her fingers up and down the scars on Tonkala's forearm.

Tonkala held her breath and tried desperately to jerk her arm away from Namid. "You lost a husband?" Tonkala questioned, knowing that Namid's one and only husband was Chayton.

"*Héehe'e,* – Yes, I lost a husband, Tonkala," Namid explained. "You lost your husband to *mato.* – bear. I lost my husband to *you.*"

With all of her strength, Tonkala jerked her arm free from Namid's strong grasp, burning her flesh in the process. Tonkala stumbled backwards, looking for a place to escape. Namid took several steps towards Tonkala. Tonkala finally realized she could never escape this intense woman, so she decided to stand her ground. Tonkala glared up at the tall woman. Namid smiled down at Tonkala, her eyes dancing with mischief.

"Do not worry, Tonkala," Namid declared. "I do not want my husband back."

"*Taku?* – What?" Tonkala asked.

"You want Chayton?" Namid queried.

"*Taku?* – What?"

"You can have Chayton!"

"*Hat'ugha?* – Why?"

"Chayton does not love me, he loves you," Namid admitted. "And I have not loved Chayton for many winters…I am not sure I ever loved Chayton."

Tonkala was stunned. She did not know what to say or how to react. Her mouth hung wide open while confusion engulfed her. Nothing came out of her mouth.

"Chayton loves you, Tonkala," Namid continued. "The River People will leave this village soon and when I leave, Chayton is yours."

Before Tonkala could think of anything to say, Namid had disappeared, leaving Tonkala standing there, shaking from fear.

***

Draping a smelly badger carcass across his shoulder, To'sarre returned to the small camp hidden at the base of the mesa. Itsee met him near the campfire and began his complaining immediately. "To'sarre, it has been too long since we have seen our families," Itsee began. "The warriors grow impatient."

To'sarre nodded, but said nothing. He had heard the same complaint countless times. He did not need Itsee to remind him.

"Perhaps, we can trade Saril for our own people," Itsee suggested, looking over at Saril sitting by the campfire with his hands and feet bound together with hemp rope.

"He is only a prisoner, To'sarre," Itsee commented. "Saril would be better off if we killed him."

To'sarre laughed, knowing that this would only infuriate Itsee. When To'sarre felt his laughter had irritated the warrior enough, he replied to the suggestion, "You will see your family soon, I vow to you, without making my nephew your sacrifice."

"When?" Itsee asked. "When will I see my family?"

"Soon," To'sarre replied.

"Saril is no good!" Itsee bellowed and then stormed away. To'sarre watched the warrior depart. To'sarre knew that the other warriors felt the same way. They all wanted to see their families. To'sarre knew he must do something soon. He knew that the other warriors would ultimately end this standoff by killing both Saril and him.

***

Mo'pie sat up in the small lean–to shelter where he slept. He looked around the village to make sure no one was walking around. He listened and only heard the crackling of firewood at a nearby campfire and crickets chirping loudly from the darkness. Behind him, he could hear the muffled drone from the nearby river. Other than that, the village was quiet. Mo'pie crawled from his lean–to shelter and then, while holding his breath, he listened again. He knew where the wolf dogs and sentries for the village would be. He would take a wide berth around the outskirts of the village to avoid them. Mo'pie stood up, rolled up his hide blanket, and placed the straps of his pouches and quiver across his shoulders. Finally, he picked up his spear thrower and spear. Then, Mo'pie vanished into the moonless night.

***

The sentry smelled the fire before he actually saw it. His nose led him downriver where he spotted the flames from a wildfire, burning out of control along the river. The sentry sprinted back to the village, yelling and screaming the entire way. Groggy hunters followed the sentry back downriver where they saw the blaze burning the cottonwood trees along the riverbank. The village erupted in chaos as every adult raced downriver to help put out the blaze. By the time people arrived, the fire had engulfed the entire grove of cottonwood trees and was quickly spreading to the dry grass of the prairie. The people soaked animal hides in the river and attempted to smother the

37

prairie fire while others dug a perimeter around the village with sharpened bison bones.

The people fought the wildfire for the remainder of the night and prevented the blaze from entering the village. The wildfire continued its journey downriver towards the prairie to the east, away from the village. As a new sun broke on an overcast sky, weary people returned to the village, exhausted, but triumphant. While two sentries remained awake to keep an eye on the departing wildfire, the rest of the tribe retired to their tipis to rest and sleep. It was later in the day when somebody noticed that Mo'pie and the rest of To'sarre's people were missing. The news spread almost as quickly as the wildfire.

Hexaka sent hunters out to search for these people, but they came back empty–handed. Finally, Hexaka sent women into their tipis to find more clues as to their whereabouts. The women noticed that weapons, food, and water pouches were all missing which made Hexaka finally realize that for the second time, his old friend To'sarre had fooled him. Standing next to Chayton and Namid, Hexaka voiced his frustration with To'sarre.

"To'sarre has bettered me for a second time," Hexaka stated.

"Second time?" Namid asked.

Chayton waved his arms at Hexaka, trying to stop the tribal elder from saying too much in front of Namid.

"After the last battle with the Mountain People," Hexaka explained with a hint of a smile, "To'sarre tricked us and stole our prisoner."

"Hexaka, we need more sentries to watch the wildfire!" Chayton blurted out.

"*Taku, Chayton?* – What, Chayton?"

"Stole your prisoner?" Namid queried. "Who was your prisoner?"

"The wildfire could change direction!" Chayton interrupted.

"Chayton, the wildfire is gone, there is no reason to be concerned," Hexaka declared.

"I –," Chayton tried to interrupt, but Hexaka had already turned around to face Namid.

"Chayton must have told you about the prisoner he was bringing you," Hexaka began addressing Namid's question.

"No."

"He captured a prisoner during the battle with the Mountain People," Hexaka answered.

"You told me that already," Namid stated while glaring directly at Chayton. Then, she asked, "Who was the prisoner?"

38

"I am worried about the wildfire," Chayton announced, but no one was paying attention to his concern about the wildfire.

"Chayton captured that little shaman," Hexaka answered Namid's question. "Chayton was going to bring him back to you as a gift, Namid."

"Shaman?" Namid asked.

"I cannot remember his name," Hexaka replied and then turning to Chayton, he asked, "What did they call that shaman?"

"*Slol wa yea shnee!* – I do not know!" Chayton bellowed. "We must go check on the wildfire, Hexaka!"

"Saril!" Hexaka blurted out, suddenly remembering the name.

"Saril?" Namid hissed.

"*Ai,* – Yes," Hexaka replied with a big grin. "Chayton was bringing Saril to you as a gift."

"Saril killed my father," Namid proclaimed.

"*Ai!*" Hexaka replied and then added, "Ha! Ha! Ha! I thought we were going to have to rescue Chayton from Saril."

Chayton was now looking for a rock to climb under.

"Saril poisoned my father," Namid fumed, turning to face Chayton. "Saril is alive and you let him go? You did not tell me?"

"Chayton did not let him go," Hexaka corrected Namid, "Saril escaped."

"To'sarre stole him from me...us," Chayton explained.

"I knew that To'sarre could not be trusted," Namid declared. "You told me to trust him."

Namid stood there waiting for an explanation from Chayton, her anger boiling out of every pore on her body. Hexaka saw the livid expression on Namid's face and finally realized that Chayton had not told Namid anything about Saril. Hexaka decided it was time for him to leave so Chayton and Namid could have some time alone.

"Uh...I must go...I must–I must speak to...uh...elders," Hexaka stammered and made a hasty retreat across the village.

Namid stood there and scowled at Chayton. Finally, her temper erupted like an active volcano.

"You did not tell me that you had found Saril!" Namid roared. "I thought I could trust you!"

"To'sarre stole him from me–us."

"Why would this friend of yours steal him?" Namid demanded.

"*Slol wa yea shnee,* – I do not know," Chayton hemmed and hawed. "His sister was–maybe...maybe to kill him...*Slol wa yea shnee.*"

"To'sarre stole this *kaga* – demon from you and you did not tell me," Namid seethed.

"I was bringing him to you as a gift."

"A gift?" Namid challenged. "A gift that you never delivered to me!"

"*Ai*, – Yes," Chayton continued. "We–we–we woke up and To'sarre was gone."

"You did not tell me!"

"I knew what you would do," Chayton whispered, "and I did not want you to leave me."

"Leave you?" Namid mocked Chayton. "Ha! Ha! Ha!"

Chayton lowered his head and looked down at the ground as if he were a wolf dog caught stealing food.

"The warrior called Mo'pie is heading to rejoin To'sarre, is he not?" Namid demanded.

"*Ai*. – Yes."

"Then that is where I must go!" Namid announced.

"*Hee ya*, – No," Chayton said, "You cannot leave."

"Why?"

"We just found each other," Chayton announced.

Namid laughed so loud that she drew the attention of almost everyone in the village. People looked at her, wondering what was so funny. When she finally stopped laughing, she turned to Chayton and said, "I will not rest until I have found Saril!"

Chayton knew it would do no good to argue with Namid. The next thing he knew Namid was bellowing orders to the River People, telling them to break camp and that they were leaving immediately. Honiahaka watched what was happening and came up to Chayton.

"Namid will not rest until she finds Saril," Honiahaka stated.

"You cannot let her go," Chayton replied.

"Ha! That would be like trying to stop a river from flowing," Honiahaka replied. "I agree with her this time. If Mo'pie leads us to Saril, then Saril will pay for the death of my father."

"I will miss Namid…and I will miss you, Cricket," Chayton mumbled.

"Ha! Ha! Ha!" Honiahaka laughed. "When you used to call me Cricket it angered me, but no more."

"*Amba, le mita kola*, – Goodbye, my friend," Chayton replied.

"*Amba, Chayton*."

Before the sun even set, the River People had left the village of the

Folsom People along *Pankesha Wahpa.* The elders met by a campfire that night to discuss whether the Folsom People would help the River People find the shaman who killed Avonaco. The elders voted that the Folsom People would stay out of the chase. An elder named He Wonjetah summed up the vote by saying, "With Namid in pursuit of Saril, it will be Saril who needs the help."

Within several suns, the Folsom People crossed *Pankesha Wahpa* for the first time and headed north in pursuit of the migrating bison herds. For many winters, the Folsom People pursued the bison, following them from the foothills of the mountains to the grasslands of the prairies.

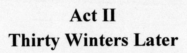

Act II
Thirty Winters Later

Chapter Four

The wings of a red–tailed hawk shimmered in the gusty winds above the sandstone bluffs. The hawk glided straight up towards the heavens and then with the slightest flip of its wings, it barreled down over the top of the bluffs, leveling off right above the rock surface. The seeing eye of the hawk watched the human at the edge of the bluffs. With another flick of its wings and tail, the hawk glided to the south, in search of food and away from the human.

Near the edge of the sandstone cliff, the old man knelt on a strip of *tatanka* – bison hide, facing the morning sun. The old man's knees nearly touched the neatly stacked rocks in front of him. He held his arms out, waving his hands over the pile of rocks and then finally resting his arms on top of the rocks. The old man closed his eyes to the bright morning sun. Tears flowed down the deep crevices of his cheeks. His lips moved in prayer, but the words were lost on the strong wind coming from the north. After the sun had cleared the hills to the east, the old man picked up the walking staff lying next to him and used it to stand up. He then carefully bent over and snatched up the strip of bison hide where he had knelt. The old man then shuffled over to another stack of rocks where he threw down the strip of bison hide and knelt down, continuing his ritual of prayer.

The three graves lay on the highest bluff, overlooking a large bowl shaped valley. Below the sandstone cliff where the old man knelt and prayed was a village made up of many small tipis. While the old man knelt at the graves, the people of the village hustled about, taking care of morning chores. While boys ran through the village with their wolf dogs pretending they were hunters, their mothers and sisters hauled water from the *wakon ya.* – natural spring. At the natural spring, the women always heard the latest gossip from their friends. The smell of grilled meat filled the air above the village while hunters sharpened the stone tips of their fluted projectile points at the ends of their spears.

By the time the sun had warmed the air on this chilly morning, the old man finished his prayers at the third grave. He pulled himself up to his feet with his walking staff. Dizzy from the physical exertion, the old man stood at the edge of the sandstone cliff, catching his breath while looking out across the valley. He watched the smoke rise from the campfires of the village while waiting for his dizziness to pass. He took several deep breaths and when the black spots in front of his eyes disappeared, he ambled off to his right, crossing the top of the rocky bluff. When the old man reached the well–worn animal trail, he turned left and carefully followed the trail down the steep incline of the bluff. He followed the trail's switchbacks until he arrived on the rich grassland that surrounded the natural spring and the village. Once on flatter terrain, the old man picked up his pace, walking steadily down the trail towards the village. Halfway to the village, a young boy sprinted up the trail to meet the old man. The boy grabbed the old man's legs and hugged them.

"*Thunkashila!* – Grandfather!" the young boy said. "*Tókiya yaún haun hwo?* – Where have you been?"

"I was visiting your *unci,* – grandmother," the old man replied with a toothless grin.

"How do you visit *unci* when she is not here?" the young boy asked.

The old man laughed loudly letting his voice carry downwind. "She is here," the old man replied while leaning over and placing two fingers on the left–hand side of the young boy's chest. The old man spoke softly into the ear of the young boy, "Cansha, your *unci* is always here. She is in our hearts."

Cansha pushed his small hand under his grandfather's two fingers and felt his own heartbeat. When Cansha felt the thumping of his heart, he smiled.

"Do you hear your *unci?* – grandmother?" the old man asked.

"*Ai,* – Yes," Cansha replied with a giggle. Then, the young boy looked up at his grandfather and said, "*Thunkashila,* – Grandfather, I do not remember *unci.* – grandmother."

"You were very small when *Wakan Tanka* – Great Spirit took your *unci,*" the old man replied. "Whenever you think of her, she will be here for you."

Cansha smiled and then said, "*Thunkashila,* I will race you down the hill."

"Ha! Ha! Ha!" the old man laughed. "*Inahni!* – Hurry! *Iyagke!* – Run!"

Cansha took off sprinting down the grassy slope of the hill towards the village, yelling, "Catch me, *thunkashila!*"

The old man laughed as he watched his young grandson race down the hill. The old man took a few steps and then stopped walking. He stood motionless on the prairie, waiting for the dizzy spell to pass. At about the same time his dizziness disappeared, his lingering cough began. The old man stood on the prairie, hanging on desperately to his walking staff, letting his dizziness and coughing pass. Finally, he thought he could continue his hike to the village. There, he would take his morning nap.

***

The old man woke up from his nap when the sun was starting its descent in the sky. He reached over and picked up his satchel. He pulled out a large red and gray striped rock and sat staring at it. He rubbed the rock between his thumb and forefinger while thinking about everything that had happened to him since he had carried the rock from the canyon. Much had happened in his life since then, some of it good and some of it bad. When the old man finished reminiscing, he gently placed the red and gray striped rock back into the satchel. Then, with satchel in hand, the old man stood up and left his tipi. When he was outside the tipi, he had to shield his aged eyes from the bright sun. He slowly edged his way to a flat boulder next to his campfire where he sat down. Then, he pulled five unfinished spear points from the satchel. He laid the unfinished spear points down on the boulder next to him and then dug through the satchel, pulling out a cylinder–shaped punch made from an antler, a large antler hammer, small squares of bison hide, and a sharp deer antler tine. He placed these items next to the five unfinished spear points. He leaned over and picked up a flat rock at the base of the boulder. He set the flat rock down next to his other supplies. When the old man looked up, a young boy was running like the wind towards him.

"*Haw!* – Hello!" the old man said to the young boy when he arrived at the campfire.

"*Haw!*" the boy replied, somewhat out of breath. "I want to watch you."

"*Waste!* – Good!" the old man declared with a grin.

The young boy sat down as close to the old man as possible without actually sitting on the old man's lap. The old man picked up the first spear point and handed it to the young boy.

"*He táku hwo?* – What is it?" the old man asked.

The boy studied the piece of chert, his face frozen in a frown as he concentrated on the old man's question. The young boy flipped the rock over in his hands, studying every surface. His eyes narrowed as he scrutinized the base of the spear point. Between the two sharp ears at the corners of the base of the spear point, the young boy spotted a tiny knob of chert, jutting out at the middle of the base.

"*Tóka he?* – What is wrong?" the old man asked, a whimsical smile on his face.

The boy flicked the tiny knob with his thumbnail and replied, "You have dulled this part."

The young boy then ran his thumb across the small knobbed platform and said, "It is smooth."

45

"*Ai, hat'ugha?* – Yes, why?" the old man asked.

The young boy used both hands to demonstrate the mechanics of what would happen to that piece of chert. "When you strike here, the rock will split," he explained.

"*Waste!* – Good!" the old man praised the boy. "What else do you see?"

Using the tip of his tiny finger, the young boy pointed at the area between the knob in the middle and the ears on both sides of the base of the spear point. "Here, you have left the rock sharp," the boy explained.

"*Waste, hat'ugha?* – Good, why?" the old man asked.

"To help the rock break," the young boy replied, his voice unsure of the correct answer.

"*Waste!* – Good!" the old man proclaimed. "We will finish a spear point."

Just then, two more boys walked up to the campfire and greeted the old man. They looked at the young boy sitting at the old man's feet, but did not say a word.

"You are late!" the first young boy scolded the latecomers.

"Late?" the older boy named Hogan challenged. "He has not started his story, has he?"

"*Hee ya,* – No, he is showing me how to flute spear points," the young boy replied, "and I will not show you."

"*Enila!* – Be quiet!" Hogan replied. "That is the old way and I already know how!"

"Be kind, Hogan," the old man said to his grandson.

The old man picked up a square of *tatanka* – bison hide. He placed it on top of his left thigh. He then picked up the flat rock and placed it on top of the bison hide. He then placed another square of bison hide over the top of the flat rock. The old man picked up an unfinished spear point and the antler punch. The three boys watched, never taking their eyes off the old man's skilled hands. The old man then adjusted the flat rock so it was on the inside of his left thigh. He pushed the tip of the unfinished spear point against the flat rock and lined up the antler punch against the tiny knob on the base of the spear point. When the old man was satisfied with the positioning of the spear point, he placed the other end of the antler punch against his right thigh.

"Move back," the old man warned the young boy at his feet.

With his right hand, the old man picked up the antler hammer. He was just about to strike the antler punch when the shadows of two more children crossed the old man's lap. The old man stopped what he was doing and looked up. He smiled when he saw two more grandchildren, Cansha and Heesha.

"You are late!" Hogan blurted out to his younger brother and sister.

"Hogan!' the old man warned his grandson.

The old man motioned for his two young grandchildren to sit down in front of him, close enough to see, but far enough away to avoid flying pieces of sharp rock. The old man readjusted the flat rock with the tip of the spear point. He then carefully positioned the groove in the antler punch with the tiny knob at the base of the spear point. When everything was to his liking, the old man picked up the heavy antler hammer and took a couple of practice swings in the air. The old man then held the antler hammer above the antler punch and swung down with enough force to transfer energy from the antler punch through the rock. The rock popped loudly and when the old man lifted up the spear point for the children to see, a flute or groove ran longitudinally up the entire length of the spear point. The children laughed as if it they had just witnessed great magic. Their eyes were as big as the moon as they looked around at each other. The old man gazed around at the children, smiling. The old man was proud of the flute in the spear point and relieved that he could still do it. However, what made him the happiest was passing down the fluting tradition to the next generation of the tribe.

"Now, I am going to give each of you one of these unfinished spear points," the old man proclaimed, "and when a new sun arrives, you will bring me a finished spear point."

"That will be easy," Hogan spouted off. "These *children* will have trouble."

The old man handed each of the children a spear point.

"*Thunkashila* – Grandfather tell us a story about the journey to the North Country," his granddaughter Heesha pleaded.

"*Ai!* – Yes!" the other children chimed in, begging the old man to tell them a story.

"If you are interested, I will tell you more about the journey of the Folsom People," the old man replied. "Where did I end the story last time?"

"The Mountain People!" Heesha replied. "The Folsom People…and the River People defeated the Mountain People!"

"Ah…I remember," the old man declared. "We defeated the Mountain People and freed the River People from slavery. We thought the Mountain People were gone forever, but they started a wildfire and burned our village, forcing us to flee north with the River People."

"What was the name of the village of the Mountain People?" the first young boy asked. "I cannot remember."

The other children looked around at each other. None of them could remember the name of the village, except Hogan. "The Mountain People lived at *Tip'e–konnie*," he informed everyone.

"*Waste, Hogan,* – Good, Hogan," the old man responded and then he asked another question, "Do any of you remember what *Tip'e–konnie* means in the language of the Mountain People?"

"Simple," Hogan blurted out, "House of Rock."

"*Waste, Hogan,*" the old man answered. "Someone else answer my next question. Why was this village called the 'House of Rock'?"

"Because their houses were rock," Hogan answered before anyone could say anything.

The old man glared at Hogan, ready to scold him, but he took a deep breath and continued his story, "We then lived with the River People in a village near a plateau where two rivers come together. After a few winters, the Folsom People decided to continue their journey to here…to the North Country."

"What happened next?" Heesha asked.

"We never saw the River People or Mountain People again until a few of us returned to the village of the River People…the village near the plateau," the old man explained. "The River People were gone…we thought they had been killed."

"By the Mountain People!" the first young boy exclaimed.

"*Ai,*" the old man continued. "The four of us discovered a village of Mountain People in a river canyon along the plateau and they attacked us."

The old man stopped talking and took a deep breath. He was considering whether to tell the children the rest of the story. His apprehension was not about frightening the children, but about his own fear of revisiting this memory.

"Tell us what happened!" one of the children blurted out. Then, the other children joined in, urging the old man to continue his story.

The old man sighed and closed his eyes as his mind traveled back to that horrendous day. "The Mountain People wounded me badly," he spoke slowly in measured words. "They…the Mountain People killed one of our bravest hunters… a hunter called Eka Huutsuu."

The old man stopped speaking and swallowed his emotions. He was not sure he could continue. His eyes filled with tears as he thought about what happened next.

"What is the matter, *thunkashila?* – grandfather?" Cansha asked, noticing his grandfather's tears.

"Ha! Ha! Ha!" Hogan laughed and then proclaimed, "*Thunkashila –* grandfather cries like a *chincá! –* child!"

"*Enila, Hogan! –* Be quiet, Hogan!" Cansha appealed to his older brother.

"*Hee ya! –* No!" Hogan replied.

The old man gritted what few teeth he had left and continued the story. "The Mountain People killed Keya…my *thanhanshi… –* cousin…*le mita kola* …– my friend."

The old man stopped talking.

"What happened?" a youngster asked.

The old man looked up at the bright blue sky hanging over the village. He began watching the antics of a red–tailed hawk floating and gliding on the wind. The old man's attention was lost on watching the graceful flight of the hawk. This daydreaming allowed the old man to escape the reality of this story, at least temporarily.

"*Thunkashila! –* grandfather!" Hogan blurted out. Then, peering around at the other children, Hogan said, "*Thunkashila* forgets all of the time."

The children looked around at each other, wondering if they should stay or leave the old man alone.

Thunkashila! – grandfather!" Hogan shouted while shaking the old man's shoulder. The old man jumped when his grandson shook him.

"*Thanhanshi Keya? –* Cousin Keya?" Hogan asked. "What happened?"

"*Te! –* Killed! Dead!" the old man bellowed. "The Mountain People killed him and then they hunted in the forest for Wiyaka and me…as if we were animals! We fled for our lives! Wiyaka saved my life!"

The old man stopped talking and looked around at the children. He could see by their empty stares that he had lost them. Their interest and curiosity were gone. The old man was recalling events and people that none of the children had ever known. The children would never really understand what it was like to lose a good friend until they experienced it on their own.

"Are you alright, *thunkashila?*" Cansha asked.

The old man was about to reply when Hogan interrupted him. "I would have killed all of the Mountain People!" Hogan bragged to the other children. The old man glared at the older boy and was about to say something, but his more patient side prevailed. *Hogan is a boy, let him be,* the old man thought.

"The Mountain People did not catch you and Wiyaka?" the first young boy finally interrupted the silence.

"*Ai...hee ya,* Yes...no," the old man replied.

"What happened to the Mountain People?" Cancha asked

"*Slol wa yea shnee,* – I do not know," the old man replied. "Wiyaka found many of them dead in a place called the Dead Pine Forest. Their bodies were broken and twisted."

"What happened?"

"Some believe *Wakan Tanka* killed them," the old man stated. "*Slol wa yea shnee.* – I do not know."

"Did you ever see the River People again?"

"*Ai,*" the old man replied, "The River People found us along *Pankeska Wahpa.* – Shell River."

"What happened?" Cansha asked.

"I will save that story for another sun," the old man replied, too weary and emotional to continue. "Finish your spear points and we will meet here in the new sun."

The children all moaned. They wanted to hear what happened next to the River People and Mountain People. The old man smiled at them, happy that he could pass on a few of the stories of the Folsom People. The children disbanded, leaving the old man to think about what happened to Keya.

"*Key kte yo!* – Wake up!" someone bellowed at the old man. Then a firm hand landed on the old man's shoulder and shook him until the old man almost fell off the rock he was sitting on.

"Dreamer!" the voice rang out. "Dream the sun away!"

The old man looked up and saw that it was his friend. "Wiyaka, you sound like brother *hexaka!* – elk!" the old man replied. "*Enila,* – Be quiet, I was in thought!"

"For you, that is difficult," Wiyaka jeered. "Thinking, that is!"

"Did you come here to ridicule me?" the old man asked.

"*Hee ya, Chayton,* – No, Chayton," Wiyaka replied, "but, I do enjoy it. I came to see if you changed your simple mind."

"*Hee ya,* – No," Chayton replied. "I have not changed my simple...I mean my mind."

"Perhaps, changed your mind is not the right words," Wiyaka continued. "Lost your mind is better."

"You are funny," Chayton said. Then, clearing his throat, Chayton spit out a glob of phlegm that had accumulated in his mouth and throat.

"You are not only feeble and old, Chayton," Wiyaka stated. "You are also *takuni slolye sni.* – stupid."

"*Iyaya, Wiyaka!* – Go, Wiyaka!" Chayton replied, putting his knapping gear away in the satchel and then struggling to stand up. Once he got to his feet, Chayton stood there, his body wobbling back and forth. The exertion had winded Chayton as he gasped for air. He coughed several times and then without saying another word, he headed for his tipi.

"You are a *gnaye!* – fool!" Wiyaka yelled at the back of his departing friend's head.

***

"Are you really leaving?" Hoka asked Chayton while they sat around the cook fire at the nighttime meal.

"*Ai,* – Yes," Chayton replied, chewing the tough bison meat on the left side of his mouth where he still had a couple of usable teeth.

"You are *witko tko ke!* – crazy!" Hoka responded.

"Respect your *até, Hoka!* – father, Hoka!" Ptecila scolded her husband.

"He is too old!" Hoka responded as if Chayton was not in the tipi to hear what he just said. "It is too dangerous!"

Chayton choked on some of the bison meat and began sputtering and coughing. Ptecila leaned over to help the old man while Hoka just glared at his father, visibly upset over Chayton's decision. Once Chayton had recovered from his coughing spell, he replied to Hoka in a gravelly whisper, "Hoka, when you were a child did I not teach you how to hunt?"

"*Ai,* – Yes," Hoka replied. "What does that matter?"

"Was it me who taught you the ways of the Folsom People?"

"*Ai.*"

"Did I teach you to survive in dangerous country?"

"*Ai!*" Hoka answered. "I do not know understand what that has to do with you leaving the village."

"I taught you the ways of a hunter," Chayton replied. "It is now time for you to respect what I want to do."

Chayton had silenced his son, at least temporarily. Then, after thinking about what Chayton just said, Hoka responded, "Chayton, your family is here…my mother…your wife…Tonkala rests here."

Hoka always referred to his stepfather as Chayton when he was upset. "I have spoken to Tonkala…your mother," Chayton replied. "She knows why I must do this…she is with me, in my heart, wherever I travel."

Hoka was too upset to reply. He could not hide the displeasure on his face. Chayton saw that his stepson was not happy, but all he could do was explain his decision the best way he knew how. "Hoka, I must do this," Chayton said

51

in a voice barely louder than a whisper. Then, to make sure Hoka heard, Chayton raised his voice and bellowed, "I will do this!"

Chayton could tell that Hoka would never accept his decision. Chayton shrugged his shoulders at Ptecila and she just shook her head. She walked over to Chayton's side of the cook fire and helped him to his feet. Chayton gave Ptecila a hug and then thanked her for the meal. Chayton then said goodbye to his three grandchildren. Before exiting the tipi, Chayton looked at Hoka, but Hoka was too upset to look back. Chayton pushed the flap of the tipi open and exited. He walked through the darkness to his own tipi, coughing and spitting the entire way.

"If you let Chayton go by himself, you bring shame to him and your family," Ptecila declared to Hoka after Chayton left the tipi.

"He is not going anywhere," Hoka replied.

"You know your *até*, – father," Ptecila continued. "If he says he will do something, he will do it."

"That is because he is stubborn," Hoka replied.

Ptecila glared at her husband, not saying a word. His wife's glare made Hoka uncomfortable and he looked away. Even though he was not looking at her any longer, Hoka knew that Ptecila was still staring at him. Finally, he had enough.

"What am I supposed to do, *mitháwichu ki?* – my wife?" Hoka demanded.

"*Iyaya*, – Go," Ptecila answered in a whisper so the children did not hear.

"*Taku? – What?*"

"Go with your father."

"Leave you and my children to follow that *witko tko ke wichah^cala?* – crazy old man?" Hoka argued.

"Be respectful, Hoka," Ptecila responded. "That *wichah^cala* – old man raised you as his own son. He did not have to do that. He taught you the ways of the Folsom People. It is time for you to repay him."

"What about you and my children?"

"We will be fine," Ptecila answered. "My brother and father will watch over us until you return."

"*Slol wa yea shnee*, – I do not know," Hoka said.

"You cannot stop the will of Chayton," Ptecila replied. "You must go with him or you will never live without shame. It is your duty as his son."

"What about Hogan?" Hoka whispered. "He needs a father."

"*Ai*, – Yes, he needs a father to teach him how to be a man…to be a hunter," Ptecila replied.

"Then I must remain here for Hogan," Hoka stated, relieved that the discussion was finally over.

"Hogan is not becoming a man in this village, his life has been too easy," Ptecila spoke softly. "You will take him with you. He will learn hardship with his father and grandfather. You will make him a hunter!"

Now, it was Hoka's turn to glare at his wife. He was wondering if she had completely lost her mind.

Chapter Five

When a new sun broke above a red horizon, Chayton was already on top of the bluff, kneeling in front of the grave of Tonkala, his departed wife. Chayton was telling Tonkala how much he loved and missed her. He told her about his forthcoming journey and asked her to watch over their family. When he had finished chatting to Tonkala, Chayton stood up and strolled over to the next grave, throwing down his piece of bison hide to kneel on. His joints creaked as he knelt down in front of the grave.

"*Was'te, Hexaka,* – Greetings, Hexaka," Chayton said to the pile of sandstone rocks on top of his uncle's grave. "You were always a father to me."

Chayton's eyes turned misty from tears as he spoke. "I am leaving and it will be many night suns before I will visit with you again," he said, wiping the tears from his cheeks. Chayton continued, "I am visiting our friend Kangi…and your son…my friend Keya."

Chayton turned his face away from the grave just in time to cough several times. He cleared his throat and spat a glob of phlegm on the ground in the opposite direction. He then turned back to the grave and tears were flowing down the wrinkled furrows along his cheeks. Once he cleared his throat, Chayton spoke in a raspy voice that was not much louder than a whisper, "I will go to the place Tarca Sapa gave his life."

Chayton closed his eyes and prayed to *Wakan Tanka*. His mouth moved while tears fell down his cheeks. He knelt there for a long time, praying and weeping. Finally, he opened his eyes and spoke to all three graves in front of him, "I will have you in my heart."

Chayton cleared his throat and then wobbled to his feet. He caught his breath in the thin oxygen of the high plains. With the help of his walking staff, he stumbled over to the third grave, the grave of Sheo, his aunt. Chayton was almost ready to kneel down when a voice called out to him. Chayton slowly turned around and saw his son Hoka standing behind him.

Chayton smiled at his son and asked, "*Does ksh kay ya oun hey?* – How are you?"

"*Waste,* – Good," Hoka replied.

"Have you come to visit your mother?" Chayton inquired.

Hoka looked over at Tonkala's grave and replied, "*Ai,* – Yes, but I am here to visit with you."

Chayton's facial expression soured. He had a suspicion as to why Hoka had walked all the way up the bluff. Hoka was still trying to convince him not to take the journey, but Chayton had grown weary of the debate. Chayton had made his decision and nothing would make him change it. Chayton hesitated while he thought about the best way to respond to his son without stirring up another argument. "I am done arguing with you, Hoka," Chayton declared. "I am leaving this valley when a new sun arrives."

"I am done arguing, as well," Hoka replied.

Chayton was relieved and suspicious at the same time. "*Waste,* – Good," Chayton said quietly, "I am happy that you found the good sense I thought you had lost."

"*Hee ya, até,* – No, father, that is not it," Hoka replied. "I am going with you. We both must have lost our good sense."

"*Taku?* – What?"

"I am going with you."

"You are going?" Chayton challenged, unsure if this was good or bad news.

"*Ai.* – Yes."

"*Hat'ugha?* – Why?" Chayton demanded.

"You cannot go alone!" Hoka blurted out.

"*Hat'ugha?* – Why?"

"You are old," Hoka replied. "I will watch over you."

"You will watch over me?" Chayton roared. "I have not had anyone watch over me since I was a *chincá!* – child! I do not need you to watch over me!"

"That is not what I meant," Hoka replied.

"That is what I heard!"

"I want to be with you."

"*Hat'ugha?* – Why?"

Hoka had to think of a better answer than the last one. He knew the wrong answer would set Chayton off on another one of his tirades. He could not tell Chayton the truth; that his wife Ptecila insisted that he go. He decided to stroke Chayton's more than decent–sized ego.

"I want to learn from you," Hoka blurted out.

Hoka waited for Chayton's reaction to this plea. It did not take too long for Chayton's facial expression to soften. Finally, he replied to his son, "I can teach you much, but you must be willing to learn."

"I am willing, *até.* – father."

"Does your wife know of your decision?"

"*Ai.*"

"She accepts your decision?"

"*Ai.*"

Chayton looked satisfied and then replied, "Let me sleep on it."

"Sleep on it?"

"*Ai.*"

"There is something else," Hoka revealed.

Chayton opened his right eye wide, curling his eyebrow upward. *I knew it,* he thought. He waited for Hoka to disclose what 'something else' entailed.

"Well?" Chayton roared.

"Hogan will be coming with us," Hoka murmured, barely above a whisper.

"*Taku?* – What?" Chayton inquired, cupping his hand around his ear and waiting for Hoka to repeat what he was sure he had not heard.

"Hogan will be coming with us–me!" Hoka repeated in a loud voice.

"Hogan?" Chayton questioned. "Your son?"

"*Ai.*"

"My grandson?"

"*Ai.*"

"*Hat'ugha?* – Why?"

Since Hoka had successfully played on Chayton's ego the first time, he decided to play on it one more time.

"Hogan needs to learn from you."

"He is only a *hokshila,* – boy," Chayton proclaimed.

"Hogan is not much younger than you were when you left the canyon," Hoka contended.

"There is a difference."

"*Taku?* – What?" Hoka asked.

"We are different," Chayton explained. "I knew how to make weapons and hunt. I knew how to live with *maka.* – earth."

"Who taught you these things?"

"Who taught me?" Chayton repeated.

"*Ai!* – Yes!" Hoka challenged. "Who taught you to make weapons and to hunt?"

Chayton had to think about the answer to that question. He then pointed at

Hexaka's grave and answered, "This hunter whose bones lay here…Tarca Sapa…Pahin…my friend Wiyaka…my father."

"And you taught me," Hoka replied.

"Not very well," Chayton sniped.

Hoka paid no attention to Chayton's insult. "My son…this boy…needs help from his *thunkashila* – grandfather."

"My journey is no place for a *hokshila*, – boy," Chayton replied.

"I will be there…you will be there."

"What is this *I will be there*?" Chayton asked. "I told you I will sleep on that decision."

"*Ai*," Hoka replied, "you can sleep on the decision about Hogan, as well."

"Ehhh!" Chayton bellowed. "If Hogan wants to go, he must make his own weapons and prepare for the journey."

Hoka started to smile. He knew he was beginning to win the debate with his father. His smile was short lived.

"You cannot help Hogan!" Chayton asserted. "If this *hokshila* – boy wants to become a hunter, he must do things that hunters do!"

Hoka listened and then bowed.

"Now, leave," Chayton demanded, "so I can say farewell to Sheo."

***

After coming down from the bluff, Chayton waited by his campfire for the five children to return with their finished spear points. Chayton had given each one of them a spear point and had asked them to flute and finish them. His grandchildren, Heesha and Cansha were the first to arrive. Cansha showed his spear point to Chayton who admired it and told him how to make the next spear point even better. Heesha's spear point was a different matter. The small girl was unable to flute the spear point at all and from her knapping of the rest of the spear point, she needed a lot more practice. Chayton praised her anyway. Two more boys showed up and Chayton inspected their work. One of the boys was on his way to becoming a master, but Chayton praised all of the children equally for their progress and effort.

"Where is Hogan?" Cansha asked after everyone had passed around the spear points for inspection.

"Hogan is in our tipi, he is sleeping," Heesha told everyone. "I will go get him."

Before Chayton could tell the small girl 'not to bother', she was sprinting through the camp on her way to wake up her lazy brother. While they waited, Chayton started another story. Then, midway into the story, they all heard

Heesha herding Hogan back to them. When they arrived, Chayton could tell that Hogan was not happy to be there.

"*Haw, Hogan,* – Hello, Hogan," Chayton greeted his tardy grandson.

"*Haw,*" Hogan replied.

Chayton waited for Hogan to show everyone his spear point, but Hogan just stood there, brooding over his sister waking him up.

Finally, Chayton asked, "Where is your finished spear point, Hogan?"

Hogan looked around at the other children who happened to be staring back at him, waiting for him to answer Chayton.

"I do not have a spear point," Hogan replied.

Jaws dropped as the children's eyes shifted from Hogan to Chayton. They waited in anticipation of the old man's famous temper to erupt.

"*Hat'ugha?* – Why?" Chayton asked quietly.

"I had other things to do," Hogan replied.

If the other children could have dropped their jaws any further, they would have hit the ground. They waited for Chayton's wrath, knowing that it would be coming as sure as a new sun. As Chayton's fury boiled up inside him, he thought about the best way to respond to the boy's insolence. Chayton's gut reaction was to lash out viciously at the boy, telling him that he was no good and that he needed to set a better example for the younger children. Then, Chayton looked down at the young faces of the children and saw they were waiting for this exact response from him. Chayton coughed and then took time to clear his throat. Then, he responded to Hogan, "If becoming a hunter is not important to you, it is not important to me."

Chayton stood up and walked to his tipi. He left the problem for the children to sort out amongst themselves. He had also now made up his mind about taking Hogan on his journey. Chayton walked into his tipi and headed straight to his bison robe to lie down. Dizziness and nausea were overcoming him. He settled onto the bison robe and soon fell into a deep sleep.

"*Key kta yo!* – Wake up!" Hoka exclaimed, shaking Chayton's shoulder. "*Hi!* – Come! Join us for food."

With Hoka's assistance, Chayton rose to his feet. As soon as he stood, Chayton began coughing until his eyes streamed tears.

"*Doe ksh kay oun hey?* – How are you?" Hoka asked, supporting the old man by his elbow.

"*Waste!* – Good!" Chayton blurted out. "*Hoppo!* – Let us go!"

When Hoka and Chayton arrived at the tipi, they entered and Chayton looked around.

"I thought we were eating," Chayton expressed aloud when he saw only Ptecila and Hoka in the tipi. "Where are my grandchildren?"

"We will eat," Hoka replied, "but, first we want your answer."

"What answer?" Chayton asked.

"Whether you will let Hoka go on your journey," Ptecila blurted out.

Chayton looked at the married couple. Chayton had hoped that Hoka had not been serious and would forget about the journey. Chayton had been too busy getting ready to worry about Hoka. Chayton did not want to appear as a forgetful fool in front of Hoka and Ptecila so he said, "If you must go, Hoka, I will allow it."

"What about Hogan?" Hoka asked, hitting a raw nerve with Chayton.

"KAAF! KAAF! KAAF!" Chayton coughed while turning his head away from Hoka and Ptecila.

Hoka waited to make sure Chayton was through coughing and then asked again, "Will you let Hogan come on your journey?"

"*Hee ya!* – No!" Chayton said bluntly.

"*Hat'ugha?* – Why?" Ptecila cried out. Hoka held up his hand in front of his wife's face, signaling her to stay out of the debate.

"*Hat'ugha?* – Why?" Hoka repeated his wife's question.

"Hogan is not a serious *hokshila,* – boy," Chayton answered. "He has no respect for our way of life or his elders."

"Hogan has no respect for you?" Hoka queried.

"Or you," Chayton replied. "I may be old, but I am not blind, at least not yet. I watch how he treats you and Ptecila. He has no respect for you or our way of life."

"The journey will teach our son to respect!" Ptecila blurted out.

"My journey is not for teaching your son respect, this is for you to do right here," Chayton declared, waving his arms in the air. "This journey will be dangerous! I do not want him along. He will only make the journey more dangerous. Your son lacks the heart of a hunter!"

Hoka jerked his head backwards in shock at Chayton's harsh judgment about his son. He started to say something in defense of Hogan, but his wife beat him to it.

"Hogan will find this heart," Ptecila pleaded with Chayton.

"A boy does not find his heart like a pebble in a stream," Chayton stated and then pounding on his own chest, he added, "Heart is here or it is not."

Hoka and Ptecila did not know what to say. The two parents and Chayton sat by the cook fire, listening to the crackling of the burning wood, all of them deep in thought. Finally, Hoka confessed, "We do not know what to do about Hogan."

Chayton shrugged his shoulders. He did not have an answer for Hoka's dilemma.

"He is your grandson!" Ptecila proclaimed.

"*Enila, Ptecila!* – Be quiet, Ptecila!" Hoka scolded his wife.

"You! *Enila!* – Be quiet!" she bit back at her husband. "Chayton forgets who helped him with his life."

"*Winyan,* – Woman, how do you know who helped me?" Chayton challenged.

"We know who was there for you when your father Chetán died," Ptecila replied, not intimidated by the old man.

"I do not like your back talk, *winyan!*" Chayton thundered.

"*Enila, Ptecila!* – Be quiet, Ptecila!" Hoka demanded.

"You had Hexaka to help you!" Ptecila declared. "You had Tarca Sapa to help you! You had others to help you! Everyone in the tribe helped Chayton, but now Chayton refuses to help our son…his own grandson!"

Hoka finally stopped trying to quiet his wife down. He sank down low near the cook fire, his hands on his knees and his eyes staring at the flames.

The encounter with Chayton visibly upset Ptecila. Tears rolled down her cheeks. "Help us, Chayton," Ptecila pleaded. "We have lost our son…we have lost Hogan!"

Chayton looked at the woman, thinking about what she just confessed. "*Slol wa yea shnee,* – I do not know," he mumbled.

Hoka looked up and reentered the fray, "Hogan will do his share of work, on my word."

Chayton sat quietly by the cook fire, pondering what to do. He remembered being a lost boy after his mother and father died, but everyone in the village helped him. Tarca Sapa did not need to help Chayton, but he did. Chayton thought about what Tarca Sapa would do in this same situation.

"Hogan can come on the journey," Chayton finally declared. "If…he shares the work."

"*Pilamaya!* – Thank you!" Ptecila and Hoka both proclaimed at the same time.

"I came here for a meal," Chayton announced. "Where is it?"

Chapter Six

A new sun came and with it the departure of the three travelers on their journey: Chayton, Hoka, and Hogan. Chayton walked around and said goodbye to everyone in the tribe, old friends and others alike. He then stood in front of the two grandchildren who were not going on the journey with him, Cansha and Heesha. Chayton knelt down in front of his young granddaughter and said, "Heesha, I have a gift for you."

"*Taku?* – What?" she whispered to her grandfather.

Chayton held out an amulet that he had made from polished bone. It was as white as fresh snow. The amulet was in the shape of a human, its arms folded across its chest. The human had no facial features, only the faint outline of a nose and mouth. The small girl looked at it and asked, "Who is it, *thunkashila?* – grandfather?"

"It is you, Heesha," Chayton leaned down and whispered to his granddaughter. "The bone is from a *wakan* – sacred animal. I carved it for you."

"What will it do?" Heesha asked.

"It will protect you through life," Chayton replied.

Heesha tightened her grip around the small amulet and then reopened her hand, making sure it had not vanished like magic. She looked up and smiled at her grandfather. Chayton gave his granddaughter a hug and then struggled to stand up.

"*Pilamaya, thunkashila,* – thank you, grandfather," Heesha replied.

Chayton smiled at the small girl and then shuffled a few steps to his right so he could stand in front of his grandson, Cansha. Chayton leaned over and whispered, "Hold out your hand, Cansha."

Cansha held out his hand with the palm up. Chayton stuck his hand in his satchel and withdrew the *inyan wakan,* the sacred red and gray striped rock, brought from Chayton's first canyon home. This was Chayton's most prized possession. Chayton stared at the *inyan wakan* and his mind drifted back through a lifetime of memories. Out of the five original sacred rocks, this was the only one left. It had been with Chayton throughout most of his life. Chayton rubbed the surface of the rock with his thumb, something he had always done. He reached out and gently placed the *inyan wakan* in the young

61

boy's hand. Cansha grabbed the rock and moved it up near his eyes, so he could see it better.

"Cansha is too young," Hoka told Chayton.

"When he becomes a hunter, he will have it," Chayton answered.

Chayton leaned down and covered Cansha's hand and the sacred rock with his own hand. Chayton leaned forward and whispered to his grandson, "Cansha, this *inyan wakan* has brought me power...It has brought me wisdom...I want you to have it. It will give you power and protect you as it has protected me."

Cansha looked into his grandfather's frosty eyes and then back at the sacred rock. Chayton stood up, struggling to straighten his bent back. Hoka watched Chayton labor to get to his feet and became even more concerned about the journey. Chayton stood there, a smile on his face, watching his grandson flip the large rock back and forth between his hands, finally dropping it in the dirt. Hoka sidled up alongside Chayton and said, "Cansha does not understand the importance of the *inyan wakan*."

"He will," Chayton replied, smiling. "Now, I must leave."

Chayton turned around and Wiyaka was standing in front of him. Chayton smiled at his old friend and his eyes immediately misted with tears. "This is my most difficult goodbye, *le mita kola*, – my friend," Chayton told Wiyaka.

"*Ai*, – Yes, for me as well, *sunka*, – brother," Wiyaka replied with a smile, then adding, "I have been waiting for you to leave for a long time."

"Always the wise one," Chayton said with a chuckle that set off another bout of hacking and coughing.

"Your breathing is *sica*, – bad," Wiyaka proclaimed. "You cannot go on this journey. You should be sleeping under a tree like the old gopher that you are."

"I will...KAAF! I will let you...KAAF!...do the sleeping for me," Chayton stammered between coughs.

"I do not think a worn–out *wichah^cala* – old man is able to go on a dangerous journey."

"*Enila!* – Be quiet!" Chayton replied. "You are as old as me! You are as worn out as me!"

"*Hee ya!* – No!" Wiyaka stated. "I will not let you go on this journey!"

"KAAF! KAAF!" Chayton coughed again and then replied to Wiyaka in a gravelly voice, "You will not let me go? Ha! Are you going to stop me?"

"What will you do *wichah^cala?* – old man?" Wiyaka demanded. "Hit me with your walking staff?"

"I will break it over your thick noggin!" Chayton exclaimed. "It will be like hitting that rock over there!"

"I am not letting you go," Wiyaka repeated.

"Get out of my way, Wiyaka!"

"I am not letting you go," Wiyaka continued, "unless I am going with you!"

"*Taku?* – What?"

"You need someone to watch out for your old hide."

"*Taku?* – What?" Chayton repeated.

"You cannot even hear!" Wiyaka responded. "How are you going to hear *igmuwatogla* – mountain lion when you cannot even hear me standing in front of you?"

Chayton was confused. He stood there with a bewildered look on his face.

"You stand there looking *takuni slolye sni!* – stupid! You look like you are lost and you have not even left the village!" Wiyaka bellowed. "You are not fit for this journey! That is why I am going along with you!"

"As slow as you are?" Chayton challenged. "I am not waiting for you!"

"I am ready to leave," Wiyaka announced, holding up his satchel and water pouch.

"You are not taking weapons?"

"Over there, by the rock, blind one," Wiyaka said with a grin.

"You must keep up with me! I will not wait for you!"

"A snail crawling in the creek can keep up with you," Wiyaka responded.

"I am not helping you on the trail."

"I will be carrying you on my back before we reach the first hill," Wiyaka replied.

"As irritable as you are, I am sure no one will miss you here."

"Are you going to walk or chatter like a deaf squirrel?" Wiyaka demanded.

"Walk!"

"Where are we going?" Wiyaka asked.

"That is for me to decide."

"We are probably going to the first hill where you will stop and take a nap."

"Eh!"

"Ha! Ha! It does not matter how far!" Wiyaka exclaimed. "I will still be saving your life, just like past journeys."

"Eh!" Chayton groaned halfway out of the village.

"Hogan!" Hoka yelled at his son. "*Hi! – Come!*"

Hogan was saying goodbye to his girlfriend on the other side of the village. When Hogan heard his father yelling at him, he just moved closer to the girl.

"Hogan!" Hoka screamed even louder.

"Hogan!" his mother shouted at him.

Hogan heard his mother, but hugged his girlfriend instead. Then, he slowly plodded towards his mother and father, his head drooping down towards the ground. When he got to his parents, he walked right past them without saying a word, following Chayton and Wiyaka down the trail. Frustrated, Hoka and Ptecila looked at each other with concern.

"Make him a hunter," Ptecila pleaded to Hoka.

"I will try," Hoka replied and then hugged and kissed his wife goodbye.

***

At their slow pace, it took the travelers nearly two suns to reach *Pankeska Wahpa,* – Shell River, the site where the Folsom People had camped for many winters. The travelers then headed south towards *Katiyimo* – Enchanted Mesa and reached it just as the sun was dropping behind it to the west. Chayton stopped in front of the shadowy slope of the mesa and looked up at the sky. He watched the golden eagles ride the wind currents, circling the mesa for food.

Hoka walked up alongside his father and asked, "Is this where we camp?"

Still smiling at the sight of the birds of prey, Chayton replied, "*Hee ya,* – No, we will go further."

Chayton continued to watch the eagles and then without saying a word, he suddenly took off walking towards the south. Wiyaka quickly followed him leaving Hoka and his son Hogan still standing under the shadows of *Katiyimo*. This gave Hogan another opportunity to complain to his father. "*Thunkashila* – Grandfather is walking as slow as a *keya,* – turtle," Hogan declared to his father. "I could have walked this far in half a sun."

"*Enila!* – Be quiet!" Hoka scolded his son. "*Thunkashila* – Grandfather can hear you!"

"*Thunkashila* – Grandfather could not hear a *tatanka* – bison if it was bellowing in his ear!" Hogan jeered with a laugh.

"Be respectful, Hogan!"

"*Até,* – Father, I did not ask you to bring me on this journey."

"I know," Hoka replied. "You are here to learn from *thunkashila.* – grandfather. He will help you become a hunter."

"I am a hunter!" Hogan blurted out.

"*Ai,* on the outside you are as tall as a hunter," Hoka replied with measured calmness in his voice, "but inside you are a *hokshila. –* boy."

Hogan started to back talk his father, but a shout from Chayton interrupted them.

"Hogan!" Chayton yelled. "*Hi! Inahni! –* Come! Hurry!"

"What does he want?" Hogan scoffed.

"Hogan!" Chayton shouted again. "*Inahni! –* Hurry!"

"*Iyaya! –* Go!" Hoka demanded, but his son did not budge.

"*Wayaka! –* Look!" Chayton shouted.

Hogan finally left his father's side and slowly ambled towards Chayton. When Hogan eventually arrived, he found Chayton pointing at something on the ground.

"What do you see?" Chayton asked.

Hogan inspected the ground where Chayton's finger was pointing. He did not see anything, but instead of telling his grandfather that he saw nothing, he decided to play along with the game. Hogan leaned down further, his nose almost touching the ground. He could barely contain his laughter.

"What do you see?" Chayton repeated.

"I see a track," Hogan answered, finally noticing what Chayton was making the fuss about.

"What kind of track?"

"A muddy track."

"*Hee ya! Hee ya! Hee ya! –* No! No! No!" Chayton bellowed and then asked, "What kind of animal made the track?"

Hogan giggled and then moved his nose even closer to the ground. "Let me smell it," Hogan jeered.

"Smell it?" Chayton questioned.

"It is a large track," Hogan smirked, "*Ai!* It is a large and muddy track."

"It is in the mud and it is large!" Chayton roared with frustration. "What animal made this track?"

Hogan started laughing as he hid his face close to the ground. Hogan pretended he was carefully investigating the track, but he had no idea what animal had left it. More importantly, he did not care.

"*Slol wa yea shnee, –* I do not know," Hogan answered and then he decided to guess. "Is it *Mato? –* Bear?"

Chayton looked over at the boy's father with a look of disbelief on his face. Hoka turned away, embarrassed that his son would say the track belonged to a bear. Chayton then turned back to Hogan and challenged him, "*Mato?* You think that a *mato* made this track?"

"Ha! Ha! Ha! That is not the track of a *mato*, *hokshila!* – bear, boy!" Wiyaka interrupted the conversation with a taunt.

"*Slol wa yea shnee*, – I do not know," Hogan replied and then he guessed again, "*Sunkmanitu tanka! –* Wolf!"

"*Sunkmanitu tanka? –* Wolf?" Hoka challenged.

"What have you taught this *hokshila*, Hoka?" Chayton challenged the boy's father. "Three lobes on the bottom of the pad, Hogan, what is it?"

Hogan could not hold back his laughter any longer.

"What is funny, Hogan?" his father demanded.

"Nothing is funny, I am not good at this," Hogan admitted.

"You must learn!" Chayton lectured his grandson. "Your life…our lives depend on you recognizing danger around us!"

"You can go ahead and get yourself killed, *hokshila*," Wiyaka blurted out, "but you will not get us killed!"

Hogan looked unconvinced and bored with the whole exercise.

"This track belongs to a dangerous animal…a hunter of humans…it passed by here before us," Chayton declared. "You must learn sign! *Wayaka!* – Look!"

Chayton followed the trail of the tracks through the muddy soil, pointing at each individual paw print. Finally, he stopped and leaned over.

"The front paw is larger than the back paw," Chayton explained to Hogan. "The tracks are wide. This animal was running."

The hunters followed the trail with Chayton pointing at each visible track as he spotted them.

"No claw marks!" Wiyaka added.

"Here, the animal stopped," Chayton informed the boy, pointing at several paw prints in a small area. "*Wayaka! –* Look!"

"What else do you see?" Chayton asked Hogan.

Hogan looked around and spotted a small pile of dirt and mud off to one side. He walked over to take a closer look. He noticed striations in the soil from claw marks on the southwest side of the pile. "The animal buried something."

Chayton and Wiyaka began laughing and then Chayton said, "*Ai*, – Yes, it buried something."

"*Hokshila*, – Boy, you do not want what that animal buried," Wiyaka added, which made Chayton laugh even louder.

Hogan now realized what the animal had buried. He then inspected the claw marks in the muddy soil. Chayton noticed Hogan's interest in the claw marks and asked the boy, "What do these claw marks tell you about this animal?"

After thinking about it, Hogan could not come up with an answer and replied, "*Slol wa yea shnee.* – I do not know."

"At least the *hokshila* knows he is *takuni slolye sni,* – stupid," Wiyaka blurted out.

Hogan's angry face blushed with red as he took a step towards Wiyaka, but his father grabbed his arm.

"Do you want to die?" Chayton interrupted.

"*Taku?* – What?" Hogan demanded.

"Do you want to die, Hogan?"

"*Hee ya!* – No!" Hogan replied. "Who wants to die?"

"Then learn," Chayton replied. "The burial tells you it was probably a male and the scratch marks tell you the direction it was most likely traveling. See, the claw marks, they are sharp on this animal."

Chayton pointed to the southwest and added, "the animal was heading towards the south, perhaps heading for water and it stopped to make *cesli.* – feces."

After the hints, Hogan realized what animal made the tracks. He looked at Chayton and blurted out, "*Igmuwatogla!*"

"*Waste!* – Good!" Chayton praised Hogan. "*Igmuwatogla!* – Mountain lion!"

"*Takuni slolye sni hokshila,* – Stupid boy," Wiyaka mumbled under his breath.

Chayton looked at the position of the sun. It was touching the western horizon. "We will camp down there, next to those trees. There should be water," he announced to the others, pointing his walking staff to the south.

***

Hoka stood up and walked over to the campfire. He turned the rabbit carcass that hung roasting over the campfire. The other tired travelers sat around the campfire, watching the flames and deep in their own worlds. It had been a long time since Chayton and Wiyaka had walked that far. Both of them could barely keep their eyes open. Chayton's eyes gradually closed as the warmth of the campfire put him to sleep.

"Where are we going, *thunkashila?* – grandfather?" Hogan asked, waking Chayton up from his newly found sleep.

"Leave *thunkashila* alone, Hogan," Hoka insisted.

Hogan started to sass his father, but Chayton opened his eyes and replied, "That is all right, Hoka, I am awake. What is your question, Hogan?"

"Where are we going?" Hogan repeated. "You have not told us and we are traveling like a *keya.* – turtle."

Chayton smiled. "We have a long way to go," he replied. "There is no hurry."

"Where are we going?" Hogan repeated, unhappy with his grandfather's response.

"We are going to see your *thunkashila*, – grandfather," Chayton replied to the persistent boy.

"You are my *thunkashila*," Hogan shot back. "My other *thunkashila* is back at our village."

"*Ai*, – Yes," Chayton answered. "We are visiting the blood father of Hoka."

"Ah," Hogan replied without fully understanding. Growing up Hogan had heard his father occasionally speak of a blood father.

"I am sure you remember people talking about Kangi," Chayton added. "He was my friend and the blood father of Hoka."

Hogan did not say anything nor did anyone else. The only sounds came from the popping wood in the campfire and the cooing of a lonesome dove in a nearby tree. One by one, the travelers drifted off to sleep. No one noticed the pair of eyes watching from the trees.

***

At first light, Hogan woke up with his face lying in the dirt next to the campfire. Out of a half–opened eye, he watched Wiyaka leaning over and throwing more wood on the campfire. His eye drifted to the left where he saw Chayton sitting next to the campfire, talking with Hogan's father. Hogan brushed the dirt from his face and rubbed the sleep out of his eyes. Suddenly, his stomach gurgled. He was having an urgent call of nature and headed for the nearby stand of trees where he would have privacy to empty his stomach. He walked into the stand of trees and began looking for grass to use for cleaning himself. Hogan found some usable grass and began pulling it from the soil by its roots, collecting it in a pile.

When Hogan stood back up, he caught the glimpse of something out of the corner of his eye. He turned his head and spotted a large beast crouched in front of him in the grass, watching him. Hogan's stomach rolled and immediately became queasy as adrenalin rushed through his body. His hands shook from fright and then tingled with numbness. His mind turned blank as he stared back at the beast. Hogan's instincts told him to run, but his feet were frozen. Hogan tried to find air to breathe, but his chest was too tight to inhale. The mountain lion opened its mouth and out came a growl from deep within its throat. For the first time, Hogan realized that his weapons were at the campfire with his other gear. If the mountain lion attacked, Hogan had nothing to defend himself, except a small stone knife hanging from a strap around his neck. Hogan's mind now screamed for him to run, but somewhere in his memory, he remembered his father telling him never to run. *Movement makes igmuwatogla attack!* His feet were as numb as clay, but Hogan still fought the urge to run. His trembling hand slowly reached for the stone knife.

The mountain lion's eyes shifted when it noticed Hogan's hand moving. The mountain lion emitted another low growl while following the movement of Hogan's hand. Hogan stopped moving his hand. Hogan's legs went limp and his sphincter muscles relaxed, releasing everything in his bowels. Then, Hogan's bladder gave way and urine ran down his leg. The stench in the air around Hogan was overwhelming. The mountain lion patiently waited for the right moment to attack while Hogan fought the urge to vomit.

Movement to the left shifted the eyes of the mountain lion away from Hogan. A raspy cough echoed through the trees. Hogan shot a glance to his left and saw his grandfather standing next to him, a flaming pine log in his hand. Chayton had become a new distraction for the mountain lion. The big male cat began padding its back legs, preparing to pounce. Chayton suddenly threw the burning torch directly at the skull of the mountain lion and the cat leapt backwards, away from the smoke and flames. With its ears flattened against its head, the mountain lion hissed and spat at the fiery piece of wood. The big cat took a step towards the torch, but when it sensed the heat, it retreated away from it.

"*IYAYA!* – GO!" Chayton screamed at the mountain lion, waving his arms wildly. The mountain lion turned and fled, bouncing over the fallen pine trees in the forest. Chayton walked over to Hogan and saw that the boy was trembling. Chayton sniffed the air and knew Hogan no longer needed to make waste. Chayton then looked down and noticed the wet grass where Hogan was standing.

"KAAF! KAAF!" Chayton coughed to rid his throat of phlegm and to expel the rancid smell of feces floating in the air. Chayton finally covered his nose with the inside bend of his elbow. Hogan stood there shaking, too terrified to move.

"This is why we notice animal sign," Chayton lectured his grandson, speaking through the inside bend of his elbow. "Clean yourself and then we will eat. We have far to travel."

Chayton turned and walked back to the camp, leaving Hogan shaking like a leaf in a strong breeze.

***

Chayton led the way, stopping often to admire the beautiful country that surrounded the travelers. He and Wiyaka were also searching for landmarks that would jog their memories as to where they were. Wiyaka remembered more than Chayton, but he let his friend find the way since this was, after all, Chayton's journey. Hoka was patiently waiting for Chayton and Wiyaka to figure out where they were when his son approached him.

"The old men do not know where we are," Hogan whispered to his father.

"It has been many winters since they were here," Hoka defended the old hunters. "Land changes…memories fade."

"We are lost," Hogan replied. "We should go back to our village, *até. –* father."

"*Enila! –* Be quiet!" Hoka exclaimed. "Do not let them hear you."

"They cannot hear me, they cannot hear anything," Hogan proclaimed, "and now they are lost,"

"*Enila! –* Be quiet!" Hogan's father thundered.

Hogan stormed off, disgusted with his father, the old men, and the journey.

By the time the sun was deep in the west, the travelers finally arrived at their destination, a place where the Folsom People once camped and where they had buried Kangi, Hoka's blood father. There was just enough light left in the day to locate the remains of the wooden burial scaffold where Kangi lay, but not enough light to see anything else.

"We will camp here," Chayton proclaimed. "Tomorrow, we will visit our friend. – *kola.*"

"Visit our friend?" Hogan questioned his father with a smile. "Does Chayton not know this is a grave?"

"Respect!" Hoka exclaimed, "He is *thunkashila* – grandfather to you."

"*Hat'ugha? –* Why?" Hogan asked. "You call him Chayton…and besides he is not of my blood! My blood *thunkashila* is up there on that pile of wood!"

Chayton could not help but overhear the bickering between father and son.

70

"Hogan, gather firewood for the campfire," he said while walking up behind Hoka and Hogan.

"*Ai, Chayton,* – Yes, Chayton," Hogan replied with a wry smile.

Chayton watched the back of his departing grandson. Hogan had never called him anything but grandfather before. Hoka quickly apologized for his son, "I am sorry, *até,* – father, Hogan respects nothing."

"Hogan is learning his way," Chayton replied, putting his arm around his stepson. "Be patient."

While Chayton and Hogan built the campfire, Wiyaka and Hoka cleaned and prepared the musky–smelling badger that Hoka had killed during the day's journey. After eating most of the badger, the travelers sat back and rested their weary bodies by the campfire. Chayton peered over at the burial scaffold and watched the light of the campfire dance on the weathered wood.

"How did he die?" Hogan asked, breaking the silence.

"Who?" Hoka asked Hogan for clarification.

"*Thunkashila,* – Grandfather," Hogan replied.

"I was a *chincá,* – child," Hoka stated. "*Slol wa yea shnee.* – I do not know."

"I was not there," Wiyaka added.

All three of them looked at Chayton whose mind had already departed back to that horrendous day when the grizzly bear sow killed Kangi.

"*Thunkashila,* – Grandfather, I mean Chayton, tell us," Hogan requested.

"*Ai,* – Yes," Hoka seconded.

Chayton was not sure he was ready to relive that day in the mountains, but he knew it was his obligation to pass on the story to both Hoka and Hogan. After thinking about where to start, Chayton recounted the story. "We were hunting in the mountains," he began. "Your father and grandfather... Kangi was leading us up one of the many canyons that reached high into the mountains. Trees lined the trail. The brush was so thick we had to crawl."

Chayton had to stop before he continued. In the darkness of the night, the other travelers could not see the tears forming at the corners of Chayton's eyes. He coughed and then looked back up at the burial scaffold, a stark reminder of the sacred ground where the travelers now camped. Chayton swallowed hard and then continued to recount what happened that day, many winters ago. "Kangi...your father...was ahead of us on the trail," he explained. "When the canyon opened up onto a meadow, two *matos*...little ones...were resting along the trail. Their mother...their protector attacked your father."

71

The travelers sat there and stared at the campfire, waiting for Chayton to continue, but he never finished the story. Chayton had no reason to finish the story. All of the travelers knew how the story ended without Chayton explaining it. Seldom did humans survive an attack from a mother grizzly bear. The quiet ended when Hogan asked a question, "Why did he not kill the *mato*?"

The three hunters looked around at each other. They had all witnessed the size and the tremendous power of a grizzly bear sow. Hogan was asking a foolish question, but he was just a boy. Chayton decided to answer it. "The *mato* was too strong…too fast," Chayton replied after clearing his throat.

"Why did you not help my *thunkashila?* – grandfather?" Hogan questioned.

"I tried…we tried," Chayton answered, recalling the terrible incident in his mind. "We were too late to help Kangi."

"You were not brave!" Hogan blurted out.

"Hogan!" Hoka thundered.

"Chayton was not brave and so my *thunkashila* dies," Hogan declared. "If I had been there, I would have done more."

"*Hokshila,* – Boy, you would have filled your pants with *cesli* – feces when you saw the *mato*!" Wiyaka roared. "Just like when you faced *igmuwatogla!* – mountain lion! Don't tell me what you–"

Chayton held up his hand to stop Wiyaka from chastising the boy. Wiyaka peered over at Chayton, not wanting to stop the verbal attack.

Chayton thought about the incident with the grizzly bear and after a long pause, he said to Hogan, "*Ai,* – Yes, we were *canl waka.* – cowards."

"Hah! Chayton was a *canl waka* and my *thunkashila* dies!" Hogan declared. The boy then looked directly at Chayton and asked, "How do you live with this, *Chayton*?"

Wiyaka sprung to his feet as quickly as a hunter did half of his age. Wiyaka reached over and snatched the boy off the ground. Wiyaka raised his arm and was just about ready to smack the boy across the face when Chayton grabbed Wiyaka's arm.

"*Hee ya, Wiyaka!* – No, Wiyaka!"

"Chayton!" Wiyaka begged. "Just one–just one hit!"

"*Hee ya,*" Chayton repeated, shaking his head. "I will answer his question."

"You do not need to answer my son, he has no respect," Hoka interrupted.

"I only have to answer to *Wakan Tanka*," Chayton replied with a whimsical smile. "But, I will also answer my grandson."

Chayton sat down next to Hogan and faced him. "I have not lived well knowing what happened to my friend Kangi," Chayton declared. "I have always wondered if I could have done more to help him."

Chayton leaned back and coughed several times in his hand. He then cleared his throat and spat a chunk of phlegm out into the darkness. "I saved the life of Kangi before," Chayton continued, "but was unable to save him a second time. *Wakan Tanka* gave Kangi one chance, not two."

This temporarily quieted Hogan. Chayton then sprawled out on the ground while Wiyaka threw more wood on the campfire. Hoka gave his son a smoldering look and started to say something to him, but decided against it. Hoka lay down and rolled over on his side, facing away from his son. Hogan remained awake, watching the campfire and thinking about his two grandfathers and their lives. Just before he fell asleep, Hogan peered over at the burial scaffold and thought to himself, *I will meet you tomorrow, thunkashila!*

***

At first light, Hogan was lying half–asleep when a moccasin–covered foot plowed into his shoulder. "*Key kte yo! –* Wake up!" the voice demanded.

Ignoring the intruder, Hogan rolled over on his other side and was just about ready to doze off when another foot connected with him, this time with much more force.

"*Wana! –* Now!" the voice exclaimed.

Hogan rolled over and opened an eye to see who was bothering him. Through his glazed eye, Hogan saw the grizzled old face of Chayton glaring down at him.

"*Kikta! –* Get up!" Chayton roared, kicking with enough force to slide Hogan's body across the ground. Hogan jumped to his feet, ready to fight the old man, but when he saw that Chayton was still larger, Hogan quickly backed down. Instead, he turned his back to Chayton and asked, "*Taku? –* What?"

"You are eating our food, but you are not providing food," Chayton replied. "It is your turn to hunt, so we can eat what you provide."

Hogan looked around to see where his father was. He spotted Hoka carrying firewood to the campfire. Hogan looked at his father, hoping he would intervene between him and Chayton.

"Listen to *thunkashila*," Hoka suggested to his son, "We share the work. We share the food."

"He is not my *thunkashila,* – grandfather," Hogan responded and then demanded, "How do I find food for four humans?"

"You only need to find food for three humans," Wiyaka blurted out. "You do not need to eat."

"You will find food with these!" Chayton interrupted Wiyaka. Chayton tossed Hogan his quiver and satchel.

Hogan caught the quiver in midair, but the satchel smacked him right in the mouth and then fell to the ground. Hogan scowled at Chayton and then reached down and picked up his satchel. Chayton set his feet right in front of Hogan, blocking the boy's path. Chayton waited for his grandson to do something.

"*Wana, iyaya!* – Now, go!" Chayton told Hogan. "Return when the sun is full, we have much work to do."

Hogan reluctantly turned around and started walking up a hill near the camp.

"Be careful of *igmuwatogla!* – mountain lion!" Wiyaka yelled at the boy. "We do not want to have to smell you! Ha! Ha! Ha! Ha!"

"Wiyaka!" Chayton blurted out, a hint of a smile on his face. Chayton then saw where Hogan was heading and yelled, "Where are you going, Hogan?"

Hogan pointed up the hill with the tip of his spear.

"*Minne!* – Water!" Chayton bellowed, pointing down the hill in the opposite direction. "You will find animals near *minne!*"

Hogan turned around and walked down the hill. He walked past Wiyaka who pretended to be sniffing the air with his nose. As soon as Hogan was out of sight, the other three travelers began laughing.

"We will make Hogan a hunter, even if he does not want to be a hunter," Chayton declared.

"I will go hunt, as well," Wiyaka offered. "I do not feel like sharing the grasshopper the *hokshila* will bring back from his hunt."

Wiyaka left and it was not long before Chayton and Hoka heard a snapping twig. Standing at the top of the hill was Wiyaka, carrying two dead rabbits. "I caught them sleeping," Wiyaka announced, hoisting the rabbits in the air by their ears.

"*Haw,* Wiyaka," Chayton greeted his friend with a toothless grin, "bring me your rabbits and I will skin them for you."

The three travelers cleaned and skinned the rabbits, then grilled them over the open campfire. They had just finished the last bite of rabbit when Hogan showed up from his hunt, empty–handed. Hogan walked around the camp and noticed the discarded rabbit bones. Hogan glared at the three travelers, waiting for an explanation.

"What food did you bring us?" Chayton asked Hogan after a belch.

Wiyaka returned Chayton's burp with his own. "*Ai, lol wah cheen!* – Yes, I am hungry! Ha! Ha! Ha!" Wiyaka proclaimed with a laugh.

"I found nothing," Hogan replied.

"You found nothing?" Chayton confirmed. "*Hat'ugha?* – Why?"

"I saw a deer, but it was too far," Hogan responded.

"I saw a deer, but it was too far," Wiyaka mocked the high–pitched voice of the boy.

"This is why you have spears," Chayton replied. "You do not have to outrun the deer and wrestle it to the ground with your hands. You can throw a good spear and it will find the deer."

"I know that, grandfa–*Chayton*!" Hogan grumbled.

"We ate the rabbits that Wiyaka killed," Chayton replied.

"I see that," Hogan replied while eyeballing the rabbit remains strewn across the camp.

"I do have some meat left on this leg bone," Chayton said, holding up a gnawed leg bone. Hogan grabbed the leg bone and held it up for inspection. There was not much meat left on the bone and the meat that remained was mushy from Chayton gumming it. Wiyaka watched and could not help but laugh. When Wiyaka finally stopped laughing, he belched as loud as a rutting elk. Then, he told Hogan, "You can have some of that! It smells like rabbit meat. Ha! Ha! Ha!"

This brought laughter from all three travelers. Hogan looked over at his father, but his father was laughing too hard to notice.

"We have much work!" Chayton finally announced when the others could not laugh any longer. "*Inahni, Hogan!* – Hurry, Hogan! Finish your rabbit, so we can go to work!"

Chayton and the others walked towards the burial scaffold while Hogan kept staring at the mutilated leg bone from the rabbit. Finally, he threw the leg bone as far as he could heave it and followed the others to the burial scaffold.

"*Le mita kola, Kangi,* – My friend, Kangi," Chayton mumbled, "You find yourself in a bad way."

Chayton inspected the burial scaffold and saw that only the lower half of the burial bundle was still intact on top of the scaffold. Scattered across the ground below the scaffold were the rest of Kangi's bones, deteriorating and bleaching in the high plains sun.

"We will need a grave," Chayton announced and then looking at Hogan, he said, "After you eat your rabbit, you will help me dig a grave."

"How?" Hogan replied, throwing his arms up out of frustration.

"I will show you," Chayton replied.

"He will dig," Hoka added.

Hogan gave his father an angry look.

"*Waste,* – Good," Chayton replied. "Find something to dig with, Hogan."

Chayton turned to Hoka and Wiyaka and said, "Collect the bones of our *kola* – friend while I help Hogan!"

Hogan followed Chayton up to some nearby pine trees where Chayton pulled out a thin stone knife and began stripping the pine needles and bark from one of the lower branches.

"Do as I do," Chayton suggested to Hogan.

Hogan took his stone knife and did exactly as his grandfather. Once both Chayton and Hogan had stripped the pine branches, Chayton instructed Hogan, "Cut around the branch back here."

Chayton cut around the tree branch with his sharp knife blade until he could break the tree branch off the tree.

"This is a digger," he announced to Hogan and then asked, "Why are you slow?"

Hogan had been watching Chayton and had forgotten to do his own work. He pushed his knife blade around the tree branch, sawing back and forth until he thought he could break it off. Hogan tried to break off the branch, but it was too green and thick.

"You could help me," Hogan said, puffing and pushing.

"*Ai,* – Yes, I could help you," Chayton agreed, but did nothing.

Hogan was now sweating a river while he continued to saw and hack away at the tree branch. Chayton watched as Hogan bent the tree branch first one way and then another. Finally, he offered Hogan a suggestion, "Save your strength, you will need it for digging the grave."

Hogan looked at Chayton and rolled his eyes. He went back to cutting the tree branch, muttering between breaths, "My knife is dull."

Chayton, not wanting to miss an opportunity to help the boy, replied, "Why is your knife dull? Do you not take care of your hunting gear?"

Hogan just went after the tree branch even harder, jerking the branch back and forth, his mind pretending he was thrashing Chayton. Finally, the tree

76

branch had nothing left to do but break with a resounding crack. Hogan sat at the base of the tree, huffing and puffing, sweat rolling off his arms and face.

"Do not stop to rest," Chayton scolded him, "we have work to do."

Before Hogan could even stand up, Chayton was down the hill and digging the grave in a likely spot. After giving up on two spots that ended up too rocky, Chayton found the perfect spot, right in the midst of a grove of pine trees.

"Your *thunkashila* – grandfather will like the view," Chayton said to Hogan as they dug the grave together with the tree branches.

"What was *thunkashila* like?" Hogan asked.

"Kangi was a brave hunter," Chayton answered. "Braver than any hunter I have ever known…except, maybe Wiyaka…perhaps Pahin…and Hexaka… probably not as brave as Waquini…or Avonaco."

Hogan continued to dig without saying anything else. He was thinking about the grandfather that he never knew.

"Hogan, we will talk about your grandfather many times on this journey," Chayton continued. "You will learn about your grandfather, you will learn about our tribe, but mostly you will learn about yourself."

Hogan did not understand how he could learn about himself. That made no sense. He did not say anything to Chayton. Hogan looked at the location of the sun. It had barely cleared the eastern horizon and he was already exhausted. He then looked over at Chayton and saw how the old man was attacking the grave with his tree branch. Hogan picked up his pace to match that of his grandfather. Hogan thrust his tree branch into the hole, loosening up the compacted soil.

"Bring our *kola* – friend over here!" Chayton shouted to Wiyaka.

Hoka and Wiyaka had collected all of the bones they could find on the ground and had retrieved the remains of the burial bundle from the scaffold. They then walked over to the grave and carefully placed the burial bundle and bones in the bottom.

"What do you remember about your father, Hoka?" Chayton asked while fumbling around in his satchel.

Hoka had to think about the answer to that question. Many winters had dulled his memory. He was young at the time of his father's death and barely even remembered what his father looked like. He remembered more about Chayton than his own father. Chayton came into his life shortly after his father's death and for Hoka, Chayton would always be his father, whether related by blood or not.

"I was young," Hoka replied. "I remember how my mother mourned for my father."

"*Ai,* – Yes," Chayton said, thinking about how Tonkala had mutilated herself after her husband's death. Chayton looked over at Wiyaka, trying to decide whether to ask Wiyaka what he remembered about Kangi. Chayton knew that Wiyaka and Kangi had never seen things the same way, so Chayton was not sure he wanted to know what Wiyaka thought.

"He was a brave hunter," Wiyaka offered without Chayton asking.

"*Pilamaya, Wiyaka!* – Thank you, Wiyaka!" Chayton replied and was relieved Wiyaka had not told the others what he really thought about Kangi.

Chayton pulled out a pouch from his satchel and opened it up. He dug into the pouch and retrieved a fluted spear point covered in a fine, red powder. He held the fluted projectile point up to the sky and said to everyone, "This is a fine fluted spear point I made to give to my friend Kangi."

Chayton gently set the fluted spear point in the grave on the remains of the burial bundle. Chayton then put his hand in the pouch and pulled out a small handful of red powder. He sprinkled red powder over the burial bundle and loose bones. He handed the pouch to Wiyaka who did the same and then Wiyaka passed the pouch to Hoka. Finally, after watching the seasoned hunters, Hogan did exactly the same thing until a light coat of the red powder covered the burial bundle and bones. Hogan handed the pouch back to Chayton and referring to the red powder, he asked, "What is this?"

"*Wasaya,*" Chayton replied.

"*Wasa...*" Hogan attempted to repeat.

"*Wasaya,*" Chayton repeated with a smile.

"*Was–wasaya,*" Hogan repeated.

"*Wasaya,* – Red," Hoka said. "The powder purifies the grave."

"*Wasaya* – Red leads us to the good trail," Chayton explained. Then, he pointed to the north and said, "A trail north is pure." Chayton then turned his arm and pointed to the south. "A trail south leads to where all life begins," he explained to Hogan.

"Are there any other words for Kangi?" Wiyaka impatiently asked the other travelers, hoping they could soon hit the trail.

The travelers peered around at each other, but no one said anything except Hogan. "I wish you were here," Hogan said, looking down at the burial bundle at the bottom of the grave. "I need a *thunkashila.* – grandfather."

Hoka glared at Hogan with angry eyes and then he turned to Chayton and said, "Hogan did not mean what he said."

Chayton smiled and swept the comment away with his hand. "He is speaking from his heart," he replied to Hoka.

The travelers pushed the dirt into the grave, covering the last of Kangi's remains. They then stacked rocks on top of the grave to prevent any disturbance. When the hunters were finished, they all turned to Chayton, wondering if he was now ready to go home.

"I will now visit my *thanhanshi, –* cousin," Chayton announced, his eyes gazing towards the south. "Hogan, you are the hunter."

Chapter Seven

"What is this place, *até?* – father?" Hogan asked.

"This is the Dead Pine Forest," Hoka replied.

"It is a horrible place," Hogan added, surveying the blowing sand and sparse vegetation.

Hoka looked around and could not argue with his son. The Dead Pine Forest was desolate and foreboding, filled with the *wanagis* – ghosts of the dead. Hoka had last crossed the Dead Pine Forest when he was just a small boy, but he vividly remembered the sandstorm that almost buried the tribe alive.

"What does he expect me to hunt in this place?" Hogan questioned.

"Who?" Hoka asked for clarification.

"Chayton," Hogan replied.

"*Ai,* – yes, *thunkashila* said you were our hunter," Hoka recalled with a smile.

"*Ai,* I am a hunter with nowhere to hunt," Hogan jeered.

"Keep your eyes keen," Hoka stated, "there is food even here."

Hogan looked at the featureless hills and gullies and saw nothing that would even remotely resemble food. Hogan thought his father was just as crazy as the old man was. A short distance ahead of Hoka and Hogan, Wiyaka and Chayton were leading the crossing of the Dead Pine Forest.

"Do you know where you are going, *le mita kola?* – my friend?" Wiyaka asked.

"*Hee ya,* – No," Chayton responded. "I do not remember."

"Ha! Ha! The last time I crossed this place it was dark and I too was lost," Wiyaka bellowed. "Then I had to return and rescue you."

"I remember," Chayton declared and then after a pause, he added, "some of it, anyway."

"The Dead Pine Forest was where we found the dead *ozuye,* – war party," Wiyaka reminisced, "ripped apart by *Wakan Tanka.*"

"I am taking you back into danger, *le mita kola,*" Chayton replied.

"*Ai,*" Wiyaka replied and then smiled. "We must watch our water, we have little left and we still have to cross the Arid Plains."

"You worry too much, *le mita kola,*" Chayton said.

"Ha! Ha! Ha! Ha!" Wiyaka laughed. "I worry because I am with you!"

"Go check our hunter, Wiyaka," Chayton suggested with a chuckle, "I see animal sign everywhere, but Hogan has never left his father's side."

Wiyaka dropped back to where Hoka and Hogan were walking.

"Does he know where he is going?" Hogan questioned Wiyaka while pointing his finger at Chayton.

"Hogan, respect!" Hoka exclaimed.

Wiyaka glanced ahead at Chayton who was weaving and wandering through the sagebrush. The sight of Chayton lost amongst the sagebrush was not too encouraging, but Wiyaka laughed anyway, "Ha! Ha! Ha! Ha!"

"What is funny?" Hogan asked.

"*Hee ya,* – No, your *thunkashila* – grandfather does not know where he is going," Wiyaka responded. "The last time he crossed this land he was close to death."

Hogan peered over at Wiyaka, making sure the old hunter was not telling him another tall tale. "He was close to death?" the boy queried.

"*Ai,*" Wiyaka continued, "he was badly wounded by a spear from a warrior."

"*Thunkashila,* I mean Chayton has not told me that story," Hogan replied.

"Chayton is not one to talk about what he has done," Wiyaka stated. "I have to do his talking for him. Chayton is my friend and I do not like anyone talking bad about my friend."

"You talk bad about him," Hogan responded. "I have heard you call him old…slow…blind."

"I have suffered with your *thunkashila* and fought many battles with him," Wiyaka replied. "I have earned the right to call him what I want and he can do the same with me."

Hoka and Hogan said nothing, so Wiyaka changed the subject. "I am not worried about Chayton finding his way across this desert," Wiyaka proclaimed. "I am worried about Hogan finding us food."

"There are no animals!" Hogan blurted out.

"You will not find animals following your father," Wiyaka replied.

Hoka held back his laughter while his stammering son tried to think up a response.

"Your father will travel with Chayton," Wiyaka suggested to Hogan, "while you and I go search for food."

Wiyaka swung his spear shaft around, whacking Hogan on the butt with it.

"Follow me," Wiyaka ordered Hogan.

Hogan looked at his father, hoping that he would intervene, but Hoka kept walking straight ahead with a smile on his face. Wiyaka took off hiking to the west, moving surprisingly well for an old man.

"What if we cannot find them?" Hogan asked Wiyaka, struggling to keep up.

"Who are we looking for?" Wiyaka questioned.

"My father…Chayton."

"Ha! Ha! Ha!" Wiyaka responded with another laugh. "They cannot lose us! I will teach you to be a hunter….before you get us all killed!"

Wiyaka walked along, studying the ground, looking for trails and tracks. Hogan walked behind him, scanning the ground while attempting to determine what Wiyaka was looking for. They walked and walked until Wiyaka finally found animal sign. He stopped to let Hogan catch up.

"What do you see?" Wiyaka asked Hogan.

Hogan studied the ground, but did not say anything.

"*Hokshila,* – Boy, what do you see?" Wiyaka repeated his query.

"I am not a *hokshila,* – boy," Hogan responded.

"Then, do not act like a *hokshila,*" Wiyaka suggested.

Hogan started to say something, but changed his mind. He leaned over and studied the ground more closely. He saw where a hoof print had broken through the hard crust of the desert soil. Upon closer examination, it became clear what was happening.

"Many animal tracks," Hogan announced.

"What kind?"

"Deer," Hogan blurted out.

"Deer?" Wiyaka challenged. "I see no deer tracks! Show me deer tracks!"

"Here!" Hogan bellowed, thinking to himself, *right here, you blind old man!*

"Tell me why this is not the track of a deer?"

"*Taku?* – What?"

"You heard me."

Hogan studied the animal tracks, trying to see what he missed or if the old man was just giving him more grief. Then, he saw it. Even the great Wiyaka could make a mistake if he only looked at a single track. This animal left a trail and that gave the individual tracks an entirely different meaning. The walking and running gaits of a deer and this animal were different.

"*Tatoke!* – Antelope!" Hogan replied.

"*Ai, waste!* – Yes, good!" Wiyaka praised Hogan.

"What do you see?" Wiyaka asked. "*Wayaka! – Look!*"

Hogan walked around, looking at the ground. Finally, he announced, "Other tracks, many other tracks."

"Recent tracks?" Wiyaka queried.

"Some new…some weathered."

"What animals?"

"Many kinds," Hogan replied. "All coming and going along this same trail."

"*Waste, – Good,*" Wiyaka replied and then asked, "*Hat'ugha? – Why?*"

"*Minne! – Water!*"

"*Waste, – Good,*" Wiyaka stated. "We must be watchful, we are near water."

Wiyaka and Hogan hunched over and snuck ahead along the trail of animal tracks. The two travelers climbed a couple of small sand hills, making sure that they did not expose themselves to any animals on the other side. They climbed another hill and on the other side of this one, they spotted a small pond of water hidden in a depression between two sand dunes. This was a desert oasis for animals and humans alike. Drinking from the pond, the two travelers spotted a *tatoke* – antelope doe. Wiyaka grabbed Hogan by the shoulder and pulled him backwards towards the backside of the hill. Then, Wiyaka threw some grass in the air and watched it float away to the north.

"We are downwind," Wiyaka declared. "I will stay here and make the *tatoke* come to me. You–"

"How will you make the *tatoke* come to you?" Hogan interrupted.

"*Enila! – Be quiet!* We have no time for questions, just watch and learn!" Wiyaka snapped at the boy.

"I jus–"

"*Enila! – Be quiet!*" Wiyaka said and then pointed to the southwest. "You hide in the brush over there, between me and the *tatoke*. When the *tatoke* walks towards me, you kill it."

Hogan still did not understand how Wiyaka was going to get the antelope to walk towards him. It made no sense. Out of patience, Wiyaka thrust his arm up in the air and pointed towards the southwest, signaling Hogan to leave immediately. Hogan reluctantly crept off, unsure of what he was supposed to do. When Hogan had been gone long enough, Wiyaka climbed back up on the hilltop. The antelope doe was still standing by the pond, but it was no longer drinking. Its head was rotating back and forth as if searching for danger.

Wiyaka pulled his shirt off and wrapped it around one end of a spear shaft. He then took the spear and thrust it in the air, waving it back and forth. The antelope's eyes locked on the object waving in the breeze. Wiyaka pulled the spear shaft down. The antelope kept staring at the spot where it last saw the object. Wiyaka patiently lay hidden in the sagebrush, waiting. Then, something else finally distracted the antelope and it forgot all about the object. Wiyaka stood up and waved the spear in the air. The antelope's sharp eyes spotted the object and it began watching it. Wiyaka continued to wave the spear back and forth, playing on the natural curiosity of the antelope. The rhythmic motion of the waving spear mesmerized the animal. Unable to curb its inquisitive nature, the antelope took a couple of steps in the direction of Wiyaka. Then, after watching further, the antelope took another step or two towards the flapping spear, never taking its eyes off it.

Hidden behind a large yucca cactus, Hogan watched the game between the antelope and Wiyaka. The behavior of the antelope was predictable. It would watch the spear, glance around to make sure there was no other danger, and then take a few steps closer. The cycle repeated until the antelope was standing alongside Hogan within easy spear range. The antelope would never get any closer to Hogan and his chances of a kill would never be better. Without thinking, Hogan stood up and grabbed a spear from his quiver. The antelope immediately spotted Hogan's careless move. Its head spun around and locked onto the predator standing on the parched prairie. Hogan fumbled with the spear, attempting to get the nock of the spear onto the spur of his spear thrower.

Wiyaka looked over the hill just in time to see the disaster unfold. He saw the antelope directly in front of him and Hogan fumbling with a spear off to his right. The antelope now recognized both threats. Wiyaka dropped the spear with the shirt wrapped around it and reached for another spear. He was just launching a spear when the antelope dropped its hindquarters and dug its hooves into the hardened soil, rapidly accelerating across the prairie. Hogan finally had his spear ready and threw it in the direction of the antelope, but the spear missed its target by a wide margin. Wiyaka started to throw his second spear, but the antelope had already disappeared over a sandy hill in the distance.

Wiyaka strutted over and picked up his first spear, cursing that the projectile point had snapped off. Then, he plodded towards Hogan, furious with the boy and livid about missing the opportunity for fresh meat.

"What happened?" Wiyaka demanded.

"*Tatoke* moved fast," Hogan replied.

"Hogan moved slowly!" Wiyaka blurted out. "You are no help at all, *hokshila!*"

Hogan started to say something, but Wiyaka had already turned on his heel and walked away. Wiyaka yelled over his shoulder at Hogan, "Gather fuel for a campfire!"

"Here?" Hogan asked, but Wiyaka was already too far away to hear, heading in the direction of the departing antelope.

With his eyes filled with tears of anger, Hogan gathered whatever fuel he could find for a campfire, realizing Wiyaka had deserted him and it would soon be dark. He was tired of Wiyaka and the journey. He vowed that if he ever saw his father again, he would tell him that he was going home. He could still find his way back to the North Country, but in a few more days, he may not be able to. He hunkered down by the small pile of fuel for the campfire and hoped that Wiyaka would return before dark.

Daylight left the Dead Pine Forest quickly and Hogan found himself sitting in the dim light of dusk waiting for Wiyaka to return. Hogan was now frightened, wondering if the three hunters had somehow forgotten about him in this desolate place. As the night turned black, every sound became a threat to Hogan.

"Why have you not started a campfire?" a voice bellowed out of the darkness. Hogan jumped to his feet, peering out into the dark night. He barely made out the shadowy outline of a human approaching him.

"What are you doing, *hokshila? –* boy?" the distinctive voice of Wiyaka echoed through the sand hills.

"I was waiting for you," Hogan responded.

"Waiting for me to start a campfire?" Wiyaka challenged and then bellowed, "Get it started, *WANA! –* NOW!"

Hogan scrambled to find his spindle and some tinder. Wiyaka stood there watching Hogan impatiently, his hands on his hips.

"*Inahni! –* Hurry!' Wiyaka bellowed, causing the boy to become even more flustered.

Finally, small flames appeared out of the tinder and Wiyaka threw some dry dung on the campfire. Before long, the campfire was burning bright.

"You did not collect enough wood and dung," Wiyaka said to Hogan. "How will we keep beasts away during the night?"

"Beasts?" Hogan asked.

"*Iyaya! –* Go! Find more wood and dung before I feed you to *sunkmanitu tanka!* – wolf!" Wiyaka responded. "I must clean this stringy jackrabbit for my meal."

Hogan reluctantly headed out in the darkness to look for more fuel to burn on the campfire.

***

"There it is," Chayton told Hoka, pointing towards a pinpoint of light on the dark arid prairie. Chayton and Hoka walked towards the light and when they arrived, they found Wiyaka and Hogan sitting next to a campfire fueled by sagebrush and dung. The first thing Chayton noticed was the skinny carcass of a jackrabbit, dangling from a spear shaft over the campfire.

"Is there a rabbit for each of us?" Chayton asked. "*Lol wah cheen.* – I am hungry."

"*Hee ya,* – No," Wiyaka responded. "This is all Hogan and I found."

"The great hunter Wiyaka could only find one scrawny rabbit after a day of hunting? Ha! Ha! Ha!" Chayton questioned, giving his friend Wiyaka a hard time over his lack of hunting prowess.

"This is all Hogan and I found," Wiyaka mumbled. "Can you not hear?"

"You are not much of a hunter, *le mita kola*," Chayton replied, goading Wiyaka even further.

The travelers sat quietly around the campfire, devouring every morsel of meat and marrow from the chewed and broken bones of that gaunt jackrabbit. Hogan finally interrupted the cracking of bones and smacking of lips with his announcement.

"*Até,* – Father, I have decided to head back to the North Country."

Hoka started to respond to his son's crazy idea when Chayton jumped in. "That is a good idea, Hogan," Chayton suggested.

Hoka glared at Chayton, wondering if the old man had a case of heat stroke. Hoka turned to reply to Hogan and Chayton interrupted him again. "We are almost across the Dead Pine Forest, so you must travel back across it...alone...but keep walking north and you have a good...maybe not so good...chance of surviving," Chayton said.

Wiyaka suddenly burst out laughing, drawing the attention of the other three travelers. When Wiyaka reestablished his composure, he said, "That reminds me of a story."

"Not another one of your stories, Wiyaka!" Chayton asserted in an attempt to discourage Wiyaka from getting involved in a family matter.

"*Ai,*" Wiyaka replied and after a brief pause, he asked Chayton, "Do you remember what happened when I crossed the Dead Pine Forest in the night?"

86

"*Hee ya!* – No!" Chayton replied bluntly. Chayton then turned to say something to his grandson, but Wiyaka just kept talking.

"I was traveling right about in this spot, it was dark, just like now," Wiyaka explained. "I was running north to warn the Folsom People about the approaching *ozuye*. – war party."

"*Ozuye?*" Hogan asked.

"*Ai*, – Yes, many warriors. Many of their *wanagis* – ghosts still roam the Dead Pine Forest," Wiyaka informed the boy. "It was night…Did I tell you it was night? I was following a star…that star, right up there. The star led me deep onto the Arid Plains, far from our people…far from anywhere."

Hogan looked over at his father to see if he was listening to Wiyaka's story. The boy leaned back against the slope of the sand hill, pretending he was uninterested in what Wiyaka had to say. Wiyaka continued anyway.

"*Sunkmanitu tanka* – Wolf came running out of the night…many of them…they almost caught me, but I was saved by a *tarca sapa* – black deer," Wiyaka claimed.

"*Tarca sapa?*" Hogan questioned, doubt in his voice. "Ha! Ha! How could a *tarca sapa* save you from *sunkmanitu tanka?*"

That *tarca sapa* – black deer led *sunkmanitu tanka* away from me." Wiyaka answered.

"There are no *sunkmanitu tanka* here," Hogan insisted and then after a pause he asked, "Are there?"

"*Ai*," Wiyaka replied. "One of our brave hunters was killed at a campfire just like this one…the hunter was lying back away from the campfire, just like you are Hogan. *Sunkmanitu tanka* snatched him up and carried him out into the night. There were more *sunkmanitu tanka* waiting in the darkness…they killed our friend and feasted on him."

"What did you do?" Hogan asked while moving closer to the campfire.

"There were too many," Wiyaka replied. "We listened to *sunkmanitu tanka* crunching the bones of our friend all night. We hoped our campfire would keep the others away. At first light, we collected our friend's bones and buried them in a small hole on the prairie. I think his *wanagi* still wanders the Arid Plains."

Hogan turned around and peered out into the blackness that surrounding the campfire. He sat up and scooted closer to the campfire.

"There are many *wanagis* – ghosts in this place," Chayton suggested.

"*Kaga!* – Demon!" Wiyaka remembered another story. "We found the *ozuye*, – war party, the bodies of warriors twisted and bent!"

87

"*Kaga?*" Hogan challenged with doubt in his voice.

"*Kaga* killed the warriors!" Wiyaka exclaimed, using his hands for emphasis. "*Kaga* twisted their bones and threw them across the prairie!"

Hogan looked over at his father, hoping that Hoka would dismiss these stories as tall tales, but Hoka just stared straight ahead, using all of his willpower not to laugh. Wiyaka was now on a roll. "Other hunters and I found these warriors," he declared. "Their bones twisted…broken…their bodies ripped apart."

"Ripped apart?" Hogan repeated.

"*Ai…*"

It became quiet around the campfire. In an attempt to spook Hogan, Wiyaka had spooked himself and the others. The hunters could deal with a war party or a wolf or two. The unknown was what frightened them the most. They listened to the sizzling dung on the campfire and the crickets chirping on the desert. Then, from a distant hill, a wolf howled and the travelers all felt a chill in the air. The travelers stared into the flames of the campfire, watching the smoke from the dry dung rise into the still air. Then, one by one, the hunters fell into a restless sleep, the unknown still on their minds.

***

At first light, Hoka woke up and saw that his son was already moving about the camp. He wondered if Hogan would follow through with his threat and leave for the North Country. Hoka turned when he heard Chayton coughing somewhere out in the darkness surrounding the camp. Chayton suddenly appeared and stood near the campfire.

"We are leaving," Chayton told Hoka and Hogan.

"Where is Wiyaka?" Hoka asked.

"He has already left. He is hunting for food," Chayton answered.

"How far before we reach the other side of this land?" Hogan asked.

"The sun will be old," Chayton replied. Chayton and Hoka looked at Hogan, expecting the boy to say goodbye to them.

"I better catch up to Wiyaka," Hogan declared. "He will need my help."

"*Ai,* – Yes, he will need your help," Chayton replied with a smile.

Act III

Chapter Eight

The game trail wove in and out of the forest, rising and falling with the ridges and valleys of the foothills of the mountains. The warrior pulled the woman down the game trail while the woman held onto the hand of a small girl. The trio ran out of the forest and headed east along a trail that followed the rocky southern rim of a rugged river canyon. As the warrior ran along the sheer cliffs of the canyon, he looked for a place to climb down, but it was too steep and too dangerous, especially for a child. The warrior then suddenly stopped and looked back in the direction they had just come. In the shadows of the pine trees, he spotted the *ozuye* – war party that was pursuing them.

"*Inahni, Moki!* – Hurry, Moki!" the warrior called Paco yelled at the woman. "They are coming!"

Moki turned around and looked for herself. She saw them. She picked the small girl up in her arms and the trio ran down the trail, heading east along the river canyon. The eight warriors who hunted the trio stopped running just long enough to confirm they were still on the trail of their prey. Their leader, a warrior called Satanta, scanned the ridges and valleys in front of him in search of the trio. Then, one of his warriors spotted them. "There!" the warrior screamed.

"Do not kill the woman!" Satanta bellowed at his warriors. "The child and warrior can die!"

As the trio attempted to escape by running east along the trail, Paco continued to search for a way to get down into the river canyon. He knew that they could not outrun the warriors for long and getting to the river was their only chance of survival. A spear whizzed past Paco's ear, narrowly missing him. The spear smashed into the ground and skidded across the rocks on the canyon rim. The warriors were now within range. Paco slowed down and stepped to the edge of the canyon rim. He saw a deep swirling pool of water, a dam of water created by gigantic boulders that had fallen into the river. Paco saw only one way to get to the river.

"*Psice!* – Jump!" Paco yelled to Moki.

"*Taku?* – What?" she yelled back.

"*Psice!*" Paco screamed, grabbing her by the hand and dragging her and the small girl to the edge of the cliff. "*Wana!* – Now!"

Paco launched himself off the canyon cliff, dragging Moki and Gad with him. Paco aimed for the center of the deep pool and smashed into the water hard. Moki followed, colliding with the surface of the water feet first, her body plummeting towards the rocky bottom of the river. Her ears exploded with pain from the pressure of hitting the water. Her nostrils burned from the surge of water rushing into them. The frigid river water caused her lungs to tighten and she expelled air as she descended through the deep column of water. On her way to the bottom of the river, Moki passed by her more buoyant daughter. She shoved her daughter Gad's foot upward, attempting to push her to the surface of the river. Then, Moki's feet slammed into the rocky bottom of the river, causing more pain to shoot up through her legs and back. Moki's legs bent as they absorbed the shock. She then flexed her legs and pushed upward, fighting to reach the precious air at the surface of the river.

Moki's body shot up through the column of water until she broke the surface of the pool. She gulped in the air. When she could finally breathe, she swam in circles, looking around the pool for her daughter Gad. Then, she saw Paco pulling the small girl out of the water on the opposite shore of the river. Moki swam to the shore and Paco reached out and helped her out of the river.

"*Inahni!* – Hurry!" he screamed at her, pointing downriver. "*Iyagke!* – Run!"

Moki grabbed Gad and climbed over the rocks and boulders that lined the river. Paco turned and peered up at the cliff from where they had jumped. He saw the warriors looking down at him. Then, several spears flew across the river, crashing into the rocks around Paco. On the cliff above, Satanta readied another spear on his shoulder. Satanta wound up and hurled his spear at Paco at the same time that other spears were speeding in the same direction. Paco watched the spears heading for him. He ducked out of the way of one spear, only to slip on the wet rocks and fall to his knees. A second spear then slammed into him, its sharp stone projectile point penetrating his body, right below his rib cage. At first, Paco felt nothing, but suddenly his side erupted in fiery pain. He screamed in agony and crumpled to his knees. He grabbed the spear shaft and pulled hard, ripping the spear shaft from his body, but leaving the stone spear point lodged deep below his rib cage. Moki heard his scream and stopped running. She saw her husband leaning up against a rock, holding his side. She scrambled back upriver, leaving Gad where she was. Moki reached her husband and grabbed him by the arm. The small woman lifted Paco to his feet. Just then, another volley of spears rattled in the rocks around them as Moki helped her husband walk downriver.

"Do not kill the woman!" Satanta roared at the other warriors. "Follow me! We will find a place to cross the river!"

Satanta sprinted down the trail, heading east along the canyon rim towards flatter terrain.

"*Inahni!* – Hurry!" Moki pleaded to Paco as she helped him crawl along the rocks heading downriver. Paco stumbled as he moved along, losing more blood with each step.

"Stay close!" Moki screamed at Gad, the deafening roar of the river drowning out her voice.

Moki looked down at her husband's wound and saw it was leaving a clear trail of blood on the rocks behind them. She pulled Paco into the shallow water of the river, yelling again at Gad, "Step on the rocks! Leave no footprints!"

"We must cross the river, Moki!" Paco mumbled.

"*Hee ya!* – No!" she replied. "They will expect that!"

"Leave me!" Paco muttered, slurring his words.

"*Hee ya* – No!" Moki responded.

With Paco's arm draped across her neck and shoulders, Moki carried her husband downriver, slipping and sliding on the slick river rocks. Exhausted, Moki searched for a place for them to hide along the canyon walls, but there was no place to hide. They would have to hide somewhere else. Moki noticed the gigantic blocks of limestone that had fallen in the river from the canyon rim. She had an idea. "Wait here! I will be back!" she told Paco and Gad.

Moki waded into the deep water of the river and then let the river current carry her into deep water towards the massive limestone blocks. She felt along the lower edges of the blocks, looking for cracks to hide in. She noticed that one of the limestone blocks had fallen directly on top of two others, leaving it only partially submerged in the river. She felt around the lower edge of this block and liked what she found. She held her breath and dove underwater. She emerged on the other side of the limestone block and found herself in a small natural chamber created by the jumbled blocks of limestone. There was a small flat surface on one of the blocks, just large enough for the three of them to lie down on. She dove back underwater and swam under the limestone block. Once in the river, Moki fought the river current to get back to Paco and Gad. She found her wounded husband draped across a flat boulder in the river, his head bobbing up and down with the waves of the water. She inspected the wound and noticed little red feathers of blood dripping into the water and vanishing in the river current.

"*Inahni!* – Hurry!" Moki told her husband and daughter. "Swim!"

"Leave…" Paco mumbled.

"Swim!" Moki demanded. "Gad, follow us!"

Moki pulled Paco into the deep water of the river, telling him, "Float on your back, I will guide you!"

Paco rolled over onto his back causing him to scream out in pain. He flattened his arms as if they were the wings of an eagle and let the river carry him. Like a rudder on a boat, Moki steered Paco towards the limestone blocks. Once there, she instructed her husband and daughter, "Hold your breath and let yourself sink into the water! Follow us, Gad!"

Paco held his breath and slowly sank into the deep pool with Moki following him. When they were deep enough underwater to clear the bottom of the limestone block, Moki pulled on Paco's shirt collar and drug him under the limestone block and then up to the surface of the water on the other side. She then labored to pull her husband onto the rock. She watched the surface of the river, waiting for Gad to surface. When Gad did not show up, Moki told her husband, "I have to go back for Gad!"

When Moki was just about ready to jump into the river, Gad surfaced, gulping large quantities of air. Moki grabbed the young girl and jerked her up on the rock. They then laid down next to Paco in an attempt to warm him against the bitter cold of the river.

***

The warriors carefully descended the dangerously steep slope of the canyon wall. They reached the riverbank without mishap and without any hesitation, each one jumped into the icy river, swimming and fighting the strong river current to cross to the other side. Finally, all of them had reached the other side of the river, freezing and exhausted. The warriors assembled around their leader Satanta. "We go upriver! The woman must live! The others die!" he instructed the warriors once again.

Satanta turned and trotted up the riverbank, jumping from rock to rock while his seven warriors followed closely behind. It did not take the warriors long to locate the area where their spears had smashed into the rocks. There, they found the bloody trail of Paco. The warriors tracked the blood trail until it disappeared into the water of the river. "The blood trail ends here," a warrior called Fala informed Satanta. "They crossed the river."

"I am not sure," Satanta replied. "Search this side of the river. Be sure the blood trail does not reappear downriver. Paco cannot travel far."

The warriors searched the length of the riverbank, looking for any sign that the trio had been there. The warriors were ready to give up the search when one of the warriors screamed, "HERE!"

When Satanta arrived at where the warrior was standing, he saw the tiny footprint from a child captured in the wet mud between two rocks.

"They are near!" Satanta proclaimed.

***

"*Ma chew ta!* – I am cold!" Gad said to her mother.

"*Enila,* – Be quiet, the warriors are near," Moki whispered and then held her daughter tight. After warming up her daughter, Moki sat up and inspected Paco's wound while there was still some daylight streaming down from above the limestone blocks. Her stomach turned queasy when she saw how bad the wound was. She carefully wiped the blood away from the wound hole with a wet piece of animal hide. She watched as the wound hole slowly filled back up with blood. She wiped away the blood again and noticed the base of the stone spear point sticking out of her husband's side. She started to pull the stone spear point out of the wound with her fingers, but then hesitated. *What would stop the blood if I removed the spear point?* She had no fuel for a fire to cauterize the wound and close it.

Moki realized they would have to leave the safety of the chamber once it was dark. She would leave the stone spear point alone until they could escape to a place where she could safely remove it and cauterize the wound. She watched her husband labor with each raspy breath. She leaned back against the rock and closed her eyes, praying and shivering in the damp cold while holding her husband and daughter in her arms.

Then, above the roar of the river, she heard someone scream 'they are near!' *They are searching for us!* Moki thought. She looked up at the open sky above the limestone blocks. If the warriors decided to climb on top of the limestone blocks and look down, the warriors would discover them. Moki tightened the embrace on her daughter and whispered, "*Enila.* – Be quiet."

Satanta stood on one of the limestone blocks above the chamber, watching his warriors comb the area where the family had entered the river. As the sun disappeared behind the mountains in the west, Fala approached Satanta and told him, "There is no other sign here."

"Keep searching!" Satanta bellowed, "She is near!"

Inside the chamber, Moki looked up at the darkening sky. She could hear the muffled voices of people yelling. She kept her eyes focused towards the top of the limestone blocks. She waited for someone to peer down into the chamber and discover them. Moki held her family close until the sky turned

94

black and then she knew it was time to leave. Moki shook her husband, but he did not wake up. She shook him harder, but still he did not wake up. She touched her husband's face and it was as cold as the river. Moki placed her hand over her husband's mouth, waiting for the warmth of his breath, but there was none. Moki ran her hand up under her husband's hide shirt and felt for the beat of his heart, but there was no heartbeat.

"My husband," Moki cried softly as tears flowed down her cheeks. She leaned over and kissed her husband's cheek. Moki began sobbing and she could not stop, even with her daughter Gad consoling her. The love of her life was gone. When Gad began weeping, it jolted Moki back to their desperate situation. Moki found her composure and told her daughter, "We leave, now."

"Is father asleep?" Gad asked.

"*Ai,* – Yes, your father is asleep," Moki told her daughter.

"We cannot leave until he wakes up," Gad announced.

Moki started to tear up again. Her sobs were now out of control as she held her hand in front of her mouth to prevent the warriors from hearing her. Gad sat there quietly watching her mother cry while her father slept. Finally, Moki had no more tears to cry. She reached over and grasped her daughter tightly, whispering, "Your father is *te.* – dead."

It took time for her mother's words to sink in, then Gad started to scream, but Moki held her hand over her daughter's mouth, whispering, "*Enila,* – Be quiet, the *ozuye* – war party will hear you."

Moki held her daughter so tightly that Gad could not scream. Moki then told her daughter, "We leave."

"We must take father," Gad murmured.

"Your father is not here," Moki explained.

"*Tuktel?* – Where?" the small girl asked.

"*Wanagi tacaku.* – Spirit path."

Gad did not understand this at all. Her mother leaned over and whispered in her ear, "We will swim under the rock. I will hold your hand. You must be as quiet as a fish. Bad people are near."

Gad was still thinking about her father and was not listening to her mother.

"Do you understand?" Moki asked, but the small girl did not acknowledge her. Moki repeated her question more sternly, "Gad, do you understand?"

"*Ai,* – Yes," the small girl eventually replied.

"We are going to swim down the river," Moki whispered. "You are a fish swimming in the river. You cannot make a sound."

Moki waited for her daughter to respond, but Gad only stared through the darkness at her father.

"Tell your father goodbye," Moki said and then began choking on her own tears.

Gad crawled over her mother and put her arms around her father's neck. She tightened her grip around her father while her tears fell down her cheeks. Moki began sobbing again as she watched her daughter say goodbye. Moki leaned over and whispered to her daughter. "We leave."

Moki reached over and pulled on her daughter, but Gad would not let go of her father's neck. Finally, Moki pried Gad's arms away from her father and pulled the girl away. Moki then retrieved her husband's spear thrower, his quiver, and hunting satchel. She put the straps for the quiver and satchel around her neck. Moki then leaned over and kissed her husband for the last time, saying, "*Amba, Paco, lotancila!* – Goodbye, Paco, I love you!"

Moki then slid into the river and pulled Gad into the water with her. She then told Gad, "Hold your breath and dive."

Both of them dove under the water with Moki holding on tight to her daughter's hand. The water was ice cold as Moki and Gad swam under the limestone block and then resurfaced in the deep pool of the river. While catching her breath in the frigid water, Moki looked around in the darkness. "Follow me," Moki told her daughter.

Moki let the river current carry her along the limestone blocks to the center of the river. When the river current began pulling on Moki, she positioned her daughter in front of her, reminding her, "Quiet as a fish."

The river current jettisoned both mother and daughter through an opening between the limestone blocks, transporting them into the wide river. As they floated along on the river current, Moki kept her eyes peeled on both riverbanks, watching for the war party. Then, Moki spotted it, the barely visible twinkle of a campfire to her left along the riverbank. As Gad and Moki bobbed up and down in the river, the campfire grew larger and cast light across the width of the river. Moki spotted several warriors standing along the riverbank, talking amongst themselves.

"*Enila!* – Be quiet!" Moki murmured to her daughter.

As Moki and Gad floated past the camp, Moki spotted another warrior, standing by himself on the other side of the campfire, staring out across the river. The flames from the campfire only lit one side of the warrior's face, but Moki recognized him, instantly. *Satanta!* Fear overcame her, stealing the air from her lungs and making her heart race out of control. She watched in terror as they floated past Satanta. Moki thought that she saw Satanta's malignant eyes staring directly at her. She almost screamed, but her lungs could not find the air. Then, Satanta's eyes drifted off in another direction, leaving the mother and daughter unnoticed. Relieved, Moki began crying as she watched Satanta disappear into the night. Moki should have felt relief at seeing Satanta disappear, but she only felt dread. She knew that Satanta would never give up searching for her.

After floating down the river for part of the night, Moki spotted a log from a tree along the riverbank. After warming themselves on the riverbank, Moki pushed the log out into the river. She and Gad clung to the log as it drifted down the river. Moki constantly asked her daughter if she was cold, knowing that when Gad was no longer cold, it was time to get out of the water. Under the light of the night sun, Moki watched the landscape change from high cliffs and pine trees to rolling hills and ghost–like prairie. Finally, she scissor kicked the water, pushing the log towards the riverbank on her right.

Moki pulled Gad out of the river and found a place to hide amongst the large rocks near the river. She then constructed a small fire hearth and gathered as much tinder and wood as she could find under the illumination of a partial night sun. She opened her husband's satchel and pulled out two large pieces of flint. She dried them off in the grass and then struck them together, creating the sparks that ignited the tinder. She had started thousands of campfires, but she had never been this cold or exhausted. Finally, the tinder exploded into tiny flames and Moki fed the new fire with more wood. She looked over at her daughter and Gad was already asleep. Moki knew they were safe at least until a new morning brought renewed danger.

Once the campfire was burning, Moki laid down next to Gad, holding her daughter with all of her strength. Without Paco to protect them, Moki was terrified of what lurked in the night. She thought about the wild beasts that roamed the hills, but no beast could be more vicious or bloodthirsty than the monster that searched for her. She tightened her grip around Gad's waist and began crying when she thought about her beloved Paco.

Moki was happy to see the first hint of light in the morning sky. She had not slept. Moki knew the warriors would be coming for her, but she still held the belief that *Wakan Tanka* would watch out for her and her daughter. Moki woke up her daughter and gave her a few roots and plant greens to eat. Moki then destroyed the fire, spreading the ashes all along the riverbank and kicking the rocks into the river. She knew that destroying the campfire would not fool the war party, but she did it anyway, mostly out of spite. She then grabbed Gad by her arm and they waded into the river, guiding the pine log out into the river current. As she and Gad drifted down the river, Moki noticed that the surrounding country was changing again. Bordering the river to the right was a massive plateau while on the river's left there were several gigantic granite cliffs reaching for the sky. Moki had never traveled this far before. She hoped that if they got far enough away, Satanta would finally give up the chase.

***

Exhausted and cold, Moki and Gad drifted down the river until the plateau disappeared and the river joined another. Moki decided that they had drifted far enough. She pushed the log to the riverbank where her and Gad climbed out of the river. They walked across a small clearing, looking around the entire time. To the west, Moki noticed the towering tip of the plateau they had just floated past. Hoping to get a better view of the terrain, Moki grabbed Gad's hand and walked towards the steep slope of the plateau.

"*Lol wa cheen,* – I am hungry," Gad announced.

"*Ai,* it will be dark soon," Moki replied. "We will find something to eat before."

Moki placed the nock end of a spear on the spur of her husband's spear thrower. She then hoisted the spear onto her shoulder. She was not a hunter, but she knew enough to be ready for any situation. The more Moki investigated the area, the more she felt safe. They would camp here and wait for a sign from *Wakan Tanka*. Moki pointed her finger towards the tip of the plateau and said to her daughter, "There is where we will camp, high up in the rocks."

As they walked towards the slope of the plateau, Moki could tell that they were walking across the remains of an abandoned village. A few decaying lodge poles still clung to each other in the air while stone circles from past fire hearths lay mostly hidden in the weeds and tall grass. Moki stopped and pondered who had lived here.

Moki felt Gad pulling on her hand and when she turned around, Gad had a piece of wood in her hand. She raised it up to show her mother. Moki gently took the piece of wood from Gad and inspected it closely. It was a broken spear shaft with a leaf–shaped stone spear point still attached with pitch and animal sinew. A chill swept through Moki as she held the leaf–shaped spear point in her hand. It was common to find old tools and spear points in abandoned villages, but something about this spear point made Moki shudder with fear.

"Bury it," she instructed Gad, handing the spear point to her daughter.

"*Taku?* – What?" Gad asked.

"Bury it deep so we will never see it again," Moki replied.

"I want to keep it."

"*Hee ya!* – No!" Moki exclaimed. "It is bad…it is evil!"

Gad leaned down and began digging in the sandy soil with her small hand. Moki's mind became obsessed with burying the spear point as she watched her daughter slowly dig a hole. Then, Moki snapped out of her trance and forced the evil thoughts out of her mind. She knelt down next to Gad and helped her daughter dig the hole. Once the hole was deep enough, Gad threw the stone spear point into the hole and then with her mother's help, they buried it. When the stone spear point was safely underground, Gad looked over at her mother and asked, "What is it? What did we bury?"

"*Slol wa yea shnee,* – I do not know," Moki replied, her voice edged in fear. "*Hi!* – Come! We must go."

Moki and Gad walked up the steep slope of the plateau until they found a place hidden amongst the rubble and boulders that had fallen from the top of the plateau. There, they built a campfire and watched the prairie in front of them. Once mother and daughter had settled in for the night, Moki instructed her daughter, "We shall grieve for your father this night, but when a new sun arrives, we can no longer grieve. For us to survive, we must be strong."

Moki let her message sink in and then she asked Gad, "Do you understand?"

"*Ai,* – Yes," Gad murmured.

"*Wana,* – Now, I will go find food," Moki said. "You stay near the campfire."

***

Moki woke up early in the morning and sat by the campfire, thinking about what she should do. She knew it would be best if she and Gad kept floating down the river out onto the vast prairie. There, they could possibly lose Satanta and his warriors. Then, she thought about her daughter. Gad could not keep up this pace for long. She needed food and rest. Moki decided to stay at the plateau for at least one more sun, to rest and wait for a sign from *Wakan Tanka*. During the day, she would brush away their trail leading from the river and find a better hiding place along the rim of the plateau. From near the top of the plateau, she could watch both humans and animals come and go along the two rivers. She turned the rock chuck that she was roasting over the campfire and woke her daughter up.

99

The warriors continued hiking downriver, looking for a sign from the family who had thus far evaded them. The warriors were now searching both riverbanks. Satanta did not know what to think about the family vanishing, except maybe that they had double backed and headed upriver. Satanta began to hear the whispers and grumbles from the other warriors. He knew the warriors wanted to go home and take care of their families. Satanta knew that he should return to his village. His father would be wondering about him. Then, the warrior called Fala found the courage to approach Satanta.

"Satanta, the warriors have asked me to speak to you," Fala informed Satanta.

Satanta did not reply.

"We…they…the warriors want to return to our village," Fala stammered.

"We will return once we find the woman," Satanta declared.

"Satanta, we have lost the trail," Fala suggested. "The family could be anywhere."

"A wounded warrior can travel little…or far…but not fast. The woman is near. I sense she is near," Satanta declared. "Tell these…other warriors that if we do not find sign in one more sun, we will head upriver and search there."

Fala was not happy with this decision and he knew that the other warriors would not accept it. However, Fala was shrewd, he knew better than to argue with the only son of the chief of their tribe. Fala would wait patiently and see what transpired. Fala watched as the warriors moved downriver, scouring the riverbanks like locusts in a field. The sun was deep in the west when Satanta and Fala heard a shout from one of the warriors.

The warriors swam and waded across the river to reach the warrior who was waving his arms in the air. When Fala and Satanta reached the warrior, they looked around and saw the spent ashes from a campfire spread across the ground. The warriors scoured the area and found footprints of a woman and child still preserved in the river mud.

"The woman and child camped here…maybe one sun…two suns ago," Fala reported to Satanta.

"What of the warrior?" Satanta questioned.

"There was no warrior here," Fala replied, "only the tracks of a woman and a child."

"We know the warrior was wounded," Satanta stated. "The woman left him behind. She is heading downriver and that is where we shall go."

Chapter Nine

Wiyaka and Hogan hiked along, enjoying the warm sun and keeping their eyes peeled for fresh game tracks. Wiyaka could tell that Hogan was still on edge from the previous night's talk about the ghosts and wolves that inhabited the Arid Plains. Wiyaka could not help but laugh at the boy. Wiyaka loved the mysterious beauty of the Arid Plains, but he also knew that with the beauty came much danger.

"Where are we heading, Wiyaka?" Hogan asked once again.

"*Taku?* – What?" Wiyaka blurted out, not hearing the boy's question.

"Where are we heading?" Hogan repeated his question in a louder voice.

"You must speak up, *hokshila*, – boy," Wiyaka replied. "Wind is loud."

Hogan held his hand up to test for wind and found nary a breeze.

"Ha! Ha! You cannot hear, you old skunk," Hogan murmured in a low enough voice where he was sure Wiyaka could not hear him.

"*Taku, hokshila?* – What, boy?" Wiyaka inquired.

"I am not a boy, I am a hunter!" Hogan blurted out, loud enough for the prairie dogs on a distant hill to hear.

"You do not become a hunter by saying you are a hunter," Wiyaka proclaimed. "You are still a *hokshila* until your deeds make you a hunter."

"Then, tell me what I must do," Hogan suggested.

Wiyaka had to think about that one. He had never had anyone ask him that question. His mind began racing through the memories of all of the hunters he had known over his lifetime and how each of them achieved manhood. The Folsom People had no common act or passage for boys to enter manhood and become hunters. If a boy survived childhood, he usually became a hunter. Finally, Wiyaka lost his patience with thinking up an answer to Hogan's question and gave up.

"We will know when you are a hunter," Wiyaka professed.

"That is no answer!" Hogan blurted out.

"I did not say I would give you an answer."

"Well, you did not give me an answer," Hogan mumbled under his breath.

"*Taku?* – What?"

"Where are we heading?" Hogan asked in a loud voice, circling back around to his original question.

"To visit a friend," Wiyaka replied.

"Who?" Hogan asked.

"You are filled with too many questions," Wiyaka replied, "when you should be searching for food."

Wiyaka split off from Hogan and walked toward the prairie dog village. At this stage, Wiyaka would not turn down a few plump, greasy prairie dogs for a meal.

***

When the sun was old, the four travelers arrived at the plateau where two rivers came together. Wiyaka and Hogan waited at the river for Chayton and Hoka to catch up. Chayton's coughing announced his arrival.

"Do you remember this place, Wiyaka?" Chayton asked when he saw his friend standing by the river.

Wiyaka did not respond, so Chayton repeated the question, "Do you remember this place, Wiyaka?"

"*Ai,* – Yes," Wiyaka replied. Then bobbing his head from side to side, he added, "Good…bad."

"*Ai,*" Chayton agreed.

"What is this place?" Hoka inquired.

"This is where we lived with the River People," Chayton acknowledged.

"What ever happened to the River People?" Hoka asked.

"*Slol wa yea shnee,* – I do not know," Chayton replied with sadness in his voice. "I have heard they are somewhere near this plateau, a place others call Sweet River."

"Will we visit them?" Hoka asked.

"*Slol wa yea shnee,* – I do not know," Chayton replied. "*Hee ya.* – No."

"Is that because Namid is there?"

"*Ai,*" Chayton replied. He stared up at the tip of the towering plateau and thought about his life. This place brought back memories about Avonaco, Honiahaka and yes, even Namid. Chayton reminisced about the twists and turns of his life and the unhappiness of sharing his early life with Namid. He thought about his cousin Keya and the Mountain People who killed him. Chayton stood there by the river, lost in a tangled web of memories. From the corner of one of his eyes, a single tear rolled down his cheek.

"Chayton!" Wiyaka roared. "*Key kte yo!* – Wake up!"

Chayton jumped when he realized he had been daydreaming.

"Do you plan on walking or just standing here like a tree all night?" Wiyaka heckled his friend.

Chayton hesitated while he tried to figure out where exactly they were. "We will camp here for the night," Chayton announced, even though he was not quite sure where 'here' was.

Wiyaka nodded his head and then spoke to Hogan and Hoka, "We will cross the river and camp in the old village of the River People."

Wiyaka pointed his spear in the general direction of the best place to cross the river. After Hoka and Hogan departed, Wiyaka turned to his old friend Chayton and asked, "*Tóka he?* – What is wrong?"

"*Slol wa yea shnee,* – I do not know," Chayton answered and then asked, "Was this journey a mistake?"

"Are you ready to go home?" Wiyaka asked.

"*Hee ya.* – No," Chayton responded.

Wiyaka just shook his head and sighed. "We will camp over there and you can rest," he told Chayton.

Without saying a word, Chayton took off walking, following Hoka and Hogan. Wiyaka watched his friend amble away. He somehow had to convince Chayton to turn around and head back to the North Country. This journey was difficult enough for young hunters and impossible for old men like Chayton and him. He watched Chayton disappear out of sight, but he could still hear Chayton coughing over the sounds of the river. He would convince Chayton to return to the village, right after their next stop.

Wiyaka caught up to the other three travelers just when they were crossing the river. After crossing, the four travelers walked up to the site of the abandoned village. As they walked along, Wiyaka noticed how strange it was to see lodge poles propped up in the air and abandoned fire hearths on the ground. After all, countless winters had passed. Wiyaka watched Chayton plod along. Wiyaka knew how hard it was for Chayton to revisit this place. When the travelers reached the heart of the old village, Chayton announced, "This is where we shall camp."

Wiyaka looked around, studying the terrain. "You rest," he instructed Chayton. "We will start the campfire and find food."

"I will start the campfire," Chayton replied, "just bring me firewood."

Hoka and Hogan quickly headed out in search of firewood while Wiyaka went searching for food. When Hogan was off searching for firewood alone, he thought about his decision to stay on the journey and not return to the North Country. He had no idea where they were going and he could tell that his grandfather's health was worsening. When Hogan's arms were fully loaded with firewood, he headed back towards the camp. Then, his eyes caught a glimpse of an animal dashing through the trees in front of him. *Deer!* Hogan thought, dropping the armload of firewood on the ground and reached for a spear and his spear thrower. *I will show that old man that I am a hunter!* It was then that Hogan realized he had left his quiver and spear thrower at their new camp. Hogan thought about running back to the camp to retrieve his spears, but then he remembered what Wiyaka had told him about manhood. How would it look if he was without his spear and spear thrower in this dangerous country? Hogan reached into his satchel and pulled out a long stone knife. He would kill the deer with his bare hands and show them he was both a man and a hunter.

Crouched, Hogan moved quietly, blending in with the trees, just as his father had taught him. Hogan held the knife out in front of him. He listened to the ground through his moccasins. His foot stepped on a twig and the pressure almost snapped it, but Hogan was keen enough to back his foot away. Hogan remained alert to the sounds of the forest, his stance relaxed and balanced. His father had taught him well and when Hogan cared, he could stalk game properly. *There it is!* Hogan caught another glimpse of shades of brown darting amongst the trees and now hiding behind a large limestone boulder. Hogan neared his prey. He slowed down his pace. He was careful not to breathe too loudly or make noise through his moccasins. Hogan approached the limestone boulder as quiet as the breeze. When he reached the boulder, he leaned up against it, letting his racing heart calm down. He breathed deep to let his nerves unwind. Then, he took a small step around the side of the boulder. Hogan waited and listened for any sound coming from his prey. He took another step and paused, listening once again to the sounds from the forest. When Hogan was convinced that the forest was unaware of him and his prey, he took a third step around the boulder. Then, he waited.

Hogan carefully repositioned his stone knife in his hand so he could stab downward. He then closed his eyes to calm down. Hogan visualized that he was the greatest hunter of all animals, *igmuwatogla.* – mountain lion. Hogan was now ready to pounce on the deer. Hogan flexed his legs and then jumped behind the boulder. As Hogan slid past his prey, it let out a scream so loud it echoed off the rim rock of the plateau. Hogan stopped in his tracks and leaped back in the direction of his prey, his knife held high above his head. Then, Hogan froze. His prey was human! His arm and the stone knife were hovering over the top of a small girl's head. Before Hogan's mind could catch up with what was happening, the small girl took off running through the forest. Hogan hesitated and then took off running after her. The girl weaved in and out of the trees, just staying out of the reach of Hogan. Then, the trees disappeared into a small clearing. The small girl sprinted as fast as she could, but her short legs were no match for Hogan's longer legs. Hogan caught up to the girl and grabbed her by the shoulder. Hogan's weight caused the girl to veer off to her right and then fall down. Hogan pounced on top of her, holding her down with his arms and legs. The short sprint had winded Hogan and he waited until he had caught his breath.

"*Táku eníciyapi hwo?* – What is your name?" Hogan finally asked.

The small girl was too frightened to answer. She squirmed underneath Hogan trying to get away.

"*Táku eníciyapi hwo?* – What is your name?" Hogan repeated.

"Gad!" the small girl blurted out.

"Gad?"

"Gad!" she repeated. "Let me go, *hokshila*! My father and his warriors are nearby. If they find you hurting me, they will kill you!"

Hogan peered around, making sure they were alone.

"*Waniyetu nitóna hwo?* – How old are you?" Hogan asked the small girl.

Gad did not answer. She squirmed like a captive animal.

"*Waniyetu nitóna hwo?* – How old are you?" Hogan demanded, pushing down on the small girl's shoulders.

"*Shakówin*, – Seven," Gad finally admitted. "Seven winters."

Hogan took some of his weight off the girl, telling her, "I am going to let you up, but do not scream or run."

Hogan stood up and grabbed the back of the small girl's hide shirt, pulling her up to her feet. Hogan held on tight to the shirt collar while guiding the girl back to the travelers' camp. The others would be impressed with what Hogan had found in the woods. After becoming lost, Hogan and the girl finally wandered into camp.

"Where have you been?" Wiyaka bellowed when he saw the boy. "What did you find?"

Both Chayton and Hoka looked up. The travelers watched as Hoka guided a small girl into camp.

"We send you for firewood and you bring back a girl!" Wiyaka chimed in. "Where is the firewood?"

"Who did you find, Hogan?" Chayton said to Hogan, smiling at the small girl.

Chayton slowly bent his creaking knees and leaned over, speaking to the child at her own level.

"*Nituwe he?* – Who are you?" he asked.

"Gad," she replied. "My tribe has many warriors and they will be looking for me."

"*Waste,* – Good," Chayton said. "They will find you unharmed."

"You will not be unharmed if my father and his warriors find you," Gad warned.

Chayton studied the girl and then stood straight up, surveying the area with his eyes and ears. He listened for this war party, but he only heard birds singing, the river flowing, and the sound of the wind whistling through the pine trees.

"While we wait for these warriors, are you hungry, Gad?" Chayton inquired.

Gad studied the face of each traveler. At first, she had thought that these humans were the warriors that searched for her and her mother. Then she realized there was only one human here who could possibly be a warrior. The other two humans were too old and the boy, well he was just a boy. Finally, she gave into her hunger and answered, "*Ai, lol wa cheen.* – Yes, I am hungry."

"Come sit–" Chayton began just when a loud piercing scream echoed through the forest.

"*INAJI!* – STOP!" a voice screamed.

The travelers turned in the direction of the sound. A woman with a spear ready to launch was standing at the edge of the camp. The travelers moved away from the campfire while the woman circled around them. Her upper body moved from side to side as she aimed the spear at each of the travelers.

"*KUTA!* – DOWN!" she screamed.

The travelers hunkered down on the ground, right where they had been standing.

"*Táku eníciyapi hwo?* – What is your name?" Chayton asked.

The woman was shaking so badly she could barely stand up. She kept circling the travelers, aiming the spear at each of them, her eyes wandering back and forth. When she reached her daughter, the woman put her free hand on her daughter's shoulder and began backing up.

"This is my mother," Gad announced to the travelers.

"*Enila, Gad!* – Be quiet, Gad!" the woman cried out.

"She is called Moki," Gad continued.

"*Enila, Gad!* – Be quiet, Gad!" the woman blurted out.

"*Miyelo ca kola, Moki,* – I am a friend, Moki," Chayton proclaimed.

106

Moki's grip on the spear relaxed a tiny bit.

"KAAF! KAAF!" Chayton coughed twice and then managed to say, "It looks like you could use some food, Moki."

Moki looked around at the travelers, unsure of what to do.

"Are you hungry, Moki?" Chayton asked. "We have little food, but we will share what we have."

With his hand, Chayton motioned for Moki to join them at the campfire. Gad smiled at her mother, reassuring her that these travelers were safe. Moki slowly lowered her spear and then walked over to the campfire. She looked at each of the travelers and then back at her smiling daughter. Finally, Moki sat down with the travelers.

**

The travelers and their two guests shared a raccoon that Wiyaka had managed to harvest and greens that both Gad and Hogan had gathered. Chayton watched as Moki kept looking out into the darkness, as if she was expecting someone or something to appear. After they ate the meal, Chayton decided to find out more about this woman and her daughter. "Where is your tribe?" he questioned.

"Our tribe is nearby," Moki answered. "They will be here soon."

"Our tribe is *sica*, – bad," Gad added.

"*Enila, Gad*, – Be quiet, Gad," Moki replied. "Our tribe is not *sica*."

"They killed my father," Gad proclaimed.

The travelers all leaned in so they could better hear what the girl was saying. Wiyaka leaned even further since he could barely hear anything. Moki did not know what to say to these strangers. She started to say something to Gad, but instead turned her face away from the campfire and began crying. None of the travelers knew what to do about a crying woman.

"They killed your father?" Hogan asked Gad.

"*Ai*, – Yes, *ozuye* – war party hunted us down and threw spears at my father," Gad responded. She looked over at her mother and then she began crying, as well. Gad grabbed her mother and both of them sat there weeping. The travelers looked at each other. None of them knew what to do, so they just sat there and hoped the crying would soon end. Finally, Moki and Gad stopped crying and sat by the campfire, still sniffling.

Chayton could not wait any longer to ask his next question, "Where is the *ozuye*... – war party...these warriors who search for you...the ones that killed your father...husband?"

"*Slol wa ya shnee*, – I do not know," Moki replied.

"Where did you come from?"

"Upriver."

"Which river?"

Moki did not understand the question. She had forgotten there were two rivers, one on either side of the plateau. She answered by pointing to the north.

"Is this *ozuye* – war party still searching for you?" Wiyaka questioned.

"*Slol wa ya shnee,* – I do not know," Moki replied. "*Ai!*"

"How many warriors?" Chayton asked.

"Seven…eight warriors."

"What do they want?" Wiyaka demanded.

Moki looked over at her daughter and then answered, "Me."

The travelers looked at each other. None of them had any idea what to do. Moki saw the look of concern on the travelers' faces and decided to keep them uninvolved. "Gad and I have a place to hide," she told them. "We will hide there. If the warriors come, we will not put you in danger."

"*Ai,* – Yes, it is best that you go hide," Chayton responded. "If the warriors show up here we will tell them we have not seen you."

"*Pilamaya,* – Thank you," Moki said, pulling Gad to her feet.

"Come back here at first light and we will talk," Chayton continued. "Now, go and if you need our help, we are here."

***

The travelers stared at the flames of the campfire for some time after Moki and her daughter left. Their thoughts remained their own until Chayton coughed and broke the silence. Hogan asked the first question, "Should we have a sentry?"

"These warriors are not here for us," Chayton replied. "We should be safe, at least I think so."

"You can stay awake and guard us, Hogan," Wiyaka said and then laughed. "Ha! Ha! Ha!"

Hogan did not reply to Wiyaka's ribbing, but instead spoke directly to his father and Chayton, "We should get far away from this woman and her daughter. They are *sica.* – bad."

Chayton did not reply. He waited for the response to come from the boy's father.

"Hogan, we…the Folsom People have always helped others," Hoka replied. "We cannot leave this woman and child here without helping them."

"We cannot help them against an *ozuye,* – war party," Hogan declared. "We are only two hunters and two old men."

108

Wiyaka' temper flared and he started to jump up, but Chayton held Wiyaka's arm, preventing the old hunter from rising.

"You mean three hunters and a *hokshila!* – boy!" Wiyaka roared.

"You are a *wichah^cala, –* old man," Hogan replied.

"*Hokshila, –* Boy, I am going to smack you across the river!" Wiyaka bellowed at Hogan.

"*Enila, le mita kola, –* Be quiet, my friend," Chayton tried to calm Wiyaka down.

"We need to leave before the *ozuye* finds us!" Hogan blurted out. "We can return to our village!"

"Perhaps, Hogan is right," Chayton said to Hoka, the boy's father. "Perhaps, it is time for you and Hogan to return to our village. My journey is not over, but it has become too dangerous. There is no reason for you and Hogan to remain here…Wiyaka can go with you, as well."

"You do not speak for me!" Wiyaka blurted out. "I go where I want to go and for now, that is with you!"

"We are not leaving you, *até*," Hoka proclaimed. "We will help this woman and girl if it is necessary."

"We will all be killed and none of you care," Hogan muttered. "I am young. I do not want to die."

"You are young and already a *canl waka, –* coward," Wiyaka blurted out.

"Stay out of this, Wiyaka," Hoka replied. "Hogan is my son."

Chayton motioned to Wiyaka to calm down. Then, after Chayton thought about the situation, he said to the others, "I have a plan!"

***

"*Inahni, Hoka! –* Hurry, Hoka!" Chayton urged Hoka to pick up the pace, stepping from rock to rock, as the pair made their way upriver. Hoka looked to his left and the high plateau seemed to rise forever, touching the deep blue sky. To his right were huge granite spires towering above the ground. Hoka and Chayton were like tiny insects as they made their way up the grandest of canyons.

"If I remember," Chayton declared, "the village of the Mountain People was up there, below those mountains."

"What was he like?" Hoka asked.

"He was a brave hunter," Chayton continued. "He died saving my life."

"Where did he die?" Hoka asked, looking around the river canyon.

"Up there," Chayton pointed at the granite spires in the distance.

"Are you sure you can climb up there, *até? –* father?" Hoka asked.

"Ha! Ha! Ha!" Chayton replied. "I could barely climb it the first time and that was many winters ago."

Chayton suddenly stopped, causing Hoka to run into the back of him. Chayton did not notice. He was completely absorbed in his own thoughts about this canyon. Hoka noticed a few tears running down Chayton's cheek.

"*Tóka he?* – What is wrong?" Hoka asked.

Chayton did not reply. His eyes kept wandering, studying the terrain. Finally, Hoka heard Chayton whisper, "Many winters…yet, so clear."

Then, as quickly as Chayton had entered his gloom, he left it. He coughed to clear his noisy lungs and then yelled, *"Inahni, Hoka, inahni! –* Hurry, Hoka, hurry!"

Hoka smiled and hurried to catch up to Chayton. The two travelers were just rounding a bend in the river when Chayton spotted a warrior walking directly towards them.

"*Wayaka! –* Look!" Chayton exclaimed and whispered over his shoulder, "I will do the talking, Hoka."

By now, the warrior was whistling loudly, calling the rest of the war party to him. When the warrior reached Chayton and Hoka, he placed the nock at the end of his spear against the spur on his spear thrower and stood in the path of the two travelers. Chayton and Hoka had no other alternative but to stop walking.

"*Was'te! –* Greetings!" Chayton said to the warrior. The warrior returned the greeting with nothing more than silence and an unpleasant expression on his face.

Chayton gazed around and saw other warriors appearing out of nowhere, all headed directly towards him and Hoka. Then, Chayton noticed the tall warrior, walking down the riverbank. This tall warrior was not in a hurry and carried himself differently. The tall warrior knew that the other warriors would take care of the two interlopers. Chayton could tell that the tall warrior was the leader of the war party. The woman had warned them about this tall warrior. When the leader finally arrived, his warriors backed out of his way, allowing Chayton and Hoka to come face–to–face with Satanta.

"Who are you?" Satanta demanded.

Chayton did not completely understand the language this warrior spoke. Chayton cupped his hand around his ear and asked the warrior to repeat what he had just said. Chayton recognized impatience in the voice of the tall warrior when he repeated his question in a louder voice, "I am Satanta! Who are you?"

The warrior did not speak the language of the Folsom People, but it was a close enough dialect for Chayton and Hoka to understand what the warrior had asked. Chayton replied to Satanta, "We are Folsom People...from the North Country."

"Why are you here, on our land?" Satanta demanded.

Chayton glanced around at the land, not realizing that land belonged to anyone, except *Wakan Tanka.* "We ask your forgiveness," Chayton replied, lowering his eyes in deference. "We are here to pray for a friend who died in this canyon, many winters ago."

Satanta listened and then thought about what he should do. "Are you alone?" he asked.

"*Ai, –* Yes, my son is with me."

"How long?" Satanta asked.

Chayton thought about his answer. "Two suns," he replied.

Satanta's angry glare softened. It appeared that he found Chayton's reply acceptable. Chayton decided to take advantage of the change in mood.

"Are you hunting?" Chayton asked, hoping his question would not anger the warrior, but Satanta's anger returned quickly. He scowled at Chayton, who quickly lowered his eyes to the ground. Satanta remained quiet for a long time and then answered Chayton's question, "We search for my sister and her daughter."

Chayton nodded his head to acknowledge that he understood.

"Have you seen a woman and child?" Satanta asked.

"*Ai, –* Yes," Chayton replied, knowing he knew something that Satanta would want to know.

Satanta waited for Chayton to answer, but Chayton just looked around and smiled a toothless grin at the other warriors. Finally, Satanta demanded, "How long?"

Chayton looked at Hoka and mumbled to him, "Two suns?"

Hoka thought about it and replied, "*Ai. –* Yes."

Chayton looked at Satanta and answered, "Two suns."

"Where?" Satanta demanded.

The hostility in Satanta's voice caused Chayton to shift his eyes back to the ground. He was once again staring at the moccasins on Satanta's feet.

"Where?" Satanta bellowed.

"Downriver," Chayton replied, "on the Arid Plains...prairie...flatlands... downriver from where two rivers come together."

Chayton made sure the warrior understood where he was talking about and then added, "They float on the water. They leave no tracks. Two or three suns…maybe more."

Chayton looked up just in time to see the determination on Satanta's face. Chayton could tell from the fire in the warrior's eyes that he would never give up looking for the woman.

"You have two suns to pray for your friend," Satanta said to the two hunters. "Do not be here when I return."

"*Ai,*" Chayton mumbled.

The warriors then headed downriver at a quick pace, leaving Chayton and Hoka standing alone along the riverbank. When the warriors were out of sight, Chayton spit a wad of gooey phlegm in their direction.

"Twenty winters ago I would have…," Chayton declared to himself and Hoka.

"*Ai, até–* Yes, father," Hoka replied. "Now, *hoppo,* – let us go, we only have two suns."

***

"*Wa nee yea due ne doe na hey?* – How many winters are you?" Gad asked Hogan as they walked along, following in the footsteps of Wiyaka and Moki.

"I am many," Hogan bellowed.

"*Hee ya,* – No, you are not many, you are a *hokshila.* – boy."

"I am a hunter," Hogan replied.

"*Hee ya,* you are not a hunter."

"I hunt with that *wichah^cala* – old man on our journey," Hogan declared, pointing his finger at Wiyaka.

"If you are a hunter, what did you kill?" she asked.

Hogan did not answer. He knew he had not killed anything. He did not want to lie or exaggerate, at least not too much. Far worse, he did not want to admit to the girl that he had not killed anything.

"With the *wichah^cala* – old man up there, I do not need to kill anything," Hogan replied. "*Wichah^cala* needs practice."

Gad looked over at Hogan. She did not believe a word of it. They could barely keep up with that old man named Wiyaka and even if he was old, Wiyaka looked like he could take care of himself. Gad gave up on the topic and moved to the next one.

"Where are we going?" Gad asked Hogan.

"You will see, little one," Hogan replied.

"You do not know where we are going," Gad declared with a grin missing

112

two front teeth. She then added, "I am not 'little one'. If I am 'little one', you are 'little one'."

Hogan did not reply. He could tell that he had met his match when it came to trading barbs with this girl. Then, Hogan took off jogging up the trail to catch up to Wiyaka. "Where are we going, Wiyaka?" the boy asked.

"To visit a friend," Wiyaka replied.

"I know that," Hogan replied.

"Then, why did you ask?" Wiyaka quipped.

"I mean where are we going?"

"We are going to visit a friend," Wiyaka wisecracked.

He knew that he would never get an answer from Wiyaka. He slowed up, dropping past Moki and then walking next to Gad.

"*Tuktel?* – Where?" Gad asked.

Hogan did not say a word.

"What did you find out?" Gad questioned. "Where are we going?"

"He would not tell me," Hogan replied.

"You are just a *hokshila*, – boy," Gad stated and then ran to catch up to her mother, leaving Hogan to bring up the rear.

Chapter Ten

Chayton and Hoka traveled up the river until the sun was low in the west. Tall granite spires had replaced the plateau and rugged foothills of the canyon. The river screamed as it pushed its way through the tight confines between two granite spires. Chayton stopped walking and looked straight up into the sky.

Seeing his father look up, Hoka did the same thing. High above the travelers were two enormous granite cliffs, coming together near their tops and forming an almost complete arch across the river. Because of its great height above the river, the two travelers could barely see the tiny sliver of sky between the tops of the two granite cliffs.

"There!" Chayton yelled against the roar of the river. "We flew across the river!"

Chayton pointed at the gap between the granite cliffs. Hoka's stomach involuntarily rolled and his fingers went numb as he thought about jumping across the sky at such a tremendous height above the river.

"Wha–wha–what happened?" Hoka asked.

Chayton motioned for them to get away from the noisy river so they could hear each other. With his walking staff picking the path, Chayton headed up a small side canyon, away from the deafening screams of the river. When they were far enough away from the river, Chayton stopped walking and turned around to face Hoka.

"The warriors trapped us on top of that cliff," Chayton explained. "We had to jump across to the other cliff or they would have killed us!"

Hoka's eyes wandered back up to the top of the granite cliffs. For as long as he had known Chayton, he had never heard this story before.

"I was badly wounded in the shoulder," Chayton said. "Keya helped me and when it was his turn to jump…"

Chayton cleared his throat and emotions caught up to him. He finally continued the story, but his voice was cracking and wavering, "I made it across…barely…Keya was the last to jump…a spear…"

Chayton had to stop. He looked away from Hoka, embarrassed that he was once again weeping like a child. Hoka stood there, not knowing whether to comfort his father or look away. Chayton finally turned back around and continued, "A spear…a spear struck Keya just as he jumped…he…he fell… he fell to the river."

"Here?" Hoka questioned. "Keya died here?"

"*Ai, –* Yes," Chayton answered. "I vowed to return…it took too long."

"Did you find him?" Hoka asked. "I mean after he fell."

"*Hee ya, –* No," Chayton replied. "The *ozuye –* war party was hunting us down."

Hoka saw that talking about the death of Keya had made Chayton uncomfortable, so Hoka stopped asking questions. Hoka was a small boy when his mother helped Chayton heal his wounded shoulder. Hoka could barely remember when that happened and Chayton had never explained what had happened to his shoulder or his cousin Keya. Even in the dim light of the canyon, Hoka could see the glistening tears streaming down Chayton's cheeks.

Chayton turned and walked away, inspecting around the base of a granite cliff as if he were searching for something. A small distance from the river, Chayton appeared to have found what he was looking for, a tiny cave carved by river floods, underneath the granite cliff. Chayton leaned over and inspected the interior of the small cave. When he was satisfied, Chayton stood up and looked back towards the river.

"What are you doing, *até? –* father?" Hoka asked.

"*Inhanblapi, –* Seeking a vision," Chayton replied.

Hoka waited for Chayton to explain, but Chayton was in a hurry.

"Find green pine boughs…long…thick…we must cover the entrance of the cave," Chayton instructed Hoka. "I will make fire."

Hoka remained standing there, still waiting for Chayton to explain what they were doing.

"*Inahni, Hoka! –* Hurry, Hoka!" Chayton snapped at his son. "Darkness comes!"

While Hoka cut and carried pine boughs back to the cave, Chayton built a large fire hearth just inside the mouth of the cave.

"Weave the pine boughs together and cover the entrance," Chayton instructed Hoka.

"*Hat'ugha? –* Why?" Hoka inquired.

"Just do it! We can talk later," Chayton replied while placing a gentle hand on Hoka's shoulder. "The *wanagis –* ghosts of the canyon are coming…Keya is coming…we must hurry."

Chayton hustled off to collect firewood while Hoka wove the pine boughs together, creating a large mat. He then lifted the pine bough mat in front of the cave entrance, effectively sealing the entrance to the cave and leaving only a small hole on the side to crawl in and out. When Hoka finished, he went to help Chayton collect firewood. When the pile of firewood stood high outside the cave, Chayton started a campfire. After the campfire was burning, Chayton instructed Hoka, "Bring me wet rock from the river and more firewood."

"More firewood?" Moki questioned, pointing at the chest high pile of firewood they had already collected.

"KAAF! KAAF! KAAF!" Chayton coughed several times. Even with the river in the background, Hoka could hear the rattling sound in his father's breathing. Hoka patiently waited for the bout of coughing to end.

"We need more firewood for your campfire," Chayton mumbled, his voice raspy and barely audible.

"My campfire?" Hoka queried, thinking that he was going to be sharing a campfire with Chayton.

"*Ai,* – Yes, build it over there," Chayton instructed, pointing to a place halfway to the river.

"What is this?" Hoka asked, pointing a finger at the sealed cave.

"*Ini ti,* – cleansing lodge," Chayton answered.

"What is it for, *até*?" Hoka asked.

"*Ini kaga.*"

"*Taku? –* What?"

"*Ini kaga...inipi,*" Chayton repeated. "It will make my *wanagi* – ghost strong."

Hoka still did not understand. He waited for Chayton to explain, but that would never happen. Chayton was stripping off his clothes and then he stood naked in front of Hoka.

"*Inahni! –* Hurry!" Chayton demanded. "Bring rocks...I need water...firewood!"

Hoka took off towards the river. When he looked over his shoulder, he saw Chayton was following him. When Hoka arrived at the river, he stepped into the icy water and started throwing river rock up onto the riverbank. Out of the corner of his eye, Hoka watched his father walk into the river and suddenly sit down. Chayton started splashing water and cleaning himself. In the light from the night sun, Hoka could see the jagged, pale scar on the left shoulder of his father. The scar was a vivid reminder of his father's last adventure into this canyon. Hoka looked around at the eerie canyon walls and an icy chill ran through his veins. His rising uneasiness caused Hoka to increase his pace at throwing river rocks onto the riverbank. Before he knew it, he had a large pile of wet rocks on the riverbank and he waded ashore. Hoka shot a glance over his shoulder at his father and yelled, "*Doe ksh kayo un hey?* – How are you?"

"*Waste!* – Good!" Chayton hollered back and then Chayton slid his head under the surface of the water. Hoka watched to make sure his father was not drowning. When Hoka saw Chayton's head resurface, he began carrying the river rocks back to the cave, tossing them just outside the entrance.

"*Ini ti!* – Cleansing lodge!" Chayton barked, walking up behind Hoka. "Put the rocks in the campfire!"

Hoka carried the rocks through the entrance of the *ini ti* and dumped them in the campfire. Steam rose as each wet rock sizzled on the hot coals at the bottom of the fire hearth. Hoka retreated from the *ini ti* just as it filled up with smoke and steam. Hoka turned to his father and asked, "Are you hungry?"

"*Hee ya!* – No!" Chayton replied. "I need firewood and water."

Hoka started to protest, but Chayton interrupted him. "*Iyaya!* – Go!" he said.

Chayton crawled through the opening of the *ini ti* – cleansing lodge while Hoka went looking for more firewood and hauling more water. When Hoka got back with a load of firewood and a full water pouch, the smoke and steam were pouring through the small gaps between the pine boughs. He could hear Chayton coughing and hacking inside. Hoka took a deep breath, then, crawled into the *ini ti*.

"Put the wood on the campfire," Hoka heard Chayton's hoarse voice speak through the thick haze of smoke and steam. "Pour the water on the rocks."

Hoka obeyed his father. When Hoka poured the contents of the water pouch on the sizzling rocks, a cloud of steam rose and filled the *ini ti*. Hoka somehow managed to breathe without coughing, but his eyes were watering from wood smoke.

"*Iyaya!* – Go!" he heard Chayton tell him, followed by a series of coughs. "Eat and keep bringing firewood and water!"

Hoka left the *ini ti* and wiped his watering eyes with the back of his hand. He walked around in the darkness, looking for rocks for his own fire hearth. After getting his campfire started, he collected more firewood for Chayton and filled another water pouch. Then, he settled down by his own campfire, hungry and cold. He looked above at the granite spires and saw a sky filled with countless stars. Hoka sat there by the campfire, staring off into space while listening to the sound of the river in one ear and Chayton's hoarse voice singing in the other.

***

Just before sunset, the war party arrived at the tip of the plateau, the place where the two rivers came together. It was the same place where the four travelers had camped and discovered the woman and small girl. Satanta did not trust anyone, including the old man who told him about seeing the woman and small girl out on the prairie. He continued to order the warriors to scour the riverbanks. It did not take long for the warriors to discover where the travelers ate and slept. The warriors also discovered another surprise, the moccasin tracks of a woman and small girl. They followed the trail of the woman and child and it led to another camp, hidden high on the steep slope of the plateau. Fala told Satanta what they had discovered and reminded Satanta what Chayton had told them.

"The old man told us he saw the woman and child on the prairie," Fala reminded Satanta.

"He was an old man," Satanta declared. "He forgot or he lied."

"There were four humans here, we met only two in the canyon," Fala queried. "Where did the others go?"

"I do not care about the four humans, Fala," Satanta admitted. "I only care about one woman. Search for the trail of the woman. This is the trail we will follow."

"What of the old man?" Fala asked.

"I do not care about the old man," Satanta replied. "Go find the tracks from this woman!"

"There is something else I must tell you, Satanta," Fala proclaimed.

"What?" Satanta demanded.

"The warriors are angry," Fala informed.

"Why?"

"They want to go home," Fala replied. "Their families need them."

"They can go home when they find the woman!"

"They say that they follow you out of respect for your father," Fala stated, "and that your father would want them to care for their families."

Satanta did not respond, but Fala took another risk when he continued, "They say that if you want the woman, you can go find her."

"Are *they* saying this or are *you* saying this, Fala?" Satanta inquired.

"I will follow you, Satanta, you know that," Fala answered.

"Who is speaking the loudest?" Satanta demanded.

Fala looked over his shoulder to make sure the warriors were not listening. When he was sure they were alone, he gave Satanta the name of a warrior called Weca.

"Weca!" Satanta bellowed, disappointed that one of his better warriors was being disloyal to him. "Once darkness arrives, Weca will be dealt with. Now, find the trail of the woman!"

***

"Let me hunt with you, Wiyaka," Hogan begged.

"I do not need your heavy feet near me," Wiyaka replied.

Hogan looked over at the woman and girl, hoping that they had not heard the disparaging remark. "I will walk as quiet as *igmuwatogla,* – mountain lion," Hogan pleaded. "Let me hunt with you, Wiyaka."

Wiyaka smiled. He caught Hogan glancing back at the woman and child. Wiyaka had just figured out what Hogan's sudden interest in hunting was all about. Hogan wanted to impress the woman and child with his hunting prowess. Wiyaka decided to have a little fun at Hogan's expense.

"Your spear flies too crooked!" Wiyaka bellowed, loud enough for everyone to hear.

"*Enila,* – Be quiet," Hogan begged.

"Ha! Ha! Ha!" Wiyaka laughed and then pointing towards a small forest to the north, he told Hogan, "Go *waziyata* – north and hunt in that forest. I will go south."

"Alone?" Hogan questioned. "I want to hunt with you. What if there are *sunkmanitu tanka* – wolf or *igmuwatogla?* – mountain lion?"

Wiyaka laughed and then replied with as much seriousness as he could muster, "Then, they will eat you and I no longer have to feed you or listen to your constant yipping like a baby coyote."

Hogan started to whine, but Wiyaka cut him off short, saying, "Do not worry, we will hear your screams before they have eaten all of you."

Hogan glanced over at the woman and child to see if they were listening to the old man's banter. They appeared too busy or polite to be listening. Hogan reluctantly walked across the meadow towards the forest to the north. Amused by his own quick wit, Wiyaka watched Hogan disappear into the trees and then instructed Moki to wait right where she was. Wiyaka then jogged toward a ridge just west of where Hogan was walking. Wiyaka's eyes studied the ground, missing nothing and looking for any subtle sign from the prey he sought. Wiyaka ran up the pine–covered ridge and then suddenly

119

stopped, listening and surveying the terrain around him. Wiyaka sensed that eyes were watching him. Then, when he was satisfied with the lay of the land, he continued hiking to the north, scrambling across the rocky slope of the ridge. Suddenly, he stopped and held his breath, listening for the sounds of the forest. Somewhere to the east, he heard the faint snap of a tree limb and the muffled sound of hooves clambering across the forest floor.

Wiyaka knew instantly that he had found deer, the most alert animal of all. Wiyaka scurried off to the northeast, hoping to outflank the deer and drive them to the southeast and into the range of Hogan's spear. Wiyaka jogged through the forest, knowing exactly where to place his feet. He smiled as he trotted along. Hunting was what he loved most about his life. Wiyaka suddenly stopped and listened. He could now hear the faint sound of hooves tromping the pine needles that covered the soil. Wiyaka's old ears pinpointed the direction of the sound and then he took off trotting to the southeast.

The shadows of the day were lengthening as Hogan slowly wandered through the pine forest. Behind every tree, he imagined the eyes of mountain lions and wolves. He stood there in a small clearing, surrounded by pine trees, trying to decide if it was too dark to hunt. Then, Hogan heard a sound in front of him, coming his way. Adrenalin shot through his limbs and his stomach heaved as he fumbled with a spear. His imagination went wild as he thought about what animal could be heading in his direction.

Then, out of the trees, five mule deer came running directly at him. Hogan ducked down as the deer suddenly halted and looked around. *They smell me!* Hogan thought. With his hands shaking like a leaf, Hogan balanced the spear shaft on his right shoulder. He would have only one chance. He selected his target, a mule deer doe that was standing broadside, nearest to him. Hogan cocked his arm behind his shoulder and was ready to launch the spear as soon as he stood up.

Hogan stood up and even this tiny sound brought an alert to the deer. Their heads swiveled towards Hogan in unison. Their eyes locked onto Hogan for the briefest of moments, and then they ran, but by then Hogan's spear was whistling through the air. The spear found its target. The sharp fluted spear tip sliced through the rib cage of the deer doe. Her bleat of pain set off a stampede for the rest of the small herd as they scattered to the winds. The wounded doe leapt forward, bouncing on the ground, attempting to free itself from the pain and the spear dangling from its side. Before the doe could rid itself of the first spear, another stone spear tip penetrated its hindquarters, spinning the doe around. The doe collapsed and then attempted to regain its feet, but the damage from the stone spear tip had paralyzed its back legs. A third spear flew over the crippled doe as it attempted to drag itself to safety in the forest.

The adrenalin surged through Hogan as he sprinted towards his prey. He positioned himself near the doe and drew back for another throw. He flung his spear and the sharp fluted spear point shattered another rib, penetrating the diaphragm of his prey. The dying doe plunged into the ground for the last time as Hogan quickly dispatched it with his stone knife. Hogan held on to his prey's neck until it finally gave up its life. Hogan lay against his dead prey, winded and his heart pounding in his chest. His arm, still encircling the neck of his prey, shook while all of the nerves in his body unwound. Sweat poured from Hogan and dripped onto the fur of the mule deer doe. Hogan closed his eyes and let his body relax. He did not know if he could ever move again.

From the trees, Wiyaka had watched the kill. He smiled at the way Hogan had dispatched the deer. It was now time to teach Hogan the next lesson. Wiyaka walked out of the trees and into the clearing.

"WHAT ARE YOU DOING?" a voice yelled from across the clearing.

Startled by the voice, Hogan jumped to his feet, still holding the stone knife in his hand.

"What are you doing with that knife?" the voice, now closer, taunted him.

Hogan looked around, unable to spot where the voice was coming from.

"I am here, *takuni slolye sni!* – stupid!" the voice bellowed.

Hogan stared in the direction the voice was coming from. Then he saw Wiyaka walking across the clearing towards him.

"*Waste!* – Good!" Wiyaka praised the boy. "I watched you."

"I–I–I thought you went *itokaga?* – south?" Hogan questioned.

"I got lost," Wiyaka replied, not admitting that he had driven the mule deer herd towards the boy.

"I told you that I was a great hunter," Hogan boasted. "You have not even killed any game."

"*Ai,* – Yes, you did well, Hogan," Wiyaka admitted, "but a true hunter is always humble."

"*Taku?* – What?" Hogan challenged. "I cannot be proud of my kill?"

"*Hee ya!* – No! You should never be proud of killing! You can be happy you have food, but never proud of killing!" Wiyaka replied. "It is now important that you honor your prey since it gave its life so that you can live."

"Honor this deer?"

"Has your father not taught you anything?"

"*Slol wa yea shnee,* – I do not know," Hogan replied.

"This mule deer died so we have food," Wiyaka explained.

"This deer died because I am a great hunter."

"*Hee ya!* – No!" Wiyaka bellowed, losing the small amount of patience he actually possessed. "We only live because of animals."

Hogan listened, but he did not understand.

"You must honor the life this deer gave you!" Wiyaka explained. "You must not brag when you take an animal or *Wakan Tanka* will punish you by starving our tribe!"

Hogan did not say anything, which only annoyed Wiyaka even more.

"Do you understand?" Wiyaka demanded.

Hogan thought about it and then replied, "*Ai.* – Yes."

"Do we come from the same tribe?" Wiyaka asked, sarcastically.

Hogan did not reply so Wiyaka continued to instruct the boy on the ways of the hunter, "You will offer a prayer of thanks to this deer and to *Wakan Tanka* for allowing us to have food."

Hogan placed his hands on top of the doe's head and then looked over at Wiyaka to make sure he was doing it right. When no protest came, Hogan closed his eyes and gave a prayer of thanks to both the mule deer doe and *Wakan Tanka.* When Hogan finished the prayer, he looked over at Wiyaka to gauge the old man's reaction.

Wiyaka looked please. "Prepare the deer, Hogan, and I will help you carry it to camp," he said with a smile.

***

Darkness set in quickly for the camp tucked behind the towering plateau. The warriors huddled around a large campfire, cooking what little meat they could scavenge during the day. Satanta stood behind the warriors, slowly walking around the perimeter of the camp. He studied the faces of the warriors, looking for any sign of deception or deceit. The warriors looked spent and their faces filthy from the long journey away from home. They had been searching for this woman for many suns and they were ready to go home, all except Satanta. As Satanta slowly circled the camp, he could hear the grumbles and complaining of the warriors as they whispered amongst themselves. Satanta picked up a piece of firewood and threw it on the campfire, causing cinders and hot ashes to explode upward. Once the flames stopped protesting, Satanta resumed his slow walk around the campfire.

"I am told you are not happy," Satanta announced to the warriors while circling behind them.

The warriors looked around at each other, trying to identify the informer. Their eyes finally settled on the only warrior not looking around, Fala. His eyes remained fixed on the campfire. Fala had betrayed the other warriors' trust. Satanta stopped walking and waited for the warriors to have the courage to confront him, but the only sound came from the popping and sizzling of wood on the campfire.

Satanta picked up another large piece of firewood and resumed his walk behind the warriors. "Tell me why you are not happy!" Satanta exclaimed. "I will listen to you."

The warriors glanced around at each other to see if others actually believed that Satanta would listen to them. Fala continued his glare at the wild flames of the campfire.

Satanta circled the warriors again, watching and waiting for someone to say anything. "You are happy with our journey!" Satanta stated. "That is good!"

Then, the warrior that Satanta suspected would find courage, found it. "No, we are not happy!" Weca declared.

"Why?" Satanta asked while still circling behind the warriors.

Weca looked around at the other warriors, hoping that they would join in and help him, but no one said anything. Every warrior joined Fala in staring at the campfire.

"Speak, Weca, do not be afraid," Satanta insisted. "You and I are the only ones who have the courage to speak!"

Weca cleared his throat and looked over his shoulder at Satanta. "We respect your father," Weca stated. "He told us to help you. We have helped you."

Satanta waited for Weca to continue, but Weca did not say anything else. "Speak!" Satanta insisted. "You warriors talk amongst yourselves when I am not near, but have no courage when I am here."

"We have followed you for three cycles of the night sun," Weca blurted out. "It is now time for us to return to our families."

"If you respect my father than you must respect his wishes," Satanta replied. "You must help me."

All of the warriors remained quiet. Weca looked around, hoping that at least one of the warriors would help him out of his predicament, but none of them even acknowledged him.

123

Satanta circled the campfire and then stopped right behind Weca. "You will see your families when this woman is found!" Satanta bellowed.

The wood on the campfire cracked and popped. The tension in the air was thick. While the warriors' heads focused on the campfire, their eyes wandered about, searching for signs from each other. They knew it was time to make a move against Satanta. Weca slowly reached down alongside his leg and tightly gripped the bone handle of his stone knife. The other warriors saw this and carefully made their move towards their own weapons. They had planned this. They would kill Satanta and then they would kill the informer, Fala. The warriors would then go home and explain to their chief how brave his son was, killed by an enemy. No one breathed as the suspense mounted around the campfire. The warriors glared at the flames of the campfire, waiting for Weca to end the unbearable tension. "Satanta, you do not understand," Weca declared. "We have made our decision and we are going home."

The treachery stunned Satanta as much as a knife wound to the heart. He could not find his breath. He breathed deeply, trying to fill his lungs, but his body fought it. He looked in Fala's direction, the only warrior he could seemingly trust. Satanta found the answer in Fala's eyes. Satanta knew what he must do. Shaking with rage, Satanta took a step closer to Weca. "Does Weca speak for all of you?" Satanta posed the question to the other warriors.

A couple of the warriors glanced around while others remained motionless, their eyes focused on the flames. Weca glared at the other warriors, hoping that they would find enough courage to support him.

"Say something!" Weca pleaded. "Do not be afraid of Satanta! He is nothing! The blood of his father makes him a warrior, not his deeds!"

CRACK! It sounded like lightning striking a pine tree. The pine log exploded into the back of Weca's head. The force of the blow was so brutal that Weca's body fell over into the campfire. The other warriors jumped to their feet, backing away from flying cinders and ashes as Satanta repeatedly struck the flailing body of Weca with the pine log. The warriors stood in horror watching their leader pummel the warrior. Weca's body shook and convulsed. His arms and legs flopped around in the cradle of the fire hearth. Satanta decided to end it all. Satanta straddled the edge of the campfire and raised the pine log above his head, he swung downward, time after time, until he had flattened Weca's skull and the warrior's blood had spilled everywhere. Too winded to continue his assault, Satanta stood next to the campfire with his hands on his hips, glaring around at the terrified warriors.

"Does Weca speak for you?" Satanta asked between breaths.

The only sound came from blood sizzling on the campfire.

***

The aroma of charred meat floated across the camp as Wiyaka and Hogan held their deer meat over the campfire. Moki and Gad lay cuddled together while sleeping on the other side of the campfire.

"They have had a difficult journey," Wiyaka commented to Hogan.

"So have we," Hogan responded.

Wiyaka looked at the boy and said, "Our journey has just begun. You have not seen anything."

Hogan did not reply. He had learned not to argue with the old man.

"Go wake them up," Wiyaka added. "Ask them if they are hungry."

Hogan slowly rose to his feet. *Why do I have to wake Moki and Gad up?* As Hogan walked over to the mother and daughter, Wiyaka said, "You did *waste* – good, Hogan,"

Hogan stopped and let the praise from a great hunter sink in. "*Pilamaya, Wiyaka,* – Thank you, Wiyaka," Hogan replied, unable to hold back his smile. He then walked over and woke Moki and Gad up. Wiyaka pulled his deer meat from the campfire and tested its warmth with his hand. He then blew on the meat and took a small bite.

"They want to sleep," Hogan told Wiyaka after returning.

While Wiyaka and Hogan ate their fill of deer meat, Hogan asked Wiyaka a question that was bothering him, "Why do we thank animals that we kill?"

"I explained this to you!" Wiyaka responded with a fury. "Did your father and grandfather teach you nothing?"

Hogan was surprised at the outburst, especially since Wiyaka had just complimented him. After thinking how to respond, Hogan answered, "*Ai,* – Yes, they have told me…you have told me…I still do not understand."

"Your food is burning!" Wiyaka said, pointing at the flaming torch that once was Hogan's deer meat.

Hogan pulled the deer meat off the campfire. The fat of the meat was on fire and Hogan had to blow it out with his breath. When Hogan was finally able to extinguish the blaze, a piece of charcoal was what he had left. He showed it to Wiyaka, making the old hunter laugh. Hogan touched the charred meat to make sure it would not burn his mouth and decided to let it cool down some more.

"*Wakan Tanka* works through all animals and humans," Wiyaka started to explain. "The eagle… hawk…deer…wolf…snake…even a mouse has power given to it by *Wakan Tanka*. Some animals use this power for *waste, –* good, some animals use this power for *sica. –* evil."

"I remember that," Hogan declared.

"*Waste! –* Good!" Wiyaka bellowed. "*Wana, enila! –* Now, be quiet!"

Both Wiyaka and Hogan looked over at Moki and Gad to make sure the outburst had not awakened them. When they saw that the woman and girl were still sleeping, Wiyaka continued, "This is why *sunkmanitu tanka, –* wolf, *igmuwatogla –* mountain lion, *hexaka –* elk and the other animals are *wakan. –* holy."

"What about us?" Hogan asked. "Humans are the most powerful!"

"*Wakan Tanka* has given no power to humans, except what comes from *sicun,*" Wiyaka explained, touching his heart with his hand.

"*Sicun?*" Hogan asked.

"*Sicun!*" Wiyaka repeated. Then, after Wiyaka thought about how to explain the meaning of *sicun,* he added, "the power of our ghost."

Wiyaka thumped his chest with a closed fist, attempting to demonstrate that *sicun* comes from within. "Humans only live if *Wakan Tanka* provides them with animals," Wiyaka proclaimed, using his arms to convey the enormity of the statement and the power of *Wakan Tanka*. "When we hunt and kill an animal, its power comes to us…we honor the animal for without it, we die."

Wiyaka had not spoken so much in a long time. He almost enjoyed it. He had no children to pass on his knowledge and wisdom so this was giving him an opportunity. He stared into the flames of the campfire, satisfied that he had explained it well enough for the boy to comprehend. Wiyaka waited for questions from Hogan, but Hogan was satisfied, at least for now.

Chapter Eleven

At dawn, Satanta rose from a troubled sleep. Finding this woman had become an obsession and killing the traitor Weca was necessary in fulfilling that obsession. He stretched his arms and looked around. Even in the dim light of a new day, his warriors were searching for the trail of the woman. Satanta smiled at the warriors' renewed enthusiasm and loyalty. Weca's death had not been in vain and if Satanta needed to kill one or two more warriors to maintain this enthusiasm, he would do so. Satanta turned around and gazed up at a nearby willow tree where the charred remains of Weca hung suspended from a piece of hemp rope. Weca's body swung back and forth in the light morning breeze. Dark blood covered most of Weca's former face and his contorted arms reached upward towards the heavens as if he begged for mercy.

"Your death served its purpose, my friend," Satanta proclaimed to the swinging corpse.

Satanta turned around and saw Fala jogging towards him. "We found her trail. She is with the girl and two men!" Fala exclaimed when he was close enough for Satanta to hear.

"Her husband?" Satanta asked.

"I do not know," Fala replied and then added, "There is something I must tell you."

"What?"

"Two warriors left in the dark," Fala explained.

"Left in the dark?"

"They are gone," Fala replied. "There are no blood trails or tracks from animals."

Satanta did not reply. His killing of Weca had a cost, after all. Now, there were only five warriors.

"Do you want me to find the trail of the warriors?" Fala asked.

"No, their trail will lead back to our village," Satanta suggested. "After we find the woman, I will deal with them."

Fala bowed his head and then asked, "Should we bury Weca?"

"No, let the birds have him," Satanta replied.

Fala bowed again and then led Satanta towards the trail of the woman.

Wiyaka rose from a deep sleep. He had found that the older he became, the better he slept. He rubbed his eyes while looking around the camp. The campfire was roaring and sitting beside it was Gad. The small girl was watching over some deer meat that was grilling over the flames. Wiyaka then noticed Hogan lying by a rock, still fast asleep. After bending and stretching to stand up, Wiyaka walked over to Hogan and kicked him in the shin.

"*Key kta yo!* – Wake up!" Wiyaka roared.

Out of one eye, Hogan looked up and then rolled over so that is face was against the ground. Wiyaka wound his foot up and kicked Hogan again, this time much harder.

"*Kikta!* – Get up!" Wiyaka bellowed at Hogan. When Wiyaka saw that Hogan was not going to budge, he moved up towards Hogan's chest and planted another kick in Hogan's ribs.

"*Wana!* – Now!" Wiyaka thundered.

Hogan finally jumped to his feet and rubbed his eyes to wake up.

"Why are you kicking me?" Hogan asked.

"To wake you up, *takuni slolye sni!* – stupid!" Wiyaka replied.

Hogan looked over at the campfire and saw Gad smiling at him through the gap in her teeth. Hogan was too grumpy to smile back at Gad or argue with Wiyaka.

"Go collect firewood," Wiyaka insisted.

Hogan looked at the large pile of firewood the women had already collected. He pointed at it and said, "We do not need firewood!"

"Do not argue with me!" Wiyaka thundered. "*Iyaya!* – Go!"

Still halfway asleep, Hogan strolled to a nearby grove of trees to collect firewood, mumbling to himself and wondering why Wiyaka had to be so mean.

"Do not burn the meat!" Wiyaka growled at the small girl.

Gad smiled, paying no attention to the cranky old man.

"Where is your mother?" Wiyaka inquired.

Without taking her eyes off the roasting meat, Gad pointed in the direction of a large clearing east of the camp. Wiyaka scanned the clearing and finally located Moki. She was in the middle of the clearing throwing spears with her spear thrower.

"What is she doing?" Wiyaka mumbled to himself.

"She is learning," Gad replied to Wiyaka's grumble.

"She cannot learn," Wiyaka dismissed the girl.

"You do not know her," Gad replied.

Wiyaka shook his head and walked over to meet Moki. "What are you doing?" he asked Moki when he reached her.

Moki hurled another spear across the clearing and then said, "I am throwing spears."

Wiyaka leaned over and picked up one of Moki's spears. He examined the feather fletching at the end of the spear. The feathers needed replacing and the sinew holding the feathers in place was in disrepair. He then examined the other end and saw that the stone spear point was shattered and dull.

"Are these your spears?" Wiyaka asked Moki.

"*Ai...hee ya,* – Yes...no," she replied. "They belonged to my husband."

"You have let them go bad," Wiyaka said.

"*Ai.* – Yes."

"Do you know how to fix them?"

"*Ai.* – Yes," Moki proclaimed, but then after thinking about her answer, she changed her mind, "*Hee ya.* – No."

Wiyaka thought about scolding her for letting the spears get into disrepair, but then he changed his mind. "I will help you," he muttered.

Moki smiled and then replied, "*Pilamaya,* – Thank you."

"We must leave!" Wiyaka insisted. "If the *ozuye* – war party has found our trail, we are in danger."

"One more throw," Moki insisted.

"*Inahni!* – Hurry!" Wiyaka pleaded.

Moki placed the nock at the end of the spear on the spur of the spear thrower and then with a running start, she heaved the spear. The spear wobbled through the air and then slammed into the ground, not far from where Moki was standing.

"*Hee ya! Hee Ya! Hee ya!* – No! No! No!" Wiyaka screamed. "There is no hope! *Iyaya!* – Go! Fetch the spear, we must leave!"

***

The sun had just disappeared behind the granite spires when Chayton finally exited the *ini ti.* – cleansing lodge. Hoka watched as Chayton stumbled naked towards the river. Hoka caught up to him and handed him his walking staff. "Are you all right?" Hoka inquired.

Chayton tried to speak, but the smoke had made his throat raw and his voice was gone from singing. Chayton continued a beeline towards the river while Hoka held on to his free arm. When Chayton arrived at the river, he handed his walking staff to Hoka and waded into the frigid water. When the water was thigh deep, Chayton sat down.

"*Lol wah cheen,* – I am hungry," Chayton finally mumbled.

"I have fish!" Hoka replied.

Chayton acknowledged Hoka by nodding his head. He then dunked his head into the river. Hoka watched Chayton cool off in the river and then he went to prepare the fish. Out of the corner of his eye, Hoka nervously watched Chayton in the river. In Chayton's weakened state, it would not take much for the river currents to wash him away. Hoka could not watch any longer. He walked back to the river and entered the fast river current. When he reached Chayton, he leaned over and grabbed the old man, but Chayton pulled away from him. Finally, Hoka just stood in the river and waited for his father to finish. Chayton eventually stood up and gingerly made his way back to the riverbank. Hoka watched his father and could not believe how frail he had become. Skin hung from Chayton's arms and back. His once strong and muscular body had disappeared with the passage of time.

Picking up his walking staff on the riverbank, Chayton slowly ambled over to the campfire and sat down. Hoka brought him a full water pouch and the fish he had grilled. Chayton took a few bites of fish and then devoured the rest of the fish with a few gulps. He drank from the water pouch and then leaned back in the grass of the canyon.

"KAAF! KAAF!" Chayton coughed and then told Hoka in a gravelly voice, "I will rest...then we will leave."

"Where are we going?" Hoka asked, but by then Chayton had already fallen asleep. Chayton slept through the night while Hoka watched over him. Chayton woke up at first light and Hoka handed him a flat rock with more grilled fish lying on top of it.

"You were up before light," Chayton said with a smile, referring to the cooked fish.

"*Ai,* – Yes, you were in the *ini ti* – cleansing lodge a long time," Hoka replied, nodding in the direction of the cave and hoping that Chayton would share what had happened. Chayton just smiled and gorged himself on every bite of the fish. Unable to contain his curiosity, Hoka finally blurted out, "What happened?"

"What do you mean?" Chayton whispered.

"*Inhanblapi,* – Seeking a vision," Hoka clarified.

"*Inipi* has made my ghost strong," Chayton answered. "I am no longer burdened with what I must do."

"*Taku?* – What?" Hoka questioned.

Chayton belched from the fish he had eaten and the water he drank. He then replied to Hoka, "We must leave. Wiyaka and Hogan are in danger."

"How do you know–" Hoka tried to ask a question, but Chayton was already standing up and putting on his clothes. When Chayton was dressed and had his gear ready for travel, he peered over at Hoka and said, "*Hoppo!* – Let us go! We must find a place to cross the river!"

"Cross the river?" Hoka challenged.

"*Ai,* – Yes," Chayton announced. "I know where they are?"

"Who?" Hoka asked. "Wiyaka and Hogan?"

"*Hee ya!* – No!" Chayton replied. "*Inahni!* – Hurry!"

Hoka thought of another question, but Chayton was already walking downriver. Hoka jogged along, trying to keep up with his father.

"We can cross the river where it is wide and shallow," Chayton mumbled and then picked up his pace, leaving Hoka behind.

"We cross the river and then climb the plateau," Chayton announced in a low voice.

"You cannot climb the plateau," Hoka expressed his doubts.

"You will have to carry me then."

"I cannot carry you up the plateau."

"*Enila!* – Be quiet!" Chayton said, stepping into the water and began wading across the river. Hoka followed, scrambling to keep up with the old man.

"What happened in the *ini ti?* – cleansing lodge?" Hoka persisted while balancing his feet between river rocks.

"You are annoying me," Chayton replied and then coughed several times to clear his lungs.

"Then tell me what happened, *até.*"

"*Wowihanble.* – Holy dream."

"*Wowihanble?* – Holy dream?" Hoka repeated.

"I hear an echo!" Chayton stated, staring up at the canyon walls.

"What happened?" Hoka asked, attempting to keep up with Chayton.

"*Wakan Tanka* told me where I must go and what I must do," Chayton answered and then stepping out of the river, he began climbing the steep slope of the plateau. "*Inahni!* – Hurry!" he growled at Hoka.

* * *

"You are a hunter!" Gad chirped to Hogan as they walked behind Wiyaka and Moki. "I thought you were just a *hokshila* until you brought us deer."

131

"*Enila!* – Be quiet!" Hogan replied while looking ahead to make sure Wiyaka was not listening. "I am not a hunter…yet."

"You told me you were a hunter?"

"I am not ready."

"You brought deer to the campsite," Gad insisted and then asked. "Did you find it dead?"

"*Hee ya,* – No, it was not dead," Hogan said. "Wiyaka helped me, I know he did."

"You would know it if he helped you," Gad suggested.

"*Ai,* – Yes, I would think so," Hogan answered. Hogan noticed that Wiyaka and Moki had climbed to the top of a hill. He followed them up the hill with his new shadow called Gad following close behind. When Hogan reached the top of the hill, Wiyaka was pointing off to the south and speaking to Moki.

"Where are we?" Hogan interrupted Wiyaka.

"*Slol wa yea shnee,* – I do not know," Wiyaka responded.

"You do not know where we are?" Hogan challenged.

"*Hee ya,* – No, it has been many winters…the land has changed," Wiyaka answered. "I have grown old and forgetful."

Wiyaka studied the terrain for a very long time, attempting to figure out where they were. He could see the Arid Plains off to the east and the mountains to the west. When he finally pieced together where they were, he said to the others, "I believe *tatanka* – bison once filled a valley to the southwest of here. We should reach that valley when the sun is old and then we should reach the river in another sun, maybe two or three. At the river, we will wait for Chayton and Hoka."

Then, Wiyaka began hiking towards the southwest, directly at the foothills of the mountains. The other travelers followed him.

***

By sunset, the four travelers had made it to the valley of the bison. The travelers were now directly north of the river where the River People's village had once been, the place where Tarca Sapa and Delshay had died in the wildfire. Wiyaka decided to camp on the edge of a pine forest that overlooked the valley to the south.

The travelers were happy as they went about their camp chores before dark. They had almost made it to their destination. While Moki unrealistically hoped that the river would stop the long reach of Satanta, the river brought back many memories for Wiyaka. For Hogan, the river meant seeing his father and grandfather again. Once reunited, they could then go home. While mother and daughter picked chokecherries and dug roots from bitterroot plants near a natural spring, Wiyaka and Hogan collected enough firewood to keep their campfire burning through the night.

After everyone ate their fill, the four travelers sang and talked while Wiyaka helped Moki repair her spears. Using fresh deer sinew, Wiyaka and Moki replaced many of the feathers on the spears that she carried. Then, Wiyaka showed Moki the way Folsom People put new tips on stone spear tips. By the time everyone dozed off for the night, Moki's weapons were ready.

***

At dawn, the mood of the camp was still good with everyone anticipating the river. While Moki and Wiyaka cooked the rest of the deer, Gad and Hogan went into the forest to gather more firewood.

"I will carry more firewood than you," Gad teased Hogan.

"Ha! Ha! You are too little," Hogan replied. "You can barely carry a twig!"

The two walked deep into the forest, laughing and joking while picking up dead tree limbs as they walked along.

"Tell me about the land you come from," Gad requested.

Hogan had no idea how to describe his home. "What do you want to know?" he asked.

"Everything!" Gad replied. "I miss my village...I miss my father."

Hogan turned around and saw that Gad had starting to cry. Hogan had no idea how to handle a small girl who was crying, so he began describing the North Country.

"Our land is north of a river called *Pankesha Wahpa*," Hogan explained, trying to get Gad's mind off her father and home. "The land is called the North Country."

Hogan leaned over and picked up some firewood.

"Our land is on the prairie, it is not in the mountains like this," Hogan continued. "The hills are not as high and there are fewer trees. There are many animals, but mostly *tatanka*. We follow the herds of *tatanka*."

Hogan's arms were now full of firewood, but he decided to pick up another dead tree limb. When he stood back up, he asked Gad, "Are there *tatanka* where you come from?"

Hogan then leaned over and picked up another dead tree limb. When Hogan stood back up, he turned around to see why Gad had not answered

133

him. WHAP! A large hand–carved wooden club smashed into the side of Hogan's skull. His body crumpled to the ground. Hogan lay on the ground, still and motionless, while the warrior stood over him watching for signs of life. When the warrior was sure that Hogan was dead, he trotted away.

Chapter Twelve

"We are almost done cooking the deer, where are the children?" Moki asked while grilling the last of the deer meat. Wiyaka looked up from what he was doing. He had forgotten all about the children. He glanced towards the forest, wondering what kind of trouble Hogan had found. Wiyaka stuffed the rest of the cooked meat in the large hide pouch he had made from the deer hide. He then hoisted the pouch high up in a nearby tree, out of reach of the forest's scavengers. Then, he instructed Moki to gather her weapons and they hurried off towards the forest, in search of the children. When they arrived at the edge of the forest, Wiyaka hoisted his spear onto his shoulder and motioned for Moki to do the same.

They walked through the forest and it did not take long for Wiyaka to find the tracks of the two children. He then discovered the footprints from two more humans, paralleling the trail left by the children. He waited for Moki to catch up and then whispered to her, "There are others here."

Moki moved a short distance away from Wiyaka and they both snuck forward, following the trail, their spears ready to throw. Wiyaka stopped several times to listen to the forest, hoping the birds of the forest would give him the answer he sought. Wiyaka and Moki followed the trail of the children until they spotted something lying in the tall grass ahead of them. Wiyaka signaled for Moki to stay where she was and then he crept forward, aware that he could be walking into an ambush. When he reached the object on the ground, he discovered it was Hogan. Dried blood covered the side of the boy's face. Wiyaka glanced around at the surrounding forest, expecting an attack at any time.

"*Hokshila,* – Boy, you found bad trouble," Wiyaka mumbled to Hogan's lifeless body. Wiyaka knelt down and touched the boy's head, but Hogan did not move. Wiyaka then took his water pouch and poured water over the top of Hogan's head. He rubbed Hogan's face with the water, attempting to wash away the caked–on blood so he could see the location of the wound. Wiyaka found a large gash above the left cheekbone on Hogan's swollen face. Wiyaka poured the rest of the water over the boy's head, but there was no response. *Dead,* Wiyaka thought. Unable to resist knowing what was lying on the ground, Moki ran over and joined Wiyaka. She knelt down alongside the boy and began examining the wound. She placed her hand in front of Hogan's nose and mouth and felt for breath, but there was none.

Wiyaka then remembered the girl. *Where is the girl?* He stood up and started to look around for any sign of the girl. He and Moki walked around the small clearing, looking for clues as to what happened to Gad. Wiyaka then found a set of footprints in the tall grass, leading away from Hogan. The footprints were too far apart for a small girl. Someone had run away from the scene and the trail led to the north.

Wiyaka turned around and glanced at Moki. He knew she had to be agonizing over her missing daughter. Wiyaka closed his eyes and listened again to the forest. He heard the breeze whistling through the pine boughs and the birds singing. The forest was back to normal. Whoever it was that attacked Hogan and captured the girl was long gone. Then, Wiyaka heard a moan.

"He is alive!" Moki announced as she ran over to Hogan's fallen body.

Surprised, Wiyaka walked back over to Hogan to check the boy himself. After, some poking and prodding, Wiyaka proclaimed, "*Te!* – Dead!"

"*Hee ya!* – No!" Moki responded. "Go find my daughter! I will take care of Hogan!"

Wiyaka followed the trail leading north. It did not take long to find another set of footprints joining the first set of tracks. He followed the trail until the tracks abruptly stopped, as if whoever made the tracks had stopped to rest. At that same spot, a third set of footprints appeared on the ground, the tracks of a small child. *Gad!* Wiyaka decided to go back and fetch Moki before following the trail further north. Wiyaka trotted back to where he had left Moki and was surprised to find Hogan sitting up.

"Where is Gad?" Moki asked as soon as she saw Wiyaka.

"They took her north," Wiyaka responded and then he turned to Hogan. "I told you to be careful, *hokshila!*"

"They?" Moki inquired.

"*Slol wa yea shnee,* – I do not know," Wiyaka mumbled. He then looked down at Hogan and asked, "What did you see, *hokshila?*"

Hogan stared straight ahead, his head wobbling on his shoulders. He did not appear to hear Wiyaka's question.

"*Key kte yo, hokshila!* – Wake up, boy!" Wiyaka roared, nudging Hogan in the shoulder with his foot. When Hogan did not respond, Wiyaka roared, "*Takuni slolye sni hokshila!* – Stupid boy!"

"*Taku!* – What!" Hogan finally responded.

"What did you see, *hokshila*?" Wiyaka demanded.

"*Ozuye!* – Warrior!" Hogan replied.

Wiyaka turned to Moki and said, "We will follow the trail north! Take this *hokshila* and go north. Follow my tracks through the grass until they stop and wait for me there. I am going back to get our food and then catch up to you!"

Wiyaka limped back towards the camp, his legs hurting and tired. Moki helped Hogan to his feet and then they hiked to the north, following the trail the warriors had left. When Wiyaka rejoined them, the trio followed the unhidden trail of two warriors and the girl. The trail eventually made an abrupt turn to the northwest, heading deeper into the foothills of the mountains.

"Their trail is clear, Wiyaka declared. "They want us to follow...to trap us."

"*Hat'ugha Gad?* – Why Gad?" Moki asked. "If this is Satanta, he does not want my daughter, he wants me."

"This Sat–Sat–Sat–warrior is using Gad to bring you to him," Wiyaka replied. "Then, he kills me and he has what he wants – you and the girl."

"You are forgetting about me," Hogan muttered. "I can help."

"*Hee ya, hokshila,* No, boy," Wiyaka responded. "I did not forget you."

"Satanta is *witko tko ke,* – crazy," Moki said on the verge of tears. "He will kill Gad once he has me!"

"*Ai,* – Yes," Wiyaka agreed, "and I will make sure that does not happen."

***

The three travelers followed the trail into the high foothills of the mountains and came to a barren ridge. Before walking out onto the crest of the ridge, Wiyaka peered over the top of its rim. He saw a large clearing with a few scattered pine trees. He smelled burning wood and then spotted puffs of smoke rising in the air. He edged his head just a little bit further over the rim rock and spotted several humans mingling around a campfire. He tried to identify the humans, but they were still too far away. He had never seen Satanta or the other warriors so he could not have recognized them, anyway. Wiyaka glanced over at Moki and asked, "Do you recognize any of them?"

Moki looked and she counted five humans standing near the campfire. Her eyes roamed to the right where she saw someone sitting on the ground. *Who was it? Gad?* She could not tell. Her eyes roamed back to the five humans. She studied them and their movements. She finally recognized one of them.

"Satanta!" Moki hissed when her eyes recognized him.

"How many warriors were following you?" Wiyaka asked.

"Eight, maybe."

"There are now only five, that leaves three of them hiding…waiting for us," Wiyaka noted. Moki focused her eyes on Satanta. She saw him leave the campfire and walk to the right, approaching the human sitting on the ground. Moki saw Satanta's arm reach out and grab the human. Satanta's arm rose up in the air and the human's body followed. Then Moki realized what was happening.

"Gad!" Moki squealed. "Satanta is lifting up Gad by her hair!"

"*Enila,* – Be quiet," Wiyaka whispered. "They will hear you."

It was too late. Moki had jumped up and was already heading across the clearing towards her daughter. Wiyaka signaled Hogan to circle around to the left while he circled around to the right. While Moki was crossing the clearing, she prepared a spear for throwing. Wiyaka hustled to his right, attempting to outflank the warriors before it was too late. He peeked over the rim rock and saw that Moki was already half way to the warriors. Wiyaka hurried to catch up. When he had run far enough, Wiyaka climbing on top of the ridge and trotted straight at the warriors, a spear on his shoulder. The warriors were so preoccupied with watching Moki that they did not notice Wiyaka coming up on their left.

Capturing the woman would be easier than any of the warriors ever imagined. The warriors started walking towards Moki while Satanta positioned himself behind Gad. Satanta pulled out his stone knife and grabbed Gad's long hair with his other hand. He jerked the small girl violently upward by her hair. Gad screamed in pain as she wobbled around on her toes, trying to take the pressure off her scalp. Satanta smiled every time Gad screamed. He knew the screams would draw Moki further into his trap. He chuckled when he realized how easy it would be to capture the woman. Moki was walking straight into his trap. Satanta's warriors would simply grab the woman and the search would end.

When Moki got closer, she reared back her arm and prepared to throw a spear. The warriors stopped, waiting for her to make her next move. Then, the warriors heard a chilling war cry coming from their left and turned to investigate. Wiyaka was standing a short distance away from Satanta, ready to hurl a spear. Then, there came a higher–pitched war cry to the right of the warriors. When the warriors turned their heads to the right, they spotted the boy Hogan ready to launch a spear at them.

Satanta's laughter started out softly, but as he continued to laugh, it grew loud with intensity. "Ha! Ha! Ha! Ha! Ha! HA! HA! HA! HA!" Satanta now laughed loud and long. The other warriors began laughing, as well. Their laughter carried from one side of the clearing to the other. When the laughter finally stopped, Satanta took his stone knife and shaved the neck of the small girl, drawing blood. Moki and the other travelers froze in their tracks.

"A woman….a boy…and an old man, attacking my warriors," Satanta bellowed.

The other warriors snickered at this ridiculous scenario.

"It does not matter," Satanta roared. "If one spear is thrown at me, I will take the head off this girl."

Moki froze while Wiyaka backed up a step.

"Take the woman!" Satanta yelled at his warriors.

A spear sizzled through the sky, striking one of the warriors in the upper thigh. "AHHH!" the wounded warrior shrieked while falling to the ground. That was enough to persuade the other warriors to stop dead in their tracks. Moki retrieved another spear from her quiver before the warriors could even react.

The wounded warrior screamed and bellowed, rolling around on the ground until he finally lay quietly, moaning softly in the tall grass. The other warriors converged on the wounded warrior. While two warriors held him down, a third warrior placed his foot on the wounded warrior's thigh and pulled hard on the spear shaft. "AHHHHH!" the wounded warrior screamed while his leg bounced up and down with each pull on the spear shaft.

"STOP!" the wounded warrior bellowed. However, the other warrior did not stop. He only pulled harder, twisting and turning the spear shaft back and forth while dragging the wounded warrior around in the grass. Finally, with a sound of ripping flesh and screams, the stone spear tip popped free and the warriors howled with glee.

"Satanta, I will kill myself if you harm Gad any further!" Moki hollered.

"I will kill the girl!" Satanta yelled back.

"You will not kill Gad because I will kill myself!" Moki cried out.

The warriors slowly retreated to where Satanta and the girl were standing, abandoning the wounded warrior. While the warriors' attention was on Moki, Wiyaka advanced several steps closer to Satanta. Out of the corner of his eyes, Satanta spotted Wiyaka's advance.

"You are an old man…your eyes are bad…your hands shake!" Satanta roared, placing the girl between him and Wiyaka, using Gad as his human shield.

"*Ai!* – Yes!" Wiyaka responded, shuffling another step forward. "I am still good enough to put this spear in your eye!"

"Ha! Ha! Ha!" Satanta howled with laughter over Wiyaka's boastful response. Then, he challenged Wiyaka, "Tell me old...blind man, why do you think you can kill Satanta when others cannot?"

"I have killed many warriors...I am still alive...they are not...one more warrior means nothing to me!" Wiyaka responded and then after a long pause, he proclaimed. "*Wayo kipi!* – It is the truth!"

Satanta contemplated what to do. His warriors were nearby, protecting him from the woman and the boy. Satanta placed the sharp edge of his stone knife against the neck of the small girl. "I might as well kill the girl, old man, if you are going to kill me!" Satanta announced with a smile.

"*Hee ya!* – No!" Moki screamed. "Move back, Wiyaka!"

Satanta turned his attention from the crazy old man to the woman. "I do not want to kill your child," Satanta told Moki. "It is you that I want."

"Leave us alone, Satanta," Moki pleaded. "I do not love you...I will never love you."

"I know you do not love me," Satanta admitted, "but as seasons pass, you will learn to love me."

"*Tóhanni Shni!* – Never!" Moki declared, taking several steps closer to Satanta.

"Then your daughter will die!"

"I will go with you, Satanta!"

"*Hee ya!*" Wiyaka bellowed. "Let me kill him!"

"Let my daughter go and I will come with you!" Moki offered.

"*Hee ya, Moki!* – No, Moki!" Wiyaka yelled out. "He will kill her, anyway!"

Satanta glanced over at Wiyaka, the sharp blade still on the girl's neck. Satanta nodded his head, acknowledging the agreement with Moki while never taking his eyes off Wiyaka.

"Untie Gad and let her walk to Wiyaka...the hunter to your left," Moki explained. "When she is safe, I will throw down my spear."

"How can I trust you?"

"You cannot," Moki replied, "but I will do nothing that will kill my daughter."

Moki's voice cracked with emotion and she fought to stop the tears that ran down her cheeks. Moki knew she had finally lost the battle, a battle where her husband had sacrificed his life. She began weeping. When Gad saw her mother crying, she began weeping. Wiyaka glared at Satanta, his spear shaking from the pent up energy.

"Let me kill him!" Wiyaka pleaded to Moki. "He will be dead before he takes another breath!"

"*Hee ya, Wiyaka!* – No, Wiyaka!" Moki blurted out. "Satanta will kill my daughter and with her death, my heart will die!"

"Where will he take you?" Wiyaka asked.

"Follow the river where you found us!" Moki answered.

Satanta leaned over and cut the hemp rope that bound Gad's wrists. Then, Satanta retreated to the campfire, hiding behind his warriors. Two warriors stood near Gad, ready to kill her if anything went wrong.

"Go to Wiyaka!" Moki said to her daughter.

"*Hee ya! –* No!" Gad replied, still crying. "I am coming to you!"

"*Hee ya! –* No!" Moki blurted out between sobs. "Obey me!"

Gad slowly walked towards Wiyaka, crying so hard she could barely walk. When she reached Wiyaka, he grabbed her by the arm and pulled her in behind him. Moki dropped her spear and walked towards the warriors.

"*Hi! –* Come!" Wiyaka yelled at Hogan who was on the other side of the campfire. "*A–ah!* Watch out!"

Hogan made a big arc around the camp, shuffling his feet sideways while never letting his eyes leave the warriors. Hogan finally reached Wiyaka and Gad.

"Back up slowly!" Wiyaka instructed Hogan. Wiyaka stepped back and Hogan did the same until they were standing on the rim rock. Then, they suddenly disappeared down the ridge, heading for safety.

"If you follow them, Satanta," Moki warned Satanta, "I will kill myself."

Satanta smiled. "You are mine!" he replied, forgetting about the old man and the girl.

*****

Wiyaka, Hogan and Gad, meandered across the hills and ridges, hoping to lose the warriors if they were following. Wiyaka found a safe place to camp for the night so he could think through the situation. Wiyaka treated the minor knife wound on Gad's neck and Hogan's gash from the warrior's wooden club. Gad had not stopped crying since the warriors had taken her mother away and Hogan was still groggy from the warrior clobbering him in the head. Wiyaka started a campfire and gave the last of the deer meat to Gad and Hogan to eat. Then, he told them that he was going hunting, but his real reason for leaving was to find a place to think. Wiyaka did not have a clear thought in his head. This was when Wiyaka could have really used Chayton's help. Chayton had always been the thinker and Wiyaka had always been the doer. He did not know what to do about this predicament. He could take Hogan and Gad to the river and wait for Chayton and Hoka to show up or he could track the warriors down and find a way to free Moki from her captivity. The first option was the easiest and Chayton would know what to do. Unfortunately, that would give Satanta a huge head start. The second option was the most dangerous. He could pursue the warriors, but he had a boy and small girl with him. If he did find the war party, how could he defeat five warriors by himself and still protect the children? He returned to the camp with two plump rock chucks for dinner and found two exhausted children, sleeping. Hogan woke up when he heard Wiyaka skinning the rock chucks.

"Wiyaka, when do we attack the *ozuye?* – war party?" Hogan asked.

"Attack the *ozuye*?" Wiyaka responded.

"*Ai!* – Yes!"

"We do not attack the *ozuye*."

"We cannot let them take Moki," Hogan declared.

"We can."

"We should attack them and get her back!"

"You not only speak like a *chincá*, – child, you speak like a *gnaye!* – fool!" Wiyaka proclaimed. "They have five spears, we have one."

"We have two spears," Hogan blurted out.

"We have one spear," Wiyaka stated. "You would not be killing rabbits or chipmunks, *hokshila*, – boy, you would be killing warriors who throw spears back at you…you cannot even kill a rabbit with your spear."

"You do not sound like the great hunter called Wiyaka, the one people speak of around campfires," Hogan replied.

"I am not that hunter, *hokshila*," Wiyaka mumbled. "I am a *wichah^cala*. – old man."

Disappointed, Hogan lay back down, leaving Wiyaka alone to ponder what they would do next.

***

The small war party marched northward, hugging the edge of the mountains. Satanta pushed the warriors to their limit, knowing that they would still be in danger until they reached the river canyon. The wounded warrior slowed their progress significantly and Moki was doing everything possible to slow them down, as well. She knew that once they reached the

142

village of Satanta's father, there would be no escape. Satanta would have someone watching her for the rest of her life. If she were to escape, it must be soon.

"Hurry!" Satanta barked at Moki, pulling on the rope that tied her wrists.

"Untie me and I can walk faster," Moki responded.

"Ha! Ha! Do you think I am a fool?"

"*Hee ya, Satanta!* – No, Satanta!" Moki replied. "I know you are a fool!"

Satanta jerked on the end of the hemp rope, pulling Moki's wrists and arms with enough force to drag her to the ground.

"Get up or I will beat you like a wolf dog!" Satanta roared. He then cocked his foot back and kicked Moki in the ribs, knocking her over onto her back. Satanta pulled out his stone knife and bent over Moki.

"Satanta!" Fala screamed, reaching out and grabbing the knife–wielding arm. "This woman will slow us down even more if you cut her up and if you kill her, our journey is wasted."

Satanta was furious, he wanting to teach the woman a lesson. Finally, his body relaxed and he told Fala, "You drag her along!"

Satanta walked away, resuming his hike to the north. The other warriors walked past Fala and Moki. Once Fala was alone with Moki, he leaned over and whispered, "Do you want him to kill you, woman?"

"Set me free, Fala!" Moki cried. "Let me go."

"I cannot…I will not die for you," Fala replied. "I have family. They will not die for you! Get on your feet or I will have to beat you."

Moki struggled to get to her feet. Her ribs ached every time she moved or took a breath. "Go!" Fala ordered her, pointing to the north.

At the end of the day, a contentious Satanta stood at the crest of a high ridge and watched the sluggish progress of the war party. Satanta did not believe the old man would follow, but he wanted to reach the safety of the canyon to the north. Satanta understood what he must do to speed up the war party's progress. Once the warriors and Moki had climbed to the top of the ridge, Satanta told them to prepare a camp for nightfall.

***

Wiyaka did not sleep well. He woke up and saw that Gad was also awake. The small girl was sitting next to the campfire, crying while rocking herself back and forth. Wiyaka was confused about what to do about the woman and the child. If Wiyaka chased the war party down, he was only one spear against many. If the war party killed him, Hogan would have to take care of the small girl and Hogan could not even take care of himself. After much consternation, Wiyaka finally made his decision. "*Kikta!* – Get up!" he roared at Hogan.

"*Taku?* – What?" Hogan mumbled.

"*Kikta!*" Wiyaka roared even louder.

Hogan sat up and rubbed his eyes, looking around and trying to remember where he was.

"I have decided that we will free Moki!" Wiyaka declared.

Gad's eyes lit up when she heard the decision. "Here is what must be done," Wiyaka continued. "Hogan, you must take care of Gad, no matter what happens to me."

"What do you mean?" Hogan demanded.

"I am going to help you attack the *ozuye*!" Hogan pleaded.

"*Hee ya!* – No!" Wiyaka thundered. "You must agree to watch over the little one. Otherwise, we go to the river and wait for your father."

Hogan sat there next to the campfire, pouting over Wiyaka's decision. Finally, Wiyaka interrupted Hogan's moping by asking, "What is your decision? The *ozuye* is getting farther away!"

Hogan looked at the small girl and replied, "*Ai,* – Yes, I will watch over Gad."

Wiyaka looked at the small girl and then back at the boy. "Hogan, you will have to become a hunter…a provider," Wiyaka declared. "Are you ready to become a hunter?"

"*Ai,* – Yes," Hogan said without hesitation.

"*Waste,* – Good," Wiyaka responded. "Eat and then we leave!"

***

The war party trudged onward, slowly moving to the north. Two warriors helped the wounded warrior along the trail. Moki saw the slow progress as a glimmer of hope. Someone could possibly rescue her before reaching the village. Satanta watched in anger as the wounded warrior passed by him with his arm draped across the shoulder of another warrior. Fala joined Satanta as he watched the wounded warrior limp away.

"Kill the warrior," Satanta said to Fala.

"What?" Fala asked.

"Kill Kohana!" Satanta ordered. "He slows us down."

"We cannot kill Kohana," Fala replied. "He has been loyal to you."

"I do not care. I want him dead."

Fala had to think fast, he did not want to disobey Satanta, but there had to be another solution. "Leave him here," Fala blurted out.

Satanta peered over at Fala, waiting for the warrior to explain himself.

"Give Kohana a spear…water and leave him here," Fala explained. "He will either keep up with us or fall behind. If he falls behind, you did everything you could for him."

Satanta contemplated the idea.

"The other warriors will not blame you if you give Kohana a chance," Fala continued. "If you kill him, they will always think they will be next."

"What if the old man finds him?" Satanta questioned the idea. "Kohana could tell him where we are going."

"That old man is not following us, Satanta," Fala answered, "and if he is, one warrior can deal with him."

"Killing Kohana is much easier," Satanta declared.

"Killing Kohana would be different than killing a disloyal warrior like Weca. What will the others think if you kill a warrior who has been loyal to you?" Fala challenged. "If you let Kohana live, the other warriors will think you are fair and wise. This will spread throughout the tribe."

Satanta thought about it. He liked the idea of being a 'fair and wise leader'. He would be like his father. "*Ai,* – Yes," Satanta finally declared, "let Kohana live."

The distance between the war party and the wounded warrior increased as the sun grew old. Finally, Kohana could not travel any further and collapsed on the ground. He knew that it was only a matter of time before the animal predators of the night would discover him.

Chapter Thirteen

While the war party struggled to make progress on their journey to the north, the three travelers made good progress. As nightfall arrived, Wiyaka's keen nose picked up the smell of wood burning somewhere to the north. He turned around and instructed both Gad and Hogan to stay put while he investigated.

"I am going with you!" Hogan argued.

"*Hee ya!* – No!" Wiyaka thundered. "*Hokshila,* – Boy, you will stay with the girl or I will smack you!"

Hogan said nothing.

"Stay alert, *hokshila*," Wiyaka added. "When you hear *jialepa,* – meadowlark, follow the sound. Until then, you and the girl climb a tree."

"*Taku?* – What?" Hogan questioned. "Climb a tree, Wiyaka?"

"*Hokshila,* you have missed the animal sign!" Wiyaka chastised Hogan.

"Animal sign?"

"*Igmu'gleŝka* – Great lion has been here," Wiyaka answered.

"*Taku?*' Hogan blurted out.

"Are you *takuni slolye sni?* – stupid?" Wiyaka demanded. "*Igmu'gleŝka!* – Great lion is near!"

"I have never seen *Igmu'gleŝka*," Hogan replied, looking all around for this new beast.

"*Hokshila,* – Boy, you do not want to see *Igmu'gleŝka*!" Wiyaka boomed. "Climb a tree... a very tall tree."

"Gad, come here," Hogan whispered while eyeballing the forest for a pine tree easy enough to climb. Wiyaka snuck forward, his spear ready to thrust into anything that got in his way. He walked with a low profile, using smell and his limited hearing to guide him through the dark forest. Then, he saw it in front of him, the twinkling light of a campfire. Squatting near the ground, Wiyaka took a step forward, letting the toe of his moccasin test the ground before putting any weight on his foot. He peered through the pine trees, watching for movement around the campfire and a camp sentry. Wiyaka then took another step, first testing the ground with the toe of his moccasin. Then, he held his breath and listened for the sounds of the forest. The forest was quiet. He listened for the sounds of humans walking or talking, but there was none. Wiyaka took another step forward, his heart and ears pumping blood at a furious rate. He took a deep breath and slowly exhaled, focusing on slowing his heartbeat down. Then, when his heart seemed under control, he listened once again. He was now close enough to the campfire to hear the popping from the burning wood. Then, off to his left, Wiyaka heard a sound! His head swiveled around and he peered into the darkness where the sound had originated. He waited and the sound came again! Wiyaka exhaled when he realized it was a hooting owl in a nearby tree. He took another step towards the campfire and stopped. He listened and somewhere off to his right, somewhere out on the Arid Plains, a coyote welcomed nightfall with several yips.

Wiyaka took a step forward and then another. He was now at the edge of the camp and could clearly see the flames of the campfire. He looked around, but saw no one. He began to panic. *I let them get behind me!* Wiyaka jerked his body around, thrusting his spear into the air, but there was no one to attack. Wiyaka could feel his heart pounding out of control. His breath was coming in shallow and uneven gasps. He closed his eyes and tried to calm down. Then, when he was ready, he turned back around and took another step towards the camp.

Wiyaka looked and listened, but saw no one in the camp. *Where are they?* Then, he heard a sound he did not immediately grasp. He held his breath and closed his eyes, focusing on the sound. Another hoot from the owl and Wiyaka heard the sound again. It was a moaning sound. Wiyaka opened his eyes and surveyed the ground in front of his feet. Then, he took a step forward. He readied his spear for an attack and then took another step forward, carefully planting the sole of his moccasin on solid ground. In front of him, Wiyaka spotted a bush where he could conceal himself from the camp. He took several steps and stopped behind the bush. With his free hand, he carefully pushed back the branches of the bush, only wide enough for him to take a gander into the camp. He watched and listened. He heard the moaning, again. His eyes focused on finding the source of the sound. He pushed the branches of the bush open a little wider. Wiyaka's eyes searched the perimeter of the camp. Then, he saw who was moaning. Lying in front of the campfire was a warrior. Wiyaka waited. *Why would there be only one warrior?* Wiyaka cautiously released the branches of the bush, letting them spring back to their original position. Then, he made the decision on what he must do.

Wiyaka slowly crept around the right side of the bush until he entered the perimeter of the camp. His spear was ready to jab any warrior that got in his way. Wiyaka closed in on the wounded warrior and when he was near enough, he waved the fluted spear point in front of the warrior's throat. Wiyaka was just about ready to jam the stone spear tip through the warrior's windpipe when the eyes of the warrior popped open. The warrior's eyes transformed from surprise to fright when he saw the stone spear point hovering close to his throat. *ATTACK!* Wiyaka knew he should attack, but for some odd reason, he did not.

"Where are the others?" Wiyaka whispered to the warrior.

"No others!" the warrior replied.

"Where are the others?" Wiyaka repeated, moving the stone spear tip closer to the warrior's exposed jugular vein.

"Gone!" the warrior replied.

Wiyaka shot a glance around the camp and asked, "The others left you?"

"*Ai!* – Yes!"

Wiyaka studied the warrior in the wavering light of the campfire. Wiyaka's gaze moved down to the warrior's leg where he noticed the dark bloodstains. He looked back up at the warrior's face, but by then, the warrior had passed out.

Kill him...kill him now...kill him now, fool... Wiyaka wrestled with his anxiety. *Ah, I cannot kill him!* Wiyaka then turned around and whistled the melodic song of a meadowlark. Wiyaka waited and finally heard a whistle in return. Wiyaka whistled the song again. This time the reply to his song was much nearer. Wiyaka whistled the song of the meadowlark a third time. Right after that, Hogan and Gad showed up at the camp.

"Keep your spear on this one while I tie his hands," Wiyaka instructed Hogan.

"He is not called *this one*. He is called Kohana," Gad declared.

"*Taku?* – What?" Wiyaka questioned. "How do you know what he is called, *wichincala?* – girl?"

"This warrior is Kohana," Gad repeated, looking at Wiyaka as if the old hunter was dense, as well as deaf.

"You know him?" Wiyaka asked, still not believing that Gad could possibly know this huge warrior.

"*Ai,* – Yes, he is from my tribe."

Wiyaka leaned down and tied the warrior's hands together in front of him. "I should have killed this Ko–Ko–Ko–warrior, but my feeble mind made me weak," Wiyaka proclaimed. "There is nothing we can do to help him. It is best if we just leave him here for the animals to feast on. If we want to free your mother, we cannot slow down and help this Ko–Ko–Ko–ah–warrior. He will make good food for *igmu'gleśka* – great lion and then *igmu'gleśka* will not be so hungry for us."

"You cannot kill him," Gad insisted. "I will heal him."

"Ha! Ha! Ha! Ha!" Wiyaka roared with laughter. "You are a *chincá*! – child! You cannot even take care of yourself and *you* are going to heal this warrior? Ha! Ha! Ha!"

The warrior Kohana was now awake and listening to the conversation.

"You cannot kill Kohana!" Gad exclaimed.

"I am not killing him," Wiyaka replied. "*Igmu'gleśka* – Great lion will kill him for us."

"I will not let you leave him!" Gad proclaimed.

"How will you stop me, *wichíncala?* – girl?" Wiyaka demanded.

"You cannot leave Kohana!" Gad insisted.

"I am surrounded by children," Wiyaka mumbled under his breath and then after pausing, he told Hogan and Gad, "We will camp here and leave at first light."

Wiyaka turned to Hogan and said, "Collect much firewood, there is danger about."

"I have to collect plants for *pecula* – medicine for Kohana," Gad announced.

Wiyaka just shook his head. He gave up arguing with the girl. He did not know what he thought about small girls, especially this one.

"*Inahni!* – Hurry!" Wiyaka instructed Gad. "Get your...your *pecula* and get back to the campfire! There is danger all around us!"

***

At dawn, Wiyaka looked at his traveling companions and said, "*Hoppo!* – Let us go!"

Gad did not look up. She was too busy applying medicine to the leg of the warrior Kohana. Hogan, sitting next to where Wiyaka was standing, did not move.

"*Hoppo!* – Let us go!" Wiyaka roared louder with some malice in his voice.

Hogan jumped a bit, but when he saw that Gad was not getting up, he stayed put.

"I am staying here with Kohana," Gad finally said, applying the herbal paste to the warrior's leg.

149

"Did you forget about your mother?" Wiyaka demanded.

"She would want me to help Kohana."

"After killing your father...hunting you and your mother down like animals, she would want you to help this warrior?"

"*Ai.*"

"I am staying," Hogan blurted out. "I told you I would take care of Gad and that is what I am going to do."

"That does not make her safe, *hokshila,* – boy," Wiyaka replied.

"We will follow your trail when the warrior is able," Hogan added.

"I should have cut his throat," Wiyaka mumbled, not meant for the girl's ears.

"You did not cut his throat," Gad replied. "He is alive."

"Ah!" Wiyaka uttered.

"*Iyaya!* – Go!" Hogan exclaimed. "The *ozuye* – war party cannot be far ahead."

Wiyaka thought about what to do. He did not want to leave the children, but he knew the girl would not leave the warrior and the war party would escape.

"You travel only with light from the sun and you follow my trail," Wiyaka instructed Hogan. "You would get lost following your own trail so I will make my trail easy for you to follow."

Wiyaka waited for Hogan to respond, but the boy did not argue so Wiyaka continued his lecture, "During darkness, you build a large campfire and do not leave it for any reason. You hear me, *hokshila*?"

Hogan nodded in acknowledgement.

"Do not untie the warrior, no matter what he tells you," Wiyaka insisted. "*Hokshila,* this warrior will slit your throat while you sleep! Do you understand?"

"*Ai!* – Yes!" Hogan replied.

Wiyaka felt a pang of guilt for leaving the boy and the girl, but what really made him mad was not having killed the warrior when he had the chance. *I have become weak and stupid,* Wiyaka thought.

Soon after Wiyaka left, Gad cut the ropes off the warrior's wrists with a stone knife.

***

By the time the sun was midway in the morning sky, Wiyaka had found where the war party had camped near a small creek flowing out of the mountains. The coals in the bottom of the campfire were still hot so Wiyaka

150

knew he was close. Wiyaka looked around and counted the moccasin tracks of four warriors and the woman. He trotted up the trail where the tracks led. When the sun was high in the sky, Wiyaka spotted a human standing on the trail in front of him. When Wiyaka approached the human, he recognized him as one of the warriors he had seen earlier. Wiyaka started to raise his spear, but then saw that the warrior was already prepared to throw his own spear. Wiyaka decided to change his tactics and greet the warrior with a warm and charming smile, the kind of smile Wiyaka seldom delivered to anyone.

"*Haw!* – Hello!" Wiyaka announced with a wide smile.

"*Haw!*" the warrior replied and then added, "*Tókiya la hwo, wicah^cala?* – Where are you going, old man?"

"*Wicah^cala?* – Old man?" Wiyaka mumbled to himself. Wiyaka's artificial smile was short lived.

"*Tókiya la hwo, wicah^cala?* – Where are you going, old man?" the warrior repeated. "Can you not hear so well?"

"*Tiyatani,* – Home," Wiyaka replied bluntly.

The warrior laughed. "I know who you are, *wicah^cala,* – old man," the warrior declared. "Stop following us or I will have to kill you and hang your old hide in one of these trees."

Kill me? I will kill you! Wiyaka thought to himself. Wiyaka forced another smile and began retreating down the same trail he had walked up. When Wiyaka was almost out of sight of the warrior, he looked back and the warrior was still laughing at him. When Wiyaka was out of sight, he left the trail so he could outflank and overtake the warrior. As Wiyaka moved through the pine trees, he heard something zip past his ear. The spear rattled when it slammed into one of the trees. Wiyaka looked to his right and the same warrior was standing on a nearby rock outcrop, just a spear throw away.

"I warned you, *wicah^cala!* – old man!" the warrior yelled as he hoisted another spear onto his shoulder. The warrior launched another spear and Wiyaka instinctively fell to the ground. The spear sped past Wiyaka and crashed into the rocks, making a tremendous racket. Wiyaka jumped to his feet and chucked the spear he had in his hand in the direction of the warrior. The spear fluttered through the air like a wounded bird, not even coming anywhere close to the warrior.

"Ha! Ha! Ha! Ha! Ha!" the warrior laughed so loud that he almost fell off the rock. Wiyaka reached for another spear, but by the time Wiyaka was ready to launch, the warrior had disappeared. Wiyaka looked around, searching for the warrior, but he was nowhere in sight. Wiyaka pulled out his stone knife and held it out in front of him. He held his breath and listened for the sound of a careless footstep, but he heard nothing. Wiyaka headed directly to the spot where he had last seen the warrior. He walked slowly, stone knife in one hand and spear in the other. He came to the outcrop where the warrior had stood. Wiyaka slowly climbed it. Standing on top of the outcrop, Wiyaka looked all around, but the warrior had vanished. Even though the war party had discovered him, Wiyaka had no other choice but to follow their trail.

***

While Gad tended to the wounds of the warrior, Hogan went hunting near the camp. He was able to run down and kill two sage hens that were too slow to escape the inexperienced hunter. When Hogan returned to the camp, Gad was still tending to the warrior.

"I need your help," Hogan told the girl, "clean and skin these birds."

Gad walked over to Hogan and took one of the birds.

"Will he be able to travel?" Hogan asked the girl.

"Ask him?" Gad replied.

"I am asking you, not the warrior," Hogan declared. "Can he travel?"

"I can travel," Kohana replied before Gad could reply.

"*Waste,* – Good," Hogan replied. "We must catch up to Wiyaka, he will need my help."

The three travelers ate the two cooked sage hens and then began their slow walk to the north. With his hands retied in front of him, the warrior limped along the trail, unable to keep up the pace and needing to stop several times to rest. By the time the sun was midway into the afternoon sky, they arrived at the campfire of the war party, but the ashes were cold if Hogan would have had enough sense to check them.

***

Wiyaka trekked north, keeping a vigilant eye on everything around him, knowing that the warrior would again try to ambush him. Wiyaka had established his routine; he would walk for a distance, then stop and listen to the forest around him. He was walking up a rocky ridge when the warrior reappeared in front of him.

"*Tókiya la hwo, wicah^cala?* – Where are you going, old man?" the warrior shouted.

"I told you!" Wiyaka yelled back. "*Tiyatani! –* Home!"

Wiyaka kept walking towards the warrior, his hand gripped tightly on his spear.

152

"I warned you," the warrior roared, "but you are a fool who does not hear."

That was it. Wiyaka's temper flared as he walked towards the rock the warrior was standing on. "Co–co–come off that rock and I–I–I will show you who is a fool!" Wiyaka stammered.

The warrior whooped with laughter. "You are the fool," the warrior replied, looking down at Wiyaka from the rock. "I do not want to hurt you."

"Come down here and we will see who gets hurt, *waglula!* – maggot!" Wiyaka bellowed.

"*Ai,* – Yes, but first I am dropping my spear," the warrior replied. "Are you brave enough to do the same, *wicah^cala? –* old man?"

Wiyaka threw down his spear, as well as his water pouch and quiver. The warrior smiled at Wiyaka and then leapt off the rock in Wiyaka's direction. Wiyaka took a step to his left to avoid a collision with the warrior, but something plowed into him from behind, knocking him to the ground. Wiyaka tried to move, but he could not. Someone was already on top of him. His body ached from the fall and he could not breathe. He gasped for breath, while he lay there in pain, unable to move. Then, the weight that was crushing Wiyaka, suddenly disappeared.

Wiyaka looked up and there were two warriors standing over him. Wiyaka tried to reach over and grab his spear, but the warrior stomped on his hand. Wiyaka jerked back his injured hand and closed his eyes, expecting the warriors to kill him. Instead, one of the warrior's hauled off and kicked Wiyaka in the rib cage. Wiyaka shrieked in pain as the kick flipped him over. Wiyaka tried to crawl away, but another kick smashed into him on the other side of his rib cage, knocking the air from his lungs. Wiyaka lay there, wheezing in and out, trying to breathe. He could hear both warriors joking and laughing at him. He lay there, unable to move, waiting for his inevitable death to come.

"*Kikta!* – Get up!" one of the warriors thundered, kicking Wiyaka in his sore ribs. Wiyaka did not move, not because he did not want to move, but because he could not get up.

"*Kikta, wicah^cala! –* Get up, old man!" the other warrior demanded.

Wiyaka tried to pull himself up with his arms, but his quivering muscles could not lift him. He did not even have enough strength left to lift his body up. Wiyaka could not even get to his knees. Then, he felt a hand under each arm and the two laughing warriors hoisted Wiyaka to his feet. Wiyaka stood in front of them, wobbling back and forth, his mouth bleeding from the fall.

"*Iyaya, wicah^cala!* – Go, old man!" the first warrior ordered, pointing towards the north.

The second warrior grabbed Wiyaka's belongings and followed Wiyaka up the trail.

***

Wiyaka walked in shame. Not only did the warriors ambush him without even a fight, but they also dishonored him by not tying his hands. The warriors had no fear of Wiyaka and that meant they had no respect for him. The warriors shoved Wiyaka north and near nightfall, they climbed a ridge where they found the camp where the war party was holding Moki.

"*Wicah^cala* – Old man was following us," the first warrior told Satanta.

"Wiyaka!" Moki screeched when she saw him. "Where is Gad?"

"She is with Hogan, they are safe," Wiyaka replied. Satanta walked over to Wiyaka and then suddenly stepped back when he saw that the warriors had not tied the prisoner's hands.

"His hands are free!" Satanta roared.

"He is weak, Satanta. He can barely walk and he has the strength of a *chincá.* – child," the first warrior replied. "He is a *wicah^cala, –* old man."

"He is not a *wicah^cala, –* old man," the second warrior replied to the first warrior, "she is a *winuhcala! –* old woman!"

All of the warriors howled with laughter while Wiyaka bowed his head in disgrace as he listened to the warriors insult him. Moki's eyes filled with tears as she looked at the broken hunter and thought about her daughter alone with only a boy to protect her.

"Kill him!" Satanta commanded the warriors.

"*Hee ya! –* No!" Moki screamed.

Satanta and the other warriors turned around and stared at the woman. "Satanta, can you not see that this *wicah^cala* is harmless?" Moki questioned. "I want you to let him live!"

Moki then smiled at Satanta and added, "You want me happy, Satanta? If you kill him, I will not be happy!"

Satanta was undecided. He kept looking back and forth between the harmless old man and Moki.

"Satanta, do you want me happy?" Moki repeated with a smile.

The decision to please the woman or rid himself of the old man tore at Satanta. Finally, he made his decision. "Tie the hands of the *wicah^cala,*" he instructed the warriors. "I will make my decision when I know this woman can make me happy."

This drew snickers and giggles from the other warriors. Satanta then looked over at Moki and added with a smile, "*Winyan*, – Woman, are you ready to make me happy?"

"*Hee ya*, – No," Moki replied. "Not until you set the *wicah^cala* free."

***

Hogan came back to the camp carrying two dead rock chucks. When Hogan saw Gad sitting next to the warrior Kohana, he dropped both of the rock chucks by the campfire and pulled out his stone knife.

"I told you not to untie him!" Hogan bellowed.

Gad did not reply, but kept rubbing the medicine on the leg of the warrior.

"*Kikta!* – Get up!" Hogan yelled at Kohana while waving his stone knife around in the air.

"Stay," Gad whispered to the warrior.

"*Kikta!* – Get up!" Hogan demanded, brandishing the knife at the warrior.

"Kohana is hurt, Hogan," Gad explained. "He is not getting up."

"Get away from him, Gad," Hogan blurted out. "He will kill you!"

"*Hee ya*, – No," she replied.

Kohana raised his arms in Hogan's direction.

"*Wahta yo!* – Watch out!" Hogan screamed at Gad.

"I will help you," Kohana replied, motioning towards the two rock chucks. "I will help you."

Gad handed Kohana her stone knife while Hogan stood there in disbelief.

***

At first light, the warrior guarding the camp rubbed his eyes trying to determine what he was looking at on the other side of the clearing. He turned around and noticed that Satanta was still soundly asleep near the campfire. The warrior knew better than to wake up Satanta without good cause. Others had done this before and ended up swinging from a tree like Weca. When the warrior turned back around, he spotted humans, many humans, walking towards the war party's camp.

"SATANTA!" the warrior blared.

Startled, Satanta jumped to his feet and ran over to the sentry. His eyes focused on the area where the warrior was pointing. Satanta spotted the line of humans walking towards the war party.

"What do we do?" the warrior asked Satanta.

"There is nothing we can do," Satanta replied.

At the middle of the clearing, all of the humans stopped walking, except four. These four humans continued to walk towards Satanta until they were

155

standing directly in front of him. Satanta did not say a word or even greet them. He waited for the strangers to speak. Finally, the tallest of the humans, spoke.

"You are on our land," the tall man said in a language that Satanta did not comprehend. Satanta shook his head and the tall man understood the gesture.

"You are on our land," the tall man repeated in a different language.

Satanta studied the tall man, and even in the dim light of morning, he spotted the pendant the tall man wore around his neck. Satanta could not quite make it out in the light of dawn, but the pendant had a blue wavy line running across the face of it. Satanta finally replied to the tall man, "We are passing through. We will only take from the land what we need. We will be at our river by the time this sun is old."

The tall man with gray braided hair looked past Satanta and noticed a woman and an old man sitting by the campfire, their hands tied. While the woman was looking directly at the tall man, the old man hid his face. The tall man did not recognize the woman.

"Who are they?" the tall man asked.

Satanta turned around and casually looked at Moki and Wiyaka, warning Moki with his eyes to remain silent. Satanta turned back around to face the tall man. Satanta did not answer the tall man's question. "We will be off your land before darkness falls," Satanta replied.

The tall man turned around and emitted a loud and shrill whistle. The other humans, who had been standing in the middle of the clearing, began walking towards the camp. When they arrived, they encircled the entire camp and the warriors. The tall man turned and whistled again. This time, three more humans came out of the morning mist, walking across the clearing. When the three humans were close enough to see, Satanta noticed that they were two men and a very tall woman. The three humans walked up alongside the tall man. Satanta recognized both of the men.

"What is your name?" the tall man asked Satanta.

"*Micaje Satanta.* – My name is Satanta."

"*Micaje Honiahaka,* – My name is Honiahaka," the tall man replied.

"This is my sister, Namid," Honiahaka said, pointing at the tall woman.

Satanta bowed slightly at Namid. She returned his bow with a seething glare.

"You have already met these two hunters," Honiahaka declared. "*Le mita kola Chayton...le mita kola Hoka.* – My friend Chayton...my friend Hoka."

Satanta finally realized that his war party was over.

Chapter Fourteen

Five humans sat around the campfire. They had just listened to Moki recount her harrowing tale about Santana, the war party, and the violent death of her husband. After she finished, Honiahaka was about to say something, but one of Chayton's frequent coughing spells interrupted him. The other four people looked on while Chayton choked on his own phlegm while attempting to clear his lungs. Finally, with eyes watering, Chayton signaled Honiahaka to proceed.

"Our hearts are with you," Honiahaka declared, looking directly at Moki, "you have lost your husband and your home."

Moki bowed her head in acknowledgement of these facts.

"These warriors have harmed you," Honiahaka stated, "but they have done the River People no harm, so any justice you seek must come from you–"

"Cricket!" Chayton blurted out, interrupting Honiahaka.

"Honiahaka."

"*Taku?* – What?" Chayton asked.

"*Micaje Honiahaka,* – My name is Honiahaka," replied Honiahaka with a smile. "I have not been called Cricket since I was a boy."

"You will always be Cricket to me..." Chayton mumbled under his breath.

"*Taku?* – What?" Honiahaka asked.

"Honiahaka...do you not recall the story of the River People and the Folsom People?" Chayton asked.

"Of course I do," Honiahaka replied.

"KAAF! I do not think you do!" Chayton continued. "The Mountain People had done no harm to the Folsom People when your father Avonaco asked for our help. Is this woman and her daughter not worthy of your help?"

"You interrupted me before I finished, Chayton," Honiahaka declared.

Chayton did not reply. Instead, he slumped back away from the campfire, cleared his throat and waved a hand for Honiahaka to continue.

Honiahaka turned from Chayton and addressed Moki. "These people have done the River People no harm," he explained, "so it is you who must decide their justice."

Honiahaka turned to Chayton to make sure the old man heard and then Honiahaka continued, "You are a friend to the Folsom People; therefore, you are a friend of ours. We will help you carry out your justice."

Honiahaka looked around the campfire to make sure everyone understood.

"You are Avonaco, Cricket…I mean Honiahaka," Chayton praised.

Honiahaka ignored Chayton's attempt at flattery.

"I will sleep and give you my answer in a new sun," Moki replied and then stood up to leave. Wiyaka rose, as well. They both bowed to the others and walked away in the darkness.

"I am sure you and Namid have much to catch up on," Honiahaka said to Chayton while standing up. "We will see you both at first light."

Namid and Chayton sat next to each other by the campfire. It had been so long that neither of them had anything to say to each other. Another bout of coughing from Chayton interrupted the awkward silence.

"You sound bad," Namid responded to the coughing.

"*Ai,* – Yes," Chayton stated. "It is getting worse."

"Our healer can help you," Namid offered.

"*Pilamaya,* – Thank you," Chayton replied and then he changed the subject, "*Doe ksh kayo un hey, Namid?* – How are you, Namid?"

"*Waste,* – Good," she replied in the language of the Folsom People, a language she had always shunned in the past.

"Have you a good life?"

"*Ai,* – Yes," she answered with conviction.

Chayton and Namid both watched the flames of the campfire, searching for the words to say to each other.

"I have children," Namid blurted out, "I have a boy and a girl."

Chayton was surprised. Children had never been a priority for Namid when they were together. Chayton always believed that Namid would never place children above other things in her life. Chayton cleared his throat and then somewhat afraid of the answer, he asked, "Who…who is your husband?"

"He is dead," Namid replied. "You did not know him."

"Dead!" Chayton blurted out before thinking.

"*Ai,* – Yes, he was many winters older than me," Namid replied. "Honiahaka always said I married my father."

Chayton looked down at the campfire, not knowing what to say.

"My husband was much like Avonaco," Namid declared.

Namid's declaration stung Chayton like a scorpion. Chayton had always known that the most important person in Namid's life was her father. Chayton had always attempted to live up to the standard set by the great Avonaco, but in Namid's eyes, Chayton always fell short. Now, Chayton was finding out that there was another man in Namid's life who had actually lived up to the standards that Avonaco had set.

"I am happy for you, Namid," Chayton declared with much sincerity.

Namid smiled and then said, "I want you to come live with us at our village, Chayton. The healer can help you and I want us to share our lives."

The proposal left Chayton speechless. He did not know what to say. Perhaps, he and Namid could finally live in peace and harmony. Chayton respected the River People as much as he respected his own people. The remainder of his life could be lived in peace with what appeared to be a much more humble Namid. A smile crossed his face when he thought about living the rest of his life with Namid and the River People. Finally, he replied, "Thank you, Namid, but let me first fulfill my vision."

Namid smiled. She understood Chayton better than he understood himself. "Fulfill your vision, Chayton, and I will be waiting for you," she proclaimed.

Chayton nodded his head, but he did not feel comfortable turning Namid's offer down. He could follow his vision, but he really did not know where that would lead him. He knew he could live in peace with Namid and the River People. The possibility of sharing a new life with Namid only confused him.

***

The same five people reconvened at the campfire at dawn to hear the justice Moki proposed for Satanta and the warriors. After greetings concluded, all eyes turned to Moki. Uncomfortable with the attention, she peered around, trying to avoid any direct eye contact with anyone. Finally, she found the courage to announce her decision.

"I want to let them go," Moki mumbled.

"*Taku!* – What!" Wiyaka blurted out while leaping to his feet. "Kill them, woman!"

"I want to let them go…let them go back to their tribe," Moki repeated.

The other three people at the campfire were too surprised to respond. Chayton was the first to find his tongue, asking Moki, "*Hat'ugha?* – Why?"

"Taking their lives will not bring back my husband," Moki replied.

"*Takuni slolye sni!* – Stupid!" Wiyaka blurted out. "Do you think this warrior…this Sat–Satanta…will ever leave you alone? He will hunt you down like a *mastinca* – rabbit and kill your daughter and then…kill you!"

Wiyaka paced around the campfire with a fury, his hands shaking and his mouth trembling as his mind tried to deal with letting the warriors go. "*Ozuye* – War party must die!" Wiyaka asserted. "I will kill them! This is a decision that should not be left to a woman!"

"Wiyaka!" Chayton interrupted, trying to get Wiyaka to calm down. "*Enila!* – Be quiet!"

"They killed her husband…they tried to kill her daughter…they tried to kill me," Wiyaka rambled on, his hands shaking and held tight into fists. "They tried to kill me."

Chayton looked at his friend and said, "Calm, *le mita kola*…Sit."

Everybody watched Wiyaka thundering around the campfire, cursing and yelling. Finally, Chayton caught Wiyaka's attention and it only took one look from Chayton to calm Wiyaka down. Chayton understood his friend as no one else did or ever could.

"Wiyaka, sit," Chayton insisted, motioning with his hands for Wiyaka to sit down. Wiyaka reluctantly sat down. Then, Chayton attempted to explain the decision to Wiyaka, "I understand, *le mita kola*, these people are *sica*, – bad, but it is not for you or me to judge them."

"They attacked me!" Wiyaka roared.

"I understand, *le mita kola*," Chayton proclaimed, now understanding where part of his friend's anger was coming from.

"Moki," Honiahaka spoke, "finish with your decision."

Moki looked at Wiyaka. She did not want to hurt Wiyaka or anyone else, but she knew he would never agree with her decision. Tears filled her eyes as she directed her explanation to Wiyaka. "Killing them will not change anything, Wiyaka," she explained. "It will not bring back my Paco or give me a home."

"He will find you, Moki," Wiyaka muttered, his voice trembling. "Sa– Sat–Satanta will hunt you down and kill your daughter. He will kill you."

"We will be like the wind, Wiyaka," Moki replied with a tearful smile, attempting to make Wiyaka smile. "He will not find us. Will you help us, Wiyaka?"

Wiyaka looked at Moki and said, "*Ai,* – Yes, I will help you, but I do not agree with this."

"Killing them makes us like them, Wiyaka," Moki added. "I am not like them."

"You do not have to kill them, Moki, I will do that for you," Wiyaka suggested, not quite understanding. Moki exhaled with a big sigh. She knew that there would never be enough suns to convince Wiyaka of her reasoning.

160

"This is *sica* – bad," Wiyaka mumbled, shaking his head in disbelief. "I hope they never find you."

"Before we let them go, we will warn them," Honiahaka interjected.

Wiyaka openly scoffed at Honiahaka's blustery statement, but Honiahaka paid no attention to the old man. Honiahaka stood up and spoke directly to Moki, "You and your daughter may live in our village. My sister Namid tells me that Chayton may be coming to live with us."

Chayton shot a glance at Namid and she smiled back at him. She stood up to join her brother. Then, brother and sister left the campfire.

Once they were out of sight, Wiyaka looked at Chayton and asked, "You are going to live with that…that…Namid?"

Chayton looked at his friend and replied, *"Slol wa yea shnee.* – I do not know."

Act IV

Chapter Fifteen

Chayton said farewell to Honiahaka, Namid, and the River People. Then he said goodbye to Wiyaka, Hoka, Hogan, and his new friends Moki and Gad. After saying his farewells, he turned towards the south and began his journey alone. Once Chayton was a good distance from the camp, Honiahaka took Wiyaka aside and whispered, "I am not sure he should be traveling alone."

Wiyaka smiled and then laughed. "The old *gnaye* – fool thinks he is alone," Wiyaka replied. "I will be close by watching out for him. Chayton cannot take care of himself."

Honiahaka looked relieved to hear this and then laughed when he thought about Chayton believing he was alone while the entire time Wiyaka was shadowing him. Honiahaka then asked, "You will be leaving soon, *le mita kola? –* my friend?"

"*Ai,* as soon as Chayton disappears over that ridge," Wiyaka answered while pointing his finger at a distant ridge.

"We will take the *ozuye* north and turn them loose near their canyon," Honiahaka said, pointing at Satanta and the other warriors lying tied up nearby.

"Give them to me and I will kill them, now," Wiyaka declared. "It will save us all trouble."

"The woman wants them to live," Honiahaka replied.

"*Ai,* a decision she will regret."

"I hope that when Chayton finishes his journey, you and he will come live with the River People," Honiahaka suggested.

"We will have to see what *Wakan Tanka* has in store," Wiyaka replied. "Who knows where Chayton is leading me. I only know that Chayton will find trouble wherever he goes, he always does."

Wiyaka and Honiahaka watched Chayton disappear over the distant ridge. Wiyaka said his goodbyes and followed his friend. After Wiyaka disappeared over the same ridge, Hoka and Hogan came and stood alongside Honiahaka. He saw that Hoka and Hogan had their meager possessions with them.

"*Tókiya la hwo, Hoka? –* Where are you going, Hoka?" Honiahaka asked.

"I am not letting those two old hunters go on this journey alone," Hoka answered.

"Ha! Ha! Ha!" Honiahaka bellowed with laughter. Then, Moki and Gad walked up alongside Hoka with their possessions.

"*Tókiya la hwo, Moki?* – Where are you going, Moki?" Hoka asked Moki.

"With you," Moki replied.

"*Hee ya!* – No!" Hoka declared. "It is too dangerous for a woman and child."

"That is why you need my spear," Moki replied.

"*Hee ya! –* No!"

"Kohana is coming," Moki added, pointing her thumb at the gigantic warrior behind her. "That is two spears."

"That warrior cannot walk," Hoka dismissed the idea.

"I will keep up!" Kohana insisted. "You will need my spear."

Hoka turned around and bent his neck backwards so he could look up at the massive warrior. Hoka knew that they could use another spear, but it was still too dangerous for a woman and child. He turned to Moki and said, "*Hee ya, –* No, you stay here, we will return as soon as Chayton is finished."

"*Hee ya! –* No!" Moki roared.

Hoka knew he was going to lose this argument and Moki would follow the old men, no matter what he said. While Hoka dealt with this strong–willed woman, Honiahaka could hardly contain his laughter. Hoka's stern face finally relaxed. "*Hoppo!* – Let us go!" Hoka exclaimed and walked out of the camp, heading to the south.

***

As Chayton hobbled along, he thought about what his vision had told him to do. Chayton knew that it was dangerous for him to travel alone, but he was not going to put others in danger just to fulfill his own destiny. Chayton stopped often to rest which usually set off another round of coughing and hacking. During his last coughing attack, he sat there on a rock until the coughing spell passed. He felt the cool morning breeze on his face and realized how very tired he was. Chayton could not understand how *Wakan Tanka* expected an old man to fulfill such a vision. He was too old and crippled. Chayton slowly rose to his feet and ambled off to the south, using his walking staff to help him along. Chayton smiled when he thought about the old friend he would reunite with in a few short suns.

Just before dark, Chayton located a safe place to camp near a natural spring. He placed his campfire near a rocky cliff where he could sleep with his back against the rock. If any humans or animals attacked, Chayton would at least only have to face them in one direction. As soon as Chayton sprawled

164

out in front of the campfire to sleep, the coughing began. Frustrated, he sat up against the cliff and stared out into the darkness. Then, he heard it, a low-pitched growl from an animal. Chayton slowly leaned over and snatched up his spear. He placed the spear on his lap. Chayton then leaned over and grabbed a piece of firewood to throw on the campfire. He gazed out into the darkness, searching for a sign from the animal he knew was watching him. Chayton's eyes remained fixed on the darkness throughout the night.

When the sun appeared over the eastern horizon, Chayton finally felt safe enough to leave the security of the campfire. He grabbed his spear and limped around the campsite, investigating the tall grass where he thought he heard the animal. Chayton found the grass trampled in several areas and was sure that it had not been that way when he arrived. He even found a spot where something had been lying down. He reached down and picked up several tufts of fur from the ground. He rubbed the fur between his fingers and then smelled it. He had only seen fur like this one other time in his life.

Chayton investigated around the natural spring for fresh animal tracks. When he first saw the tracks, his stomach rolled with both anxiety and fear. Chayton was staring at two massive animal tracks, deeply imbedded in the dark organic mud near the water. These enormous tracks did not belong to one of the large hooved animals that Chayton hunted for food. Nor did the tracks belong to the wolf or the mountain lion. These tracks belonged to a much more dangerous predator, a beast that hunted and preyed on every other animal, including humans. The beast had taken its time drinking water at the natural spring, unafraid of the human who slept nearby.

From a ridge to the north, Wiyaka watched Chayton wandering around, inspecting the grassy field surrounding his camp. With the sun already growing old, Wiyaka worried that Chayton had not started his day's journey. This was unlike Chayton. He had been doing many strange things lately and Wiyaka could sense that something was wrong. Wiyaka stood on the ridge and watched Chayton until finally he had enough. He marched down the steep slope of the ridge towards Chayton, but Chayton was too busy to even notice. When Wiyaka got within earshot, he yelled, "What are you doing, Chayton? You did not even see me coming!"

Finally, Chayton looked up and saw his friend. He smiled and waved, but Wiyaka was not in the mood for pleasantries. When Wiyaka reached Chayton, he immediately began scolding the old man like a child, "Did you not hear me, Chayton?" Wiyaka demanded. "What if I was the *hohe?* – enemy?"

165

Chayton just continued to smile at his old friend, finally asking, "What are you doing here, Wiyaka?"

"I knew you could not travel alone!" Wiyaka snapped, "As soon as I am not around, you wander around your campsite like a lost and bewildered wolf dog pup! You worry this campsite like a prairie dog searching for roots!"

"I am not lost," Chayton replied. "Follow me, you old fool!"

Chayton shuffled over to the natural spring and with his walking staff, he pointed at the colossal animal tracks in the mud. Wiyaka stared at the tracks, speechless. He could not believe what he was looking at.

"Speak, you old fool!" Chayton finally blurted out.

"They are an old sign," Wiyaka declared, his voice filled with more hope than fact. Chayton laughed and then replied, "*Hee ya,* – No, they are not old, *le mita kola,* they are fresh."

Chayton reached down and poked his finger in the mud, demonstrating to Wiyaka the freshness of the tracks. Wiyaka looked around at the surrounding hills, his hand instinctively tightening around the shaft of his spear. "I saw these same animal tracks when we were following the *ozuye,* – war party," he finally confessed to Chayton.

"I have only heard the stories around campfires about this beast," Chayton proclaimed. "Some say it is a *wanagi* – *ghost*...much larger than *igmuwatogla* – mountain lion...faster than *mato* – bear...and it does not hunt alone...it hunts with many."

"*Wanagi?* – Ghost?" Wiyaka questioned.

"*Ai,* – Yes," Chayton replied. "Stories say this beast is everywhere, but nowhere."

"Everywhere, but nowhere?" Wiyaka repeated, visibly shaken. "I must go find Hoka and Hogan."

"They are in the camp of the River People."

"*Hee ya.* – No."

"Where are they, Wiyaka?"

"I followed you," Wiyaka explained and then with a sheepish grin, he added, "They followed me."

"It is your fault they are here!" Chayton thundered. "I told you I must be alone!"

"You are lucky I am here," Wiyaka expressed. "This *wanagi* is hunting you! It wants a taste of your old smelly bones. With me here, you are safe!"

"Safe?" Chayton scoffed. "I saw you tied up in the camp of the *ozuye!*"

"I would have gotten away," Wiyaka declared. "I was ready to escape."

166

"*Ai!* – Yes!" Chayton said. "It looked like you were ready to escape."

Chayton was upset with Wiyaka. He was counting on Wiyaka to watch out for his son and grandson. Now, they had to go find Hoka and Hogan and warn them about the beast, delaying Chayton's journey even further. Chayton thought about making Wiyaka go find Hoka and Hogan, forcing them to return to the village of the River People, but he knew that Wiyaka was too stubborn and dense to leave him. Finally, he turned to Wiyaka and said, "*Hoppo,* – Let us go find Hoka and Hogan!"

"They are here," Wiyaka responded.

"*Tuktel?* – Where?" Chayton questioned.

Embarrassed, Wiyaka peered up at the same ridge where he had been spying on Chayton. Wiyaka waved his arms back and forth. He then motioned his arm in the direction of Chayton and him. Before long, five humans, not two, appeared on top of the ridge and started walking down the slope of the ridge.

"Wiyaka, you said only Hoka and Hogan followed," Chayton blurted out, "did you invite the entire tribe?"

"*Ai,* – Yes, I mean *hee ya.* – no. "

"I count five," Chayton informed Wiyaka.

"You were always good at counting."

"Who are they?" Chayton demanded.

"*Slol wa yea shnee,* – I do not know," Wiyaka sighed.

Chayton looked at Wiyaka with anger in his eyes. His solitude journey was becoming less solitary with each passing breeze. When Hoka and the others arrived, Chayton's anger boiled over when he scolded Hoka in front of the others, "Hoka, I told you not to follow me! What are you doing here?"

"We are not following you!" Hoka replied with the slight crease of a smile. "We are following Wiyaka!"

Wiyaka tried to hold back his laughter and for a short time, it worked. He stood there covering his mouth and snickering to himself. Then, he made the mistake of looking at Hoka who still had a sheepish grin on his face. Hoka's goofy expression was more than Wiyaka could handle. He opened his mouth and out came an explosion of laughter, making everyone laugh, everyone that is, except Chayton.

"This is not funny!" Chayton scolded them all.

"It is done, Chayton," Wiyaka replied. "We will face danger together, just like we always have."

167

Wiyaka then turned to Hoka and said, "I am not happy that you brought a woman and two children with us."

"I am not a child!" Hogan responded.

"As you said, Wiyaka," Hoka responded to Wiyaka, "it is done. They cannot return to the River People by themselves and I am not leaving you two."

"You will need us by the time the journey is over," Moki added.

Wiyaka opened his mouth to respond to Moki, but Hogan interrupted with a question for his grandfather, "We watched you from the ridge, what are you looking at?"

"Animal tracks by the *wakon ya,*" Wiyaka replied.

"*Enila, Wiyaka!* – Be quiet, Wiyaka!" Chayton thundered, but it was too late, Hogan was already running to the natural spring with his father following.

"*Igmuwatogla!* – Mountain lion!" Hogan blurted out, remembering his earlier lesson.

"*Hee ya,* – No, I do not think so," Chayton replied.

"What is it?" Hogan questioned his grandfather.

"*Slol wa yea shnee,* – I do not know," Chayton replied. "I pray to *Wakan Tanka* it is *igmuwatogla.* – mountain lion."

"*Thunkashila,* – Grandfather, that is funny," Hogan stated. "You pray it is *igmuwatogla?* You would want it to be *igmuwatogla?*"

"The foot is too large for *igmuwatogla,*" Wiyaka declared.

"You do not know, *le mita kola,* – my friend," Chayton butted in, not wanting Wiyaka to frighten the others. "We will walk together with a hunter at the front and a hunter at the back."

"I will be the hunter at the back!" Hogan proclaimed.

"Chayton said hunter, not *hokshila,* – boy," Wiyaka expressed.

Chayton finally noticed the warrior. He looked up at the warrior and asked, "*Nituwe he?* – Who are you?"

"His name is Kohana," Gad blurted out.

Chayton smiled at the small girl and then asked, "Does the warrior not have a tongue?"

Gad answered, "He can speak our tongue, but he does not speak much…he wants me to speak for him."

Chayton smiled and looked the warrior over. Chayton was a tall hunter and he still had to look up to see the much taller warrior. After studying the warrior, Chayton said, "The warrior can walk–"

"Kohana," Gad interrupted.

Chayton smiled at the small girl and then continued, "Kohana...can walk in the front. He is big enough to frighten any beast away."

***

The seven travelers made good progress during the day and found no other sign from the beast that left the tracks at Chayton's campsite. Before the sun had set, the travelers arrived at a small creek along the edge of the dark forest. Chayton decided that this was where he would camp and that the others could join him, if they wished.

"Gather much wood," Wiyaka instructed Moki, Hogan and Gad. "We will take this warrior hunting with us. I want to see if he is a hunter or only a warrior."

"Kohana should guard the wood gatherers," Hoka suggested. For once, Wiyaka did not argue.

The three hunters headed to the pine forest and spread out, keeping each other in sight. They quietly walked up the tree–lined creek. Chayton walked along with his spear on his left shoulder and his walking staff in his right hand. He studied the ground, looking for any sign of prey. Near the creek, he spotted a track in the mud, a track that he had hoped he would never see again. The same type of beast that had visited him at the natural spring had left a track in this forest. He called out to Wiyaka and Hoka and they came running. Together, they followed the tracks deeper into the forest.

"*Wayaka!* – Look!" Wiyaka exclaimed, pointing at the trunk of a large Ponderosa pine tree. The three hunters inspected the trunk of the tree. An animal had raked and stripped the bark off the pine tree, leaving long deep furrows and gouges running lengthwise up the trunk of the tree. Hoka stretched his arm, trying to reach the top of the damage, but even standing on his toes, he could not reach it. Chayton brushed his fingers across the deep claw marks in the tree and shards of wood fell to the ground. "They are new," Chayton said in regards to the claw marks. Wiyaka and Hoka peered around at the dark forest surrounding them, expecting to see the beast at any time.

"*Hexaka* – Elk did this," Wiyaka suggested, referring to the damage that a large bull elk can do when raking its antlers against a tree.

Chayton laughed. "*Hee ya, Wiyaka,* – No, Wiyaka," he replied. "You know better, *le mita kola.*"

The three hunters did not say a word while their minds processed what to do. They stood quietly listening to the pine forest. The only sound came from a light breeze whistling through the pines. The forest was too quiet, not even

169

a bird sang its song. Pointing at the deeply gouged claw marks on the pine tree, Hoka finally said, "This beast is warning us. This forest belongs to it."

No one replied. They did not need to. They knew Hoka was right. The beast had claimed this territory and the humans were trespassing. Chayton interrupted the eerie silence with a cough that startled both Wiyaka and Hoka.

"We should get back to camp," Wiyaka suggested. "Darkness comes."

* * *

Honiahaka and the hunters from the River People made their way towards their village near the plateau. When they came to the place where the River People would head west, Honiahaka stopped the hunters so they could release the prisoners. The hunters drug Satanta and the other warriors in front of Honiahaka and he cut the hemp ropes off their hands.

"You will go north until you reach your land," Honiahaka told Satanta. "We shall never see you again."

Satanta was a defeated man. Unable to look Honiahaka in the eyes, he mumbled, "We will go to our village. You will not see us again."

"Go!" Honiahaka ordered while pointing his finger to the north.

Satanta and the other warriors hiked north until they were out of sight of the River People. Satanta then abruptly stopped and turned around, headed back to the southeast, just enough to the east to skirt around the path of the River People.

Surprised by the change in direction, Fala caught up to Satanta and asked, "Where are we going?"

"The woman!" Satanta exclaimed. "I am going to find the woman!"

* * *

After seeing the claw marks on the pine tree, the three hunters hurried back to the campsite empty handed. Food was no longer their biggest concern. After ensuring the others were safe, the three hunters helped gather wood and dung for the roaring campfire they would need. The three hunters kept the discovery of the claw marks a secret from the others. There was no reason to frighten them. They would huddle together against a brightly lit campfire throughout the night and then head south after the sun had risen. Hungry, the travelers settled down for a long night around a raging campfire. The bright light from the flames would keep this animal away. After all, that is how it had always worked.

* * *

In the starlight, her body looked gray and ghostlike as she crept quietly through the tall grass. She was the perfect predator, the top of the food chain.

170

As she stepped, she lifted her legs high, careful not to brush up against the stalks of tall grass. The soft pads on the bottom of her feet made little sound as she glided over the rugged terrain. She had always been exceptionally careful, but tonight she was ravenous and impatient to find food. Even though she had nothing to fear, surprise was her element.

Her nocturnal eyes picked up the tiny twinkle of light near the edge of the forest. She cautiously advanced. Her instincts made her mindful of danger. She meandered across the area, staying downwind from the light and studying the lay of the land as she quietly advanced towards her target. Occasionally, she stopped and lifted her snout high in the air, searching for smells. She had yet to pick up the scent of prey. Then a sound drew her attention. It came from the direction of the light. With her belly dragging the grass–covered ground, she slowly crept towards the source of the sound. As she moved closer, the brilliant light blinded her sensitive eyes. She smelled something new, a scent locked somewhere in her memory. Out of her throat came a low–pitched rumble.

Chayton coughed. He was very tired, but between the wheezing and coughing, he was unable to fall asleep. Instead, he sat there staring at the flames of the campfire. Then, he heard something, a sound drifting in from the darkness. Chayton's eyes shifted from the brilliance of the flames to the blackness surrounding the camp. His eyes darted from one spot to another, frantically searching for the source of the sound. Everywhere Chayton looked, he saw nothing. Chayton had almost convinced himself that the noise originated from his own imagination when he caught a glimpse of something. Hovering over the ground were two, barely visible orbs of light. Chayton adjusted his eyes and focused on those tiny points of light, but he could not tell what he was looking at. He needed a closer look. With the help of his walking staff, Chayton pulled himself up to his feet, but when he stood up, the dim points of light vanished. His eyes searched the darkness surrounding the campsite, but there was nothing. Then, off to his left, the two points of light reappeared.

Adrenalin surged through Chayton's body when he realized that he was looking at the reflective eyes of an animal and from the distance above the ground, it was a very large animal. Chayton felt nauseous as he held on tightly to his walking staff. He shuffled a couple of steps to his right, never taking his eyes off the two points of light. He slowly moved the end of his walking staff towards the dozing head of Wiyaka. Chayton thumped Wiyaka in the head with the end of his walking staff. When Wiyaka did not budge, Chayton thumped him harder with the walking staff, whispering, "*Key kta yo. –* Wake up."

A walking staff to the noggin was enough to wake Wiyaka up. He shot straight up and looked around. He saw the walking staff hovering over his head and blurted out, "*Taku?* – What?"

"*Enila,* – Be quiet," Chayton responded and then pointed a wrinkled finger out into the darkness. "*Wayaka,* – Look," he whispered.

Wiyaka peered out into the darkness, unable to see anything. The eyes from the animal had vanished. Chayton scanned the blackness surrounding the campsite, but the animal was no longer there. Wiyaka glared at his friend, angry that Chayton had awakened him from a sound sleep by thumping him on the head. "*Gnaye!* – Fool!" Wiyaka blurted out.

"What is the matter?" Hoka mumbled after the two old men woke him up.

"Nothing," Wiyaka replied. "Your father is a *gnaye*. He imagines things in the dark. He is like a large *chincá!* – child!"

Wiyaka lay back down and was soon snoring away while Chayton kept his eyes fixed on the darkness until the sun broke the eastern horizon.

***

With little for the travelers to eat, it took less time for them to prepare for the day's journey. Chayton spent that time searching the grass for evidence of what he thought he had seen the night before. The grass showed that something had walked through it, but Chayton found no visible tracks. He located the spot where he thought the eyes of the animal had been watching him. There, the grass was matted, but Chayton still found no tracks. While Chayton was on his hands and knees inspecting the area, Wiyaka walked up.

"*Le mita kola,* – My friend," Wiyaka said with a mischievous grin on his face, "what is it you think you saw in the darkness, perhaps another *tarca sapa* – black deer that came to rescue us?"

Chayton looked up at Wiyaka with a dour expression on his face. "Something was here! *Wayaka!* – Look!" he proclaimed.

"Animals always watch us from the darkness, you are old enough to know that…you are old enough to know much more than you actually do," Wiyaka responded. "It does not mean that the eyes you imagined are from the same beast that clawed the tree."

Chayton was not going to argue with his friend. He looked towards the south and changed the subject. "We should reach the river in two, maybe three suns," he declared.

"We will spread out and hunt as we head south," Wiyaka suggested.

"*Hee ya!* – No!" Chayton blurted out, adding, "Too dangerous."

"We need food!" Wiyaka challenged, "This *wanagi* – ghost you think you saw will not come out in the sun."

Chayton did not waver. "We stay together," he declared and hobbled away.

***

The seven travelers had little incident during the day, but by staying together on the trail they had little opportunity for finding food. Chayton kept his eyes glued to the ground the entire time, searching for the tracks that would convince Wiyaka that they were not alone and that he had not gone crazy. Chayton finally let the warrior Kohana and Hoka spread out and search for game, as long as they promised to stay within eyesight of each other. By the end of the day, the travelers had made good progress. Chayton and Wiyaka found a suitable place for a campsite, up along the foothills of the mountains. The campsite was on a treeless hill with a small natural spring near its base. Even though the campsite was out in the open and exposed in every direction, Chayton felt it would be safer than sleeping in the nearby forest. They collected firewood for the night and then Hoka and the Kohana showed up with a jackrabbit and a good–sized turtle. By the time dusk came, the travelers had eaten and settled down for what would be another long and worrisome night for Chayton. As soon as Chayton lay down on the ground to sleep, his incessant coughing began. Moki crawled over to him and gave him a handful of dried sage.

"Chew this," she told him. "It will help."

"*Pilamaya,* – Thank you," Chayton replied, placing a bit of the herb on his tongue. He did not tell her, but he thought the sage made him cough more. As night fell, Chayton could no longer stay awake and he fell into a deep sleep.

***

She had picked up their trail and was circling the campsite. The painful light from the campfire prevented her from getting closer. She watched and listened to the travelers concealed behind the bright light. She was being cautious with this unfamiliar prey, searching for a weakness and not underestimating their strength. This was how her species had survived for millions of years. As a cub, she had learned to be wary of prey from her first encounter with a porcupine. She would wait and let her prey make the first mistake. She quietly circled the campsite, closing the distance. She was now close enough to catch the rich aroma of the humans. She remembered the aroma from somewhere in her past and she recalled the taste of the meat. She lay on the ground, crouched on her belly, her back arched like a bow, ready to spring at any moment.

Chayton's wheezing and snoring woke Wiyaka up. He leaned over and threw more firewood on the blaze. Wiyaka watched the hypnotic flames of the campfire while listening to the sounds of sleep around him. He finally closed his eyes, hoping to get more sleep, but all he could see were the flames of the campfire in his mind's eye. He opened his eyes and looked out into the blackness surrounding the campfire. As his eyes drilled deeper into the darkness, he spotted a subtle flicker of light from what appeared to be an ash ember rising from a campfire. Wiyaka blinked and refocused his eyes on the same spot. There, he saw it again, appearing and disappearing with a blink of an eye. Wiyaka slowly leaned over and grabbed a large chunk of firewood, throwing it on the campfire. The campfire protested with sparks and embers floating into the sky. The dry firewood caught on fire quickly, illuminating the area surrounding the campsite. Wiyaka peered out into the night and spotted a reflection of something. He glared at it while the flames of the campfire danced and flickered against a veil of darkness. For a brief moment, Wiyaka spotted her, exposed by the surging light of the campfire.

A growl instinctively escaped her throat. She sensed that her prey had discovered her. Her advantage of surprise was gone. She focused her eyes on the human, waiting for her prey to fight or flee. Her instincts screamed at her to attack, but caution held her back, at least temporarily. Her back legs twitched as nervous energy surged through her body.

"*Key kto yo!* – Wake up!" Wiyaka whispered while elbowing Chayton on the shoulder.

"*Tóka he?* – What is wrong?" Chayton blurted out.

"*Enila,* – Be quiet," Wiyaka whispered while pointing his finger out into the night.

Chayton's eyes were half–open and he could not see a thing. He took his fists and rubbed his eyes, trying to clear up his vision. When his eyes adjusted to the light, he looked at where Wiyaka was pointing and saw light from the campfire reflecting off a pair of eyes.

"*Igmu'gleška!* – great lion!" Chayton bellowed, much too loudly.

Startled by Chayton's loud voice, the lioness did not strike, but instead turned and crept away, circling the perimeter of the camp while looking for an opening to attack. She had no fear, but remained cautious.

"*KEY KTO YO!* – WAKE UP!" Wiyaka screamed at the others.

The lioness's ears flattened against her head when she heard her prey

174

scream. She took a step backwards and crouched down, curious about her prey. EEEHHHHHH! When Gad caught a glimpse of the lioness, she let out a high–pitched scream that carried across the surrounding hills. The lioness took another step backwards.

"Scream!" Chayton shouted at the others. "Spears outward!"

Everyone screamed as loud as possible. The travelers shoved their hand–held spears out into the darkness. The screaming temporarily confused the lioness and she retreated outside the light of the campfire. There, she hunkered down and waited.

"Use the fire!" Chayton yelled while brandishing a half–burning log off the campfire. Chayton advanced in the direction he last saw the lioness, hobbling along into the blackness of the night with a spear in one hand and blazing log in the other. The lioness retreated further, finally disappearing into the starlit night. Wiyaka and the warrior Kohana joined Chayton with spears and torches. They peered out into the shadows, but saw and heard nothing. The three travelers slowly retreated to the safety of the campfire. Everyone sat next to the campfire with spears facing out towards the darkness.

"What was it?" Hogan asked.

"*Igmu'gleška,* – Great lion," Chayton replied, his voice still trembling.

"*Igmu'gleška?*" Hogan repeated.

"*Igmu'gleška! –* Great lion! KAAF!" Chayton explained between coughs. "Much larger than *igmuwatogla, –* mountain lion. KAAF!"

Then, from the darkness of the night came a frightening animal roar that brought shivers to every one of the travelers. The roar echoed through the hills while the travelers held their breaths, waiting for the sound to disappear. Then, another roar erupted out of the south. That roar hung on the air long enough for a third roar to penetrate the night.

"We are surrounded," Wiyaka declared.

"Ai, – Yes," Chayton mumbled. "*Wakan. –* Holy."

"*Taku? –* What?" Hoka his son asked, still trembling from fear.

"*Wakan, –* Holy," Chayton repeated, even louder. "*Igmu'gleška, wakan. –* Great lion, holy."

Then a fourth roar pierced the stillness of twilight. Chayton peered out into the darkness and explained his comment. "*Igmuwatogla –* Mountain lion hunts alone," he told the others. "*Igmu'gleška –* Great lion hunts like a tribe."

"There is more than one?" Hogan asked.

"*Ai, –* Yes," Chayton replied. "There are many."

Chapter Sixteen

The encounter with the great lion had terrified the travelers. When the sun appeared over the eastern horizon, Wiyaka was attempting to convince Chayton to turn and flee to the River People's village in the north. Chayton was not listening.

"Wiyaka, you take the others north," Chayton replied. "I must continue my journey."

"You just want to cross that river to visit that old *wanagi!* – ghost!" Wiyaka declared.

"I am following my vision."

"Your vision? Ha!" Wiyaka challenged. "Did your vision tell you to feed this woman and these children to *igmu'gleška?*"

"I am not a child!" Hogan exclaimed.

"*IYAYA! –* GO!" Chayton bellowed loudly. "KAAF! KAAF! I did not ask you to follow me! I did not want you here! KAAF! KAAF!"

The arguing initiated another round of intense coughing from Chayton. He leaned over and coughed several times, finishing up by vomiting blood on the ground.

"You are not well, Chayton!" Wiyaka reasoned with his friend. "We will go back to the village of the River People. They can help you."

Chayton sat down on the ground and put his head between his legs. He sat there letting the dizziness pass.

"Eat this!" Moki said while kneeling next to Chayton and handing him some ground up sagebrush.

"*Pilamaya, –* Thank you," Chayton replied, taking the dried sage from Moki and placing it on his tongue, sucking the dryness from it. Chayton put his head between his legs and spit up more blood. Wiyaka saw the pain his friend was in and did not know what to do. He walked over and knelt down alongside Chayton, putting his hand on Chayton's shoulder.

"*Hecheto aloe, le mita kola, –* It is finished, my friend," Wiyaka insisted. "We are heading north."

"*Hee ya, –* No," Chayton answered. "I must finish what I started."

"I will follow you anywhere, Chayton," Wiyaka attempted to reason with the old hunter, "but we are putting the others in danger."

"*Ai!* – Yes!" Chayton concluded. "That is why I must go alone."

"We are not leaving you, *até!* – father!" Hoka proclaimed after eavesdropping on the conversation between Chayton and Wiyaka.

"You must take the woman and child away from here," Chayton mumbled, his voice barely audible.

"My child…Gad stays with me," Moki declared, "and I stay with you…we have no home…we have no place to go."

"KAAF! KAAF!" Chayton coughed and leaned forward. He let a mouthful of bloody drool drip from his mouth onto the ground. When he could finally speak, he replied to Moki in a gravelly whisper, "Go to the village of the River People, I will meet you there when I am finished."

"*Hee ya!* – No!" Moki exclaimed. "We remain with you."

Exasperated with Chayton's stubbornness, Wiyaka stood up and walked around the campsite, thinking about what he should do. Finally, he gave up thinking about it and said, "We are one sun…maybe two from the river. If we stay together and only travel with the sun, we might survive."

"And then what?" Chayton challenged. "Will the river stop *igmu'gleška*?"

"*Slol wa yea shnee,* – I do not know," Wiyaka replied to Chayton. "After we cross the river, your *wanagi*…Tarca Sapa will protect us."

Chayton looked up at Wiyaka to see if he was serious. The two friends burst out laughing at their private joke.

***

The travelers continued their march south, staying near each other and counting every step to the river. The warrior Kohana shadowed Moki and Gad, watching over them and never letting them out of his sight. Moki continued to practice her spear throwing and Kohana was always nearby to retrieve her thrown spears. The travelers saw no sign of the great lions, giving them hope that they had passed through its forbidden territory. By the time the sun was deep in the west, the travelers reached the edge of a rocky ridge that looked out across the prairie to the south. As the travelers stood on the edge of the rim, Chayton finally saw what he had been seeking. "The river!" he yelled. "We have made it!"

In the distance, the shimmering river meandered across the prairie, winding its way to the east. The travelers smiled and laughed at their good fortune. "We should be there by dark," Wiyaka declared and started to climb down the slope of the ridge.

"*Inaji!* – Stop!" Hoka cried out.

Wiyaka stopped and looked over his shoulder at Hoka. "What is that?"

177

Hoka asked, pointing off in the distance at some dark spots on the prairie.

"*Tatanka!* – Bison!" Wiyaka exclaimed with a laugh. "They once filled this valley."

"*Hee ya!* – No!" Hogan blurted out. "Not there! Over there!"

The travelers followed where Hogan's finger was pointing. In the middle of the prairie, between the travelers and the river, there was other movement. "What is it?" Hoka asked.

Chayton focused his eyes and shrugged his shoulders, replying, "*Slol wa yea shnee.* – I do not know."

All of the travelers stared at that spot on the prairie, trying to determine what it was they were looking at. Wiyaka put his right hand against his face, attempting to shield his eyes from the setting sun. Then he finally recognized what it was. Wiyaka laughed and blurted out, "*Tatoke!* – Antelope!"

Filled with relief, everyone smiled and laughed. Hoka started to follow Wiyaka down the ridge when Kohana reached out and grabbed Hoka by his shoulder. The powerful arm of Kohana brought Hoka to an immediate stop. "*Hee ya, tatoke! Igmu'gleška! A–ah!* – No, antelope! Great lion! Watch out!" Kohana announced to the other travelers.

"*Hee ya!* – No!" Wiyaka replied while focusing his gaze on what he was sure were antelope.

"*Hee ya, igmu'gleška!* – No, great lion!" Kohana argued. "*Wayaka!* – Look!"

"Kohana is right," Hoka agreed, staring at the distant spot on the prairie. "They are feeding on a *tatanka.*"

The travelers stood on the rocky ridge, still unsure of what they were looking at and what to do.

"How many?" Wiyaka asked, finally relenting to the younger eyes of Kohana and Hoka.

Kohana took his time and counted the pale–colored animals. When he finished counting, he told the others, "*Wikcémna.* – Ten."

"*Wikcémna?* – Ten?" Wiyaka challenged. The rest of the travelers were too stunned to say anything. Most had never seen a great lion and now there were ten of them between them and their river destination. Kohana recounted the animals just to be sure.

"*Hee ya!* – No!" Kohana said after a long pause. The other travelers felt a sense of relief when they thought Kohana had made a mistake or perhaps the spots on the prairie were antelope, after all.

"*Aké wanji.* – Eleven." Kohana blurted out.

No one spoke. All of the travelers' thoughts were wrapping around the reality that eleven human–eating great lions lay between them and the river. Chayton was the first to break the long silence by saying, "I will find a way to the river, Wiyaka...Hoka. It is time for you to head north, away from this place. I will finish what I must do and then follow you."

"I am staying with you, Chayton," Wiyaka murmured.

"I am staying with you, *até*," Hoka added.

Wiyaka threw some dry grass in the air and watched it float off in the direction of the great lions. "We are upwind, we must move before they discover us," Wiyaka said while looking around. "Chayton, we can follow this ridge to the west. From there, we can avoid this valley and still reach the river through the mountains."

"We must set up camp," Hoka added. "We do not want to be without fire when it is dark."

"*Ai*, – Yes," Wiyaka replied, looking up the ridge towards the west. "We must build a campfire soon."

Wiyaka and Hoka herded the other travelers along the ridge, heading them west towards the mountains. Before darkness came, the travelers had located a place to camp that afforded them a rock formation to their backs. The travelers struck camp and collected as much firewood as they could find before the disappearing sun no longer protected them. It would be another hungry camp, but by dark, the travelers were safely huddled around the bright flames of the campfire.

In the dark of night, Wiyaka looked up and saw that the moon was only a sliver of white. The night would be pitch–black which meant good hunting for the predators of darkness. Throughout a sleepless night, the travelers heard the sound of roars, coming from different distances and directions, but they never saw any great lions. Just before first light, the exhausted travelers finally fell asleep by a blazing campfire, relieved that they had somehow survived another night. When dawn arrived, the drowsy travelers woke up, one by one. It was not long before they noticed that Chayton was missing.

"Search the area around the camp!" Wiyaka ordered the others, peering around the sparse pine forest surrounding the campsite. The travelers searched the area, but none of them found any sign of Chayton. As the sun lit up the sky, the travelers became braver and wandered even further away from the campsite, but still no sign of Chayton. Then, the big warrior Kohana discovered a footprint heading to the east across the ridge they had crossed the previous sun. The travelers concluded that the footprint could only belong to Chayton.

"Where is that *gnaye* – fool going?" Wiyaka asked while inspecting the track.

The travelers followed Chayton's tracks back across the ridge to the same spot where they had stood and observed the eleven great lions on the prairie. The hawk eye of Kohana first spotted Chayton. "There he is!" Kohana exclaimed, pointing at a barely visible spot on the prairie below. Chayton's walking staff had given his identity away.

"He is walking towards the river...right through *igmu'gleška!*" Wiyaka exclaimed, once he had located Chayton with his own eyes. Wiyaka shifted his eyes away from Chayton to the great lion pride directly south of him. The great lions were lounging and sunning in the tall grass. Hoka started to climb down the ridge after his father, but Kohana stopped him. Hoka tried to break free from Kohana, but the warrior's grip was too powerful.

"Start a fire!" Wiyaka suddenly blurted out.

"*Taku?* – What?" Hoka questioned Wiyaka. "*Wana?* – Now?"

"Start a fire!" Wiyaka demanded. "*Inahni!* – Hurry!"

The travelers ran to the nearby trees and collected tinder and firewood for a campfire. Hoka struck two pieces of chert together, creating a spark that started the fire. The travelers fed the small flames until they had a blaze going. All this time, Wiyaka kept his eyes glued on Chayton, hoping that his friend would suddenly change course and turn around. "*INAHNI!* – HURRY!" Wiyaka cried out to the other travelers. "We need torches!"

The travelers dipped the ends of the dry pine logs in the campfire and let them catch on fire while Wiyaka watched Chayton walking directly towards the great lions. The great lions finally noticed the human. Showing little interest, two lionesses rose to their feet, yawned, and stretched their legs. Finally, they joined the other great lions in watching the human prey walking directly at them. One of the lionesses decided to mosey on over and greet Chayton.

"Does that *gnaye* not see *igmu'gleška?*" Wiyaka blurted out to no one in particular. Chayton kept steadily walking towards the great lion pride, staying on course with the river.

"Here!" Hoka said, handing Wiyaka a pinewood torch.

"*Hoppo!* – Let us go!" Wiyaka shouted. "Kohana, go around to the west! Take Moki and the children to the river!"

This time, Hogan did not argue with Wiyaka about calling him a child.

180

Hogan was more than happy to go west with Kohana and circle around the great lion pride. Wiyaka and Hoka made their way down the rocky slope of the ridge and ran as fast as they could across the prairie, following Chayton's trail. Once they were closer to the great lion pride, Wiyaka and Hoka used their torches to set the grasslands on fire.

***

The lioness watched Chayton walk right past her. As Chayton walked amongst the great lion pride, he quietly prayed to *Wakan Tanka* and sang his death song. The great lions were unsure of what to do about the human who walked amongst them. A few great lions rested on their haunches while others stood there like statues. They all gawked at the human. Both Chayton and the great lions were experiencing something novel. Chayton had never been this close to so much danger and the great lions had never seen prey fearlessly walk amongst them. As Chayton sang his song, his frightened voice cracked and wavered. He had never been so terrified in his entire journey through life. The great lions' heads followed Chayton as he walked away from them. When Chayton had passed the last great lion, he shot a glance over his shoulder. Miraculously, the great lions were not following him. *How could this be?* Chayton let go of a raspy cough and then looked upward at the deep blue sky, giving thanks to his creator. The river was near and on the other side was his destination, the village site where his friend and mentor, Tarca Sapa, had died in the wildfire. Chayton smiled at knowing that he would soon see his friend.

Behind Chayton's uneventful march across the grasslands, complete chaos had erupted. With torches burning, Wiyaka and Hoka continued to start fires everywhere on the prairie. The breeze out of the northwest took care of the rest, pushing the wildfires in the direction of the great lions. The great lions smelled the smoke and completely forgot about the human walking away from them. Most of the great lion pride headed east, away from the approaching wildfire, while two young great lion males caught sight of Kohana and the others sprinting across the prairie to the west. It was too much temptation for the immature male lions. The humans ran like deer, the great lions' favorite prey. While the rest of the great lion pride retreated to the east, the two young males loped towards the west in pursuit of their prey.

The travelers ran towards the river while Kohana, half–carrying Gad, brought up the rear. They had almost reached the river when, out of the corner of his eye, Kohana caught sight of the two great lions bearing down on him and the other travelers.

"*IYAGKE!* – RUN!*" Kohana screamed. Moki looked over her shoulder and saw that Kohana had stopped running. She reached back and grabbed Gad's hand, pulling the small girl towards the river. Kohana pulled a spear from his quiver, whispered a prayer, and hoisted the spear onto his shoulder. He waited until the great lions were well within range and hurled the spear at the nearer of the two great lions. The spear sizzled through the morning air and struck the great lion in its shoulder, spinning it around and causing it to tumble head over heels on the ground. The great lion snarled with pain when the stone spear point remained stuck in its shoulder muscle.

Kohana was preparing to launch the next spear just as the second great lion sped past the wounded one. Kohana flung the spear at the great lion, but the young male easily avoided the projectile. Kohana quickly launched another spear, but he was too hasty and the spear streaked over the top of the great lion. When the great lion reached Kohana, it leapt through the air, plowing into the warrior. The big cat's velocity and weight leveled the gigantic warrior and Kohana collided into the ground with a thud. The great lion hooked its claws into the muscular biceps of the warrior. Kohana fought to escape, but the great lion was too powerful. The great lion's massive fangs bit down on Kohana's face and head, looking for the warrior's vulnerable neck. Kohana screamed out in agony as the large fangs crushed the bones in his face and skull. In spite of Kohana's courage and strength, the mauling by the great lion was too much for him. The great lion eventually reached the dying warrior's throat and gripped it between its incisor and canine teeth. The young male lion repeatedly bit down, each time advancing its jaws further onto the warrior's thick neck. Finally, the great lion locked Kohana's throat between its razor sharp carnassial teeth. It closed its powerful jaws and its knifelike teeth sliced through Kohana's carotid artery. Blood flooded the sky as the neck gash widened. Bathed in a flow of blood, the great lion pinned the mighty warrior to the ground while ripping the warrior's throat wide open. The blood of Kohana spilled on to the land as the warrior's dying eyes flickered for the last time.

Crying, Moki pulled both Hogan and Gad into the shallow waters of the river. They waded at first, but then the deep river forced them to swim. Moki held onto the back of Gad's shirt with one hand guiding the young girl across the treacherous water. When they reached the other side of the river, they waited for Kohana, but he never showed up. Moki sat down along the riverbank with Gad in her arms and they wept for Kohana.

Act V

Chapter Seventeen

After fording the river and joining the others, Wiyaka and Hoka searched for Chayton along the smoke–filled river valley. They were hoping that Chayton had actually made it across the river before the wildfires reached him. After searching up and down the riverbank, Wiyaka decided it was time to go further upriver near the old village of the River People. Wiyaka surveyed the terrain trying to get oriented. It had been nearly forty winters since he had last been to this place. The land had changed and his memory had faded. Evidence of the large village that had once stood there was gone. Thick groves of cottonwood trees had replaced tipi poles.

Wiyaka gazed up at the tops of the cottonwood trees and watched the limbs bend in a strengthening wind. Wiyaka and the others reached a small clearing where the windblown grass and weeds rose as high as a human's knees. Wiyaka stopped to look around, searching for clues that his old friend had been there. Then, Wiyaka heard a sound carried across the wind, a muffled cough. He heard it again and then another raspy cough. He glanced in the direction of the sound, surveying the wind–whipped, yellowing grass. In the midst of the waving grass, Wiyaka noticed a bare spot on the monotonous grasslands. A rattling cough urged Wiyaka towards this bare spot. Leaning into the strong breeze, Wiyaka headed towards the sound and the hole in the sea of grass. He held his spear ready until he was near enough to identify an unconscious Chayton, sprawled out in the grass.

Wiyaka leaned over and poured the contents of his water pouch over Chayton's head. He then gently slapped Chayton's cheek several times in an attempt to wake him up. Chayton's body moved, but he did not wake up. Wiyaka grabbed Chayton by the back of the shirt and jerked him up into a sitting position. Wiyaka then slapped Chayton's cheeks hard, several times. Finally, Chayton coughed and his eyes blinked open. Chayton glared at Wiyaka, but there was no recognition in Chayton's eyes that he even knew Wiyaka.

"It is me, Wiyaka, you old *gnaye!* – fool!" Wiyaka roared.

"Wi–yak–a!" Chayton finally proclaimed.

"What are you doing, *le mita kola*?" Wiyaka demanded. "Do you want to die? Walking amongst *igmu'gleška*! I have never seen such foolishness!"

Chayton smiled and held out his hand. Wiyaka looked and saw an object cradled in the palm of Chayton's hand.

"*He táku hwo?* – What is it?" Wiyaka asked.

"*Wayaka!* – Look!" Chayton insisted.

Suspicious of what Chayton could have possibly picked up, Wiyaka carefully plucked the object out of his friend's hand and held it up against the overcast sky. The object appeared to be an animal bone, shaped and polished by a human.

"*He táku hwo?* – What is it?" Wiyaka repeated.

"Tarca Sapa," Chayton mumbled.

"*Taku?* – What?" Wiyaka questioned. "This is a bone from Tarca Sapa? I doubt it, his bones are gone–"

"*Hee ya!* – No!"

"*Taku?* – What?"

"This belonged to Tarca Sapa," Chayton answered. "This was his amulet."

Wiyaka pulled the amulet up to his eyes for a better look. He studied and admired the hand carved detail on the amulet. Finally, a grin formed on Wiyaka's face and he said, "I remember."

"It came from a beast that lived in the time of the First People," Chayton explained.

"This was strong medicine for Tarca Sapa," Wiyaka stated.

"Let me look," Hoka said, standing alongside Wiyaka. While Wiyaka held onto the amulet, Hoka studied the tan–colored ivory.

"Where did you find it?" Wiyaka asked.

Chayton pointed at the ground where he was lying. "This is where Tarca Sapa told me it would be."

"Ah…Tarca Sapa told you where to find it?" Wiyaka challenged Chayton with doubt in his voice.

"*Ai,* – Yes," Chayton replied.

"He is dead, Chayton," Wiyaka responded. "Tarca Sapa is not going to tell you anything."

"He did."

"When did he tell you?" Wiyaka asked suspiciously.

"*Inhanblapi.* – Seeking a vision."

Wiyaka did not believe much that came out of the vision quests by hunters. *Without food…water, who knows what a human will see or hear?* If there was anyone in the Folsom People tribe that was a skeptic, it was Wiyaka. This time, however, Wiyaka actually believed Chayton. The *wanagi* – ghost of Tarca Sapa had once saved Wiyaka's life on the Arid Plains, so what Chayton just told him seemed reasonable. Wiyaka turned his head and looked around, expecting to see the *wanagi* of the old healer, Tarca Sapa, standing nearby. Wiyaka then turned to the other travelers and announced, "It appears Chayton found what he was seeking. We can now go home."

The other travelers grinned and laughed at knowing that they would soon escape this perilous land. Wiyaka looked around and noticed a rock outcrop to the west. "We will camp there, against those rocks," he told the other travelers.

"What about *igmu'gleška?* – great lion?" Hoka asked.

"The rocks will help keep us safe, but if *igmu'gleška* hunts us, there is little we can do," Wiyaka answered. After a short pause, Wiyaka smirked and said to Hoka, "Your father said Tarca Sapa is nearby to protect us."

Hoka could not tell if Wiyaka was serious or not. Hoka found little comfort in the ghost of a long–forgotten healer protecting them. The travelers would be camping across the river from a large pride of great lions. To protect them from the great lions, the travelers would need more than a ghost.

"Gather wood for a campfire," Wiyaka instructed. "Stay near when you hunt."

"What about Kohana?" Gad asked.

Wiyaka stared at Gad with a bewildered look. He was not sure what she meant.

"The warrior," Hogan clarified.

Wiyaka looked around and for the first time, he noticed that the warrior was missing.

"Where is he?" Wiyaka asked.

Gad began crying.

"*Igmu'gleška,*" Moki answered. She did not need to explain. Everyone understood what she meant. Moki reached down and held her weeping daughter.

"He is already the dung of that *igmu'gleška,*" Wiyaka declared. "There is nothing we can do for him…we can say a prayer, maybe…*Ai,* we will say a prayer…a long prayer."

"We must go bury him, Wiyaka," Hoka replied.

"Did you not hear me, Hoka? There is nothing left to bury," Wiyaka argued. "*Igmu'gleška* has chewed him to dust. They will spread him across the prairie."

Wiyaka's comment only increased the wailing from the small girl. Moki held Gad tight and comforted her, but it did not help.

"We must try to bury Kohana," Hogan jumped into the conversation.

"*Iyaya, hokshila! – Go, boy!*" Wiyaka blurted out. "We will be here if you come back."

"My father once told me you buried several warriors…several *hohe –* enemy who died on the prairie," Hoka said to Wiyaka.

"*Ai, –* Yes, but there was only one *kaga, –* demon," Wiyaka replied. "There are many *igmu'gleška –* great lion here."

Hoka turned to his son and said, "Hogan, if Wiyaka is afraid, I will go with you."

Wiyaka groaned and kicked the tall grass with his moccasin. Wiyaka knew he could not let them go by themselves and Hoka knew this, as well. "Let this warrior's bones lie," Wiyaka pleaded with them. "He will be dust soon enough. He is our enemy!"

"He is my friend," Gad announced through sobs.

"Ahh!" Wiyaka responded and then after thinking about it, he mumbled, "Moki and Gad, we need a campfire and greens gathered for food."

Wiyaka then turned to Hoka and Hogan and said, "Once *igmu'gleška* has had time to eat your friend, we will go bury what is left of him."

Then, Wiyaka knelt down alongside Chayton and whispered, "*Doe ksh kayo oun hey, le mita kola? –* How are you, my friend?"

"*Blue gxoe cha ah snee wa key yea, –* I am tired," Chayton mumbled.

"*Ai,*" Wiyaka said. "Now that you have the amulet, it is time to go home."

"*Ai,*" Chayton mumbled. "It is time to go home."

***

The sun was deep in the west when Wiyaka, Hoka, and Hogan swam the river. They had waited too long in the day to go bury the warrior Kohana. Wiyaka had stalled the others from going any earlier. He wanted to make sure that the great lions had eaten their fill before the travelers showed up. Now, they were racing with another demon, the demon of darkness. Hogan led the way to the spot where he had seen Kohana fall while Wiyaka and Hoka followed him with spears poised to throw. The trio reached the top of the hill where the great lion had attacked Kohana, but when they got there, they were not alone. The trio stopped in their tracks when they saw a great lion lying amongst the bones, eating scraps of flesh from the warrior. The great lion had already sensed the humans' arrival and was glaring at them.

"It sees us," Hogan whispered.

"*Ai,* − Yes," Hoka replied.

"What do we do?" Hogan murmured.

An answer to Hogan's question did not come from Hoka or Wiyaka. Neither of them knew what to do in such a situation. The trio stood at the top of the hill, too petrified to move and too terrified to run. The great lion stared at the humans with eyes the color of fire.

"Why does it not move?" Hogan asked.

Hogan never did get a response from Hoka or Wiyaka. They were too stunned to talk. Wiyaka finally found his tongue, but only muttered two words, "Spread out."

While keeping his eyes glued on the great lion, Wiyaka slowly shuffled to his left, his spear arm ready to throw. Hoka moved in the opposite direction from Wiyaka to encircle the great lion. Hogan remained standing in the same spot. The great lion watched the humans and demonstrated its displeasure by roaring loudly. The great lion attempted to stand up, but could not. Finally, the male lion gave up and settled back down. This was when Wiyaka noticed the spear shaft dangling from the shoulder of the great lion. *The warrior wounded this igmu'gleška!* As Wiyaka moved further to the left, he was able to see the damage caused by the spear. Dried blood caked the great lion's shoulder and leg.

"*Owa sicha!* − Bad wound!" Wiyaka yelled.

"What should we do?" Hoka asked.

With great effort, the great lion rose to its feet. Its maimed leg hung in the air, curled up under its belly.

"It cannot run!" Wiyaka informed the others. He glanced over his shoulder, ensuring no other great lions had decided to join this one.

"What should we do?" Hogan repeated his question, his voice an octave higher than normal.

"We back away from this *igmu'gleška* until we reach the river," Wiyaka said, "and then we swim for our lives!"

"We told Gad we would bury Kohana!" Hogan reminded Wiyaka.

"If we stay here, we will be burying more than a few bones from this warrior!" Wiyaka bellowed out.

"We told her!" Hogan insisted.

"Ahh!" Wiyaka bellowed out. He knew what he had to do.

Wiyaka resumed his circling of the great lion while Hoka and Hogan kept their spears aimed at the beast. The eyes of the great lion now followed Wiyaka's every move.

"*Kte, Hoka!* – Kill, Hoka!" Wiyaka instructed the hunter. "Hogan and I will be ready to throw if you miss or if it attacks you."

"You–you–you want me to throw?" Hoka stammered.

"*Ai,*" Wiyaka replied and then he peered over at Hogan and said, "Did you hear what I said, *hokshila*? Get ready!"

"*Ai,*" Hogan squeaked with the boldness of a field mouse.

The great lion took one painful step towards Wiyaka, roaring and exposing its massive canine teeth. "Are you ready?" Wiyaka asked both Hoka and Hogan.

"*Ai!* – Yes!" Hoka thundered.

"Do not miss!" Wiyaka bellowed.

"*Ai!*" Hoka yelled.

"*Hokshila,* are you ready?" Wiyaka bellowed when Hogan did not respond promptly.

"*Ai,* I am ready!" Hogan confirmed, the pitch of his voice wavering.

"I will keep *igmu'gleška* busy!" Wiyaka stated while continuing to move to the left. "*Wana, Hoka!* – Now, Hoka, while its side is towards you!"

Hoka's spear shook on his shoulder as nerves took control of his body. He decided where to aim and then took a step towards the beast, hurling the dangerous spear at it. The spear flew straight, but at the last moment, the great lion sensed it coming and fell backwards in an attempt to avoid it. The spear sped past the big cat. The great lion bounced up from its fall and even with its enormous pain, it attacked with vengeance. Before Wiyaka could react, the great lion had hobbled half way to him. Wiyaka jerked the spear off his shoulder and held it out defensively in front of him with both hands. Wiyaka thrust the spear in the direction of the wounded great lion, but even with its lack of mobility, the great lion was still a formidable predator.

"THROW!" Wiyaka screamed while poking his spear at the snapping jaws of the great lion.

Hoka was ready to launch another spear, but Wiyaka had gotten in the way. Hoka moved to his right to find a better shot while Hogan flung his first spear at the great lion. The spear flew true and the sharp fluted projectile point penetrated the upper rib cage of the beast. The great lion roared in pain, jumping straight up in the air and falling backwards. The big cat flopped over on its side, reaching with its claws in an attempt to extricate the spear from its side. Wiyaka advanced quickly while the great lion was thrashing around on the ground. Wiyaka poked and prodded the massive cat with his spear, but could not get close enough to do any damage.

"GET BACK!" Hogan screamed at Wiyaka who did not need further encouragement. Wiyaka took off running to get away from the gnashing jaws of the beast. Hogan launched a second spear. The spear struck the great lion in its underside, causing more damage. Before the big cat could react to its new attacker, Hoka's second spear struck the maimed great lion in the neck. The great lion flailed about in the dirt, roaring and making a frightful ruckus with jaws snapping and its one claw swiping at the air. It attempted to get up several times but only fell back down. It lay there taking in shallow breaths and bleeding freely from its wounds. Finally, the great lion laid its head on the ground and fell asleep, forever.

The trio stood clear, too frightened to move. They waited longer than necessary to ensure the beast was dead. No one wanted to discover it was still a wounded great lion. When Wiyaka was sure that the big cat was not going to rise from the dead, he began digging a grave with one of Kohana's discarded long bones. "We will bury them together." Wiyaka announced.

"*Taku?* – What?" Hoka asked. "Animal with human?"

"They were both warriors," Wiyaka replied. "We bury them together."

The trio worked until they had dug a grave deep enough for the bones of Kohana and the carcass of the massive great lion. Wiyaka cut off one of the legs from the great lion for food and then the trio pushed and pulled the gigantic beast to the grave. Sweating and out of breath, the trio finally shoved the great lion into the grave where it settled at the bottom with the bones of Kohana. They poured dirt into the grave and placed rocks on top. Wiyaka jammed the spear that Kohana had used to wound the great lion into the rocks of the grave, pointing the spear tip towards the sky. When the trio was done, they stood back and quickly recited a few prayers to *Wakan Tanka*. Then, Wiyaka looked to the west and saw that the sun was dropping below the horizon. "We must go. We are in danger," Wiyaka told the others. The trio hiked back to the river and then to the campsite.

***

Just as the sun disappeared from the land, a storm from the north blew in. Winds roared, stirring up the sand and dust from the prairie. The travelers huddled around the campfire, feeding the fire with enough wood to keep the flames as high as possible. Exhausted from their traumatic ordeal, the travelers eventually fell asleep until the shrouded light of a new day woke each of them up. After walking around the campsite, Hoka noticed that again one of the travelers was missing.

"Where is my father?" Hoka asked against the roar of a vicious wind.

"Maybe, he makes waste, I do not follow him around," Wiyaka replied. The travelers went about their routines, preparing for the journey back to the North Country. When the travelers were ready to go and Chayton still had not shown up, they spread out and searched the area around the campsite.

"CHAYTON!" Hoka screamed into the wind while Wiyaka hiked the area, looking for tracks on the windswept prairie. Wiyaka did not find any of Chayton's tracks or that of great lion. He was relieved when he did not find any blood trails leading from the camp.

"I see no sign of *igmu'gleška,* – great lion," Wiyaka informed the others when they reconvened around a dying campfire. "If *igmu'gleška* were here and got Chayton, we would have found tracks and blood."

"I am going to search for my father," Hoka said, gathering his weapons.

"I will go with you," Wiyaka replied. "Moki, stay near the campfire with the *cinca.* – children."

Moki nodded her head, but when Wiyaka turned around, he saw Hogan was gathering his weapons. "Where are you going, *hokshila?*" Wiyaka asked.

"I am going with you and my father," Hogan replied.

"*Hee ya,* – No, you are a *chincá,* – child," Wiyaka stated. "You stay here with Moki and the girl."

"I was not a *chincá* when you needed me to kill *igmu'gleška,*" Hogan blurted out.

"Hogan is right," Hoka said to Wiyaka. "He killed *igmu'gleška,* not you, not me."

"I still do not believe it," Wiyaka mumbled under his breath.

"He killed the beast," Hoka responded.

"He is my *thunkashila!* – grandfather!" Hogan stated. "I am going with you!"

"Hogan, stay with the woman and the girl in case *igmu'gleška* returns," Wiyaka said.

"We will be fine," Moki added. "I have my spears."

Wiyaka's face could not disguise his frustration with no one listening to him. "You do not listen!" he roared at Hogan. "You are just like Chayton! He is off somewhere and left me behind! I do not know why I follow him!"

"Hogan can come with me, Wiyaka," Hoka interjected.

"You watch out for him, not me!" Wiyaka declared and then mumbled under his breath, "That *hokshila* will become food for *igmu'gleška.*"

"Moki, remain at the campfire," Hoka told the woman. "*Igmu'gleška* will rest until nightfall and we will back by then."

"Hoppo! – Let us go!" Wiyaka thundered. "Do you expect to find Chayton around the campfire?"

Hoka restrained himself from saying anything further to the cantankerous old man.

"The first place we will check is north of our campsite," Wiyaka announced. "Your father may have started north without us."

As soon as the trio stepped out from behind the rock outcrop, a blast of northerly wind almost picked them up and carried them away. They spread out just far enough to cover more ground, but close enough to protect each other with a spear throw. Walking into the sand–filled wind, the trio shielded their eyes, which made the search even more difficult. They could barely see or remain standing, but they continued their search.

"Chayton has always been trouble for me," Wiyaka mumbled to the wind as he walked along, trying to remain standing up.

***

The trio found no sign of Chayton's whereabouts to the north. The wind continued to pepper them with sand and silt, making the search almost impossible. Unable to withstand the wind and sand any longer, the trio took refuge behind another large rock outcrop. While Hoka and Hogan rested and rinsed their eyes with water, Wiyaka sat staring out into the sandstorm, thinking about where his friend could have gone. *What sign has he left me?* Wiyaka thought and thought. Then, the answer finally came to him.

"I know where he is!" Wiyaka blurted out, not meaning to disclose this to Hoka and Hogan.

"Tuktel? – Where?" Hoka asked while standing up and walking over to Wiyaka.

"Hoka, listen to me," Wiyaka said as calmly as he could. "I will find your father, but I want you to take the woman and the children north."

"I am not a child!" Hogan reminded Wiyaka once again, but Wiyaka paid no attention to the boy.

"Where did my father go, Wiyaka?" Hoka repeated.

"Slol wa yea shnee, – I do not know," Wiyaka declared. "I only think I know. It is dangerous where I am going and I could be wrong. We do not need the woman and children roaming the Arid Plains with me."

"I am going with you, Wiyaka," Hoka insisted. "If my father is in danger, I must help."

"We cannot take the woman and children," Wiyaka pleaded to Hoka, shaking his head from side to side.

"Wiyaka, they cannot stay here...*igmu'gleška* – great lion is near," Hoka replied. "They must stay with us."

"Ah!" Wiyaka responded with a grimace. "This will be no place for a woman and child!"

"We will gather Moki and Gad," Hoka suggested to Wiyaka, "and then you will take us to my father."

***

With nothing to stop the wildfire, the winds pushed it deep onto the Arid Plains to the east, leaving scorched prairie in its wake. Satanta and the other three warriors hiked across the smoldering remains of the prairie. A strong wind on their backs pushed them south and now a river lay in front of them. Satanta stopped hiking to take a drink of warm water from his water pouch. He shielded his eyes and looked up into the dusty sky above the scorched prairie. He noticed several vultures navigating the winds in the sky above. Satanta laughed at the sight of the birds. "I am not ready for you, my friends," Satanta mumbled under his breath. He scanned the terrain with his eyes, searching for the source of the vulture's interest. He spotted several more vultures on the ground to the southwest. Satanta signaled the other warriors to follow him and then he hiked upwind, towards the feasting vultures.

As Satanta and the warriors neared the vultures, the birds screeched warnings and flapped their wings, unwilling to give up their feast. As the warriors drew nearer, the vultures relented and hopped across the prairie, feigning injury in a ploy to lure the warriors away from their newly found food. The ploy did not deter Satanta and the vultures eventually took to the air.

The war party looked around the site and noticed the blood stained grass. Satanta plucked a fragment of human bone from the ground. Blood stained the freshly crushed bone and Satanta noticed teeth marks on its gnawed end. Then, he spotted the pile of rocks and the new grave. He leaned over to inspect the spear jutting out of the top of the grave and immediately recognized the hand–carved spear shaft. The spear belonged to Kohana, the wounded warrior who Satanta abandoned on the trail. *What was Kohana doing here? Who killed him?* Satanta scanned the horizon in every direction, searching for a clue for what happened to the warrior.

"What did this?" Satanta asked while looking around at the carnage.

His frightened warriors had nothing to say.

"We continue south," Satanta stated. "The woman is near!"

Before Fala could protest, Satanta was trotting towards the river. The other two warriors peered over at Fala, hoping he would do something to end Satanta's madness. Fala stood there while he pondered what to do. He took a couple of steps towards the river and his feet suddenly stopped. Then, he changed his mind again and followed Satanta to the river. When Satanta arrived at the river, he waded into the shallow water and looked over his shoulder to check the whereabouts of his three warriors. He saw Fala and the other two warriors standing on the riverbank.

"Hurry!" Satanta roared. "The woman is near!"

Fala and the others did not move. Satanta waded back to the shoreline. "Follow me! Hurry! She is getting away!" he ordered the three warriors.

"No, Satanta," Fala replied. "This is finished."

"What?" Satanta demanded.

"Our journey is done, we are going home," Fala answered. "We will cross no more rivers for you and this woman."

Satanta climbed up the riverbank where Fala was standing. SMACK! Before, Fala could duck his head; Satanta's wooden spear thrower had smashed into Fala's face. Fala's head snapped back as his body fell backwards to the ground. Fala grabbed his injured jaw and held on to it. While holding his glare on the other two warriors, Satanta waited for Fala to climb back up on his feet. Fala finally staggered to his feet and stood teetering in front of Satanta, his chin bleeding from a long, jagged wound.

"We go!" Satanta exclaimed.

Fala moved his jaw muscles to make sure he could still talk and then he replied to Satanta, "We have followed you…but it stops here."

Fala turned around and began walking up the hillside, heading north. The other two warriors vacillated between following Fala to the north and remaining with Satanta. They finally made their decision and followed Fala.

"My father will reward you!" Satanta blurted out.

Fala slowed down and then stopped. Fala looked at the other two warriors to see what their reaction was and then he slowly ambled back towards Satanta.

"If you help me, my father will give you power," Satanta proclaimed to Fala. "More power than you will ever have."

"Why should I trust you?" Fala demanded, holding his jaw in his hand.

"I want the woman," Satanta replied. "If you help me find the woman, my father will reward you!"

"No woman is worth this," Fala declared.

"My father will reward you."

Fala turned around and gauged the reaction of the other two warriors to Satanta's proposal. Fala could tell the other warriors were going to leave the decision up to him. Fala thought about Satanta's offer and eventually made up his mind. "*Ai,* – Yes, we will help you for three suns," he replied to Satanta. "Then, we head north, with or without you, with or without the woman."

Satanta thought about thrusting his spear right through the midsection of Fala and ending the treacherous warrior's life. Satanta did not like ultimatums, especially from one as lowly as Fala, but he needed Fala for just a bit longer and then he would deal with his treachery. Satanta smiled at Fala and said, "If we are to search for only three suns, let us go."

Satanta turned around and waded into the water of the river, dog paddling once he reached the deeper water. Fala and the two warriors followed. Satanta climbed the opposite riverbank and began hiking south. His obsession to find Moki would never end.

***

She lay hidden, crouched in the tall, windswept grass. She spotted the humans in the distance and watched them walk right past her. She yawned, exposing her large yellowish–colored canine teeth. She rose to her feet, stretching her front legs and then her back legs. Then, she slowly ambled off in the direction of the humans.

Satanta and the other three warriors discovered the recent camp of the travelers. Satanta checked the ashes in the campfire and found them still warm. He smiled at his good fortune. The warriors investigated the campsite and found footprints from the woman Satanta sought and her child. The warriors unraveled the trail and soon pieced together the direction. Satanta signaled the other warriors to follow him and then took to the trail of his prey. Out of the corner of his eye, Satanta noticed an animal slinking through the tall grass to the east of the warriors. Satanta stopped to investigate, letting the other warriors catch up.

"What is wrong?" Fala asked, once standing alongside Satanta.

Satanta said nothing. He was too preoccupied with relocating what he had seen. Satanta eventually replied to Fala's question, "It was only the wind blowing the grass." Satanta turned and continued his march to the south.

She knew her prey had discovered her. She would wait. She had patience. A soft purr erupted from her throat as she watched her prey attempt to escape. When the prey left her sight, she let out a roar that carried on the wind.

Downwind from her, the roar brought another lioness to full alert. When the lioness caught a scent of humans floating on the breeze, she began stalking the prey.

On a small hill further south, Satanta stopped to look back again. He studied the terrain they had just traveled, seeking movement in the grass. At last, he saw. Satanta spotted the top of the beast's head, popping above the tall grass and then disappearing. The beast was stalking the warriors. Satanta's heart skipped a beat and adrenalin took over his body. Satanta now knew what had killed Kohana. Satanta and his warriors had become the hunted.

Fala noticed the fear in Satanta's eyes. "*Tóka he?* – What is wrong?" he asked.

"*Wayaka!* – Look!" Satanta replied.

"*Tuktel?* – Where?" Fala inquired. He looked and saw nothing.

Satanta did not reply. He looked around for a place to run or hide, but he knew he could never run fast enough. He was not an antelope. Satanta gripped his spear so tightly that his knuckles turned white. All of the warriors were now watching the waving grass, searching for what Satanta thought he saw. Satanta grabbed his spear in both hands and walked up behind Fala. He swung his arms backward and with all of his might, Satanta thrust the spear forward.

"AAWWWHHHH!" Fala screamed. "AAAAAAAHH"

Satanta twisted and turned the spear shaft, ripping open the back of Fala's knee with the sharp stone spear tip. Fala reached down and grabbed his wounded knee. He tried jumping out of the way, but fell to the ground. Fala lay on the ground, grabbing the back of his knee and whimpering like a child.

"Ahhhh," Fala moaned while rolling around on the ground in front of the other warriors. Fala tried to stand up, but the pain was too intense and he only had one good leg. The other two warriors stared in fright while Fala rolled around on the ground. The two warriors first looked at Satanta and then back to Fala. Finally, their eyes settled on Satanta.

"Leave him!" Satanta ordered the two warriors. "*Igmu'gleška* – Great lion is hunting us and now we have provided it with food!"

Satanta turned and walked south. The two warriors watched Fala writhing around on the ground, whimpering like a child. The two warriors took a wide berth around Fala, jogging to catch up to Satanta and leaving the wounded prey for the beasts.

The war party was now three.

Chapter Eighteen

High above the Arid Plains, the sun was shining and the high plains sky was deep blue. At the surface of the Arid Plains, a different situation existed. Day was night as gale–force winds filled the air with sand and silt. Wiyaka gripped Moki's hand tightly as he fought his way through the blinding sandstorm. His eyes streamed tears and his throat was raw from the gritty sand. While Wiyaka drug Moki along, she drug her daughter Gad along. Behind them, Hogan and Hoka followed, staying near enough not to lose them in the swirling sand.

Wiyaka continued to watch the sky, hoping to catch a glimpse of the sun and determine the direction they were walking. Wiyaka was hopelessly lost and knew they must find shelter to wait out the storm. Ahead of them, Wiyaka spotted a small ripple in the otherwise featureless prairie. With no other alternatives, he headed straight for it and luckily discovered a small arroyo. Wiyaka cautiously climbed down its nearly vertical embankment, helping Moki and Gad to ensure they did not fall. Once at the sandy bottom of the arroyo, Wiyaka collapsed on the ground dragging Moki and Gad with him. Wiyaka laid there in the sand, staring up at the raging sky while sand and silt rained down on them. His eye caught Hogan sliding down the embankment, head first, and crashing into the bottom of the arroyo. Wiyaka peered in the direction of the boy to make sure he was all right. When Wiyaka saw Hogan crawling towards him, he relaxed and closed his eyes, shielding them from the onslaught of sand. Hoka was the last to enter the arroyo. He methodically made his way down the embankment without incident.

Physically drained, the travelers laid there along the steep slopes of the arroyo and soon they were all asleep. The vicious winds streaked overhead while sand and silt rained down on top of them. Nothing could wake the travelers. When Wiyaka finally woke up, he shook the thick layer of sand off his clothes and then took a big gulp of water from his water pouch, swishing the water around in an attempt to wash the grit from his mouth and throat. The others eventually woke up and Wiyaka shared his water with them. Hoka then scooted over alongside Wiyaka and making sure that the others could not hear, he whispered into Wiyaka's ear, *"Tókiya la hwo, Wiyaka?* – Where are you going, Wiyaka?"

"Slol wa yea shnee, – I do not know," Wiyaka replied.

Hoka glared at the old man, not sure how to respond. They were wandering aimlessly around the Arid Plains and Wiyaka had no idea where they were going or where his father had gone.

"I know–I think I know where Chayton–your father is going," Wiyaka declared after reading the concern on Hoka's face.

"My father is not well," Hoka declared. "He could never cross the Arid Plains by himself. He did not come this way, Wiyaka. You are wrong!"

"Your father is strong, Hoka," Wiyaka responded. "I have seen him survive with little more than hope."

Hoka did not reply. He was not going to get into another argument with the temperamental old man. Wiyaka placed a reassuring hand on the shoulder of Hoka and said, "Go rest, Hoka, you must trust me."

***

The travelers remained in the arroyo until that evening when the gale–force winds finally subsided. Much of the sand eventually settled to the ground and by nightfall, a few stars peeked through the suspended dust above the Arid Plains. The travelers emerged from the arroyo and looked all around. Under the glowing light of a yellow–ringed moon, the travelers could see remarkably well across the prairie.

"Wayaka, hanhepi wi, – Look, night sun," Hoka said, pointing his finger at the strangely– colored moon, "What does this mean?"

"Wanagis, – Ghosts," Wiyaka replied in a voice barely above a whisper. *"Hoppo! –* Let us go!"

Hoka laughed to himself. He had known Wiyaka for a long time and whenever Wiyaka did not understand something, he always blamed it on ghosts. "How do we know which direction we are traveling?" Hoka challenged Wiyaka. "Everything looks the same."

"We walk opposite the star of the north," Wiyaka responded.

"Slol wa yea shnee, – I do not know," Hoka said with doubt.

"You will have to trust me, Hoka," Wiyaka replied, turning and pointing his spear tip at the North Star, "or you and the others follow that star back to the North Country."

Wiyaka stared at Hoka, waiting for the young hunter's response. When Hoka did not reply, Wiyaka knew that Hoka understood his message. "I am going there," Wiyaka informed Hoka while jabbing his spear tip in the opposite direction of the North Star. The old man then walked away.

"Where are we going?" Hogan asked his father.

Hoka had to think about the answer to that question. He was not sure. Should they follow this crazy old hunter and his whim or head back to the North Country in hopes that Chayton was heading there? Hoka looked up at the North Star and then back towards Wiyaka. The old man was already disappearing into the endless sea of sand and sage. If Hoka wanted to follow Wiyaka, he needed to decide.

"*Hoppo!* – Let us go!" Hoka told the others.

***

Chayton woke up disoriented, his fever and hallucinations much worse. His ears buzzed from a high fever and each time he took a step, he became dizzy and almost fell over. The ravaging fever had eaten away most of Chayton's judgment. He was confused and lost. He was not even sure if it was morning or evening. Chayton glanced around and the prairie looked the same in every direction. There was sagebrush, sand, and then more sagebrush and sand. He reached down and touched the outside bladder of his water pouch. His water was almost gone. Chayton sat down on his haunches and looking up at the sky, weeping and praying to *Wakan Tanka*.

A harsh cawing from a crow brought Chayton out of prayer. He peered across the desolate prairie and watched a single crow hopping around on the ground in front of him. "What are you doing here?" Chayton mumbled to the bird.

The crow showed no fear of the old man. Delirious from fever, Chayton just sat there and watched the crow hopping around and staring at him. Then, two more crows landed on the ground and they started their dance in front of Chayton, hopping and strutting around. Then, more crows arrived, landing on the ground and perching on the tops of sagebrush. Now, everywhere Chayton looked, there were crows. The ground was black with crows. Soon after all of the crows had arrived, they took off in flight, landing in the distance. Chayton watched as even more crows joined the original crows. Before long, the alkali soil of the prairie was black with crows.

Chayton could no longer ignore the taunts and jeers from the murder of crows. Aided by his walking staff, Chayton pulled himself to his feet, setting off another loud explosion of cackling from the birds. Chayton plodded forward in the direction of the crows, taking a step at a time. Chayton eventually reached the black shoreline in a sea of birds, only to have the murder of crows take off and land on a distant hill. The ritual continued with Chayton following the feathered creatures across the prairie. As the veiled sun disappeared below a red horizon, Chayton finally caught the murder of crows and found them washing their feathers in a small desert pond. Chayton collapsed along the shore of the pond, submerging his feverish head into the cool water. After drinking his fill, Chayton looked up and within arm's reach was a crow, perched on a small rock and staring at him. The bird bobbed its head at Chayton in one direction and then another. "*Kangi* – Crow, you would make a good meal," Chayton mumbled to the bird.

The crow cawed and fluffed its feathers. It seemed to have understood what Chayton said and immediately flew away, leaving Chayton lying at the edge of the pond alone. Chayton managed to scrounge up some fuel for a small campfire and ate the last bit of rabbit he had with him. He was not hungry, but he knew he must eat. His fever still raged and his body went from freezing to burning up and then back to freezing. Chayton lay down next to the campfire and coughed repeatedly until his mind entered a dream–filled sleep. The crows continued their clatter until well after dark and then as suddenly as they had appeared, they disappeared.

***

Chayton woke up to a sun that was already well above the eastern horizon. He looked around, trying to remember where he was and how he got there. His campfire was a pile of cold ashes. He listened, but he heard nothing but the wind making its way across the prairie. He thought he remembered something about birds or crows, but he could not be sure. He grabbed his walking staff and hoisted himself up onto his feet. He stood there, hanging on to his walking staff and fighting his dizziness. By the time his dizziness passed, the coughing began. After the coughing stopped, Chayton focused on determining where he was. The terrain was flat with no landmarks, whatsoever. Finally, he decided to keep walking with the morning sun on the left side of his face. Chayton picked up his gear and continued his journey. The crows had helped him get this far, now he would have to make it on his own.

***

By midday, the winds were blowing hard across the prairie, creating massive clouds of sand and silt. The skies overhead turned black and visibility was low. Chayton made little progress as he meandered back and forth across the prairie. He stopped to rest and plopped down in the middle of the prairie. He raised his water pouch to his dusty lips and drained the last few drops of water. Between bouts of coughing and dizziness, he had been stopping to rest far too often. After struggling to get to his feet, Chayton stumbled forward, slowly marching across the prairie. Then, in the haze,

Chayton spotted a group of humans walking parallel to him on his right. He waved his walking staff to draw their attention and they eventually spotted him. Chayton had no more strength left to walk so he plopped down on the ground and waited. When the humans arrived, Chayton noticed that animal hides covered their faces.

With the help of his walking staff, Chayton hoisted himself up to his feet and waved his arm in a sign of friendship to the people. *"Was'te! –* Greetings!" Chayton yelled into the wind.

The leader of the humans pulled the animal hide mask from his face, and for a moment, Chayton thought he was looking at himself, thirty or more winters earlier. The leader was tall and his long, black hair blew across his face in the fierce wind. The leader studied Chayton, but never responded to Chayton's greeting. Chayton greeted the humans again, but the leader only returned a puzzled look. Finally, the leader spoke, but Chayton did not understand a single word. Chayton greeted the leader and the humans for a third time, but they just stood there, staring at him.

The leader then turned and spoke to his people. Two young boys came running. The first boy handed Chayton a full water pouch while the second boy held out a small rabbit hide. Chayton took the water pouch and bowed to the young boy. Chayton lifted the pouch and took a long drink of cool water. He then handed the water pouch back to the young boy and smiled. Then with another nod of his head, Chayton accepted the rabbit hide from the second boy. Chayton saw that the rabbit hide was covering something. Chayton slowly pulled the edges of the rabbit hide back and found dried pemmican to eat. Chayton smiled and thanked everyone with a loud laugh.

Chayton was in a predicament. He had nothing to give these humans in exchange for their gifts of food and water. He opened his satchel, dumping out the sand and silt that had accumulated in its bottom. In the corner of his satchel, Chayton located his last remaining fluted spear point made from the red and gray *inyan wakan* – sacred rock of the canyon. Chayton looked down at the beautiful spear point. He did not want to give it up. The spear point was his last possession from the canyon where he was born. He would have to find something else to give them. He started to put the spear point back into the satchel, but then changed his mind. He reluctantly handed it to the leader. The leader plucked the spear point from Chayton's fingers, immediately inspecting it with his eyes. The leader knew this type of rock. He knew the power that this rock and spear point possessed. He smiled at receiving such a wonderful gift for only food and water.

The leader turned and held the spear point high in the air, showing everyone in his small tribe. The humans instantly moved closer to have a better look. They jabbered and talked about that fluted spear point in their strange tongue. One after another, they began pointing their fingers to the south. They were trying to tell Chayton something about his gift, but Chayton did not understand. The leader turned to Chayton and held out the spear point, attempting to give it back, but Chayton held up his hands in protest. The leader touched the fluted spear point with his index finger and then pointed to the south. He said something to Chayton, but Chayton still could not understand. The leader rubbed the spear point between his thumb and index finger and pointed to the south, once again. Chayton looked towards the south just as the dust briefly settled on the surface of the prairie. For the first time, Chayton caught a glimpse of the sandstone bluffs to the south.

"Big Creek," Chayton mumbled. The leader laughed when he saw that Chayton finally knew where he was.

The leader started hiking to the south and the tribe followed. Urged along by two giggling boys, Chayton followed the humans. The leader turned around to ensure Chayton was following. He smiled when he saw the two boys pushing and shoving Chayton along the trail. The leader then covered his face with the animal hide mask and marched towards the headwaters of Big Creek.

***

Wiyaka and Hoka reached the top of a windy knoll and looked out across the vast prairie. In every direction, they saw sagebrush and blowing sand. Hoka again challenged Wiyaka. "*Tókiya la hwo, Wiyaka?* – Where are you going, Wiyaka?" Hoka yelled into the wind.

"*Itokaga, – South,*" Wiyaka replied.

"What is in the south?" Hoka demanded.

"Your father is in the south," Wiyaka answered.

"How do you know?" Hoka challenged.

"*Slol wa yea shnee, –* I do not know," Wiyaka responded. "I believe he is there."

"How do you know?" Hoka repeated his question, hoping for a different answer.

Wiyaka knew there was no simple answer to this question, but that he owed Hoka an explanation. "Your father is my *sunka, –* brother," Wiyaka yelled into the wind. "When my *sunka* feels pain, I feel pain…your father is in pain…I am in pain…I know where my *sunka* is heading."

Hoka decided not to argue the point. He knew that Wiyaka was the only one who had any chance of finding his father.

"Where is your son?" Wiyaka asked, looking around and not seeing the boy.

"He is hunting!" Hoka stated.

"In this wind?"

"*Ai!*"

"That is stupid!" Wiyaka declared. "He will get lost and then we will be searching for him and your father!"

Hoka realized his mistake, but before he could do anything about it, Wiyaka bellowed out, "Find him and keep him near us!"

***

As the tribe marched south, Chayton watched the bluffs grow nearer. As he ambled across the terrain, the humans took care of him with food and water. By the end of the day, the tribe reached the bluffs and camped near the natural spring at the head of Big Creek. Chayton tried to orient himself to his surroundings. It had been a lifetime since he had been at the headwaters of Big Creek. He looked to the south and saw the creek disappearing into the canyon, just as he had remembered it. As dusk set in, he climbed up a small hill at the edge of camp and in the fading light, he located the pile of rocks that marked the grave of one of the bravest hunters Chayton had ever known, a hunter called Pahin. Chayton got down on all fours and started pulling the tall grass and weeds away from the pile of rocks. When he came across a stray rock, he picked it up and threw it back on top of the grave. Darkness set in, but Chayton did not quit. When he finally looked up from his task, he noticed that the entire tribe was helping him clean up the grave.

The leader came up behind Chayton and gently touched Chayton's shoulder, startling the old man. Chayton jerked his body around and then realized the hand belonged to the young leader. He breathed a sigh of relief and then said to the leader, "Pahin saved my life."

Chayton knew the leader did not understand his words, but he repeated what he said, "Pahin saved my life…a life of happiness…and hardship."

Even in the darkness, Chayton could tell that even though they spoke different languages, the leader understood. Chayton moseyed back down the hill and sat down by one of the campfires. The people brought him more food and water. After eating, the exhausted old man fell into a deep slumber, filled with dreams about his life.

***

At first light, the humans were already up and doing chores around the camp. Unable to sleep with the sound of this early activity, Chayton decided to get up. With assistance from his walking staff, Chayton stood up and then stretched his arms. Then, all of a sudden, his coughing returned. He leaned over and repeatedly coughed in the direction of the ground. He coughed so violently that his throat burned and his eyes watered. Finally, he was able to stop, but the coughing had taken its toll. Chayton stood there, wobbling back and forth, clinging onto his walking staff so he would not fall over. He was too dizzy to take a step. He squeezed his eyes shut to let the dizziness pass, but it only made matters worse. When he reopened his eyes, a small boy with food and water stood in front of him. Chayton forced a smile and then gathering what little strength he had left, Chayton released the walking staff and grabbed the water pouch. He hoisted the water pouch to his lips and drank deeply. He then took the food and thanked the boy. However, he could not eat it. When Chayton was finally able to depart, the leader turned and led the small tribe towards Chayton's birthplace.

As Chayton limped along, he looked around at the land where he was born. The landscape had changed dramatically since he had left the canyon as a young hunter. At that time, the drought had dried up the creek and the vegetation was brown and dead. As Chayton ambled along the trail, his thoughts returned to the past. He thought about Tonkala and Tarca Sapa. He reflected on the unfortunate deaths of his own father and mother. He remembered the wolves that took Pahin's life and the young hunter Mato who died near the lair of a mountain lion.

At the upper end of the canyon, the leader stopped to let the tribe rest while filling their water pouches from the nearby creek. Chayton plopped down on the nearest rock he could find. The leader came up and stood next to Chayton. *"Tiyatani!* – Home!" Chayton announced with a smile. *"Ehanni!* – Long ago!"

The leader smiled at Chayton, a gesture of kindness more than understanding. The leader then shouted to his people and everyone rose to their feet. The people waited for their leader to take them into the canyon. Chayton followed the others, smiling at the two boys who walked on either side of him. They walked all afternoon with Chayton observing everything around him. It had changed so much that he hardly recognized the land. The grass was green and the trees were full of leaves. They walked around a bend in the creek and Chayton saw something he remembered as if he saw it yesterday.

"Wagichun Wagi!" Chayton bellowed loud enough for everyone to hear. The leader stopped and when he did, all the people stopped. Chayton kept walking towards the sacred cottonwood tree called *Wagichun Wagi*. The old tree stood high above the ground, but there was nothing left of it but a skeleton of broken branches and rotting wood. The sacred tree had lived out its life. Chayton stared up at the sacred tree and a feeling of melancholy came over him. Memories floated through his mind as he reflected on his own mortality.

"Te! – Dead!" Chayton cried out. *"Te!"*

Chayton was distraught. The sacred tree of the Folsom People was dead. Chayton was too heartbroken to look up at the sacred tree. Instead, he let his eyes drift towards the ground in front of him. *What does this mean for the tribe? What does this mean for me?* He thought. A small boy ran up to Chayton and stepped in front of him, blocking Chayton's view of the ground. The boy reached out and tugged on Chayton's hand, pulling him along. The boy led Chayton around to the backside of *Wagichun Wagi*. When they reached the other side of the tree, the small boy pointed up. Chayton's eyes followed the boy's finger and saw that a new cottonwood sapling was sprouting up alongside the weathered trunk of the dead sacred tree. Chayton began to cry. He realized that *Wagichun Wagi* and the Folsom People shared this same circle of life.

The tribe patiently watched as Chayton walked around the tree. Chayton then strolled across the area, finally locating another pile of rocks marking the grave of Mato, a young hunter killed by a mountain lion. Chayton bent down and began gathering rocks that had strayed from the grave. A few of the tribe members came to help Chayton gather rocks while the rest pulled the tall weeds surrounding the grave. Once the grave was clean, Chayton knelt down and prayed to Mato, asking the ghost of the young hunter for forgiveness. Chayton's mind revisited his life again. He attempted to understand why *Wakan Tanka* had blessed him with a full life while cutting Mato's life short. By the time Chayton finished praying and meditating, the sun was behind the canyon walls to the west and the tribe was preparing a camp. Chayton left the grave and hobbled over to where the tribe was camping along the creek. The leader of the tribe walked up to Chayton and with a kind smile, he said, *"Natan uskay!"*

The leader spoke in the language of the Folsom People, but Chayton was unsure of the meaning of the message. *"Taku?* – What?" he questioned the leader.

"Natan uskay!" the leader repeated and then after a long pause, he repeated the warning for a third time, *"Natan uskay!* – The attackers are coming!"

The leader placed a hand on Chayton's shoulder and gently squeezed. He then let go and walked away, leaving Chayton alone to unravel this mysterious message.

During the night, Chayton's fever returned and his coughing had never been worse. His dreams were wild and unpredictable, filled with images of hostile Mountain People and catastrophic storms. When Chayton finally woke up next to the campfire, he was all alone. The leader and his tribe were gone. Spread out on the ground in front of Chayton was a deer hide. On top of the deer hide were offerings of food and water. Chayton shuffled around the campsite and found no evidence that anyone except him had ever been there. He limped down to the pond along the creek, the same place he had watched the tribe draw water, but Chayton found only his footprints. *Was I dreaming?* He turned around to confirm that *Wagichun Wagi* was still there and it was. Then, he remembered the warning from the young leader, *"Natan uskay!"*

Chapter Nineteen

He heard a sound. He watched and listened. There it was again, coming from somewhere in the shadows of the canyon. He scrunched his eyes to see better into the darkness of the canyon walls. Then he saw it, a momentary flicker of movement between two trees. He crept down the rocky slope of the canyon, listening and watching as he went. Thickets of willow trees filled the narrow canyon floor. He located a large rock near the animal trail and hid behind it. He held his breath and listened. His ears pounded from the blood coursing through his head while his heart beat loudly in his chest. Then, he heard what he knew was coming, the clear and rhythmic sound of footsteps. He peeked out from behind the boulder and saw the patches of animal hide flickering through the trees. He remained hidden until the sound was alongside the boulder and then he reached out and yanked the human to the ground. He jumped on top of the human, pinning the human's arms to the ground with his knees. He raised his knife and was ready to plunge it downward into the human's heart when he realized it was his grandson.

"What are you doing here?" Chayton demanded, taking his knees off Hogan's thin arms.

Hogan glared up at his grandfather with terrified eyes.

"Hogan, what are you doing here?" Chayton repeated, shaking the boy's shoulders with his hands.

"Se–se–searching for you, *thunkashila!* – grandfather!" Hogan stammered.

"Where are the others?" Chayton demanded.

Hogan did not respond quickly enough for Chayton so he shook the boy and repeated, "Where are the others?"

"Behind me," Hogan replied.

"*Natan uskay!* – Attackers are coming!" Chayton exclaimed.

"*Taku? Tuktel?* – What? Where?" Hogan questioned.

Chayton's mind raced to come up with a plan. "Go to the other side of the canyon and stay hidden!" he instructed Hogan. "Let your father and the others walk right past us!"

"Let them walk right past us?" Hogan questioned.

"*Ai!*" Chayton blurted out and then added, "When the enemy follows them, you kill the enemy."

"Kill them?"

"Kill them all."

Chayton struggled to stand up. Then, he grabbed Hogan by the front of his hide shirt and hauled him to his feet. "*Iyaya!* – Go!" Chayton said, shoving his grandson towards the other side of the canyon.

Hogan wandered across the canyon floor, stopping once or twice to look back at his grandfather. Waving his arms, Chayton urged the boy to hurry up and take cover. Finally, Hogan located a spot to hide in the brush and knelt down, facing up the canyon.

***

Wiyaka led the way down the canyon as the travelers walked single file through the grove of trees. He needed no tracks or trail to show him where he was going or where he would find Chayton. He knew exactly where Chayton would be and they were almost there. Wiyaka was excited to reunite with his old friend and he picked up the pace. Wiyaka walked around the bend in the canyon and spotted *Wagichun Wagi* ahead. When Wiyaka reached the sacred tree, he looked to his right and spotted a smoldering campfire. He smiled and breathed a sigh of relief. Wiyaka had guessed where Chayton would be and he was right.

***

Hogan watched the humans walking through the grove of trees, heading straight towards him. His chest tightened, he could not breathe. His stomach was queasy, fluttering with anxiety and fear. *How many? What should I do?* Hogan felt sick, but he swallowed hard to keep his stomach contents down. With hands shaking, he placed a spear on his shoulder. He never imagined he would have to kill another human, but that was what his grandfather told him to do. He waited for the humans to appear out of the trees.

The lead warrior stepped out of the grove of trees and immediately spotted the boy aiming a spear at him. The warrior stopped in his tracks and waited for Hogan to make the first move. Hogan froze, too terrified to move. Hogan's delay was all the the warrior needed. By the time Hogan could react, the warrior was sprinting towards the boy. The warrior's momentum carried him into Hogan, slamming the boy into the ground. Before Hogan could do anything, the warrior was sitting on his chest, pinning the boy's arms to the ground with his knees.

Hogan gasped for breath. The nasty fall and the weight of the warrior on his chest were too much. He could not find air to breathe and he was suffocating. The warrior peered down at the trapped boy and smiled, knowing what was in store for the boy once Satanta showed up. Chayton wound up his walking staff and swung hard. The walking staff made a wide loop around Chayton's body, gaining speed as it traveled. WHAP! The heavy wood of the walking staff smashed into the back of the warrior's head. The warrior's body trembled for a moment and then crashed face first on top of Hogan. Chayton pushed the warrior off Hogan.

"*Inahni!* – Hurry!" Chayton urged Hogan. "*Natan uskay!* – The attackers are coming!"

Hogan crawled across the ground, still wheezing and huffing. He finally found his wobbly legs and managed to stand up. Hogan's eyes searched the ground for his lost spear at the same time an airborne spear whizzed past Chayton. The spear struck Hogan in the shoulder, slicing through his shoulder muscle. The impact spun Hogan around as he screamed out in pain and fell to the ground. His high–pitched scream echoed through the canyon.

"Hogan!" Hoka thundered when he heard his son's scream. Hoka took off sprinting up the canyon in the direction of the scream, but Moki was already ahead of him. Wiyaka looked around and saw that they had left him behind with the small girl Gad.

"Ah!" Wiyaka bellowed with disappointment. Then, he turned to Gad and said, "Stay close, *chincá!* – child!" Wiyaka grabbed his spear and slowly began creeping up the canyon in the direction that Moki and Hoka had run.

Before Chayton could turn around, a second warrior crashed into him, knocking both of them to the ground. The warrior jumped up and peered down at the old man. Chayton tried to move, but he could not. Every muscle and joint in his body screamed in agony. The warrior pulled a stone knife from its scabbard and leaned over to finish Chayton off. Hogan regained his feet and saw his grandfather lying on the ground. Hogan ran straight at the warrior and plowed into him, knocking them both to the ground. Pain shot through Hogan's shoulder as he lay there, trying to catch his breath. Woozy from the collision with the boy, the warrior struggled to his feet just as Chayton got up to one knee. The warrior kicked Chayton in the face, knocking the old man back down on the ground. Chayton attempted to crawl away, but the warrior kicked him in the ribs, knocking Chayton over onto his back. Hogan jumped up and ran into the warrior again, but this time the boy just bounced off the much larger warrior. Hogan swung at the warrior with his one good arm, but the warrior easily ducked it. The warrior backhanded Hogan and the boy flew through the air, landing on the ground again. This time, Hogan did not get back up.

Satanta, hiding in the protection of the trees, walked out into the small clearing and stood near the second warrior. He peered down at the conquered old man and boy.

"Where is the woman?" Satanta demanded.

"There is no woman here," Chayton replied. The warrior sidled up alongside of Chayton and kicked him in the ribs again. Chayton grunted with pain, but said no more.

"Where is the woman, old man?" Satanta repeated, pulling his own stone knife from its scabbard.

"I am here!" Moki cried out from the other side of the clearing.

Satanta's head spun around in the direction of the voice he longed for. A smile came to his face when he spotted the woman he sought. "I found you!" he yelled back to Moki.

"And I found you!" Moki screamed as she hurled a spear in the direction of Satanta. The weakly thrown spear wobbled through the air, barely making it as far as Satanta.

"Ha! Ha! Ha!" Satanta laughed. "That is no way to treat your husband!"

"I would rather die than to be your wife!"

"You are lucky to be alive with an old man and a boy protecting you," Satanta mocked Chayton and Hogan.

"I am no boy!" Hoka bellowed from the edge of the clearing. "What can you do to me?"

Satanta turned his attention to Hogan's father on the other side of the clearing. Satanta smiled and then replied, "We will hang you from the same tree as this old man and boy."

Hoka dropped his spear and spear thrower on the ground. Then, he threw down his satchel and quiver. He jerked the hide strip holding the stone knife around his neck and ripped it in half. Knife in hand, Hoka marched towards Satanta. The second warrior looked over at Satanta, who nodded his head, acknowledging what he wanted the warrior to do. Poised with his own knife in his hand, the warrior walked towards Hoka.

Then, out of the trees flew Wiyaka. He jumped on to the back of the second warrior. The warrior stumbled to his right and then spun his body around in circles, trying to rid himself of the pest on his back. Wiyaka held onto the warrior's neck for dear life while Chayton crawled across the ground and grabbed the warrior's ankles, desperately hanging on while the warrior kicked and screamed. With a running start, Hogan plowed into the second warrior, knocking everyone to the ground. The two old men and the boy

210

wrestled with the second warrior, barely able to subdue him. Hoka marched right past the fracas on his way to challenge Satanta.

When Hoka reached Santana, he circled the warrior, his knife slicing the air in front of him as he feigned an attack. Satanta did not reach for his stone knife, but instead extended his spear out in front of him, poking and jabbing the sharp spear point at Hoka. Hoka slowly circled Satanta, sparring with the spear while attempting to find an opening in Santana's defense.

"*Até!* – Father!" Hogan yelled, still lying on top of the warrior with the two old men.

"Stay back!" Hoka yelled while circling the warrior to the right. Hoka jabbed his knife at the warrior while Satanta thrust his spear at the hunter. Moki nocked another spear onto her spear thrower and put the spear up on her shoulder. She slowly moved to her right, trying to get a clear shot at Satanta. Hoka lunged at Satanta with his knife while the warrior countered with his own thrust of his spear. The sharp stone tip of the spear grazed Hoka's right bicep, opening up a deep wound. Hoka stepped back as pain shot up his arm and shoulder. Blood filled the wound cavity quickly and began dripping onto the ground. Hoka shifted his knife from his right to his left hand and then continued to circle the warrior. Satanta smiled, knowing the hunter would soon be defeated.

Hoka took a step backwards when the sharp stone tip of Satanta's spear grazed his chest. Satanta laughed. He knew that the hunter's life belonged to him. Moki continued to circle the fight, searching for an open shot. For a split moment, she had one, but she hesitated too long. Satanta again closed the gap between him and Hoka. Blood flowed from Hoka's wounded arm as he desperately fought for his life.

"*Até!* – Father!" Hogan hollered while the second warrior continued to squirm his way out from underneath the two old men and the wounded boy.

Hoka was now in full retreat as he backed up across the clearing. Then, Satanta, tired of the game, stopped and nocked the spear onto his spear thrower. He watched Hoka and placed the spear on his shoulder. Hoka looked for a place to run, but there was nowhere to hide on the clearing. Satanta took aim and began his wind up just as another spear point whizzed past him, severing Satanta's windpipe. Satanta instantly fell to his knees and grabbed his throat, trying to breathe and stop the flow of blood from the deadly wound. His eyes looked in the direction where the spear had come. He saw the woman he loved.

"That was for my husband!" Moki hollered. "That was for Paco!"

211

Satanta pressed his hands against his throat in a futile attempt to breathe and stop the massive flow of blood. His look of surprise turned to fear as his face drained of color. His life ended as his body slumped forward on the green grass of the canyon.

No one said anything. After watching Satanta die, the second warrior quit struggling. He understood his fate. Moki ran over to Hoka to help him bind his wound while Gad ran over to Hogan to help him with his wound. Wiyaka finally released his grip from around the neck of the second warrior. The warrior lay on the ground, not moving a muscle. Wiyaka reached over and grabbed the warrior's shirt collar, saying, "*Wakan Tanka* has blessed you."

The warrior did not understand the meaning of the message. He waited for his pending death.

Wiyaka pointed at the first warrior, only now waking up from the collision with a walking staff. "*Iyaya!* – Go!" Wiyaka exclaimed to the second warrior. "Take that one with you."

The second warrior still did not understand.

"*Iyaya,* – Go, before I change my mind!" Wiyaka bellowed.

The second warrior untangled his legs from the grasp of Chayton. Wiyaka glared at the warrior and warned him one last time, "*Iyaya!* – Go!"

The second warrior needed no further encouragement. He ran over and collected the first warrior and both of them escaped the clearing, leaving their weapons behind. Wiyaka looked down and saw that Chayton was not moving.

***

Chayton waded across the wide and shallow river. Each step took enormous effort as he slogged through the knee–deep water. Chayton thought he would never reach the other side of the river, but he did, only to find a forest so thick that it would not allow him to leave the water. Chayton plodded through the water downriver, hoping to find a way into the thick forest, but eventually he gave up. He turned around and toiled his way back upriver. When Chayton was about to give up, he spotted what appeared to be a narrow, well–hidden trail leading into the shadows of the trees. He clamored ashore and entered the secluded trail on the edge of the dark pine forest. Before entering the blackness of the forest, Chayton turned around one last time and peered out across the translucent water of the river. A fire–enflamed sun was rising above the river, casting its brilliant light across the water. Chayton stared into the dazzling redness of the sun, his eyes unable to turn away. *Wasaya! I am on the right trail.* The rays of the sun reflected off the rippled surface of the water, creating sparkles of glimmering light that danced on the foliage of the pine trees. Chayton had never seen anything quite so beautiful.

Chayton pondered what to do. Shall he walk towards the red sun and river or follow the trail into the blackest of forests? Finally, Chayton turned his back on the red sun and ambled up the shadowy trail into the sunless forest. The narrow trail wound its way through the pine trees and after a great distance, Chayton emerged onto a large clearing, filled with the greenest of grass and brightest of wildflowers. Chayton turned his gaze upward towards the sky and watched as the ascending sun cast its colors across both sky and land. Chayton gazed up the trail and caught sight of another human, standing on the path in the middle of the clearing. Chayton cautiously walked towards the human, contemplating who else could possibly be in this strange new land. When Chayton arrived, he saw that the human was a man with long dark hair. The man was clothed in a beautiful robe made from the hide of a bison. Chayton studied the man's features and was sure that he had met this man before, but he could not remember where.

"*Was'te, Chayton,* – Greetings, Chayton," the man said, knowing who Chayton was.

Chayton peered over at the man while his memory dealt with remembering who it was. "*Was'te,*" Chayton replied after a long pause. Then, after an even longer pause, Chayton asked, "*Nituwe he?* – Who are you?"

"Ha! Ha! Ha! Ha!" the man laughed so loud that it actually frightened Chayton. When the man finally stopped laughing, he stood there and glared at Chayton, but he never answered Chayton's question.

"*Nituwe he?* – Who are you?" Chayton repeated.

"You know who I am," the man replied.

"*Slol wa yea shnee.* – I do not know."

"My heart is heavy if you do not remember me."

Chayton studied the features on the man's face, but he still did not recognize him. "*Slol wa yea shnee,* – I do not know," Chayton finally confessed.

The man said nothing. The two men stood there studying each other for the longest time, neither of them wanting to be the first to break the silence.

"You are young," Chayton eventually observed.

"*Wayaka!* – Look!" the man pointed a long finger at Chayton's hands. "You are young!"

Chayton looked down at what he last remembered were gnarled and

213

scarred fingers, the hands of an old hunter. What Chayton saw were the hands of a young man. He reached up with his other hand and felt the muscular forearm and bicep on his other arm.

"Where am I?" Chayton asked.

"Where is my amulet?" the man inquired, not answering Chayton's question.

"*Taku?* – What?"

"My amulet!" the man roared when he saw it. "There it is, around your neck."

Chayton reached up and touched the amulet hanging from his neck. Still perplexed by the encounter, Chayton continued to study this stranger's face.

"Ha! Ha! Ha!" the man laughed when he noticed how bewildered Chayton appeared. "You still do not remember me, do you?" the man inquired.

"*Hee ya!* – No!"

"*Micaje Tarca Sapa.* – My name is Tarca Sapa!"

"*Tarca Sapa te.* – Tarca Sapa is dead."

"*Ai,* – Yes."

"Why are you here?" Chayton asked. "Where are we?"

"This is my home."

Chayton looked around. It was a beautiful place with a strange–colored sky and beautiful flowers.

"How did you find me...uh...how did I find you?" Chayton asked.

"I have been waiting for you," Tarca Sapa replied.

"You knew I would be here?"

"*Ai,*" Tarca Sapa answered and then added, "Others are waiting for you."

"Others?"

"*Ai.*"

"Where am I?" Chayton asked loudly.

"*KEY KTO YO!* – WAKE UP!" Wiyaka screamed, shaking Chayton's shoulders violently.

Chayton's eyes fluttered open.

"*Key kto yo!* – Wake up!" Wiyaka exclaimed, continuing to shake Chayton until he was sure he was awake. "You were dreaming!"

"Where am I?" Chayton muttered.

"You are here with me at *Wagichun Wagi*," Wiyaka replied. "You were dreaming, *le mita kola.*"

Chayton's eyes darted around and he saw all of the other travelers kneeling alongside him. Wiyaka and Hoka were near Chayton's head and

Hogan was kneeling alongside Moki and Gad. Chayton looked around and everyone was crying, but now that he was awake, they all began laughing through their tears.

"*Haw, até,* – Hello, father," Hoka proclaimed.

Chayton looked towards the voice and saw his son Hoka with tears streaming down his face. Chayton reached up and gently touched Hoka's cheek. Chayton began weeping when he realized he was back with his family. "*Lotancila, Hoka,* – I love you, Hoka," Chayton proclaimed, his gravelly voice barely above a whisper.

"*Lotancila, até,* – I love you, father," Hoka replied.

"*Haw, thunkashila,* – Hello, grandfather," Hogan said.

"*Haw, Hogan,* – Hello, Hogan," Chayton whispered, tears filling his eyes. Chayton looked over at Moki and Gad. He saw that they were sobbing while laughing at the same time.

"Are you hungry?" Wiyaka asked.

"*Lay he huh nee keyn oh snee,* – It is cold this morning," Chayton replied.

"Cover your father," Wiyaka ordered Hoka.

"*Minne?* – Water?" Wiyaka offered, but Chayton refused it.

"*Blue gxoe cha ah snee wa key yea,* – I am tired, so I rest," Chayton mumbled and then he reentered the world of unconsciousness.

"CHAYTON! CHAYTON!" Wiyaka screamed. "*KEY KTO YO!* – WAKE UP!"

Chayton found himself on the same trail, standing in front of Tarca Sapa. Chayton studied Tarca Sapa and finally announced, "*Cheek se ya, Tarca Sapa!* – I remember you, Tarca Sapa!"

"Ha! Ha! Ha!" Tarca Sapa laughed and then replied, "*Ee yo monk pee!* – I am happy!"

"Where am I?" Chayton asked.

"*Wanagi Casaku.* – Spirit Path."

"*Hat'ugha?* – Why?"

"Others are waiting for you," Tarca Sapa replied.

"Others?" Chayton asked. "Who?"

"Your father and mother…Hexaka…Sheo…"

"*Hat'ugha?* – Why?"

"They are waiting for you, *le mita kola,* – my friend," Tarca Sapa answered.

"I am not ready."

"*Ai, hecheto aloe, le mita kola,* – It is finished, my friend," Tarca Sapa declared.

215

Chayton said nothing; he just gazed around at the new world surrounding him.

Wiyaka poured water over the top of Chayton's head while Hoka shook his father. When the water was gone, Wiyaka slapped Chayton in the face. "*Key kto yo, le mita kola!* – Wake up, my friend!" Wiyaka yelled with a wild look in his eyes.

Chayton's eyelids flickered and his glazed eyes partially opened. Chayton stared up at the blue sky, not acknowledging the travelers kneeling around him. With tears pouring down his cheeks, Hoka leaned over and tried to draw his father's attention, but Chayton's eyes remained fixed on the sky. Hogan rocked back and forth praying that his grandfather would snap out of it.

"*Lela oosni,* – very cold," Chayton mumbled. Chayton then turned his head towards his lifelong friend Wiyaka and murmured, "*Hecheto aloe, le mita kola.* – It is finished, my friend." Chayton's eyes went dim while he continued to stare up at the heavens.

"*HEE YA!* – NO!" Wiyaka roared.

"*Key Kta yo, até!* – Wake up, father!" Hoka cried out while Moki and Gad wept.

***

Chayton found himself back on the trail, but this time, Tarca Sapa was nowhere in sight. Chayton looked around and noticed another human walking towards him on the trail. He focused his eyes, trying to see who it was, but he could not tell. Chayton's expression changed from bewilderment to joy when he finally recognized the human.

"*Doe ksh kay oun hey, Chayton?* – How are you, Chayton?" the woman asked.

Chayton moved towards the woman and embraced her. He held her tight and felt the love he had missed for so many winters. Tears fell from his eyes as he held the woman in his arms. The woman ran her fingers through Chayton's black hair and kissed him gently on the lips. Then, she reached up with her hand and wiped away Chayton's tears. Chayton held Tonkala tight. He would never let her go.

***

Far to the north, near the village of the Folsom People, lightning filled the sky as black clouds rolled in from the west. Chayton's grandson Cansha and his friends had been hunting and were now running down the steep slope of the bluffs, trying to reach the safety of the village before the storm arrived. The red and gray *inyan wakan* – sacred rock bounced up and down in the satchel where Cansha kept his grandfather's gift. As he sprinted to the village, Cancha never noticed that the red and gray sacred rock had fallen out of his satchel and landed on the trail. Later, a vicious thunderstorm struck the village, flooding the grasslands and creeks while burying the red and gray sacred rock. The red and gray sacred rock lay buried on that prairie for well over ten thousand winters until another human came along and discovered it eroding from a dry streambed.

***

Wiyaka was a broken man. He remained kneeling by the lifeless body of his friend. Moki and Gad continued to weep while Hoka and Hogan, still nursing their wounds, remained close to each other. Night fell and the bullfrogs from the nearby pond greeted a new moon while the evening breeze rustled the leaves in the nearby cottonwood trees. No one left Chayton's side. One by one, the travelers rose and collected more wood for a campfire. Then, they gathered up the remaining food and divided it equally amongst themselves. Wiyaka never left the side of Chayton, holding onto a small hope that Chayton was sleeping and would eventually wake up. When the night was old, Wiyaka finally collapsed from exhaustion and slept.

At dawn, the camp was quiet as everyone went about the chores. Wiyaka began digging his friend's grave, alongside the grave of the hunter Mato. Moki redressed Hoka and Hogan's wounds and once she was done, she and Gad went to the creek to gather sweet grass for the burial ceremony. After collecting the sweet grass for burning, Gad helped Moki prepare the deer hide for Chayton's burial bundle. It was the same deer hide that the leader and the mysterious tribe left Chayton at *Wagichun Wagi*. By the time the sun was overhead, Wiyaka had the circular grave dug. Then, Moki and Gad spread the deer hide across the bottom of the grave in preparation of Chayton's corpse.

The travelers burned sweet grass on the campfire while they carried Chayton to his new grave. They placed Chayton on top of the deer hide, his knees tucked tight and his face pointing east towards the new sun. They then arranged Chayton's scant possessions beside him in the grave. The travelers then pulled the outer edges of the deer hide up around Chayton as far as it would go and tied it together with strips of deer hide. Each of the travelers placed a personal item in the grave for Chayton to take along on his journey into the spirit world. They then covered the grave with soil and built a monument of rocks over the top. For two suns, the travelers prayed and mourned at Chayton's grave. At dawn on the third day, Hoka approached Wiyaka and told him, "We are ready to leave for the North Country."

Wiyaka did not reply, but instead continued staring at Chayton's grave. Hoka finally gave up and left, but soon returned. "We are ready, Wiyaka," Hoka requested. "Winter is coming."

Wiyaka still said nothing. Hoka went off to get everyone prepared to leave for the North Country while Wiyaka remained alongside Chayton's gravesite. Hoka returned once again and stood over Wiyaka, waiting for the old man to get up, but Wiyaka did not budge. "*Hoppo!* – Let us go! The snows are coming!" Hoka insisted.

Wiyaka looked up at Chayton's son and then looked around at the other travelers who were waiting for him. Wiyaka's eyes then drifted back to his friend's grave. The travelers stood there, waiting on the old hunter while listening to the rustling of the changing leaves on the cottonwood trees. Finally, Wiyaka spoke, "*Iyaya!* – Go!*"

Hoka did not understand what this meant. He waited for Wiyaka to explain, but no other words came. Hoka turned around and looked at the others for guidance.

"We are ready, Wiyaka," Hogan declared.

"*Iyaya!* – Go!" Wiyaka replied, using his hand to shoo the travelers away.

"We cannot leave you here, Wiyaka," Hoka proclaimed.

"*Iyaya!* – Go!" Wiyaka insisted and then added, "I have always been there for Chayton and I will watch over him now."

Hoka did not know what to say or do. He looked over at the others, but they were just as confused. Hoka finally reached down to pull Wiyaka to his feet, but when he grabbed Wiyaka's hide shirt, Hoka changed his mind.

"*Amba, le mita kola,* – Goodbye, my friend," Hoka said, squeezing the old hunter's shoulder, instead. Hoka slowly backed away from the grave and began walking across the clearing. Hoka motioned for the others to follow. The travelers slowly walked across the clearing while keeping their eyes on Wiyaka the entire time, hoping that he would change his mind. Suddenly, Hogan ran back to Wiyaka and embraced the old hunter. "*Amba, Wiyaka!* – Goodbye, Wiyaka!" Hogan exclaimed with tears running down his cheeks.

"You are a hunter, Hogan!" Wiyaka proclaimed, looking up at the boy and smiling. "I am proud to call you *le mita kola.* – my friend."

Hogan smiled and then rejoined his father and the others. Hoka stopped and waited for Wiyaka one last time before disappearing into the trees of the canyon. That was when Hoka finally realized that both Chayton and Wiyaka would be fine.

CPSIA information can be obtained
at www.ICGtesting.com
Printed in the USA
FFOW03n2144231014
8310FF